I0724436

KINGDOM OF LOCKS

THE KINGDOM TALES BOOK FIVE

DEBORAH GRACE WHITE

LUMINANT PUBLICATIONS

KINGDOM OF LOCKS: A RETELLING OF RAPUNZEL

By Deborah Grace White

For Ruth, a loyal reader from the start,
and in warm memory of Dorothy.

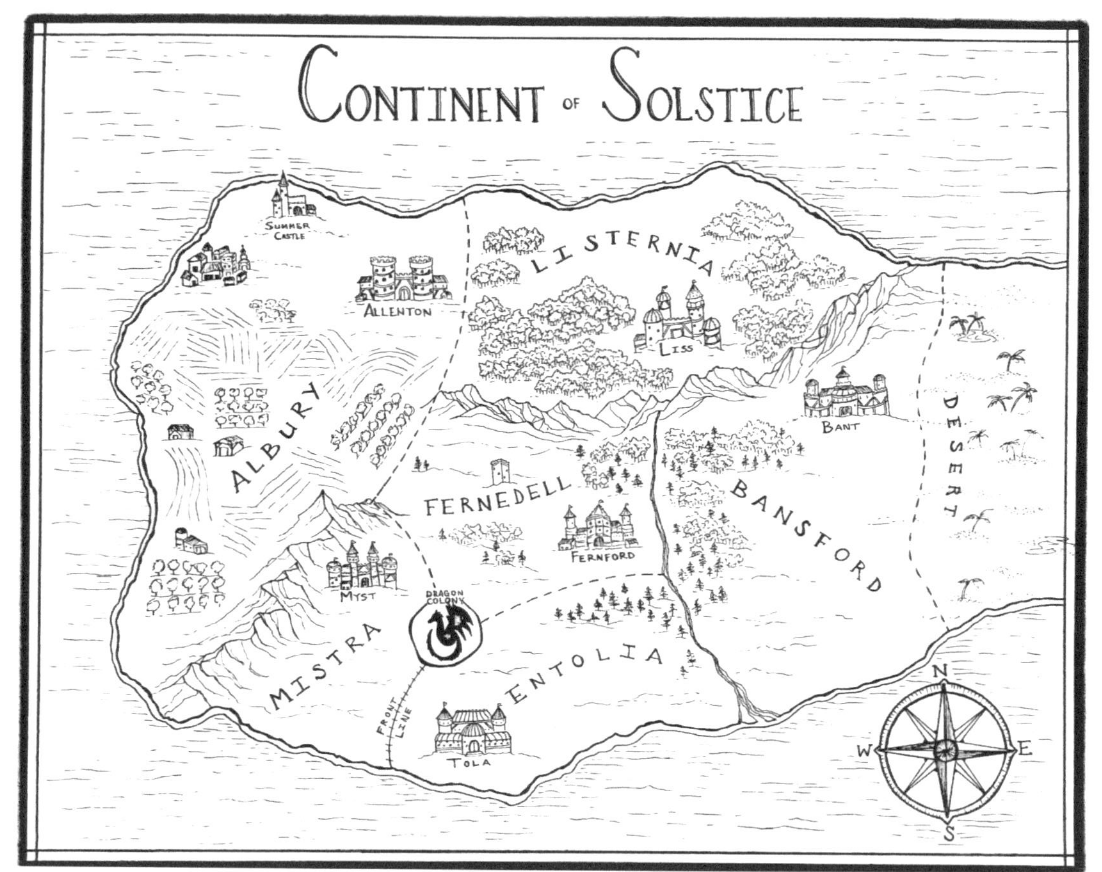
CONTINENT of SOLSTICE
SUMMER CASTLE
ALLENTON
LISTERNIA
LISS
BANT
DESERT
ALBURY
FERNEDELL
BANSFORD
FERNFORD
MYST
DRAGON COLONY
MISTRA
ENTOLIA
FRONT LINE
TOLA
N
E
S
W

PROLOGUE

Racquel, Albury's young queen, laughed at the antics of the small copper-haired child rolling in the wild-flowers before her, reflecting that the little girl was like her mother Imelda in more than just looks.

"Won't she get her gown dirty?" Racquel asked her friend. "Or injure herself?"

"I don't think so," smiled Imelda, watching her daughter fondly. "I can't imagine her getting hurt badly enough to cause concern, just from rolling in the grass. And as for the gown, what does it matter?"

Racquel shook her head in disbelief. "Your children certainly enjoy more freedom than mine ever will."

"Well, I'm not the queen, am I?" Imelda pointed out. "The lack of a title does have its benefits. I'm very content as a commoner, you know."

Racquel sighed, not relishing the reminder of her elevated standing. It was one of the reasons she so enjoyed spending time with Imelda. Her oldest friend rarely mentioned Racquel's status as queen, and spoke to her as though they were still equals.

She didn't mention any of that, however, instead giving her friend a speaking look. "Don't let the head of your clan hear you calling Albury's most powerful merchant family mere commoners, Imelda."

Imelda grimaced. "My family are a little full of their own importance, aren't they? But influence or not, we're commoners just the same. And strictly speaking, I stopped belonging to the clan when I married." Her eyes rested warmly on her daughter, who was now chasing a butterfly. "Gustav and I are our own clan, and we don't have any desire for titles."

"Well, I know better than anyone that titles don't bring happiness on their own," said Racquel sadly. In spite of the day's warmth, she pulled her silk shawl a little more tightly around herself. "I was happier as a lady than I am as a queen. Not that anyone would believe that." She saw that Imelda was watching her with distress, and attempted a smile. "Your husband's fleet gives you financial security, that's all that matters. You certainly don't seem to need a fancy title to be happy."

"Racquel," Imelda said, reaching out a tentative hand.

"Did Gustav take your son with him to the regional market?" Racquel asked quickly, eager to change the subject.

She was glad that Imelda had found happiness with her husband, but she hated the pity she saw in her friend's eyes any time Racquel's own marriage came up. Racquel had no doubt that Imelda knew as well as she did that love had played no role either in the formal arrangement that had brought Racquel into the royal family, or in the relationship that stemmed from that arrangement. Her sole value in her husband's eyes lay in the fact that her father was a highly influential member of King Justus's court.

"Yes," said Imelda, still sounding hesitant. "A five-year-old is too young to be underfoot when Gustav is working, of course, but he's never been good at saying no to Ambrose. He'd spoil the boy if I let him get away with it."

Racquel smiled, but the expression was pained. Again, it was impossible not to draw comparisons. If only her own son—who wasn't much older than Imelda's—enjoyed such favor from his father.

"Will Prince Justin be traveling here from the capital with his father tomorrow?" Imelda asked delicately, her mind clearly taking a similar route.

Racquel nodded. "Are you sure you can't come back to the Summer Castle?" she pressed. "Even just for a few hours? We could have refreshments, and—"

Imelda was already shaking her head. "I'm sorry, Racquel, but Gustav and Ambrose are expecting us back at the inn soon. It took us half an hour to walk here, and we'll have to walk back yet. We can probably only stay for another fifteen minutes."

"I understand," said Racquel, swallowing her disappointment. She knew Imelda had no interest in castles, but she would have loved the company. "And there's no need for you to walk. I can have a carriage brought around."

Imelda smiled in amusement. "A half hour stroll isn't a hardship, Racquel. We both enjoyed the walk over immensely."

Racquel opened her mouth to reply, then gasped abruptly as she received a solid kick to her stomach. "Ooh! That was a big one."

"Was it?" Imelda asked delightedly. She looked over at her daughter. "Fliss, the baby is kicking! Come and see."

"You can't exactly see anything," laughed Racquel. "But she can feel if she likes."

"Can she really?" Imelda asked brightly. She smiled at the three-year-old who had run over, hands full of wildflowers. "Her Majesty said you can put your hand on her tummy, and try to feel the baby."

The little girl's eyes were round as she did so, and she gave a delighted squeal of laughter when the baby kicked again.

"Is it a girl this time?" she asked Racquel innocently.

The young queen smiled. "I don't know for sure, but I think it is."

Imelda gave her a scrutinizing look. "You think, or you hope?"

Racquel smiled. "Don't tell Justus, but both. He wants another boy—an heir and a spare, you know—but I think a girl would be just lovely."

Her eyes became a little distant as they roved over the peaceful meadow where they were walking. Their meeting place was far enough from the royal estate that Racquel could no longer see the spires of the Summer Castle, and they were alone but for the half dozen guards loitering in a loose circle around them.

"A girl would have an easier life, too."

At this addition, Imelda cast a sideways look at her friend. "I have noticed that King Justus is...a little hard on Prince Justin."

Racquel grimaced at the understatement, but didn't respond. Here was another thing she couldn't bring herself to discuss with her happy friend. Guilt lanced through her at the thought of her son, and the pressure he already faced. But what was the point in dwelling on it? She knew she'd never be able to stand up to Justus, not when it came to raising his son and successor. But a sweet baby princess...might not her mother be allowed more say in her upbringing? Surely it would be considered the queen's province to choose what kind of instructors and companions should surround and educate a princess.

"Imelda," she said.

Her friend seemed to sense her sudden nerves, because she straightened up from alongside her daughter and gave the queen her full attention. "What is it?"

"Well..." Racquel twisted her gown between her fingers. "I know you're happy as you are, but I wondered if you might consider accepting a position in the castle, back in Allenton."

"In the castle?" Imelda looked startled.

Racquel swallowed. "If this is a girl," she said, rubbing her belly protectively, "I wondered if you would consider being her lady-in-waiting." She saw Imelda's hesitation, and hurried on. "I know there would be a cost to your own family, but the title does come with some benefits. Access to the castle, perhaps even additional education for your children."

She met her friend's eyes, a plea in her own. "There's no one else I trust, Imelda. You're my oldest friend—my *only* friend from my life before I became queen. I want this child to be surrounded by love, not by..." She trailed off, but she knew she didn't need to finish. Imelda was already far too aware of the cold calculation that typified King Justus's every move.

"The title doesn't interest me in the slightest," said Imelda frankly. Her eyes softened. "But for the sake of our friendship, Racquel, I would gladly do it."

"Thank you," the queen cried, enveloping her friend in an embrace, partly to hide the tears building behind her eyes. Now she just had to hope that the baby truly was a girl.

As she pulled back from Imelda, her eyes fell on a crumbling stone wall partway across the meadow. It was so overgrown, she hadn't even noticed it at first.

"Did you ever crave anything strange when you were pregnant?" she asked her friend.

Imelda looked bemused at the sudden change in topic. "Nothing too strange. Why?"

Racquel gave a self-conscious laugh. "That honeysuckle looks unbelievably good right now."

Imelda followed her gaze to see the flowers creeping over the crumbling stone.

"You can't eat flowers, silly," chimed in the little girl.

"Felicity!" scolded Imelda. "You're speaking to our queen!"

"Oh," said Felicity, eyes wide and curious. "Can you eat flowers if you're a queen?"

Racquel just laughed. "Not usually," she explained. "But honeysuckles can actually be eaten."

"Go on, then," encouraged Imelda.

Racquel shook her head. "Oh no. I was just being foolish."

"Racquel," Imelda scolded her. "You're Albury's queen. If anyone can get away with eating whatever they like, it's you."

"Justus wouldn't approve," Racquel sighed.

Imelda looked like she wanted to roll her eyes. "The king isn't here, Racquel. And many physicians believe that if a woman craves food while she's expecting, it's because her baby needs it. I'll even fetch it for you."

Racquel let out a final feeble protest, but Imelda was already marching across the clearing. The young queen followed in her friend's wake, not sure whether to be amused or embarrassed by the sight of the other woman scrambling up onto a moss-covered log in order to reach some of the trailing flower.

"Here you go!" Imelda cried triumphantly, jumping nimbly to the ground again with a sprig of yellow blooms in her hand.

Still a little self-conscious, Racquel took them and nibbled at one of the petals.

"Well?" Imelda demanded.

Racquel let out a reluctant laugh. "It tastes delicious."

"Good," said Imelda firmly. "I'm getting you some more." She stepped back up onto the log.

"What is this place?" Racquel asked, frowning up at the wall. "I didn't realize there were any estates this close to the Summer Castle."

"Probably because there aren't anymore," grunted Imelda, stretching up to reach more honeysuckle halfway up the wall.

"Judging by how overrun it is, I'm guessing it hasn't been a functioning estate for years."

Her questing fingers had just closed around a new lot of honeysuckle when a loud crack made both women jump. Alarmed, Racquel spun around to see the vines growing over a nearby patch of wall shake and then part, as someone forced open an overgrown gate from behind them.

"Thieves!" The angry cry preceded the young man who strode out into the clearing. His gaze fixated on Imelda, who had barely managed to keep her footing on the log at his abrupt appearance. "What gives you the right to come here and steal my flora, you little rodent?"

"That's enough," said Racquel, her anger rising at hearing her friend spoken to in such a way. "She was picking them for me."

"And what gives *you* the right?" he sneered, turning his attention to Racquel.

He received his answer without her having to say a word. Her guards had obviously seen his arrival, and Racquel felt them converging behind her, silent menace in their posture.

The newcomer's gaze passed from the guards to Racquel's face, and sudden understanding hit. "You're the queen!" he gasped.

"That's right," chimed in Imelda, hopping down from the log at last. "So show a little respect."

The man barely glanced at her as he responded, his voice cold. "Respect for thieves, come to steal from my garden? Not likely."

Imelda drew in a sharp breath. "What nonsense! How were we to know the estate was inhabited? You should take better care of your property. Besides, the honeysuckle is on the outside of the wall, *and* it's little better than a weed!"

"A weed?" scoffed their accuser. "You clearly know nothing

of magic. Honeysuckle is a valuable plant, useful for many kinds of enchantments."

At the mention of magic, Racquel's guards had fallen into formation around her, and she had to lean around one of them to watch the ongoing confrontation. One of the guards, she was glad to see, was keeping Imelda's daughter safely back from the action.

"An enchanter, are you?" said Imelda, with disfavor. "Then you have even less excuse for your rudeness."

"Just as a queen has even less excuse for stealing," he said coldly, his eyes on Racquel.

She stared back in growing anger, his sheer audacity momentarily robbing her of speech. She wasn't normally vain about the position that brought her mostly pain, but it was a little much for this stranger—barely twenty years old, by the look of him—to speak so to his queen.

"I will pay you for your honeysuckle, if that's what you desire," she said icily, drawing on her court training as she raised one sculpted eyebrow. "But I won't tolerate your rudeness a moment longer."

The enchanter wasn't listening to her. His eyes were fixed on her bulging stomach, understanding suddenly dawning.

"You're expecting," he declared, as if he'd made an impressive discovery. "Is that why you wanted the honeysuckle?" A gleam of interest shot into his eyes. "Some enchanters think that denotes susceptibility to magic in the child." He shook his head slightly. "An old wives' tale, most likely, but no matter. Either way, a baby is just what I need." He met her eyes at last, his own shining in triumph. "I'll take the baby as payment for your theft."

Racquel barely heard Imelda's angry gasp, her senses swimming in her own shock and alarm. "How dare you?" she demanded, her hand flying protectively to her stomach.

"You said you'd pay me," the enchanter replied, his voice hard and angry.

"In coin!" Racquel said coldly.

"I don't want your gold," the man retorted, his tone dismissive. "I want the baby." He rubbed his hands together. "A prince or princess of Albury...quite apart from the vessel, the political uses could be invaluable."

"You're mad," said Racquel blankly, taking a step back. But even as she said the words, a sick unease gripped her. The calculating gleam in his eyes wasn't consistent with madness. He was utterly unreasonable, but she was fairly sure his mind was sound. Which made his calm demands all the more terrifying.

"That's enough," said one of her guards, stepping forward with his weapon raised suggestively. "Move back from the queen, or we will remove you."

"You all heard her!" the enchanter said angrily. "She said she'd pay me! And I've named my price. The child for the honeysuckle. That baby is mine by right, and I will claim it."

"You were warned," growled the guard. He raised his spear and took a step toward the man. But before he could lay a hand on him, there was a bang, and thick smoke suddenly filled the air.

Everyone in the group lifted their arms over their faces, coughing as the smoke began to dissipate. When Racquel could again see the clearing, there was no sign of the enchanter. With a frantic gesture, she felt her stomach, half afraid that the baby would somehow be gone.

But of course her passenger was still there, even giving a reassuring kick under Racquel's hand.

"Of all the theatrical, self-aggrandizing weasels!" exclaimed Imelda.

Racquel turned a colorless face to her friend. "Who was

that? What did he mean he'd claim the baby? What was all that about a vessel?"

Imelda hurried to her side, gripping her arm reassuringly. "Don't give him another moment's thought, Racquel," she said, her voice soothing. "He was a big-headed lunatic, and he'll never be allowed to get anywhere near you or your baby."

"But he's an enchanter," said Racquel, still fighting a creeping sense of panic. "Who knows what he's capable of?"

Imelda snorted. "Not a very powerful one. If he had strong magic, he wouldn't resort to such paltry tricks as creating a cloud of smoke to make it look like he'd disappeared." She looked down. "It's all right, Felicity."

Racquel chewed her lip anxiously, staring without seeing as her friend knelt down and reassured her daughter, who was clinging to her leg in alarm, having run to her mother as soon as the guard released her.

In spite of Imelda's reassuring words, Racquel couldn't help the fear that had lodged beside her heart. She passed a hand back and forth over her stomach in a convulsive rhythm, gripped by a fleeting and illogical wish that the baby could stay in there forever, where she was safe. If the baby was a she, of course.

"Don't tell Justus about this," she said suddenly. Her own fear was enough. She didn't want to deal with his anger as well.

As weeks turned into months, Racquel all but forgot about the unsettling encounter with the enchanter. The guards had found no sign of him when searching the estate. It had supposedly belonged to a family of Alburian nobles which petered out when the only descendant, a woman, married a Fernedellian and left the kingdom. Whether the enchanter was descended from the family, or just a bold traveler who'd taken up residence in the abandoned estate, Racquel doubted she'd ever know.

As she'd sensed, the baby was indeed a girl. Princess Aurelia was everything the queen had hoped she'd be. Born with her mother's golden hair and her father's clear blue eyes, she'd enchanted everyone in the castle from the moment she was born.

Everyone except the father who'd wanted another son, of course. But Racquel did her best to keep the baby out of Justus's sight as much as possible. She knew he had little patience for crying infants. Justin, on the other hand, was very interested in Aurelia, and Racquel was encouraged by the softness the six-year-old showed toward his baby sister.

As an infant, Aurelia was too young to have an official lady-in-waiting yet, but true to her word, Imelda's visits to the castle became more frequent, and when Racquel was unable to be with little Aurelia—which was often—Imelda shared the role of caring for her with her various nursemaids.

Because unfortunately, while Aurelia might so far have an easier life than her royal brother, the arrival of the princess did nothing to make the queen's role less demanding. King Justus still expected his wife to fulfill all the state duties of a queen, and in his view, caring for an infant who could be handed off to any number of servants didn't fall under that description.

Outings such as the rambling walk Racquel had shared with Imelda and her daughter during her visit to the Summer Castle remained rare. More times than she could count, Racquel watched with tears firmly held at bay while her friend took her baby daughter out in her place, the queen deprived of both her daughter's company and the fresh air she so desperately needed.

"Racquel."

On one such occasion, her husband's impatient voice called Racquel's attention back to the council room where the two of them awaited the king's advisors.

Racquel drew her eyes from the window with reluctance. Imelda was climbing the steps into a carriage, baby Aurelia in her arms and several guards mounting up beside the vehicle. The visit to the river had been Racquel's idea. And now she wasn't even to take part.

"Why do I have to be here, Justus?" she burst out, in uncharacteristic defiance. "It's not as though I'm allowed to actually speak up in these meetings. Why must I attend the council?"

"You are the queen," scowled Justus. "And you will not neglect your responsibilities for an infant."

"*Our* infant, Justus," said Racquel, a little desperately. "She's our daughter!"

"And she is perfectly safe in the care of her nursemaids and her guards," said the king dismissively. "Your place is here, not in a nursery."

A nobleman entered the room at that moment, and Racquel fell silent. But inside she burned with frustration and helplessness. It was all she could do to maintain the emotionless facade expected of her at these events. Sometimes she thought Justus's coldness would kill her. But no. She brushed such selfish thoughts aside. However disheartened she might become, she would never be so weak as to succumb to death. There might not be much she could do for poor little Justin, but Aurelia needed her, and Racquel would never abandon her daughter.

The meeting lasted for hours, and Racquel heard barely a word of it. She was watching the carriageway, waiting for Imelda and Aurelia's return. The advisors were finally winding to a close when Racquel saw a single rider speed across the flagstones, his horse lathered in sweat. A shot of fear went through her, as if her heart already grasped something her mind couldn't possibly know yet.

Within minutes, there was a smart rap at the door. A guard entered, wild-eyed and shaking, and knelt beside his king. Racquel couldn't hear the quiet words he spoke, but her fear turned to terror as Justus barked for the advisors to clear the room.

Racquel didn't move, frozen in place like the statue she'd been trained to resemble.

"Repeat that," Justus said curtly.

The guard swallowed visibly before speaking. "The...the princess, Your Majesty. She was being carried by her minder, and...and...they both..."

"What?" Racquel cried, suddenly on her feet. "They both what?"

The man bowed his head. "They both fell into the ravine, Your Majesties. We have men searching the river. Their bodies haven't yet been recovered, but...but it's a fifty foot drop."

Racquel's eyes passed to her husband's, barely able to comprehend the words through the numbness that had descended over her. For the briefest instant, she thought she saw genuine pain in Justus's eyes, but the expression was gone so quickly, she placed no reliance on it.

"How?" he asked, in a voice more awful than anything she'd ever heard.

"How?" she whispered, something hysterical rising up within her. "HOW? You wouldn't let me care for my own daughter, that's how! I should have been with her! I should have been the one to—"

She buried her face in her hands, sobbing brokenly as the terrible truth crashed upon her. Wave after wave of grief engulfed her, and she made no attempt to keep her head above the surface. She'd lost not only her precious daughter, but her oldest, closest friend, whose own children would now be motherless.

Abandoning any attempt at dignity, she sank to the floor, not even trying to hold on to the will to continue as she felt it slip away from her, away to wherever Aurelia had gone.

SEVENTEEN YEARS LATER…

CHAPTER ONE

Aurelia

"A little higher...a little higher...that's it! Perfect. Well done, Aurelia. Excellently done."

Aurelia looked down at the older woman beaming up at her, a wry expression twisting her own features.

"I'm placing a curtain rail, Mama Gail. Not performing life-saving surgery."

"A job well done is a job well done," said her mother firmly. "And don't make me regret letting you read that physician's guide."

Aurelia chuckled as she looped her dark braid—three times as thick as her arm—around a large metal hook suspended from the stone wall. Holding the tension with the ease of long experience, she lowered herself back to the stone floor.

"It was fascinating. And you never know when it might come in handy. If you slash your leg open by accident, I could stitch it up for you!"

Mama Gail shuddered. "I'm sure I'd be grateful for whatever help you could give me in that situation, but there's no need to sound so gleeful about it."

Aurelia's grin fell away as she stood beside her mother, looking up at the curtain rail. "I don't know why we need a curtain, really. We only get one window onto the world. Covering it up is the last thing I want to do."

Mama Gail put an arm around her shoulder and squeezed. "I know, sweetheart. But it would get cold at night without the insulation. Plus Master Mulehead would make a fuss if he saw we'd knocked down the curtain, and who has the energy to put up with that?"

Aurelia laughed, even as a small shiver went over her. She'd always admired Mama Gail's daring—personally she was too much in awe of their captor to call him names, even behind his back. The mention of him sobered her, and she glanced out of the window. Sunset was approaching. Trying to emulate Mama Gail's unbreakable spirit, she didn't give voice to her dread.

"*I* have the energy," she informed her companion instead. "Energy is the one thing I have an endless amount of. Well, one of two things," she amended. "That and time."

"Nonsense," said Mama Gail briskly. "No one has an endless amount of time. Everyone has the same number of hours in a day, and we're no exception."

"And this particular day is drawing to a close," Aurelia told her pointedly.

Mama Gail sighed. "You're right. Well, the sooner he comes, the sooner he'll leave. Come on."

Following her lead, Aurelia set about tidying the two rooms that formed the only home she'd ever known. Most of the tower's single story was taken up with a large open space, with a second room containing two beds for the building's two inhabitants. It wasn't messy—Mama Gail had always insisted on tidiness and routine. But they still undertook this process every day, hiding their treasures, and any signs of activities their captor might disapprove of. The aim was for nothing in particular to catch his eye during his nightly visits, so that he'd be less likely to linger.

Or, as Mama Gail liked to so succinctly put it, "The sooner we can bid good riddance to bad rubbish, the better." Aurelia smiled to herself at the thought of her mother's fierce expression as she stashed the pages she'd copied out of the physician's guide under the lid of a bench seat.

Straightening up, she watched a little enviously as her mother twisted her copper hair—only just beginning to show streaks of silver—into a simple knot on top of her head. It looked so easy and comfortable. Aurelia ran a hand down her own thickly braided mass of hair.

"Is your head hurting again?" Mama Gail asked, noticing the gesture immediately. "Should I re-braid it?"

Aurelia shook her head. "No, it's fine. Just, you know… annoyingly long."

Her mother nodded sympathetically, then glanced out the window. "Do you think I have time to return this to the study?" she asked, lifting a heavy volume on botany. Not a fascinating subject, as it turned out.

Frowning as she followed the other woman's gaze, Aurelia shook her head. The sun was nearing the horizon. "Too risky, I think."

"You're right," Mama Gail agreed. "I'll hide it under the chamber pot. He'll never go near there."

Aurelia choked on a laugh, but it died on her lips as a hatefully familiar voice rang out from outside the window.

"Honeysuckle! Throw me my rope!"

With a grimace, Mama Gail hid the stolen tome, then moved to the opening. "You forgot to say please," she called out irritably.

"Don't upset him," pleaded Aurelia. "It's not worth it."

Her mother lifted her hands in surrender, stepping back to allow Aurelia to approach the window.

As Aurelia moved forward, she pulled at her braid. Mama Gail helped her, and between them they soon had Aurelia's dark tresses free of the complicated plait into which her mother threaded them after their visitor left every night. Unrestrained, the hair was much longer, pooling around Aurelia's feet in many loops that made it hard to move without tripping. Not even glancing out of the window, Aurelia gathered her hair and threw it over the metal hook she had used to lower herself to the floor. Except this time, she threw the rest of her hair out the window, wincing slightly as it pulled against her scalp on its journey down to the ground far below them. She didn't need to prompt her mother to help—they were too practiced at this routine. Both women looped Aurelia's locks around their elbows with quick, expert flicks, making sure that their arms would take the weight of their visitor rather than Aurelia's scalp.

"All right," Aurelia called out, hating the quaver in her voice. The next moment, she felt the tug indicating that the enchanter had transferred his weight from the ground to her hair. Bracing her feet against the wall of the tower, she held the tension in her straining muscles as their visitor pulled himself, hand over hand, up her hair.

When a well-known form appeared in the window, Aurelia had the fleeting thought—not for the first time—that if she let go at just the right moment, he'd fall, perhaps to his death. She brushed it aside, ashamed of herself, as a tall man climbed through the window and into the tower.

"Good evening," he said, straightening.

The two women just looked back at him, taking in his closely cropped dark hair, fine clothes, and general air of authority. He raised an eyebrow at their silence, his gaze settling on Aurelia.

"Where are your manners, Honeysuckle? Anyone would think you were raised in a hovel, instead of this luxurious dwelling."

Aurelia could feel Mama Gail's anger beside her, and she felt the usual surge of irritation herself at the stupid name the enchanter had given her. But both women knew perfectly well that their lives would be much easier if they didn't goad their captor. The last thing either of them wanted was to endure one of his hypocritical lectures.

"Good evening, Master Enchanter," said Aurelia quietly, using the form of address he insisted upon from her.

"What brings you to our *luxurious dwelling*, Cyfrin?" Mama Gail asked curtly, apparently not placing quite as high a value as Aurelia did on keeping their visitor's feathers unruffled.

Cyfrin narrowed his eyes. He never failed to take offense at Mama Gail's refusal to recognize his right to visit them, or his ownership over the building in which they lived.

"I'm in no mood to argue with you tonight, crone," he sneered.

Fortunately Mama Gail wasn't as easily offended as the enchanter was, and she simply rolled her eyes. Aurelia would have copied the gesture if she dared. It was absurd to call Mama Gail—not much older than forty, and glowing with health from the tip of her copper-haired head to the soles of her worn slippers—a crone.

Cyfrin turned to Aurelia, his eyes raking over her unrestrained hair. A flash of approval passed over his face. Nothing else about Aurelia ever elicited that reaction, and she took no pleasure from him directing it at her hair. If she had her way, she'd slice the whole lot off before bed that very night.

But Cyfrin didn't see her impractically long tresses as a nuisance.

"Ah, my Honeysuckle," he said, a caress in his voice that made Aurelia's skin crawl, even though she knew it was directed at her hair rather than her. "If you could only feel the potency of the power that leaks from you. It's breathtaking."

"She can feel it, all right," said Mama Gail dryly. "She'll hardly be able to hold her head up soon. It's too heavy for her."

Cyfrin ignored her. Stepping up to Aurelia, he stooped and picked up a loop of dark hair. "Shame about the color," he sighed, for what must have been the hundredth time. "It was supposed to be as golden as honeysuckle, like your mother's was." He shot Mama Gail a nasty look. "It was golden when I adopted you. I still don't understand how it changed."

Aurelia's mother rolled her eyes. "How would I have changed her hair color? Many babies start with pale hair only to have it darken."

But Cyfrin had turned back to Aurelia, uninterested in Mama Gail's words. "Shame," he repeated thoughtfully, clearly talking to himself. "Golden hair would have been an excellent foil for mine."

Aurelia blinked in confusion. She had no idea what he was talking about, and her eyes slid to Mama Gail, seeking clarification. What she saw made her stomach clench uncomfortably. Her mother, who usually made a point of never showing a hint of vulnerability in front of their captor, looked deeply uneasy. When her gaze moved to Aurelia's, she quickly sent her a reassuring smile, but it was too late to hide her initial reaction.

"Well," said Cyfrin briskly, apparently unaware of their silent exchange, "no sense in wasting any time. Let's get to it."

Aurelia turned around obediently, so that she faced away from Cyfrin. She felt the familiar sensation of his hands tangling through her hair, and suppressed a shudder. It felt so soothing when Mama Gail ran her fingers through her daughter's hair, whether to gently work out the knots, or just to comfort her after a difficult day. But when Cyfrin did it, it made Aurelia's skin crawl.

Although perhaps that was the magic.

As soon as he grasped her hair, the enchanter began to mutter. The language wasn't one Aurelia knew, but she recognized the odd phrase from her and Mama Gail's clandestine studies of magic. Not that she needed to know the details to understand the concept. Cyfrin had been pouring his magic into her hair every night of her life for as long as she could remember. She knew from rifling through his own notes that she now carried more power on her person than a hundred enchanters combined.

If only she had the magic in her blood that would allow her to access it. But Mama Gail had assured her regretfully that no one in her family had ever had magic. Aurelia had made her peace with the unpleasant fact that she was nothing more than a passive vessel. The routine was so familiar that she'd barely thought about it when she was a child. But lately she'd been growing increasingly uneasy as she considered what Cyfrin's plans might be for his accumulated power, and what her role in those plans would require from her. She didn't need specifics to know she wanted no part of any scheme of his.

After several minutes, Cyfrin stopped muttering and released her hair, giving it a fond pat as it fell back into place.

Aurelia stepped quickly away from him, gathering up the locks and winding them around her arm to keep them from his reach. She may not have the means to stop him from furthering his plans with the use of her hair, but she drew the line at letting him stroke it like some kind of living pet.

"I've been working on something new," mused Cyfrin, his eyes passing from Aurelia's tresses to her face. "Something for your benefit, Honeysuckle. I haven't worked out the details yet, but I hope to be able to start the process soon."

"What have you been working on?" demanded Mama Gail, who had moved to stand alongside Aurelia.

Cyfrin's eyes flicked to her with the usual irritation. "That's between me and Honeysuckle."

"No such thing," contradicted Mama Gail. "Anything involving Aurelia involves me."

Anger flashed across Cyfrin's face at her refusal to use the ridiculous name he'd chosen for Aurelia. "Don't overstep your boundaries, *Abigail*," he said, turning the name into a sneer. Without giving his opponent a chance to respond, he shifted his attention back to Aurelia.

"Have you made any progress on the task I set you, Honeysuckle?"

Aurelia lowered her eyes. "No, Master Enchanter," she said. "I can't think of any way to make my hair more like a ladder."

"Can't you even complete one simple task?" Cyfrin snapped, losing his temper with his usual rapidity. "You have nothing else to do all day up here. Do you realize how much effort it takes to haul myself bodily up a formless rope each night?"

Mama Gail leaped to Aurelia's defense, as usual. "What a hardship for you," she said with biting sarcasm. "I've no idea how she's supposed to turn her hair into a ladder. Of course, we could probably do it quite well if we cut it all off."

"Don't you dare snip a single strand!" Cyfrin shouted, firing up with painful predictability. "You know what will happen if you do. What use would I have for either one of you if the hair stopped growing?"

Aurelia's eyes were still on her feet, but she could sense his gaze shifting to her. She braced herself for further recriminations, but to her surprise his tone was milder when he next spoke.

"Well, I'd have no use for Abigail, anyway."

Aurelia dared to look up, unnerved by his unusual manner. His eyes hardened slightly as they met hers. "I'm disappointed that you couldn't even find one solution, Honeysuckle. I expect you to do better."

Yes, Master Enchanter. Her standard obedient response was on the tip of Aurelia's tongue, but something made her hold it back. Perhaps it was simply Mama Gail's palpable annoyance beside her. Or perhaps it was something deeper, some underfed instinct of defiance that recognized that she was no longer a child, and refused to be forever silenced. Whatever the cause, she couldn't bring herself to feign submission, not this time. She just stared into Cyfrin's eyes, giving him no answer.

She could see the anger growing with each passing second, but somewhat surprisingly, he made no comment. Instead he turned away from both women, striding across the large living space. He bypassed the door into their bedroom, pausing instead outside the only other door in Aurelia's world, a door she'd never been able to pass through. After muttering something inaudible—presumably checking that his protective enchantment remained in place—Cyfrin opened the door and disappeared into his study.

Aurelia let out a sigh.

"Well done," said Mama Gail quietly, and Aurelia didn't have to ask what she meant. The older woman shot an annoyed look toward the now-closed door. "I was hoping he wouldn't want to work in there tonight."

"I hope that every night," said Aurelia fervently. "But," her tone turned optimistic, "maybe he won't be in there for long."

Mama Gail smiled encouragingly at this bright comment, but both women held themselves tensely as they went through the supplies Cyfrin had brought, discussing their evening meal. The food was simple, but Aurelia didn't mind that. Presumably Cyfrin ate more lavishly than they did, back at whatever home he occupied when he wasn't with them. And she would rather eat rocks than partake of any food interesting enough to tempt him to stay for the meal.

The solid door notwithstanding, neither of the tower's occupants ever relaxed while Cyfrin was in the building. Still, Aurelia couldn't help but feel that her mother's unsettled air went beyond the usual irritation.

"What is it, Mama Gail?" she asked at last, after the third time her mother had slammed a dish down with a little too much force. "Why are you afraid?"

The other woman froze, turning startled eyes on Aurelia. "Afraid?"

Aurelia raised an eyebrow. "Don't deny it, Mama. You promised you'd never lie to me, remember?"

"Of course I remember," said Mama Gail, her expression softening. "I just hadn't put it in so many words, I suppose." She laid down the pot she was holding, considering her answer. "You're right. I am afraid, a little."

"But you're never afraid," said Aurelia, alarmed.

Mama Gail laughed. "Of course I am, darling. Everyone is sometimes. No matter how old." She sighed. "Perhaps I'm worrying over nothing."

Aurelia sent her a skeptical look. Her mother wasn't one to worry even over things Aurelia thought were alarming, let alone over nothing.

"I won't lie to you, Aurelia," said Mama Gail seriously. "But that doesn't mean I'm going to tell you everything I'm thinking. I will say, however, that I don't like not knowing what Cyfrin is planning. All his talk of working on something new has put me on edge."

"Yes, I was surprised by that as well," Aurelia said thoughtfully. "He's never mentioned a secondary project before, has he? And what did he mean it's for my benefit?"

Her mother shook her head, but further conversation was halted by the abrupt opening of the door into Cyfrin's study. Both women paused, watching silently as the enchanter strode back across the room.

"I'm ready to leave, Honeysuckle," he said lazily, his eyes drifting across the floor, where her hair lay in coils.

Without a word, Aurelia stepped forward and gathered her hair up. In no time at all, she had it looped through the hook, and she and Mama Gail were lowering Cyfrin down to the ground below their sole window.

When his feet touched the grass, he turned his face back up to his audience. "I'll anticipate a better solution tomorrow night, Honeysuckle," he said sternly. As always, he ignored the presence of the other woman.

"And that's the very best view of him," commented Mama Gail dispassionately, as Cyfrin sauntered into the tree line with his back to them.

Aurelia fell back, letting out a sigh of relief. Her heart felt light, as it always did when Cyfrin's nightly visits were over. A whole day before they'd have to look at his self-satisfied face again. Her thoughts became more troubled, however, as they drifted to her mother's face.

Mama Gail's eyes were once again uneasy as they followed the enchanter's form, and she was actually chewing on one lip anxiously. Aurelia frowned. For all the other woman's calm assurances, Aurelia could never remember her mother to have shown fear regarding Cyfrin before. What had Aurelia missed in the evening's visit that had so rattled her mother?

"Mama?" Aurelia prompted.

Mama Gail started slightly, turning to her companion with a smile. "Sorry, lost in my thoughts. Shall we eat?"

Aurelia nodded, collecting bowls from the simple kitchen situated on one side of the room. Her thoughts ran back over the visit, trying to solve the puzzle of her mother's worry, and her temporary good cheer fled when she remembered Cyfrin's parting words.

"How am I going to figure out how to make a better ladder out of my hair before tomorrow night?" she asked Mama Gail.

The other woman snorted. "You're not even going to try, darling. It's a stupid request, that only a stupid person would make."

Aurelia was silent for a moment. She appreciated her mother's constant reassurances, but it was dawning on her as she grew older that the unwavering support may have hindered her ability to recognize when she really was deficient.

"It is one simple task," she said, repeating Cyfrin's words. "And I couldn't even think of the hint of a solution." She let out a sigh as she ladled soup into a bowl. "I really am useless, aren't I?" Lifting a strand of dark hair, she attempted a smile. "I can't even get my hair color right. It's not exactly the color of honeysuckles, is it?"

"Of course you're not useless!" said Mama Gail sharply. "Now you listen to me, Aurelia. That man is a liar and a thief. He doesn't know you, and he has no right to make any comments about your capability. Your name is not *Honeysuckle*," she said the word with disdain, "and your hair is precisely the color it's supposed to be." She nudged Aurelia's shoulder. "Would a useless person have been able to save someone's life when they were only a baby?"

Aurelia rolled her eyes, even as a smile tugged at her lips. "I don't think I can take credit for that," she said dryly.

"Of course you can," Mama Gail contradicted comfortably. She settled into her seat, shifting her shoulders against the hard wooden chair to find a more amenable position. "It was seventeen years ago, on a bright spring morning."

"Mama Gail," protested Aurelia, recognizing the familiar opening to a story she'd heard many times before. "Don't you think I'm a little too old for this story?"

"Not at all," said her mother calmly. "Now, as I said, it was a lovely morning, and my dearest friend Racquel had entrusted me with the honor of taking her precious baby for an outing to the river."

"She wanted to come," Aurelia chipped in, entering into the spirit of it. "She would have if she had her way."

"Precisely," nodded Mama Gail approvingly. "But she couldn't, so all the cuddles fell to me."

"Are babies *very* cuddly?" Aurelia asked, with a wistful note in her voice. "I would like to hold one someday." She'd never seen a child, other than her memories of herself in her childhood, which didn't count at all.

"They're extremely cuddly, and you'll get to hold many in your lifetime, I trust."

Aurelia bent a skeptical look on her, which Mama Gail ignored. "So we went to the river, you and I. We had a picnic, and went for a walk, and you tried to eat a caterpillar."

"I had discerning taste," interjected Aurelia, on cue.

Mama Gail returned her grin. "All was going well, in short, and you'd fallen asleep in my arms. I left the picnic area, thinking it would be pleasant to stretch my legs. I didn't intend to go anywhere near the ravine, of course."

"But then," Aurelia interrupted in a dramatic voice, "a rabid animal appeared from nowhere, chasing you toward the edge!"

Mama Gail chuckled appreciatively. "That's it in a nutshell, yes. I held you close and ran from it, and by the time I realized which direction I was going, I was dangerously near the edge. I turned away, but before I knew what was happening, something grabbed my ankle and pulled me over."

"With me still clutched in your arms," supplied Aurelia.

"Of course," smiled Mama Gail. "I wasn't about to let go of you. It must have looked to the others in our group like we'd fallen right off the edge." Her eyes took on a faraway look. "I can still hear the screams." She shook off the memory, her voice becoming brisk. "But of course we hadn't plummeted to our deaths. We'd actually been pulled into a hidden alcove just below the cliff's edge. Before I could so much as blink, Cyfrin the Skunk had put a silencing enchantment on me, and we were dragged into a tunnel that I'm sure no one else knew about."

She drew a breath, and once again Aurelia marveled at the warmth in her mother's smile as she remembered such a terrible event.

"And that's when you saved my life."

Aurelia laughed in spite of herself. "It really doesn't count, Mama Gail."

"It does," contradicted her mother firmly. "Cyfrin snatched you away from me, babbling nonsense about how he was claiming his payment."

Aurelia nodded. She knew all about the bizarre confrontation that had occurred between Cyfrin and both the mother who gave birth to her, and the one who raised her. Mama Gail had made no secret of the fact that she hadn't told Aurelia everything about her history, but she told her the truth where she could.

"He wanted you, not me," Mama Gail went on. "He was going to get rid of me, there's no doubt about it. Then you started wailing, and you reached for me. As soon as you were in my arms, you stopped crying. And the dimwit who was stealing you realized for the first time how little he actually wanted to raise a baby." She rolled her eyes.

"So really," Aurelia pointed out, "I saved you by stopping crying."

Mama Gail chuckled. "My way of saying it is better."

Aurelia stirred the soup around her bowl, her thoughts far from the simple fare. "You've never mentioned others in the group by the river before," she commented. "Who were they?"

"Employees of your parents'," said Mama Gail simply.

Aurelia looked up sharply. "You mean servants?"

Her mother shrugged. "Some of them were servants, yes."

"Who were my parents, Mama Gail?" Aurelia pressed, as she had many times before. "They must have been wealthy to have multiple servants."

Her companion held her gaze with a serious expression. "They were wealthy," she acknowledged. Her eyes searched Aurelia's carefully. "Does that make it harder?"

"What do you mean?" Aurelia asked, puzzled.

"I mean, is it harder being trapped up here with nothing, knowing that you were born to a life of luxury?"

Aurelia considered the point. "Maybe it would make a difference if I understood what a life of luxury entails. But it's all just make believe to me." She gave her mother a faint smile. "And I don't have nothing. I have you."

Mama Gail's answering smile was a little sad.

"So were my parents merchants?" Aurelia pressed again. "Like you and Gustav? Is that how you became friends with my mother?"

Mama Gail let out a sigh. "I know it's frustrating, Aurelia, but I think for now it's still easier for you if you don't know so many details. Can you trust me?"

Aurelia hesitated only for a moment. "It is frustrating," she acknowledged. "But yes, of course I trust you."

"Thank you," said Mama Gail, squeezing her hand with a

serious expression on her face that told Aurelia she really meant it.

They ate the rest of the meal in thoughtful silence, but as soon as they were done, the older woman rose.

"Well, he's long gone by now. Time for my nightly snoop, do you think?"

Aurelia nodded, trying to look as unconcerned about the risks as her mother always seemed to be. "Don't forget to return the book on botany."

Retrieving the book in question from under the chamber pot, Mama Gail strode across the space to the study door, which Cyfrin hadn't even bothered to lock.

"I'd love to know what he writes in those notes of his," she said innocently. "Such a shame that he's put an enchantment on the door to keep out Aurelia, also known as Honeysuckle, and Abigail."

She smirked over her shoulder at Aurelia before pushing the door open and tripping lightly in. Aurelia moved slowly across the space, but didn't bother trying to enter the study. She knew from many attempts that Cyfrin's enchantment was effective at preventing her from entering.

"I wish I knew your real name," she said softly.

Mama Gail poked her head back out the door. "I know, Aurelia, and I'm sorry. But names have power, it's one of the few things I knew about magic before ever we were locked in here. And if nothing else, the enchantment on this door has proved how wise a decision it was never to give Cyfrin my real name."

"Can't you trust *me* with that power?" Aurelia asked, without much conviction. It wasn't the first time they'd had this conversation.

"I trust you completely," Mama Gail assured her. "But Cyfrin can't be trusted. And until we're free of his control, it's better for you not to have information that might be dangerous."

"You told me *my* real name," Aurelia pointed out.

Mama Gail stepped fully back into the room, a frown creasing her forehead. "That's because it's important for you to know who you are. And you are not who he's tried to mold you into."

Aurelia nodded, although her mother's words did little to touch the hollow feeling in her chest.

Perhaps sensing this, Mama Gail stepped forward and placed a hand on Aurelia's cheek. "If you want to use a name other than Abigail, what's wrong with Mama? That's as real a name to me as the one I was born with. I've carried it for more than twenty years."

Aurelia gave a weak smile, chivvying her mother back into the study.

"I'm all right. Go see what he wrote today." She fell silent, listening to the sound of Mama Gail rifling through papers. "I don't really understand," she mused after a moment. "If the enchantment on the tower can keep anyone but him from entering or exiting, why doesn't he put the same enchantment on his study?"

"Uses too much magic," grunted Mama Gail, emerging from the study with a thick leather tome Aurelia recognized well. "If I've understood what I've read, that's an incredibly powerful enchantment he's put on this tower. It would take only a fraction of the magic to craft a protection keeping only the two of us out of the study, and it must seem a safe bet to him given no one else can get into the tower."

Aurelia smiled. "Except he underestimated your deviousness in giving him a false name."

"Indeed," agreed Mama Gail solemnly. "And it's always a mistake to underestimate my deviousness." She flipped a few pages in the volume, and a frown settled onto her brow.

"What is it?" Aurelia asked curiously. "Isn't it working?

Hasn't the news changed since yesterday? Perhaps the enchantment on the book has worn out."

Mama Gail shook her head, her eyes scanning the page rapidly. "No, the magic is still working. This is today's news, sure enough." She raised her eyes to meet Aurelia's, her expression grim. "And it's not good."

CHAPTER TWO

Amell

"Well," said Amell cheerfully, glancing over at the man riding beside him. "That was a very nice wedding."

"Very nice, Your Highness," agreed Sir Furnis, only the tiniest hint of a smile betraying his thoughts.

Amell chuckled. "Yes, you're right, Furn. I found the ceremony itself long and dull. But having it on a clifftop was exciting. And there were dragons there, which always adds some interest."

"I'm just glad Entolia and Mistra are no longer at war," said Sir Furnis mildly. "A royal wedding is as good a way to celebrate that as any."

"True, true," said Amell absently. He glanced around at the rest of their group. The few members of his father's court who had accompanied the delegation had opted to ride in carriages. He and Furn were as alone as they could hope to be, the rest of his guards riding in formation at a respectful distance behind the prince and his personal guard.

"To tell you the truth, Furn," Amell went on in a conspiratorial voice, "the really interesting part of our visit to Entolia wasn't the wedding. King Basil called a council of royals from each kingdom the day before the ceremony."

Sir Furnis showed a flicker of interest, turning slightly in his saddle to face his charge. "Is that where you disappeared to? I was half afraid you'd fallen into the ocean when I couldn't find you."

Amell chuckled good-naturedly at the entirely plausible explanation for his absence. "King Basil wanted to keep it pretty quiet, but I can trust you."

"Of course you can, Your Highness," said Sir Furnis, sounding resigned more than curious.

The stoic guard had more experience than anyone at being the recipient of Amell's sometimes overblown confidences, but this time Amell was fairly sure even Furn would be interested.

"Well, he's been wondering if there's a connection between the attacks on the various royal families over the last few years. The curse that turned King Justin into a beast, the enchantment that put Princess Azalea to sleep, the whole princes into swans thing in Mistra..."

Sir Furnis shot him a sharp look, clearly grasping the significance of the idea as quickly as Amell had expected him to. "A connection? You mean some organized group behind it all?"

Amell shrugged. "Maybe. That's what Basil wondered." He gave a sudden chuckle. "Fernedell is just about the only kingdom not to have been targeted if so. Are we secretly behind it, or are we just being passed over? Because I take offense if it's the latter."

"But you'd have no problem with the former?" Sir Furnis asked dryly.

Amell's easy grin didn't falter. "My father is maddening at times, but even I can acknowledge there isn't a dishonorable bone in his body. I think we can rule out the Fernedellian crown as the shadowy player behind these attacks."

Sir Furnis shook his head at the flippant words, but there was a smile on his face nevertheless. It was one of the things Amell liked best about his personal guard. Furn might be incredibly strait-laced when it came to his duty, but he was never uptight, and he never scolded. Amell considered him a close friend, at least as much as was possible with someone who insisted on calling him 'Your Highness' in spite of every protest.

"Who could it be, I wonder?" Sir Furnis mused. "If there is a conspiracy, of course."

"No idea," said Amell brightly. "We're all going to give our Enchanters' Guilds a once over, so I suppose that's somewhere to start. Seems unlikely it'll lead anywhere, though. Still, imagine if we were the ones to figure it out, Furn! What a lark that would be."

The guard just shook his head, his expression a mixture of exasperation and indulgence as his charge drifted into grand visions of single-handedly uncovering a nefarious plot against Solstice's crowns.

This cheerful state of mind didn't last. The closer the group traveled to Fernedell, the further Amell's mood dropped. The trip to Entolia for his old friend's wedding had been a welcome point of interest in his frustratingly predictable life, but he knew that as soon as he reached the castle in Fernford, he would be back under the restrictions that so chafed him.

"It would be an adventure, though, wouldn't it?" he said, a touch wistfully. "Having to fight off some powerful magical attack?"

Sir Furnis shot him a look. "It's a strange thing to wish for, Your Highness."

"I suppose it sounds bad," acknowledged Amell. "But the other royals at that table managed to overcome their curses."

"Not without significant cost," Sir Furnis reminded him gently.

Amell sighed. "You're right of course," he said, the words lacking conviction. They'd all seemed fine to him. Most of them even appeared to have found love through the experience. His thoughts flew to an old fantasy, of himself swooping in heroically to save some beleaguered damsel, and earning her eternal love and gratitude into the bargain. She'd be beautiful, of course. Long flowing hair, sparkling eyes, a look of utter trust and admiration on her face when she gazed at him.

He smiled self-consciously at the childish image. He'd outgrown those sorts of daydreams years ago, of course. But he still craved adventure. And he wasn't sure what was more disheartening—the fear that the royal duties laid out in an endless trail before his feet would beat that desire for adventure out of him, or the fear that they wouldn't, and that he'd spend his entire life not only bored, but bitterly frustrated.

With a sigh, he cast a glance over his shoulder, back toward the distant dragon colony. He'd wanted to go by a less direct route so as to pass near the area and try to catch a glimpse of the mysterious realm of the dragons. But the captain of the guard responsible for the delegation wouldn't hear of it.

Around noon of the second day of travel, they approached the city of Fernford. It was pleasantly situated on a large grassy plain, surrounded at some distance by four sizable groves. They rode through the southern grove at a quick pace, everyone eager to reach their destination now they were so close. When they emerged from the trees and Amell caught sight of the city, he tried to assess it dispassionately. It was a pleasant place, bustling with activity and bursting with color. Everywhere spring flowers bloomed from window boxes and market squares, and even the poorest classes favored cheerful fabrics that made the capital seem alive with the constant movement of bright colors. And the castle rising up from the center, many red flags flapping in a brisk breeze, was the prettiest part of the picture.

It brought him little joy.

"Take heart, valiant prince," Furn said softly, as they rode into the castle courtyard.

Amell glanced over, lifting an eyebrow in surprise at his guard's sympathetic smile.

"You face a particularly difficult monster to vanquish," Furn continued, "but I have faith in you."

A little bemused, but heartened all the same, Amell dismounted and handed his horse off to a hovering groom. Never one to hang back, even from a less than pleasant task, he took the steps two at a time and charged the nearest page with notifying his parents of his arrival. Furn kept pace behind him, and soon the two of them were striding through the castle in the direction of a small private dining hall used by the royal family.

Amell located not only his parents, but his sister eating a luncheon inside.

"Tora!" he said, smiling in genuine pleasure at his only sibling after greeting his parents more formally. "Did you miss me?"

"It was certainly quiet in your absence," said the princess tartly. She softened the words with a grin, and rose to embrace him. "Hello, little brother." She turned to Amell's guard. "And hello, Furn. Good to see you brought him safely home again."

"Of course, Your Highness," said Furn, bowing deeply.

"Tora," said Queen Pietra reprovingly. "That's hardly an appropriate way to address Sir Furnis."

"Oh, I forgot," said Tora innocently. "You refer to him as Sir Very Patient Man, don't you? You're not wrong, of course." She sent Amell the ghost of a wink.

The queen colored faintly, and Amell knew his mother was once again deeply regretting the comment she'd once made in exasperation, and which her children had never grown tired of repeating.

"You must be hungry," said Tora, resuming her seat. Her eyes flicked to Furn. "Both of you. Do join us."

Furn, who'd remained silent and unmoving through the entire exchange regarding himself, shifted slightly in place.

"I wouldn't dream of intruding, Your Highness," he said, his voice a little stiff.

"Your decorum does you credit," said Queen Pietra firmly. Her children, having waited in vain for her to follow the words with a gracious invitation for Sir Furnis to nevertheless eat with them, scowled at each other. But neither of them pushed the point. It would just make Furn uncomfortable. And even Amell was honest enough to admit that, as his personal guard, the poor fellow already had enough to put up with.

Amell seated himself across from his sister, reaching out for a cold ham in the center of the table.

"Did I miss anything exciting while I was gone?" he asked, as Furn assumed a place against the wall behind him. The guard was really too experienced and too senior to stand in the position of a manservant, but he clearly knew as well as Amell that the king and queen would want a report from him before he was dismissed.

"Nothing of note," said Tora calmly, buttering a roll. "A late thaw on the western side of the mountain range led to some flooding. But no homes were affected. Only some pastureland."

Amell grunted, unsurprised that nothing interesting had happened in Fernford during his absence.

"I'm meeting tomorrow with the farmers who were impacted," King Bern informed his son. "You will join me, Amell."

"Yes, Father," said Amell dutifully, although he made no particular effort to hide his lack of enthusiasm for the dull task.

"How was the wedding of King Basil and Princess—or I should say Queen Wren?" Queen Pietra asked. She clucked her tongue. "A couple of teenagers to be monarchs. A sad state of affairs for Entolia. And it's little better in Albury—worse in some ways, since their young queen is a commoner."

"Are you so disparaging of commoners?" Amell asked, a little surprised by his mother's words.

"Of course not," she said mildly. "A prosperous kingdom is built on a population of happy, hardworking commoners. But they shouldn't be brought into a royal family lightly. Albury is at a disadvantage with one of its monarchs having received no court training prior to her marriage."

Amell shrugged, not especially interested in discussing Alburian politics. "Well, I don't envy Basil," he said candidly. He raised his wine in his father's direction. "Speaking of which, to your good health and long life, Father."

King Bern indulged in a rare smile of amusement as his son drained the goblet before continuing.

"But I think he and his new queen will do a good job of leading their kingdom into better days. They have plenty of wealth to assist in the process, thanks to their mines."

"Yes," said Queen Pietra, studying her son with what she evidently felt was a casual air. "Entolia is certainly a kingdom on the rise. How did you find Princess Zinnia?"

Tora almost choked on her wine in an attempt to suppress a laugh. "Subtle, Mother," she said appreciatively.

Amell just rolled his eyes. "Princess Zinnia was in excellent health, Mother, and as uninterested in marrying me as I am in marrying her."

"What's this?" King Bern interjected, his startled expression suggesting that someone at least had missed the queen's not-so-subtle hint. "You're not after the boy about getting married, are you, Pietra? There's plenty of time for that. Eighteen is much too young to be hassling him."

"I wasn't hassling anyone," said the queen with dignity. "Not but what marriage might steady you, Amell. I merely asked how

Princess Zinnia is. Just because she happens to be one of the eligible princesses who—"

"Must I marry a princess?" Amell interrupted with a touch of anxiety. "Because Zinnia and I really wouldn't suit, Mother, and she's not *one of* the eligible princesses—she's the *only* eligible princess in Solstice! Her sisters are all too young for me, and none of the other kingdoms have unmarried princesses."

"No, you don't have to marry a princess," said his father. The words were made less reassuring by the dampening tone he always used when he felt Amell was getting too excited. "There are many perfectly appropriate young women within the court right here in Fernford. But as I say, there will be time enough to think of such things."

Amell nodded, a little relieved, but his mother apparently wasn't finished.

"You can marry within our kingdom, of course," she said, with a hint of regret. "But an alliance would certainly be nice. Now that Entolia and Mistra have a marriage alliance, as well as the one between Bansford and Listernia, we're at risk of being left behind." She turned to her daughter, her expression brightening. "I'm forgetting the Mistrans again. Now that they're no longer swans, there are five unmarried princes."

"Oh good," said Tora dryly. "I can be the lucky offspring to sacrifice myself to an alliance." She glanced at her brother. "You're off the hook, Amell."

"Much obliged." He grinned at her, raising his re-filled goblet in her direction. "Shall I drink to your marital happiness now?"

"All this nonsense about sacrifices," scolded the queen.

Tora gave her mother an innocent look. "I'm just trying to clarify, Mother. So the prerequisites for my groom are that he be a prince, and a human? No other requirements?"

The queen scowled at her daughter. "This is no time to be

flippant, Tora. At twenty years old you should be taking this matter much more seriously. I was not only married but expecting you by the time I turned twenty."

"What happened to not hassling anyone?" protested Tora hotly.

Amell sent her a sympathetic wince, and he heard Furn shift slightly behind him. For all his complaints about their overbearing ways, Amell knew that in some regards his parents were even harder on Tora. He'd often commented on it to Furn, and although the guard never expressed an opinion aloud, Amell had the sense that he agreed.

"Your situation is different from Amell's," said the queen crisply, "as you are well aware."

"We're not doing this again, Mother," Tora said with evident frustration. "Not here." Her eyes flicked to Furn, and Queen Pietra's followed.

"Oh, Sir Furnis," she said, seeming surprised to find him still standing at attention behind Amell. "You must be eager to return to your own home after such a long journey. You needn't stay."

"Hold on, Pietra," said King Bern patiently. "He's waiting to give his report on the Entolian trip." He nodded to the guard. "Go on, Sir Furnis."

With a bow, Furn delivered a succinct but informative summary of their journey, to which Amell listened in mild surprise. He wasn't sure whether to be impressed at all the guard had observed, or embarrassed at how much had gone over his own head.

"Thank you, you are dismissed," said King Bern.

With another bow, Furn strode from the room with such quick steps that Amell wondered if he really had been itching to leave. He'd hidden it well, if so.

"Now that we have privacy," Queen Pietra said, turning back

to her daughter with a purpose that made Amell search his mind for a way to turn the conversation. But Tora's reprieve came from an entirely different source as a sharp knock at the door caused them all to turn.

A servant hurried forward to intercept the messenger who had appeared in the doorway, and a moment later the newcomer was hurrying to the king.

"A message from the warden, Your Majesty," he said, bowing low.

"The warden?" King Bern repeated sharply, reaching out for the sealed billet in the messenger's hand.

The rest of the family stilled, and Amell and Tora exchanged tense glances. An urgent message from the prison couldn't bode well.

King Bern's face grew visibly harder as he read, and his wife's patience soon gave out.

"What news, Bern? Is it bad?"

"Very bad," he said, laying the parchment flat on the table with a bang. "There's been a breach."

CHAPTER THREE

Amell

"A breach?" Amell repeated, over his mother's gasp. "You mean a prisoner has escaped?"

"Not just one," corrected his father grimly. "An entire wing of the prison was blown open, and all its inmates got away."

"All of them?" said Tora, startled. Her face was paler than Amell had ever seen it. "How many prisoners is that?"

"Three dozen, according to the warden." The king met the eyes of each member of his family in turn. "I don't need to explain to any of you how serious this is."

"You certainly don't," said Queen Pietra, her voice not quite steady. "I always thought it was a bad idea to build that prison."

"Pietra," said the king sharply, and she fell silent. He called a servant over. "Send the captain of my guard to me at once." Turning to the messenger, he added, "Return to the prison immediately, and tell the warden that three squadrons will leave Fernford within the hour. He should hold his position, and focus on making sure the remaining wings are secure."

With a hasty bow, the messenger departed in the wake of the servant who'd already run to retrieve the captain. Amell had no doubt that the news would be all over the castle within half an hour, and the city soon after.

The moment they were alone again, the queen's restraint fled. "This was bound to happen, Bern! We should never have agreed to build a prison for the riffraff of the continent. I don't know why—"

"Nonsense," her husband cut her off impatiently. "This wasn't bound to happen. It should never have been possible with the protections on the prison. It's the most reinforced site in Solstice. And you do know why it was worth building the prison, so let's not be dramatic."

Tora was frowning thoughtfully. "Of course it was worth it. It's one of our primary sources of revenue."

Amell nodded absently, his mind turning over the dire implications of the news. Although he'd only been a child at the time, he perfectly remembered the decision ten years before to build the prison. The problem had been common to several of the kingdoms—what to do with enchanters and enchantresses who had broken the law but, due to their powers, couldn't be reliably contained through normal means. When the idea had been raised of a special prison, designed to hold the magic-wielding criminals from across the continent, and reinforced with all the magical protection the combined kingdoms could afford to provide, it had made excellent sense for Fernedell to volunteer. Not only was the kingdom centrally located in the continent, but its economy wasn't as strong as most of its neighbors. Being the only landlocked kingdom on Solstice had its detriments.

But now, Fernedell's economy was thriving. And it was largely thanks to the handsome contributions paid by the other kingdoms for the service of housing their convicted enchanters and enchantresses.

"Never mind that, though," Tora was continuing. "The question is how in dragon's flame a breakout happened."

"Tora," the queen said reprovingly.

Amell wanted to roll his eyes. It was hardly the moment to worry about Tora using an unladylike expression.

Apparently his father was equally unconcerned about such trifles. "It was no accident, that much is certain," he said darkly. "There was an explosion, but even before that, the magic-users among the guards reported feeling an intense surge of power approaching the facility."

"So it was sabotage," said Amell, sitting up straighter. "An intentional attack."

King Bern nodded. "And one with great power behind it, we have to assume."

"But that's amazing!" exclaimed Amell. All three of his family members looked at him with identically raised eyebrows. "Sorry," he said, trying not to laugh at his own ill-timed excitement. "It's terrible, of course. I just meant...it's our turn, after all."

"And what," asked King Bern icily, "do you mean by that? You think we deserve this misfortune?"

"No, no, that's not what I mean," said Amell, exasperated. He lowered his voice. "I just attended a meeting with King Basil, who thinks there might be a connection between the various magical attacks against royals in recent years. I commented, just joking you know, that we were feeling a little left out, but this certainly fits the description, doesn't it?"

"Are you telling me," King Bern demanded, sounding angrier by the second, "that you invited this calamity? That you baited whoever might have been listening to target us for—"

"What?" protested Amell. "Of course not! The conversation wasn't the cause—I just meant that this development supports

Basil's theory." He saw that his father still didn't look convinced. "It was a very private conversation, Father."

"If you were involved," said his father cuttingly, "I don't think we can put much reliance on the meeting's privacy."

"That's not fair," said Amell, stung. "I'm perfectly capable of keeping things to myself. I've kept plenty of—"

A pointedly cleared throat from his sister caused Amell to fall silent, rethinking what he'd been midway through blurting out. Quite apart from the fact that many of the secrets he'd kept over the years had been Tora's, he wasn't going to win any favor with his parents by boasting about how he took every opportunity to hide his activities from them.

He scowled internally, half wishing he'd kept Basil's theory to himself. Of course his father not only refused to take Amell's information seriously, but found some way to blame him for the disaster at the prison. Not that Amell really imagined for a moment that his father believed the attack at the prison had been caused by a casual conversation of Amell's. He surely knew as well as Amell did that the prison break must have been in planning for some time.

"I'll oversee the manhunt myself," King Bern was saying distractedly. "But I suspect we'll have to call in assistance from the other kingdoms. Over thirty fugitives! And all with magic at their disposal."

Amell leaned forward in his seat. "I'd like to assist, Father. I can help coordinate the search."

The king pinned him with a look. "This isn't some chance for showy heroics, Amell. This is a serious threat to our people."

"I understand," Amell insisted. "I'm taking this seriously, believe me. I don't want criminally minded enchanters roaming freely over our kingdom, subjecting innocent citizens to their malice. I want to help round them up, and—perhaps even more importantly—help figure out who was behind the incident, and make sure they can't do any more mischief."

His father was silent for a moment, searching Amell's eyes closely, as if trying to measure his earnestness.

"You're exactly correct about my two main priorities," he said at last. Amell brightened. "And I applaud your eagerness to assist," the king added. "This has the potential to be an excellent learning experience for you. But to be frank, Amell, I'm not sure I want *you* roaming freely over our kingdom, especially with thirty-five criminals on the loose. You're still too young and, dare I say it, have too often proven yourself lacking in responsibility to be entrusted with such a crucial task without proper supervision."

With an effort, Amell swallowed his irritation over his father's total lack of faith in him. It smarted, but he knew expressing any resentment over the slights would only reinforce his father's opinion that he was too young and hotheaded for any serious responsibility.

"I didn't say I wanted to wander the kingdom unsupervised," he said calmly. "Just that I want to help."

"I know you didn't," acknowledged the king. "But this crisis is of sufficient severity that neither I nor my chief leaders can afford to be burdened with your oversight."

"Furn's old and responsible," Amell suggested hopefully.

His father gave him a pointed look. "Twenty-five is not old, Amell." He paused. "Although I will acknowledge that Sir Furnis has shown himself to be unusually responsible for his age. Otherwise he would not have been given the role of heading your guard so young. Given the antics you've still managed to pull off, I shudder to think what trouble you would have gotten yourself into without him these last five years."

"It's all right, Father," smiled Amell ruefully. "You don't need to pretend. I know perfectly well that you gave the role to someone young in the hope they'd have more success reaching me, and I'd be less likely to give them the slip. And you were quite right. I can never bring myself to go behind Furn's back. It would be such a poor thing to do, somehow."

"Well, I'm glad one of my strategies in curbing your activities has proved successful," said King Bern dryly. He drummed his fingers on the table. "Well, you'll never grow into your role if I don't give you the opportunity to learn, I suppose," he said at last. "When I ride for the prison, you and Sir Furnis may join me."

Amell sprang out of his seat, ready to run in search of his guard immediately.

"Amell, will you calm down?" his father chastised him wearily. "The poor man's just been released from your last journey. I won't be riding out immediately. I'll need to meet with my captain first. It's possible I won't go in person until tomorrow."

"And do we need to remind you that *you* have only just returned from a lengthy absence?" Queen Pietra added. "Can't you even sit through a single meal with your family without running off in search of adventure?"

"Of course I can, Mother," said Amell, with as much dignity as he could muster while lowering himself back into his seat. "I just didn't want to hold Father up, that's all."

"I've said you can come," said King Bern. "I'm not going to leave without you."

"I want to hear more about this theory of King Basil's," said Tora, re-entering the conversation. "Do you really think it's possible that this attack at the prison is linked to the curses some of the other royals have experienced?"

"It fits, doesn't it?" Amell said eagerly, pleased that someone was taking his comment seriously.

"Not really." His father's tone was dampening. "I don't see how a prison break can be considered an attack against the royal family. There are many more plausible motivations for someone breaking prisoners out.”

“All the other attacks had more personal motivations as well,” said Amell. “That doesn’t mean there isn’t a wider connection.”

“Well,” said King Bern, rising from his seat, “we can certainly discuss it further. But I think you’re grasping at straws, Amell.” He picked up the billet from the messenger. “My captain will be waiting for me.” His gaze passed over his family, a crease between his eyes. “I’ll have the guard around the castle doubled while we decide how to contain this disaster.”

“Is that the best use of—” Tora started, but the king had already paced from the room. Amell stared thoughtfully after him, wondering if his father’s parting words had indicated some small openness to the idea of an attack targeted on the royal family.

He turned back to find his mother looking at him pointedly, and stilled his tapping foot. He knew the habit irritated her, but he hadn’t even realized he was doing it. It was just so hard to sit sedately at lunch when such dramatic events were occurring. Grim as he knew the situation to be, he couldn’t help being glad that the captain had refused to sidetrack the delegation as Amell had requested. It would have been maddening to have arrived back from Entolia only to find he’d missed the opportunity to play a role in his father’s response to the prison break.

An explosion, his father had said. What could cause such a thing? It was clearly magical in nature if the magic-users employed at the prison had felt a surge of power approaching.

As soon as it was polite to do so, Amell extricated himself from the dining room. Remembering his father’s admittedly pertinent reminder, he didn’t go in search of Furn straight away. The guard deserved an hour to himself, particularly if he was going to be dragged from the capital again within the day.

He made no attempt to find his father, either. If the king had been willing for his son to join him in his interview with the captain of his guard, he would have invited Amell.

Instead, pausing only to change out of his traveling clothes, the prince left the castle. It was only a short walk down the cobbled streets to his destination. He stopped outside the imposing stone building, his eyes lingering on the elaborate scrollwork over the doorway.

Enchanters' Guild, it read, etched in large letters into the stone.

Amell felt a swell of determination as he strode through the doorway. His father might not take him seriously, but he intended to follow his hunch regarding the attack. And even before this latest incident, he'd already been planning to make inquiries with the Fernedellian Enchanters' Guild, to satisfy himself that there was no reason to think his kingdom might be harboring magic-wielding conspirators. If he was going to be occupied with the situation at the prison for some time to come, it would be just as well to snatch this opportunity to make contact with the guild.

The fact that it meant he could be doing something, instead of sitting around waiting for his father to decide things were well enough in hand to involve his flighty son, had nothing to do with it. Of course not.

"Your Highness." The clerk manning the guild's lobby greeted Amell with evident surprise as he entered the broad, well-lit space. "What an honor." He rose, bowing low, but Amell waved an airy hand.

"No need for formalities," he said cheerfully. "I'm not here on official royal business. I was just hoping to speak with Bartholomew."

The clerk blinked at this casual reference to one of the

guild's most senior enchanters, but he quickly bent into another bow.

"Certainly, Your Highness. He's in the building, meeting with the recruiters. I'll let him know you're here."

The man scurried from the room, and Amell was left loitering in the lobby. He strolled over to a bookshelf, running his hand along the leather bindings of a series of books on magical theory. He'd never studied it much. He remembered his excitement as a small child when the concept of power had been explained to him. And then his disappointment when he learned, not only that no amount of training could give him the aptitude for magic some were simply born with, but that studying the craft without being able to actually do it was just about the most boring topic in his education.

He turned with a sigh from a tome called, 'The Basic Principles of the Counterforce', and wandered over to the other side of the room, where a stand was displaying a worn leather glove. The placard read, 'Fernedell's first known artifact'.

He studied the item dispassionately. He knew the tales as well as any royal would. No one knew exactly when dragons had come to Solstice, but it was generally accepted that humans had been there first, and that before the advent of the beasts, the human population had carried no magic. But once the dragons arrived, and started flying around, involuntarily shedding their magic everywhere they went, it slowly became clear that some humans had the capacity—equally involuntary—to absorb that magic and carry it in their own right.

And so power had entered human bloodlines.

It had taken some time for the magic-wielding humans to study their new ability sufficiently to learn the craft of pouring their magic into items that could later be used. And apparently, the first known Fernedellian enchantress to create an artifact had felt the need for gloves that kept her hands warm perpetually.

"What a mundane use of something so exciting," muttered Amell, turning away from the object, from which all magic had long ago leaked.

His face brightened at the sight of the clerk, returning with a familiar figure in tow.

"Bartholomew!" Amell cried, striding forward to meet the elderly enchanter. "I was lucky to find you here."

"Not so lucky, Your Highness," chuckled Bartholomew. "I'm mostly to be found here. I'm delighted you came looking. What can I do for you?"

Remembering the secrecy with which Basil had told him of his theory, Amell glanced at the clerk. "Walk with me?" he asked Bartholomew, tilting his head toward the open door, and the bustling street beyond.

"Certainly," assented the enchanter, and within moments they were out on the street, strolling at a sedate pace comfortable for the elderly man. "It won't be much satisfaction for you, walking with me," smiled Bartholomew. "I move so slowly, you may as well be standing still."

Amell flashed him a cheeky grin. "I thought you knew me better than that, Bartholomew. I never stand still."

The old man chuckled. "Truer words were never spoken," he assented. He bent a shrewd look upon his visitor, the keenness of his gaze at odds with his frail frame. "What's brought you to see me, Your Highness?"

"A matter of some delicacy," said Amell at once. "I'd be grateful if you'd keep it to yourself."

"Of course," agreed Bartholomew readily.

Amell smiled gratefully, not doubting the enchanter for a moment. Bartholomew had been the castle's resident enchanter all Amell's life. His natural magic was one of healing, and in addition to providing sundry magical services to the crown, he'd been the one to patch Amell up when his foolhardy exploits had landed him in strife.

Which had been often.

In short, Bartholomew was as familiar to Amell as his old nurse, and the prince had been sad when the elderly man withdrew from his active role to take up some training responsibilities within the Enchanters' Guild. He was one of the guild's governing members, and rightly so. Few in Fernedell had more experience in magic than he did.

"How confident are you in the guild's leadership?" Amell blurted out, with the lack of tact that was the despair of his family.

Bartholomew came to a stop, throwing him a startled look. "Do you have reason to doubt the guild, Your Highness?"

"Not really," admitted Amell. "It's just come to my attention that a series of attacks have been carried out against the various royal families of Solstice over the last few years, all of them using inexplicably potent magic. I want to be sure that if there's some organized group of criminal enchanters, Fernedell isn't harboring any of them."

Bartholomew frowned, still unmoving in the street. Passersby wove respectfully around the prince and the senior enchanter, and Amell searched Bartholomew's face for any sign of unease. He saw only a pensive consideration.

"I would be astonished to discover any such person within the guild," Bartholomew said at last. "Although the idea of a broader connection between these attacks is worth further consideration. I must confess I hadn't thought of it. If there is a conspiracy, we can only be thankful Fernedell has so far escaped being targeted."

"Actually," said Amell grimly, "we may not have." With

lowered voice, he told Bartholomew of the prison break, watching as the old man's eyes widened in horror.

"So you're confident no one from the guild had any hand in such an attack?" Amell pressed.

"I suppose I can't be completely confident without any investigation," said Bartholomew, raising his hands. "But I can't believe it. To unleash so many violent magic-users on the unprotected community! It doesn't bear thinking about."

"So there hasn't been any tension recently?" Amell asked him. "No debate regarding the ethics of the prison, or," he lowered his voice further, "discontent with the crown, or anything like that?"

"Not that I've heard," shrugged Bartholomew. "The guild operates very smoothly. We have our disagreements of course, but we haven't had true tension of the nature you describe in almost twenty years, not since Cyfrin."

"Cyfrin?" echoed Amell, stumbling over the unfamiliar name. "Who or what is that?"

"He was an enchanter," sighed Bartholomew. "Well, still is, I suppose. He disappeared after he was denied a position with the guild, but I can't imagine he's dead. He was a young man when it all happened, not much older than you."

"When what happened?" Amell asked impatiently, bouncing slightly on the balls of his feet.

Seeing the gesture, Bartholomew smiled and began walking again. "His father was an enchanter, and a senior member of the guild. He passed away quite suddenly, and it quickly became clear that Cyfrin expected to inherit his father's position."

"Is that how it works?" Amell asked, surprised.

Bartholomew shrugged. "Not necessarily, but it certainly can happen, if the guild considers the successor an appropriate candidate."

"But they didn't think that about Cyfrin?"

"No," said Bartholomew dryly, "we certainly did not. Cyfrin's father was a good man and a good enchanter, but his son was a rotten apple. Plus there was the issue of divided loyalties," he added as an afterthought.

"Divided loyalties?" Amell asked, confused.

Bartholomew nodded. "His father was Fernedellian, but his mother was from Albury. A position in the Enchanters' Guild holds considerable influence in matters of court—ideally candidates would have absolute loyalty for your father."

"But that wasn't the main issue?" Amell asked.

"It was barely a factor when compared with his other...indiscretions."

Amell raised a questioning eyebrow, and Bartholomew sighed.

"How much do you understand about the role of vessels in magic?"

Amell gave him a sheepish look. "It rings a bell from my studies, but I'm afraid..."

"You remember little of them," Bartholomew finished with a smile. "You understand about artifacts, I suppose?"

Amell nodded. "Of course. Are they what you mean by vessels?"

"They're the primary example of them, yes," said Bartholomew. "They can receive and store magic for later extraction. The quantity of the magic, the quality of the power once extracted, depends on the item chosen, as well as the skill of the magic-user. Some objects lend themselves to magic more than others."

"A bit like how some people have the aptitude for magic, and others simply don't," chimed in Amell.

Bartholomew nodded. "Precisely." He hesitated. "Although that cuts to the heart of what Cyfrin was proposing, actually. He was...frustrated by the natural limits of inanimate vessels."

"Inanimate?" Amell echoed, looking sharply at his companion. "You mean he wanted to use living creatures as vessels?"

"That's exactly what he wanted to do," said Bartholomew grimly. "By the time it came to the attention of the guild, he'd waded very deep into experiments with animals. And he was quite right about one thing—living beings do not suffer the same limitations as objects. The results of his experiments were quite impressive, in one sense. The amount of power he could store in the creatures he selected surprised me, if I'm honest."

"So why did the guild disapprove?"

Bartholomew smiled, but it wasn't a happy expression. "Because of the cost. Do you think he was the first to think of such a thing? The potential use of animals as vessels has been explored before. And quite apart from the ethical issues with using a living creature as a passive vessel for your power, when that creature has no choice or control in the matter, there was one fairly significant problem with his experiments."

"Which was?"

"The power becomes wrapped inextricably around the creature's life force. In short, the animals all died when the power was extracted from them. Without exception."

"That's a bit grim," said Amell.

"It got more so," Bartholomew assured him. "Cyfrin wanted to progress his experiments. Having achieved impressive results with animals, he had already become once again frustrated with the limitations of his vessels. He wanted to store more power than the creatures could hold. His own magic wasn't especially strong, but he was incredibly clever, and resourceful. He'd realized that if he could save his magic up in a vessel, he would no longer be limited to his natural level of power."

"What do you mean he wanted to progress his experiments?" Amell asked.

"He wanted to begin using humans as vessels," said Bartholomew simply.

"What?" Amell protested. "Knowing they would die when he accessed his power? How could he think the guild would approve that?"

"He had a theory that a human vessel wouldn't die. Our bodies are stronger, and our cores more capable of interacting with magic. That much we know. But naturally, the guild wasn't willing to take that chance with a person's life."

"I should think not," said Amell emphatically. He frowned as he thought the other man's words over. "So he wanted to pour his power into another enchanter? One with capacity to receive it?"

"Certainly not," said Bartholomew tartly. "Such a person would be able not only to receive the power, but to use it as they wished. That was the last thing Cyfrin wanted. He wanted to choose some random magic-less peasant and use him or her as a passive vessel, stuffing them full of his magic, knowing they would have no way to access or use it themselves. And, of course, willing to take a gamble that they might not survive the experience. He said it was worth the risk for the cause of advancing magical knowledge."

"He didn't place much value on others' lives, did he?" Amell said, disgusted.

"You could say that," agreed Bartholomew dryly. "To make matters even worse, his research had led him to believe that the younger a person was, the more receptive their body would be to someone else's power. He proposed attempting the process with a child." He shook his head. "You can see why he wasn't given a position of leadership within the guild. When he refused to acknowledge the inappropriateness of his proposal, his membership was revoked altogether. He disappeared completely. It makes me uneasy to think about it sometimes, but we haven't heard rumors of any suspicious activity that would suggest his experiments continued."

"And it's unlikely his experiments have anything to do with the prison break," mused Amell, a little disappointed. "None of the curses against other royals fit the description, either."

"That's a good thing," Bartholomew said, smiling again. "Trust me. It's much better if Cyfrin isn't involved."

"Of course," said Amell absently. He was reassured on one point, at least. If the Enchanters' Guild was unified in taking a strong stance on experiments like Cyfrin's, it was unlikely to be harboring any treasonous magic-users.

Amell's eyes flew up to the castle. "I should probably return. I'm to accompany my father to the prison, and I don't know when he's leaving." He smiled at the enchanter. "Thank you for making time to answer my questions."

"Of course," said Bartholomew. "And try not to get yourself into any trouble, Your Highness."

Amell's smile grew. "I'd best not make promises I can't keep."

CHAPTER FOUR

Aurelia

Aurelia glanced nervously out the window. "It's almost sunset."

Mama Gail's eyes passed around the space. "I think we're ready."

Aurelia nodded, although her thoughts didn't match the action. She never felt ready for Cyfrin's visits, no matter how tidy they'd made the tower.

"Do you think he knows about the prison break?" she asked the older woman.

"Without a doubt," Mama Gail said dryly. "I imagine the news hadn't appeared by the time he left yesterday evening. He didn't seem concerned then, and I doubt he'd be able to hide his reaction. But we can be sure he has better sources of news than we do." She gestured to their sole window, a reflection of Aurelia's own irritation crossing her features. "He spends his days out there, doesn't he? In the world."

Aurelia moved to the opening, leaning her elbows on the windowsill. Her eyes passed over the small patch of grassy ground that surrounded the tower, before the view was obstructed by trees. She had no window on the other side of the tower, but if Cyfrin's information was to be trusted, the forest ringed their little clearing on all sides.

But then, how was any of Cyfrin's information to be trusted? As with everything, they had no way to check whether he was telling the truth. No way beyond the enchanted news-carrying volume he kept in his study, of course. And they were very careful never to let him know they had access to that. Not that it covered such mundane topics as the geography of their little patch of the world. It just mirrored major news announcements from each of Solstice's capitals. And that was a good deal better than the nothing Cyfrin usually told them about the world outside.

"He's always said it's dangerous out there," Aurelia sighed, her eyes passing over the peaceful forest scene below. A fox slunk across the open ground, disappearing into the trees. "It sounds like he might actually be right."

Mama Gail sighed as well, approaching with soft footsteps. "There are always dangers in life. But the world is not primarily a wicked place. He just tells you that in the hope it will keep you docile. Still," she leaned her own elbows on the windowsill, matching Aurelia's posture, "I can't deny that this prison break news is alarming." She made a face. "Not that we have much call to be alarmed on our own account, of course. Since no one can get in here apart from Cyfrin."

"Except that the inmates who escaped all have magic, don't they?" said Aurelia. "Do you think it's possible they might be able to break Cyfrin's enchantment and get in here after all?"

Mama Gail frowned. "Their magic would have to be very strong. And don't forget what I've read in his notes about the powerful concealment enchantment over this whole place. They wouldn't even be able to find us in order to attempt to break their way in."

Aurelia was silent for a moment, thinking this over. She wasn't sure whether to be relieved or disappointed.

"Are they all like him, do you think?" she asked softly. "Was the prison full of enchanters like Cyfrin, who've just been unlucky enough to actually be caught in their misdeeds?"

"I suppose so," said Mama Gail. She straightened, clapping Aurelia on the shoulder. "Which is cause to hope, isn't it? They were caught, which means Cyfrin can be, too. He'll be made to face justice one day. You mark my words."

Aurelia didn't answer, her eyes still fixed on the lengthening shadows beyond her window. Her mother had been saying that for as long as she could remember. And she'd always believed it, because Mama Gail wouldn't lie to her. If Aurelia was certain of anything, she was certain of that. But she wasn't a child anymore, and she was starting to understand that there was a difference between intentionally lying, and simply being mistaken. Mama Gail might believe they'd be free one day. But that didn't mean they actually would be. Or that it would be anytime soon.

A shiver went over Aurelia at the thought of spending her whole life in the tower, locked away until she was older than Mama Gail, her youth wasted, her future snatched away as surely as her past had been.

But no, she realized with a fresh shot of dread. She wouldn't be in here forever. Because at some point, Cyfrin would decide it was time to claim the magic he'd stored in her hair. When that time came, things would surely change. If she survived the experience, which she didn't assume she would, whatever his notes theorized.

And what would happen to her then? Did he have some further sinister plan to follow in case of her survival? Or would she be discarded like a broken pot, no longer of any use? That last thought was actually quite appealing. She didn't mind being thrown friendless on the world, if it meant she could be out of the tower. And she'd never really be friendless, because her mother would never desert her.

"If we do get out," she asked idly, "where will we go? Back to Albury?"

"Of course," said Mama Gail brightly, seating herself and continuing the mending she'd been working on most of the afternoon. "That's where our family is."

"Your family," Aurelia corrected. "Since my original parents are both dead now."

She frowned as she turned the memories over in her mind. She'd been too young to be aware when the mother who gave birth to her died. But she did remember Mama Gail telling her, at the age of four, that her father had passed away. Aurelia could picture the other woman now, coming out of Cyfrin's study with a somber air that had frightened the little girl. But Mama Gail had never adequately explained where she acquired the information. She couldn't have read it in Cyfrin's news-book. That tome only gave broad news, not specific details like individual people's births and deaths. Perhaps Cyfrin had kept tabs on the family from whom he'd stolen a baby, and had made a note of their deaths for his own records.

"My family *is* your family," Mama Gail said firmly, unaware that her companion was lost in memory. "Ambrose and Felicity will be all grown up now, just like you. You'll like having a brother and a sister. And Gustav will love you as much as I do."

She spoke with such firmness, Aurelia sometimes wondered if she was trying to convince herself as much as her daughter. If the idea of joining Mama Gail's family was a reality rather than a distant—and likely impossible—dream, she would feel nervous about how they would receive the interloper who'd stolen their mother away from them.

"Plus," said Mama Gail, "you're forgetting your other brother."

"Justin," Aurelia repeated absently. She wondered about him sometimes, but it was hard to feel too attached to a brother she'd never met. Especially since Mama Gail hadn't interacted with him much before her capture, and so couldn't tell Aurelia a great deal about what he'd been like.

All such reflections fled from her mind as she saw a figure emerge from the trees down below. She pulled back from the window, but Cyfrin had clearly seen her.

"Ah. Honeysuckle," he called, his voice tight and clipped. "My rope."

Swallowing her distaste, Aurelia pulled her hair free of the intricate braid which was the only thing that allowed her to move around freely. In a minute, she had her tresses over the hook and out the window, Mama Gail helping to brace her as Cyfrin pulled himself up.

Aurelia steeled herself for further recriminations about her failure to find an easier way for him to climb up. But Cyfrin didn't say a word about it. It was apparent from the moment he slipped through the window that he was in a foul temper, and apparently the matter had been driven from his mind.

"Took you long enough," he snarled at Aurelia. "You should have your hair unbound before sunset in future. No reason for me to wait around on your convenience."

Aurelia shot a tense look at Mama Gail, hoping the other woman wouldn't leap to her defense and set Cyfrin's back up further. But although her mother's lips were pressed into a thin and disapproving line, she held her peace. They had both been prepared for their captor to be angry.

"Well, let's not waste more of my time," snapped Cyfrin. None too gently, he buried his fingers in Aurelia's hair, muttering his usual incomprehensible monologue. He fell silent after no more than a minute, stepping back.

Aurelia turned in surprise, gathering her hair protectively. "So short today," she said, without thinking.

"Well, I had to waste time and power reinforcing the protections around your haven, didn't I?" Cyfrin snapped. "You should be thanking me, not complaining. Little do you know how vulnerable you would be to this world's dangers without my intervention, Honeysuckle."

Aurelia and Mama Gail exchanged silent looks. Impressed by her mother's calm demeanor, Aurelia tried to relax her posture. They both knew how important it was that Cyfrin not have any suspicion that they already knew the news that was making him so irritable.

"Dangers, Master Enchanter?" Aurelia asked hesitantly. "Is something amiss?"

"I knew it was a terrible idea," growled Cyfrin, ignoring her question. "I could have told them at the time. I'm amazed it took ten years for such a disaster to occur. What fools does the king have in the Enchanters' Guild, to be advising him to make Fernedell the dumping ground for every disgraced magic-user in Solstice? But I know what fools he's got running the guild—the kind who are too narrow-minded to know progress when they see it. The kind that would rather hang on to their power than see magic advance."

Aurelia remained silent, trying to mold her expression into one of bewilderment. In actual fact, she had a fairly good idea what Cyfrin was talking about. She didn't know the full details of his falling out with the Fernedellian Enchanters' Guild—his ledgers were full of notes on his experiments, not personal journals recounting the events of his life. But she and her mother had gleaned enough to gather that he'd fallen from the guild's favor on account of his unorthodox methods. It wasn't hard to imagine, given the way he'd experimented on her hair all her life. The fact that such projects had caused him to be thrown out of the guild gave Aurelia great faith in Fernedell's other enchanters.

Thanks to the news Mama Gail had read before, she also understood his other comments. Although she'd been a young child at the time, she could still remember Cyfrin's fury when the decision had been made, ten years earlier, to build the magic prison a short distance to the south east of the tower's location. From the way he'd spoken, anyone would have thought the king chose a site so close to them out of personal malice, rather than being completely unaware of Cyfrin's illicit tower.

"What disaster are you talking about?" Mama Gail asked curtly. "If you want to be understood, you'll have to be a little plainer."

"I have no need to be understood by you," snapped Cyfrin. "But I'll have you know that all my predictions have proved correct. There's been a mass break out from the prison, just as I said there would be."

"You predicted a break out?" Mama Gail asked coldly. "I have no memory of that." Cyfrin's face darkened, but she pressed on. "How many escaped? Are we in danger?"

"A hundred criminal magic-users are on the loose now," said Cyfrin, with relish. "And the only reason you're safe is because of my protections." He turned to Aurelia, his expression softening slightly. "Don't forget that."

Aurelia kept her face blank with difficulty. It was so like Cyfrin to lie and exaggerate the numbers. She knew from the official record Mama Gail had seen that the number was less than forty. But the enchanter would want her to be more afraid than the truth warranted. He was truly deluded enough to think he could frighten her into actually *wanting* to be trapped in the tower. The worst part was, if Mama Gail hadn't always been there, contradicting his lies the moment he left, it probably would have worked.

"Never mind all of that," said Cyfrin, his features contorting into a smile that was even more alarming than his scowl had been. "Did you miss me, Honeysuckle?"

"Did I...what?" Aurelia blinked, taken aback both by the strange question, and by the sudden switch in manner. Was Cyfrin trying to be...kind? It wasn't convincing.

"Did you miss me?" he repeated, his voice betraying only the tiniest flicker of irritation at her obtuseness. "I saw you waiting for me by the window. Counting down the hours?"

Mama Gail snorted, but Aurelia was too bemused to even see the humor. Did Cyfrin *want* her to look forward to his visits? He'd never shown any hint of it before. He clearly expected her to see him as her benefactor—supposedly protecting her against the world—but he'd never tried to endear himself to her on a personal level before.

"Actually, I was just...enjoying the view," she said blankly.

Again annoyance crossed Cyfrin's features, but he quickly stifled it. "I was looking forward to seeing you," he said, his smile once again not quite natural.

His gaze drifted to her hair, and Aurelia gathered it to herself uneasily. Why was he behaving so strangely? She preferred his angry rants to this falsely gentle tone. What lie was he trying to sell her now? Whatever his motivations, they weren't genuine. That much was a given.

"Just because I don't have much magic available to store," he went on, "doesn't mean this evening needs to be a total waste. There are other aims to pursue."

"Other aims?" frowned Aurelia. "Are you talking about the new project you're working on?"

"You remembered," said Cyfrin, sounding pleased. Aurelia

stared at him, still utterly bemused by his demeanor. He cast a lazy glance over his shoulder at Mama Gail. "I want to speak to Honeysuckle alone, crone. You can wait in the bedroom."

"I don't think so," said Mama Gail, her voice as hard as the stone that formed their tower. "I'm not going anywhere."

"I think you are," said Cyfrin grimly. "This is between Honeysuckle and me."

"I've already told you," snapped Mama Gail, moving to stand beside Aurelia, "anything involving Aurelia involves me."

"Her name is Honeysuckle," spat Cyfrin. "And her time is mine to command, not yours. She was given to me in payment for a theft. *You* formed no part of that bargain. If you know what's good for you, don't remind me how dispensable you are to my plans."

"It's all right, Mama Gail," said Aurelia, alarmed by the stubbornness she saw in her mother's eyes. It wasn't the first time she'd been afraid the other woman would push too far and tip Cyfrin over the edge. If he decided he no longer wanted to house and feed Mama Gail, Aurelia didn't like to think what he would do. "You can go into the other room for a moment, surely."

"I most surely cannot," contradicted Mama Gail. "And I will not."

Aurelia frowned. Mama Gail was always determined, and she made a point of being defiant when it came to Cyfrin. But usually she knew where to draw the line to avoid a level of confrontation more painful than it was worth. Aurelia couldn't understand her mother's sudden intensity. Cyfrin was unpleasant, but he'd never been violent toward them. Why was Mama Gail so determined not to leave Aurelia alone with him?

"In the other room," growled Cyfrin. "Now."

Mama Gail planted her feet firmly, her stubbornness written clearly across her face. Aurelia opened her mouth to again urge her mother to let it go, when Cyfrin's arm suddenly flashed out. Before Aurelia well understood what was happening, he had her mother in a painful-looking armlock. Both women shouted in protest, but he ignored them completely. With a brutal twist, he spun Mama Gail around and marched her forcibly across the tower before practically throwing her into the room where she and Aurelia slept and slamming the door behind her.

CHAPTER FIVE

Aurelia

In a movement so swift Aurelia could barely follow it, Cyfrin produced a large silver key and turned it in the lock. Mama Gail's furious shouts could be heard from behind the door, and judging by the frantic banging, she was pounding her fists against the wood.

Cyfrin stalked back over to Aurelia, his face still heavy with anger. For a moment they stood in silence, Aurelia staring at him in mingled alarm and astonishment. What had come over everyone? Why did he want to speak with her alone for the first time in her entire life, and why was Mama Gail so adamant he not do so?

Taking in her expression, Cyfrin drew a deep breath. "Now," he said, his pleasant tone so forced Aurelia winced slightly. "We can talk more comfortably."

Her mouth actually fell open. "Comfortably?" Mama Gail's angry shouts and continued attempts on the door drew her gaze, and she felt a sudden surge of anger. "Let her out."

"I will in a minute," said Cyfrin dismissively. "She needs to learn a lesson about obedience."

Aurelia relaxed slightly. Infuriating as it was, this self-satisfied assumption of authority over his prisoners was at least a more familiar role from Cyfrin. As her eyes passed over him, she saw again that large silver key, and a frown settled on her face.

"You have a key to our room?" she demanded. "You've never told us about that."

"You've never needed to know," Cyfrin said smoothly, stowing it in his pocket. "Now, to more important matters."

"No," said Aurelia, surprising herself by her own defiance. "You had no right to keep it from us. And you have no right to take it with you. You should leave it here."

"No right?" One of Cyfrin's thin, dark eyebrows shot up. "I have every right where you're concerned, Honeysuckle."

His tone had grown angrier with each passing word, and for the briefest of moments Aurelia winced, waiting for her mother's inevitable defense of her, and the enchanter's equally inevitable explosion of wrath. But of course neither came. Mama Gail couldn't hear a word they were saying, and her continued protests were nothing more than a muffled pounding and wordless yelling.

Cyfrin followed her gaze to the locked door, and a smug look crossed his face. Clearly he too was reflecting on the lack of retort.

To Aurelia's own surprise, she felt neither relief over the avoidance of confrontation, nor fear over being undefended. Instead, as she took in Cyfrin's smirk, she felt a surge of something powerful that she'd never experienced before. All at once, standing alone before the enchanter for the first time ever, she understood what Mama Gail's explanations had never been able to make clear. She couldn't have explained it in words, either. She just knew it was important to defy Cyfrin, even without a hope of stopping him from doing whatever he wanted.

"You don't," she said clearly, pleased at the steadiness of her voice. "You don't have any right where I'm concerned."

Cyfrin's eyes widened in a look of shock that quickly gave way to anger. But just as he opened his mouth to cut her with his words, he seemed to suddenly recollect something. Drawing another deep breath, he narrowed his eyes thoughtfully.

"You should trust me, Honeysuckle," he tried again. "And you shouldn't believe everything that woman tells you."

Aurelia's confusion at his uncharacteristic restraint was drowned out in the sudden flare of anger brought on by his last words. How dare this man, who'd stolen her from her family and lied to her all her life, tell her not to believe the only person who'd ever cared for her?

"You need to leave," she said coldly. "I don't want to talk to you."

Again anger crossed Cyfrin's face, and this time he wasn't as successful at controlling it. "I've let you grow up too wild," he spat. "You *will* listen to what I have to say."

"I won't listen to a word until you let my mother out," Aurelia said stubbornly.

Cyfrin made a derisive noise in his throat. "You know she's not your mother, Honeysuckle. Just one of the many lies she's told you."

"She's *never* told me a lie," Aurelia retorted. "Unlike you. What do you want me to believe, that you're my father?"

To her mingled amazement and irritation, Cyfrin threw back his head and laughed. "Your father? That's the last thing I want you to believe." He wiped his eyes, his voice mocking. "Oh, Honeysuckle, you ignorant child. I see you're in no humor to hear about my new project tonight. But there's always tomorrow night."

He reached out a hand toward her hair, but she drew it back out of his reach. Again surprising her, he just let out another light laugh.

"Here," he said, withdrawing the key and holding it out to

her. "It's fitting, isn't it, for me to give you the key? Take it as a sign of my goodwill."

"Of your what?" Aurelia asked bitingly. "You don't know what that is."

A hint of irritation showed for a moment on the enchanter's face, but he banished it with the shrug of a shoulder. "You don't know as much about me as you think you do, child. I hope to show you that with a little time."

Aurelia reflected that she knew much more of her cruel, selfish captor than she ever wished to, but she didn't say so. She didn't want him to change his mind about giving her the key. Reaching out slowly, she pulled it from his hand, both unnerved and irritated by the indulgent smile lingering on his face.

"I'll take my leave now," he said carelessly. "You can let the woman who *isn't* your mother out once I've gone. I have no desire to deal with her ill manners further tonight."

With the key safely in her hand, Aurelia allowed her anger to show. "Don't talk about her like that. And I can't lower you without her help."

"Yes you can," said Cyfrin impatiently, ignoring her rebuke. "You don't need her." He met her gaze, and she had the unsettling impression that he was trying to communicate silently with her, although she had no idea what. "*We* don't need her."

Before Aurelia could decide how best to respond, Cyfrin had stooped down and seized the end of her hair. He didn't pause to admire it, thankfully, just threaded it expertly through the metal hook above his head. Tugging it much less gently than Mama Gail did, he pulled it through until he could lower himself down.

Left with little option, Aurelia braced herself against the wall as usual, holding the tension with her arms and hoping it would be enough. Again she wondered what would happen if she let him fall on purpose. Even if she'd been bold enough, she wasn't confident the fall would kill him. And he'd be so enraged by the attempt, she didn't want to think about how he'd react. Not to mention they wouldn't be able to survive without the supplies he brought them each day. They didn't know enough about magic to understand whether the enchantment keeping them in the tower would lift simply because Cyfrin died.

She was therefore feeling anxious as Cyfrin stepped out from the window, trusting his whole weight to her hair as he shuffled his feet down the outside of the tower. But somewhat to Aurelia's surprise, she found that with the help of the metal ring, she was able to lower Cyfrin by herself.

The lightness she felt when his weight finally shifted onto the ground went beyond the fact that her hair was no longer weighed down by him. It even went beyond the usual relief she felt at his departure. For the first time in her life, she'd faced something without Mama Gail by her side, and she hadn't been a complete failure.

The thought of her mother reminded her of the other woman's predicament, and she yanked her hair back through the ring with painful haste. Hurrying across the room, she fitted the key into the lock with fumbling fingers. The moment she turned it, the door flew violently open, and Aurelia only just jumped out of the way in time.

"Aurelia!" Mama Gail gasped, the moment she grasped that they were alone. "Where is he?"

"He's gone," said Aurelia simply. "Are you all right?"

"Am *I* all right?" Mama Gail repeated, sounding more distressed than Aurelia had ever heard her. She stepped close to Aurelia, running her hands down either side of the younger woman's face, searching her for signs of Aurelia hardly knew what. "What did he do to you?"

"Nothing," Aurelia shrugged. "He just...talked to me."

"And what did he say?" Her mother's eyes were keen, that unnerving air of fear back around her.

"Nothing much," Aurelia admitted. "Certainly nothing to justify all the fuss." She peered at her mother anxiously. "Are you sure you're all right? I'm sorry he locked you in the room like that." Her face darkened. "I can't believe he had a key all this time. As if we're not locked up enough as it is."

"Never mind me," said Mama Gail impatiently. "Aurelia, what did he say? What did he do?"

"I told you, nothing," Aurelia insisted. "Honestly, it was kind of nice. I mean," she hastened to add, "not him forcing you into the room like that."

The fear was palpable on her mother's face now, and it sobered Aurelia more than any other of the night's bizarre events.

"Aurelia," said Mama Gail, taking her hands and pressing them almost painfully. "No matter how nice he tried to make himself appear, you mustn't forget all he's done. You mustn't forget what he is."

Aurelia laughed incredulously. "*He* wasn't nice, Mama Gail. He's a snake—what could possibly make him appear nice? I meant it was...strangely satisfying. He was his usual obnoxious self, and I actually stood up to him! I wasn't even afraid."

Her mother drew a shaky breath, attempting and not quite managing to smile. "I'm proud of you, Aurelia," she said. "But I still don't want you left alone with him again."

"Well, he won't find it so easy next time," smiled Aurelia, proudly holding out the key to her mother.

With a satisfying gasp, Mama Gail grabbed it, lifting it up to examine it. "How did you get it off him?"

Aurelia shrugged. "He just gave it to me. As a sign of good-will, apparently." She rolled her eyes.

Mama Gail's frown was back. "I think you'd better tell me

exactly what he said," she pressed. She glanced around. "You're sure he's gone?"

"Of course," Aurelia assured her. "I lowered him to the ground myself."

"Without any help?" Mama Gail asked, startled.

Aurelia nodded. "I said I couldn't do it without you, but he said I could. And he was right, actually." Her voice turned dry. "Probably the first true thing he's ever told me." She cast her mind back over their conversation. "As for what he said, it was mostly just strange. He said the usual nonsense about having every right to do whatever he wants, and how I should trust him instead of you." She shook her head in irritation.

"What did he say about this new project of his?" Mama Gail asked.

Aurelia frowned. "Nothing at all. He said he could see I wasn't in the mood to talk about it, but he'd tell me tomorrow night. Or something like that."

She'd expected the tension in Mama Gail's shoulders to relax, but if anything, it increased.

"It was all a bit bizarre," she mused. "He said I didn't really know him, and he'd hope to change that." Her expression darkened. "He also said that you're not my mother. If he really wants me to listen to him, he'd know better than to say such outrageous things."

"Oh, Aurelia," said Mama Gail, her posture softening at last. She laid one of her hands against Aurelia's cheek, a gentle smile of reassurance on her face as she met the younger woman's eyes. Aurelia was sure her mother could see the insecurity she tried so hard to hide. "He's wrong about pretty well everything," said Mama Gail calmly. "So it should come as no surprise to us that he's wrong about that as well."

Aurelia nodded, closing her eyes briefly. Her mother's hand was rough from years of effort, but it was comforting nonetheless. For a moment, Aurelia was a small child again, her heart shattering and her world falling apart as Mama Gail tried to explain why Cyfrin had ridiculed Aurelia for calling her Mama that evening.

She could still remember the feeling of being unmoored when the only mother she'd ever known explained for the first time about the parents who'd brought Aurelia into the world. About the mother who'd loved her and lost her, and who was now gone forever. About the father who, at that time, was still out there somewhere, but about whom Mama Gail seemed reluctant to talk much.

"So you're not my real mother?" Aurelia had whispered, her little heart breaking a tiny bit more.

"Not real?" She could still picture Mama Gail's indignant face. "Don't I look real to you?"

Aurelia hadn't answered, her gaze dropping to the floor as tears dripped down her nose. All at once, she'd felt a familiar hand tilting her chin up, until two pairs of blue eyes locked.

"I'm as real as you are," Mama Gail had assured her in her steady way. Taking Aurelia's small, pudgy hand, she'd laid it over her own heart. "My love for you is as real as this heartbeat. And nothing can ever take it away. Don't listen to what that man says. None of it is real." She'd leaned her head forward, until her forehead and Aurelia's were touching. "But we're real," she'd said. "You and me. Mother and daughter."

And just like that, the crippling loneliness had drifted away. Isolated as they'd always been, Aurelia had never felt alone again, no matter what poison Cyfrin spewed at her.

The seventeen-year-old Aurelia opened her eyes, looking into a familiar face that was more lined than it had been back then, but no less determined. And currently watching Aurelia with a searching gaze.

"What else did Cyfrin say?"

Aurelia sighed, pulling back from both her mother's comforting hand and her own memories.

"I don't know, Mama Gail. I got angry when he said you're not my mother, and he laughed at me for accusing him of trying to be my father. He said that's the last thing he wants to be." She grimaced. "As if it's a surprise that he wouldn't want to be associated with me. Now, if he could claim my hair as his offspring..."

She trailed off, frowning as she saw tension return to her listener's frame.

"I don't like it," Mama Gail muttered, apparently to herself. "I don't like it at all." She frowned toward the closed door of Cyfrin's study. "Can you get started on dinner without me, Aurelia? I want to look through his notes again, see if I can find anything about this new project of his."

"But he didn't even go in there tonight," Aurelia objected.

Mama Gail was already halfway to the study, and she didn't break stride. "Yesterday it sounded like he was almost ready to begin whatever it was," she said over her shoulder. "He must have been planning it for a while. As far as I can tell, he keeps any notes that could be incriminating here, where no one can ever find them. Surely there's something in there about his plans." Her voice dropped to a mutter again, and Aurelia barely heard it as she passed through the protected doorway. "And if it's what it seems, it'll happen over my dead body."

A thrill of fear went over Aurelia at the image. Whatever her mother wasn't telling her, she had a terrible feeling it was going to change everything. And not for the better.

CHAPTER SIX

Amell

Amell sat astride his horse, trying not to fidget as he waited for his father to appear.

"You're making the poor creature nervous, Your Highness," said Furn, his lips tilted in a smile.

Amell sighed. "No, I'm not. She's used to me." He stroked the horse's side absently. "Aren't you, old girl? Plus, I'm sure you want Father to hurry up as much as I do."

"I daresay he'll be here any minute," said Tora calmly, giving her own mare's mane an affectionate stroke. She glanced at the robed representative of the Enchanters' Guild who formed part of the group. "Is he bringing more enchanters with him? I thought he'd want magical protection in addition to guards, given the nature of the fugitives."

"I don't think any more enchanters are coming with us," Amell said distractedly, still craning his neck to check the castle's entrance. "But the guild and the guards have combined teams on a roster. They've been patrolling the main highway since yesterday, making sure it remains safe and clear for traffic. I think they're putting protective enchantments on it and everything. We'll be staying on that route for sure."

He tapped two fingers against his thigh in a frantic rhythm. "Two hours' ride," he said abruptly. "Only two hours from here to the prison. I can hardly believe Father didn't go yesterday, and even this morning he's dallying."

"Somehow I doubt His Majesty is *dallying*, Prince Amell," added Furn, a laugh in his voice. "Also, you should brace yourself. While it might take you and me two hours of hard riding to get there, it will probably take this cavalcade twice that."

He nodded toward the assembled group of guards, investigators, and various others, including the enchanter from the guild.

"Your father sent some of his most trusted representatives yesterday, and he remained in Fernford because he was needed to make decisions regarding the large scale troop movements the crisis will require. Plus I imagine he sent letters to each of the other monarchs in Solstice, alerting them and seeking their assistance. Sometimes a king needs to look at the bigger picture."

"Yes, yes, I know all that, of course," said Amell impatiently. He sent his friend a wry smile. "I'm just eager to be off."

Furn's own smile showed no surprise.

"I must say, Furn," Amell commented, "you seem to have a good grasp of it all. Maybe you should consider working toward a role as a senior advisor. It wouldn't be the first time Father has drawn an advisor from the more genteel of the guards."

There was a different edge to Furn's smile now, this time harder to place. "I don't have such large ambitions, Your Highness."

"What are your ambitions, then?" Amell asked, his interest piqued. Furn was undeniably capable of a more challenging role than the one he currently held, and he was a fastidious and driven man. Amell had no doubt the guard had dreams of his own, but he'd never heard Furn talk about them.

"Nothing to speak of," said Furn, with a firmness that effectively closed the topic.

Amell raised an eyebrow. He was certain there was something behind Furn's light words, but apparently he wasn't to know what. He hadn't quite decided whether to press when Tora took the decision out of his hands.

"I can't believe you have *no* plans, Furn," she said, her voice a little too smooth. "There must be something you intend to pursue."

The guard shot her a swift look under his brows, but still said nothing, his expression stonier than Amell had ever seen it.

"Remind me again, Princess Tora," Furn replied at last, "how you convinced His Majesty to allow you to accompany the group today?"

"Oh, I didn't," said Tora airily. "Amell is going to convince him for me."

"I'm what?" Amell demanded, distracted from Furn's uncharacteristically taciturn behavior. "Tora, doesn't he know you're here?"

"Not a clue," Tora replied cheerfully. "But I don't see why you should have all the excitement. Besides, you'll need someone to watch your back."

"I believe that's my role, Your Highness," said Furn, in the disapproving voice Amell so often heard from his other guards, and so rarely heard from Furn. It awoke such a familiar frustration that almost in spite of himself, Amell was goaded to his sister's defense.

"No need to scold, Furn," he frowned. "She's not wrong about there being no good reason for her to miss the excitement."

"This isn't a festival, Your Highnesses," Furn said, his tone clipped. "It's a visit to the site of a violent crime, that site also being a prison containing the continent's most dangerous criminals."

"Yes, we're aware of our destination, thank you," said Tora pleasantly. She turned slightly in her saddle to face her brother. "You'll speak up for me to Father, won't you, Amell? Tell him you think I should be allowed to come?"

Ever sympathetic to a plea to be included in the action, Amell shrugged. "I'm willing to, Tora, of course I am. But I'm not sure how far my word will go. Honestly, Furn would be more likely to convince him."

"But Furn is determined to be disagreeable where I'm concerned," Tora informed him calmly, without looking at the guard.

Amell did so, however, and was amazed to see that Furn's expression was more deadpan than ever.

"You're not going to be disagreeable, are you, Furn?" he asked.

"It's never my intention, Your Highness," Furn replied, his voice mild enough. "But I must confess, I don't think it's a good idea for the princess to come."

"Why not?" Amell demanded.

Furn cleared his throat, avoiding looking at Tora at all. "I do not wish to speak ill of my peers, Your Highness, but I have sometimes felt that the princess's personal guards are not as competent as one might wish."

"Oh yes, we all know Tora's guards are embarrassingly easy to dupe," said Amell matter-of-factly, glancing back at the two mounted men sitting just out of earshot. "But it's not a bad thing, Furn. Her life would be insufferable if she could never shake them, or hoodwink them into doing what she wanted. She doesn't have someone understanding in charge, like I do."

This compliment failed to wipe the grim look from Furn's face. Peering at his friend, Amell realized Furn was genuinely troubled. Perhaps he was anxious about his ability to keep both of the young royals safe if Tora's guards failed to do their duty in the event of danger at the prison.

But seeing the hardness around Furn's jaw, Amell couldn't help but wonder whether the guard's refusal to aid their cause actually sprung from annoyance at their earlier prying into his personal affairs. It wasn't like Furn to be so reactive, even on the many occasions Amell had shown much less sensitivity than he and Tora had just now.

Amell opened his mouth, but before he could put his foot in it, as he surely would have done with any attempt to peel back Furn's suddenly stiff outer layer, his father appeared in the castle's entranceway, and his thoughts returned rapidly to the matter at hand.

The king's gaze passed over the assembled travelers, lingering on his children for only a moment before he turned to exchange words with the captain of his guard. Once he was mounted, however, he urged his horse toward their little group.

"Amell, I'm glad to see you here punctually." He nodded in acknowledgment of Furn's presence.

"Of course, Father," said Amell. "I wouldn't hold you up."

The king nodded without much conviction, his eyes traveling on to his daughter. "Tora, what are you doing here?"

"I thought I'd join the visit, Father," said Tora placidly. "I can ride with Amell and Sir Furnis."

The king scowled. "It's not an expedition of pleasure, Tora. This is a serious affair. Your presence was never part of the deal."

"I understand the situation, Father," Tora said. "And I'm taking it seriously, I assure you. I simply want to understand what's going on, so I can better support the response from back here in the castle. Surely this is the safest time for me to visit, when I can travel in the midst of such a large group of trained fighters."

The king's gaze passed skeptically to her two guards, who were sitting to attention in their saddles, but looked visibly nervous under their king's scrutiny.

"If safety is truly the issue, Father," Tora pressed, "you needn't worry. I'll stay with Amell the whole time, and Sir Furnis will look after me." She threw the guard an innocent look. "Won't you, Sir Furnis?"

Furn's jaw worked for a moment, his eyes meeting Tora's at last. Then all at once he bent his head in a stiff bow to the king. "Of course I will do so if that's your desire, Your Majesty."

King Bern sighed, looking distractedly back at the captain of his guard, who was waiting for him. "Oh, very well. If Sir Furnis is willing to take responsibility for your safety, I suppose this is the best opportunity we'll get for you to view the site. But it's a one time visit, understand? You will return to the castle with the group this evening, and stay here."

"Yes, Father," said Tora brightly, struggling to hide her delight.

The king had already turned away, but Amell didn't miss the anxious look on Furn's face.

"It's a lot to ask of you, Furn," Amell said repentantly. "Of course you're right that if there is any genuine danger, the ineptitude of Tora's own guards could be a bit of an issue."

Tora opened her mouth, a clear protest in her eyes, but when her gaze flicked to Furn, she seemed to deflate a little.

"It is a big ask, isn't it?" she admitted. "I'm sorry I threw you into it, Furn. Perhaps I had better stay."

The guard's steely expression softened slightly. "Nonsense, Your Highness," he said, his voice still a little gruff. "It's no trouble. I don't anticipate any danger."

"Don't you?" Tora asked, a smile instantly breaking across

her face at her victory. "Not even a *little* danger? That's disappointing."

Furn's tension returned instantly, and Amell gave his sister a look. She was bouncing in her saddle, showing no sign of the dejection that had softened Furn. When had she become adept at using emotion to manipulate people? He'd never noticed it before.

"You're shameless," he muttered to her, as she turned her horse around to exchange a few words with her guards.

"You have no idea," she assured him, a small smile tugging up one corner of her lips.

She was still speaking with her guards a moment later, when King Bern once again approached his son.

"We should be there within four hours. Don't wander off from the group. I'll meet with the warden as soon as we arrive. You can join me."

Amell nodded dutifully, but as soon as his father was gone, he turned a dismayed face to Furn. "Four hours? You were right about the group traveling slowly, Furn." He made a face. "I can't even suggest we ride on ahead, can I? Since Father's just told me not to *wander off*, like a small child."

Furn smiled, but kindly refrained from pointing out what Amell already knew—that his indignation at his father's warning lost some weight given he'd just admitted a desire to do precisely what his father had predicted.

The king's assessment of time proved to be depressingly accurate. It was past noon by the time the group arrived at the magically reinforced prison. Amell let out a low whistle when the road emerged from the dense forest and the facility came into view.

It was a surprisingly pleasant building for what it was. Its three wings formed three sides of a square, the open edge revealing an enclosed outdoor area in the middle. The whole structure sat in the center of a large cleared section of forest, its surroundings remarkably peaceful for a prison.

Or at least, it must have been pleasant and peaceful a few days before. The view that met Amell's eyes was one of industry, with guards swarming all over the clearing. And the building's gray stone walls and neat tiled roof were somewhat marred by the blackened pile of rubble that had once formed one end of the horseshoe.

"Explosion was no exaggeration," Amell commented to Furn.

The guard nodded, his troubled expression suggesting that he found the sight as confronting as Amell did. It was one thing to hear about a prison break. It was quite another to see with their own eyes the violence that had achieved it, and be reminded of the mischief the fugitives might even now be perpetrating across the countryside.

"I don't see any prisoners," Tora commented.

"Would you expect to, from out here?" Amell asked.

In answer, Furn nodded to a nearby section of clearing, and Amell realized that it was a currently abandoned logging yard.

"Oh, the prisoners must work there sometimes," he mused aloud. "Father told the warden to focus on securing the rest of the inmates. I'm guessing they're all locked inside until this crisis has been addressed."

"I'm sure you're right, Your Highness," Furn agreed.

The mention of the warden sent Amell's eyes wandering in search of his father, who was speaking with a uniformed guard a short distance away. Amell urged his horse toward the pair, Tora beside him and Furn following at a respectful distance.

"Ah, Amell," said King Bern, turning as his son approached. "The warden is on his way."

Even as he spoke, a short middle aged man with a balding

head and an unemotional expression strode swiftly through the entrance to the prison.

"Your Majesty," he said, bowing low to King Bern. His eyes traveled to Amell, and he bowed again. "Your Highness. Please join me in my office."

Amell's father nodded, taking a step forward before turning back to Tora, whom the warden didn't seem to have noticed.

"My guards will accompany Amell and me," he said curtly. "Sir Furnis, you will stay outside to guard Princess Tora."

Furn visibly paled, clearly dismayed at being denied the right to guard his true charge. But to Amell's surprise, Tora didn't look disgruntled at being excluded. On the contrary, she appeared quite satisfied with her situation, her eyes scanning the area with bright interest. Amell narrowed his eyes suspiciously at her, but she just threw him an innocent smile. Determining to interrogate her later, he directed an apologetic look at Furn and followed his father into the prison.

He'd expected to pass dank cells full of moaning captives, so it was a bit of a surprise to find himself in a clean, bright corridor, no bars in sight, and pleasant views of the forest through every window. He saw no sign of any prisoners between the entrance and the warden's study, and realized they must have crossed a part of the prison accessible only to guards.

Almost as soon as the warden had gestured his royal visitors into his own study, a knock at the door announced the arrival of a lean serving man in the strangest uniform Amell had ever seen. He wore gray from head to toe, and it couldn't be called flattering. The only thing that kept the loose fabric from being completely formless was the bunching at the ankles and wrists that prevented it from flowing over the man's hands and feet. His hair was also badly cut, as if he'd taken a pair of scissors to it himself. Amell tried not to stare, but it was a strange spectacle. He wasn't surprised that his father's guards, stationed at the door of the study, looked at the man askance. Amell couldn't imagine the formidable housekeeper back in Fernford allowing any of the castle's numerous servants to present themselves in such a state before a baronet, let alone before the king.

Unobtrusively, the man placed a small plate of biscuits on the warden's desk before bowing himself out.

The warden had barely begun to repeat the basic summary of the incident when a second knock sounded, and another servant entered, this one a woman. Amell's eyes followed her in astonishment as she placed a tray on the desk, steam rising idly from the silver teapot at its center. The uniform looked even worse on her, and—perhaps most astonishingly of all—her hair was also shorn in the same way as the man's had been, unevenly cut just above the ears.

"Thank you, Inmate," said the warden curtly, as the woman bowed herself out.

"Inmate?" Amell repeated, startled. "Are they prisoners?"

"Certainly, Your Highness," said the warden, inclining his head. "Prisoners from the low security wing sometimes fill the role of servants in the guards' quarters." His eyes passed to Amell's father. "Naturally only those in whom I have the highest level of confidence were selected to wait on us today, Your Majesty."

The king nodded, apparently unsurprised by all this, but Amell was fascinated.

"Is each wing a different level of security, then?" he asked. "Do different rules apply across them all?"

The warden nodded. "Precisely, Your Highness. We're currently in the low security wing, which attaches to the guards' area. The middle wing is medium security. The wing on the other end of the building is—or was—high security."

That effectively dampened Amell's enthusiasm. "So the fugitives are all considered the highest risk?"

"I'm afraid so," said the warden grimly. "Downright nasty some of them are, too."

"Have any more been apprehended since yesterday?" King Bern asked, and Amell brightened. He hadn't even been aware any had been caught.

"Yes, Your Majesty," said the warden, sitting up a little straighter. "Two of the enchanters among the guards got lucky when combing the woods early this morning, and sensed a signature of magic. They found two prisoners hiding out in a cave, obviously having been trapped within the perimeter created yesterday by the enchanters you sent from the guild."

"Good luck indeed," said the king approvingly. "How many are still at large?"

"Twenty-five," said the warden. "And we've combed the whole area again this morning. I think it's safe to say that the remaining fugitives made it beyond the ring before the perimeter was set."

"Where were the eleven found?" Amell asked curiously.

The warden pulled out a map and spread it across his desk, pushing aside the untouched tea tray to do so.

"The two this morning were here," he said, pointing at two red crosses.

Leaning close, Amell saw the prison marked at the center of the map, and a red ring drawn around the whole area, presumably delineating the magical perimeter set up by the urgent delegation of enchanters the guild had sent the day before.

"And the others, as you can see," the warden said simply, gesturing at the various other crosses marked on the map.

"No pattern to their locations, is there?" mused the king, frowning.

"Not that we can spot, Your Majesty," the warden acknowledged. "The whole thing is utterly perplexing if I may say so. Based on the account of those guards who were in the wing in question, and those who've apprehended prisoners since, it seems the inmates were taken as much by surprise as we were. If there was a coordinated plan for what to do once the explosion took place, we've yet to find any evidence of it."

"And the wall was definitely blown in from the outside?" Amell's father pressed.

The warden nodded. "Undoubtedly. I'll take you to the site myself, Your Majesty, and you'll be able to see it. It doesn't take an expert to recognize."

"It's not exactly a pattern," Amell interjected, still caught up on the previous point, "but I notice that there haven't been any fugitives apprehended anywhere in this whole section." He pointed to the north western quarter of the marked circle, which was empty of any crosses. "What's out there?"

"Nothing," shrugged the warden. "Just forest. The area's been searched, of course. There simply weren't any prisoners hiding there."

Amell frowned, considering the map again. The large blank space was quite noticeable. If there wasn't anything there, why hadn't any of the inmates caught within the ring chosen to hide in that direction? Perhaps it was worth him and Furn going for a quick look, just in case. It would certainly justify his inclusion in the trip if he found some fugitives who'd slipped through the net.

He was so captured by this idea, he barely heard the rest of his father's discussion with the warden. He trailed behind the other two men as the warden took them to the site of the explosion, where cleanup was still very much underway. Most of the wing had been secured now, and the warden invited the king to personally interview the recaptured escapees.

"Yes, I've come prepared to do so," Amell's father nodded. "Since we couldn't securely transfer them to the capital for questioning, I've brought my top interrogators with me today.

I'll summon them to join us." He glanced at Amell. "Perhaps you'd better return to Tora and Sir Furnis, Amell."

Amell looked up from the blackened stone he'd been examining, aggrieved. "I'm not so squeamish, Father," he protested.

The king gave him an unimpressed look. "It's not a question of squeamishness, Amell. Nothing untoward is going to be done to the prisoners. But interrogation is a delicate business requiring a high level of skill and training. A poorly timed interjection could ruin any chance of acquiring useful information."

Amell opened his mouth to protest the assumption that he would interrupt the interrogation, but then thought better of it. He'd wanted a chance to explore that north western section of the perimeter.

"Very well, Father," he said with dignity. "I'll ensure that Tora is keeping out of trouble."

"Yes, do that," said the king, his attention already returning to the warden.

Amell strode through the ruins of the high security wing, scanning the group still gathered outside the building for sight of a familiar face. He'd expected to find Furn and Tora still mounted, so he felt a flicker of surprise when he'd scanned all of the riders without spotting them.

He did, however, come across Tora's two guards, still astride their horses and chatting with a group of soldiers.

"Where's my sister?" he demanded of them, and they both sprang to attention.

"Examining the prison's kitchen garden, Your Highness," one of them said.

"Sir Furnis is with her," the other added hastily.

Amell refrained from asking the obvious question—*why aren't you?*—instead striding around the side of the building in search of this kitchen garden. As soon as he rounded the corner, Tora's familiar figure—too tall for beauty, she'd often informed him wistfully—came into view. She was in conversation with a gray-clad prisoner among the rows of vegetables, Sir Furnis in attendance. Once glance was enough to show Amell that his guard was as tense as the prince had ever seen him.

"Tora, what are you doing over here?" Amell asked, approaching the trio.

The prisoner bobbed a clumsy curtsy, her gaze curious as it passed over the prince. Her arms were full of herbs, and Amell could only assume that she was one of the trusted low security inmates the warden had mentioned.

"Hearing firsthand about the break out," Tora said, glancing briefly at him before returning her attention to the prisoner. "So you felt it coming?"

"I don't know if I'd say that exactly, Your 'Ighness," she shrugged. "I felt some kind of surge, but it weren't nothing I recognized. Too powerful by 'alf to be from someone inside. I wouldn't've guessed what was coming or nothing."

"I think we should rejoin the main group now," Furn said tightly.

The prisoner cast him an amused glance. "Bless you, lad, I'm no threat to anyone. There's a reason we don't have a fence round the place. It's not physical barriers keeping us restricted. That power surge did more than take out the walls. It broke the enchantment on the 'igh security wing, and a mighty complex enchantment that was, too. No idea how anyone would even *know* the way to break it. But the one round the property is back now, even if it's weaker'n it was." She rolled her shoulders, a look of concentration coming over her face. "I can feel it now."

"No need to test it," Furn said dryly.

She chuckled. "Relax, guard. I'm not going to do your princess no 'arm. I'm not the violent type, or I would've been over in that blown up wing. 'Sides, I'm due for release in a month. I'm 'ardly going to do anything to mess that up."

Furn grunted, not sounding entirely reassured, but Tora sent Amell a grin.

"I like her. Even if she's disappointingly danger-free."

The long-suffering look that passed over Furn's face told Amell that he'd missed some joke, but he didn't press.

"If you're looking for something more interesting to do, I might have a suggestion," Amell said instead, giving her a meaningful look.

Tora stepped away from the prisoner at once, nodding her thanks for the woman's time. After casting another amused glance at Furn's strained expression, the inmate returned to picking herbs.

The three of them moved halfway back toward the rest of the guards, pausing where no one would overhear.

"Father's going to be occupied for some time interrogating the fugitives who've already been recaptured." Amell said. "And I want to use the time to explore."

"I thought we weren't going to wander off, Your Highness," said Furn, although he already sounded resigned.

Amell grinned. "That was on the journey. Now we're here, we may as well be useful."

"Useful?" Tora echoed, sounding intrigued.

Amell eagerly explained what he'd seen on the map, and how it had piqued his curiosity. Tora looked unconvinced.

"Doesn't sound like there's much chance of finding anything," she said skeptically. "Not if the area's already been searched."

"No harm in it, though," Amell argued. "And as you said, it's already been searched and cleared by the guards. They've pronounced the prison perimeter secure, so we're not strictly doing anything dangerous."

"How disappointing," smiled Tora.

Amell raised an eyebrow at her. "Since when are you so determined to get into danger?"

"I was only joking," she said quickly. "I doubt we'll find anything, but we may as well look." Her voice turned dry. "I'm guessing Father didn't invite you to assist him with the interrogations."

"Not exactly," Amell agreed. He turned to Sir Furnis. "What do you think, Furn?"

Amell expected Furn's usual unruffled willingness to follow his charge into whatever foolish situation he was determined to pursue. But the guard's eyes flicked between the two royals, a crease appearing between his eyebrows. Well used to Amell's impulsive ways, however, he made no attempt to talk him out of it.

"Don't worry, Furn," Amell assured him, as they collected their horses. "We won't be going outside the magic perimeter set up by the Enchanters' Guild."

Furn nodded, looking only faintly reassured. Amell couldn't help frowning at his friend's serious demeanor. Furn had been acting strangely all day.

Tora's guards fell in behind them as they directed their horses to the north western edge of the prison. Amell noticed that Tora looked none too pleased about their presence, but she made no effort to actually lose them. For some time after they entered the tree line, the group rode in easy silence, Amell and Tora searching the trees from their mounted position, Furn taking in every detail of their surroundings with eagle intensity. Every now and then they passed sentries from the prison, patrolling the trees. They all sprang to attention when they recognized the royals, but Amell didn't stop to speak with any of them.

His eagerness to explore faded quickly, and after almost an hour of fruitless searching, he was ready to return to the prison.

He was about to say so when a particularly dense clump of trees drew his attention. Figuring he may as well examine one more section of forest before turning around, he urged his horse toward it.

"Tora, Furn, look at this," he called over his shoulder once he'd reached the trees.

"What is it?" Tora's horse picked its way across the uneven forest floor, its head appearing suddenly beside that of Amell's mount.

"Probably nothing," Amell said. "The trees are just so thick there, I wondered if it might be a good hiding place."

"Let's have a look," Tora said brightly. She swung down from her horse, ignoring Furn's noise of protest. Amell joined her, Furn following close behind, and the three of them approached the clump of trees.

"It does look like a good hiding place," Furn admitted uneasily. "If you could get in, it would be very hard for anyone to see you."

Getting in, it turned out, was precisely the problem. The dense patch was larger than Amell had at first supposed, and it took the better part of a quarter of an hour to walk all the way around it. And at no point in that walk did he find any gap large enough to allow him to force his way inside. The trees grew so close together, and the general foliage was so thick, he simply couldn't get through.

"Well, if we can't get in, I doubt a fugitive did," Tora said matter-of-factly, once they'd returned to their original position.

"Unless they're using magic somehow," Amell suggested.

Furn shook his head. "The search parties all included magic-users. Some of the prison guards were talking about it while you were inside. They would have sensed magic coming out of those trees from a mile away. The use of magic would make any hidden inmate easier to find, not harder."

Amell nodded slowly, still not entirely convinced. He continued a short distance around the thick trees again, his eyes scanning the forest on the other side.

"Is that the edge of the trees?" he demanded, surprised. Striding forward, he confirmed that the trunks really were beginning to thin on the far side of the clump. "But surely that's not right," he mused, picturing the map the warden had shown him. "I thought the forest went on quite a bit further than this."

"We must have come further than we realized," said Tora.

"And if we're almost at the edge of the tree line, we've left the protective perimeter," Furn pointed out, his voice slightly uneasy.

"True," Amell acknowledged. "I don't know how we covered that ground so quickly."

"I think we'd better be getting back," Furn said.

"Lead on, Furn, and I'll follow," said Tora amicably.

For some reason, at these polite words, a strange look flitted across Furn's face. But he did as he was bid, and led the group back to their mounts. Within the hour they had emerged back into the clearing where the prison was situated.

After mounting his horse, Amell had pulled a small knife from his belt. As they passed through the woods, he scored a series of marks on the trees. He made no mention of these marks to his companions, and Furn didn't seem to notice. When they exited the forest, Amell took note of their location. Twisting in the saddle to check the tree line, he nodded in satisfaction. He was fairly confident he'd be able to find that clump again if he chose.

"Everything all right, Your Highness?"

Amell turned back around to see Furn waiting for him with a questioning lift to his eyebrows.

"Yes, of course," he said lightly, once again keeping the path he'd marked to himself.

He felt a prickle of guilt as he drew his horse alongside Furn's. It wasn't his usual style to hide things from his guard. But Furn hadn't quite been himself since their return from Entolia, and if Amell did decide to go back to the strangely thick clump of trees, he didn't want to be hampered by his friend's sudden increase in caution. The very fact that Furn was distracted enough for Amell to get away with any kind of subterfuge showed just how unsettled the guard was.

As soon as they rounded the corner of the prison, however, any misgivings were driven away by the sight of two enormous dragons crouching calmly before the ruined building.

CHAPTER SEVEN

Amell

"Of course something exciting happened the moment we leave," Amell muttered, his eyes dwelling in disgruntlement on the dragons.

Furn threw him an amused glance, but Tora ignored him altogether. Amell didn't blame her. The two imposing reptilian figures were enough to hold anyone's attention. The three riders pulled their horses to a stop, examining the beasts from a sufficient distance to take in their entire forms.

"What would dragons be doing here?" Tora asked, sounding a little awed.

It was Furn who replied. "It's not altogether surprising, is it? As magical creatures, surely they'd have an interest in the escape of a group of criminal magic-users into the continent at large."

"Maybe," said Tora skeptically. "If by interest, you mean pure curiosity. They wouldn't have any personal stake in it."

"She's right," Amell agreed. "Dragons are far too powerful to be concerned about the magic of a measly twenty-five human enchanters."

"Maybe they've come to help round up the fugitives," Furn suggested.

Amell shook his head. "No, they won't offer to help. And Father won't ask. Surely you remember the rules, Furn. It's the most basic principle of dragon-human interaction. They don't use magic on us, either to help or hinder, and we don't use magic on them."

"Yes, I remember," said Furn. "Although it still doesn't entirely make sense to me. Wouldn't they be able to track down the escapees with ease compared to us?"

"That's not the point," Tora informed him. As a royal, she, like Amell, was well trained in matters of dragon lore. "We gain more than we lose by the agreement. We're better off going without their help if it means we're safe from their magic being used against us. They could annihilate the entire human population if they chose."

"And according to rumor, some wanted to when they first arrived," Amell chimed in, his eyes traveling over the sharp triangular plates that ran down the back of the nearest dragon, all the way to the tip of its tail. "They were sick of humans constantly asking for their help, and they thought it would be simpler to just wipe us out. But fortunately the ones who thought that weren't the ones in charge, and instead we formed the agreement."

"And as you can hear," Tora grinned, "even Amell isn't foolhardy enough to disrespect the agreement."

"You're one to talk," sniped Amell. "I thought you were supposed to be the responsible sibling, but from what I can see, all you've done today is look for danger."

"And tragically found none," said Tora lightly. "I *am* the responsible one, little brother. It's all relative. At least I never hunt out danger for no reason."

"What's your reason, then?" Amell asked skeptically.

His sister ignored the question. "It's a while since I've seen a dragon up this close," she said instead. "Is it just me, or are these ones huge?"

"It's not just you," Amell assured her. "The ones at Basil's wedding were much smaller and brighter. These must be very old, judging by their size. And look how dark their scales are. I wouldn't be surprised if they're elders."

"I thought the elders hardly ever left the colony," Furn interjected.

Amell nodded. "I think I've only seen an elder once before, when I was a child." He frowned. "Do you remember that, Tora? One came to meet with Father in Fernford."

"Yes, that's right," Tora said. "Wasn't it when the prison was being built?"

"Was it?" Amell shrugged. "I don't remember the occasion."

"It was," Tora said, with growing conviction. "They were intrigued by the methods being discussed for containing magic. I suppose they've never had any call to do so among the dragon population. They're supposed to always be very harmonious, aren't they?"

Amell snorted. "Not to mention they're much too powerful to be contained by anything."

"Father will be mortified to have them come and witness our disaster," Tora said with a grimace.

Amell's eyes had been latched on to the dragons, but he shifted his gaze to the ground at their feet, searching for his father's familiar figure. The king was standing before the creatures—which were at least six times his height—his posture straight and his expression calm. But Amell wasn't fooled by these signs. He was sure Tora was right, and he winced in sympathy for the chagrin his father must be feeling.

"Should we go and greet them?" Tora asked suddenly. Her voice brightened. "Meeting a dragon can never be considered completely danger-free, can it? Maybe today won't be a total loss."

A slightly strangled noise from Amell's right alerted him to Furn's feelings on this foolhardy attitude from one of his charges.

"Dragon's flame, Tora," Amell said mildly. "I don't know what's put you in this humor, but the sooner we can return you to your own guards, the better. Poor Furn's heart can't take the strain of being responsible for two graceless fools."

Tora laughed lightly. "Oh, I'm sure he's fine. Aren't you, Furn?" Without waiting for a response, she spurred her horse forward, toward their father and his distinguished guests.

Amell threw his guard an apologetic look. "I don't know what's gotten into her today."

"Don't you?" Furn asked, sounding a little helpless. "I was hoping you might be able to explain it to me. To be frank, Your Highness, I thought I had my hands full with you. Princess Tora's guards have my pity."

Amell smiled, but he couldn't help shaking his head as well. "She's definitely not quite herself."

Not wanting to be left out of an event as notable as a dragon visit, he abandoned further discussion in favor of following his sister, swinging down from the saddle once he was within hailing distance of his father.

King Bern was speaking when the pair approached, but he paused, turning to welcome them with the formality favored by dragons.

"Tora, Amell," he inclined his head toward the dragons, "we are honored by a visit from Tanin and Idric of the dragon colony. Mighty Beasts, these are my offspring, Her Royal Highness Princess Tora, and His Royal Highness Crown Prince Amell."

The dragons both transferred their unblinking gaze to the

newcomers, and Amell tried not to fidget. He felt almost hypnotized as he looked back at the closest one, whose scales, seen up this close, were a deep burgundy. Bearded ridges ran along its temples, and its tail was tipped with a cluster of spikes that made Amell swallow nervously in spite of himself.

"Greetings, Mighty Beasts," he and Tora chorused together, in accordance with custom.

The burgundy dragon looked back at King Bern, apparently losing interest in the prince and princess.

"Our questions have been answered. I trust you will have all success in containing the risk you are facing."

With this faint sentiment of goodwill the royals had to be satisfied, because the dragons suddenly tensed into identical crouches. A moment later they'd launched themselves into the air with a rush of wind so powerful the trees at the edge of the prison clearing were momentarily bent sideways.

To King Bern's credit, whatever mortification he felt, he didn't show it, either during or after the dragons' visit. He turned to his son and daughter, his expression a little stiff.

"I suppose I should have expected a visit from the dragons, but I confess I didn't."

"What did they want, Father?" Amell asked.

The king's expression gave little away as he answered. "To understand how such an event occurred." His tone turned brisk. "Which is what I would like to know, as well."

"Did the interrogations yield anything interesting?" Amell asked.

His father sighed. "Not really. If the breakout was the result of a concerted plan by those inside, they're hiding it well. None of the enchanters who accompanied us from Fernford have the ability to detect when someone is lying, but I will request such a person be sent by one of the other kingdoms. I don't expect much from it, though. The captain of my guard doesn't believe the recaptured fugitives were lying about how unexpected the explosion was, and even without magic, he's experienced in such matters."

"Dragons can all tell when humans are lying, can't they?" Amell mused, thinking of Furn's comments. "Shame we couldn't have asked them to have a look over the prisoners while they were here."

"Amell," said King Bern sharply, sounding genuinely alarmed.

"Don't worry, Father, I know the rules," said Amell easily. "I was just thinking aloud."

"Hm." The king didn't seem entirely reassured. "Where have you been all this time?"

"Exploring the area," Amell said casually. At his father's expression he hastened to add, "within the perimeter line."

"Well," King Bern said briskly. "Those returning to Fernford today need to leave shortly in order to reach the capital before dark. I've instructed half of the force to bivouac in the clearing. I won't be going back to the castle until tomorrow at the earliest. There's a great deal more to be done here, and I wish to oversee it myself." His gaze measured his son for a moment. "You may remain with me if you wish, Amell."

"I do," said Amell quickly, hardly able to believe his luck. "Thank you."

"I'd like to stay too, Father," Tora interjected.

"Absolutely not." There was no compromise in the king's voice. "You were never supposed to come in the first place, and the accommodations here aren't suitable for a lady of your station."

Amell couldn't help but chuckle internally at his sister's disgruntled expression, but there was sympathy in the look he cast her. It must be very trying to be a princess.

King Bern's gaze passed over Furn, and on to Tora's guards.

"I'm trusting you to ensure the princess travels safely back to the capital."

"Yes, Your Majesty," they chorused. But Amell didn't miss the resigned look that flashed across Furn's face. Clearly his guard intended to take it on himself to make sure Tora left with the group. He was probably wise, given the bizarrely defiant mood the princess seemed to be in.

"The warden is to accommodate me in the guards' quarters," King Bern told Amell. "I daresay he can do the same for you."

"No need," said Amell quickly. "We'd rather camp with the soldiers, wouldn't we, Furn?"

The guard inclined his head in acknowledgment, and a rare smile flitted across the king's face.

"To be young again, assured of a good night's sleep wherever you lay your head," he muttered.

Amell grinned, bouncing slightly on the balls of his feet in his excitement at being allowed to stay. When his father glanced at him, he stilled the movement with an effort. The king wasn't usually as irritated by Amell's restlessness as Amell's mother was, but he still didn't want to give his father any reason to change his mind.

King Bern turned to the captain of his guard, who seemed to have hung back while the dragons were present, but was now approaching. Apparently dismissed for the moment, Amell opened his mouth to ask Furn a question, only to find his guard's eyes fixed searchingly on the princess and her guards. Amell followed his gaze.

"How about I go and find us a place to sleep in the camp," he said lightly.

"Good idea, Your Highness," Furn agreed, his eyes narrowed slightly as he watched Tora talking with her guards, out of earshot.

Amell slipped away without another word, his thoughts on

the marks he'd left on the trees. He felt another flash of guilt at taking advantage of Furn's distraction. But after all, how much harm could he really come to in the protected grove?

He led his horse around the building, only mounting once out of sight of the main group. It didn't take him long to find the place where they'd exited the forest earlier, and he was soon following his own trail. With a clear direction, he moved more quickly than they had before, heading straight for the thickened clump of trees. He knew he was unlikely to find anything, but without Tora and Furn watching, he'd have more chance to poke around.

Except he never made it to the clump. He was perhaps halfway there when his horse suddenly shied, without any clear cause. Amell pulled the animal to a stop, scanning the area cautiously. He could neither see nor hear anything. Prodding his mount forward, he continued through the trees, moving more slowly now.

One of his own scores directed him around a thick mass where three trees had grown from a common patch of ground. Rounding the blockage, the pair almost walked straight into a large scaled back, its bright yellow hue standing out bizarrely against the dark trees.

At their appearance, the dragon whipped its head around, and for a moment the prince and the beast stared at each other silently, wide gray eyes meeting cat-like orbs.

The expression on the dragon's face was so reminiscent of Amell's own feeling of being caught in wrongdoing that he almost laughed. He couldn't help relaxing slightly, dropping his eyes from the dragon to focus on his horse.

The poor creature was prancing nervously on the spot, and it was all Amell could do to keep it from trampling the dragon's tail.

Apparently thinking the same thing, the beast straightened,

whipping its tail across the forest floor with such speed that it left a deep gouge in the tree trunk with which it connected. Fully extended, the dragon towered above Amell, fitting impossibly into the space below the trees, which should have been too small for it.

Amell considered the creature curiously. It was perhaps three times his height. Its size, along with the brightness of its yellow scales, told him it was much younger than the elders who had recently spoken with his father.

The dragon's gaze passed from the prince to his horse, which was still sidling uneasily. Leaning down, it placed its head before the horse's, opening its jaws in what looked like a yawn. Amell watched, fascinated, as it exhaled gustily all over the horse's face. The creature relaxed at once, all the tension draining from its muscles.

Amell, on the other hand, bounced a little in the saddle. He'd never seen dragon magic up so close before. What kind of power had the beast used to settle his horse?

Before either human or dragon could speak, a quiet rustling drew Amell's attention to a patch of foliage behind the dragon. His eyes latched on to a gash on the tree, and he realized that the magical creature had been examining the prince's own trail when Amell's arrival interrupted him. But that point was soon driven from his mind as he caught sight of a second dragon emerging from the trees with almost silent movements.

Amell blinked in amazement as he took in the creature's bright purple scales. The sight of the two dragons together triggered his memory, and he blurted out his thoughts before he could stop himself.

"I recognize you. You were both at Basil's wedding."

Both dragons fixed unblinking yellow orbs on him, and he found himself fidgeting again.

"I mean, Greetings, Mighty Beasts," he said, inclining his

upper half in as good a bow as he could manage from horse-back. "I am Prince Amell of Fernedell, and I believe I have been honored to see you before now."

The dragons unbent slightly, the purple one tilting its head to the side as it examined him. "I am Dannsair, and my companion is Rekavidur."

Amell bowed again, noting that the voice identified the dragon as a female.

"I recognize you as well, Prince Amell of Fernedell," Dannsair went on. "You are a friend of King Basil's?"

Amell nodded, his eyes passing to the other dragon. Their names were vaguely familiar. He remembered Basil mentioning that the two of them were friendly with the Entolian princesses, and that they'd taken some kind of interest in Basil and Wren's situation. Amell didn't know how he hadn't recognized the yellow dragon immediately. He'd spent most of the wedding watching the two of them, and he'd formed the distinct impression that they were a pair, to use the dragons' own terminology for mates.

"And you're a prince, you say," the other dragon, Rekavidur, commented. "Your father's heir."

It didn't seem like a question, but Amell nodded anyway, sitting a little taller in his saddle. "I am."

The dragons exchanged a silent look, which Amell couldn't read.

"He might know," Dannsair commented thoughtfully.

"If he's in his father's confidence," Rekavidur mused, just as if Amell wasn't there. "Which I wouldn't count as certain. Humans are often reluctant to trust their young, and he seems particularly young for a fully grown man."

"I know what you mean," Dannsair agreed, nodding wisely. "But his very youth makes it unlikely he will take questions amiss."

"True," Rekavidur said brightly. "It is decided, then." Both dragons turned back to Amell, studying him with undisguised curiosity.

Trained to show dragons the utmost respect, Amell had listened to this somewhat startling exchange in unresponsive silence. But under their combined and somber gaze, he found himself overcome with a sudden desire to laugh. Coughing into his hand in an attempt to cover it, he made his tone as polite as he knew how.

"Is it possible that you wish to ask me a question?"

"Precisely," Rekavidur said, his gravelly voice calm. "Your arrival," his gaze flicked to the empty forest behind Amell, "unaccompanied, may prove to be fortuitous to our inquiries."

"Inquiries?" Amell repeated, a little startled. "Is the dragon colony conducting its own investigation into the prison break?"

"I did not say so," Rekavidur responded, his placid voice sounding a little too careful.

Amell narrowed his eyes, thinking of Dannsair's stealthy movements, and Rekavidur's evident surprise at his arrival. His thoughts flew to the elders' visit to the prison, from which this younger pair had been conspicuously absent. Suddenly it all fell into place. The dragons were sneaking around as surely as he was. The thought was so bizarre, he once again had to fight the urge to laugh.

"What's your question?" he asked, warming to his fellow rebels.

"Are you aware of what enchantments have been put in place by the humans around this site since the break out?" Dannsair interjected.

"Since the break out?" Amell frowned slightly as he thought back over the briefing he'd sat in on the day before, when exactly this matter had been covered. "The protective enchantments on the prison itself have been reignited. Apparently they weren't destroyed by the explosion, just temporarily rendered ineffective. And the fencing magic around the site has been put back in place, although weaker than it was before. They'll need reinforcements from the other kingdoms' Enchanters' Guilds in order to return them to full strength." He paused, thinking it over. "Plus a basic perimeter was put in place around the area, designed to prevent anyone with magic from crossing out of it."

The dragons exchanged an amused glance, and Amell amended hastily, "To prevent any *human* with magic from crossing out of it, I should say."

Two reptilian heads bobbed slowly on snakelike necks. "All that we have detected," Dannsair confirmed. Her gaze turned searching as it settled on Amell's face. "You made no mention of a concealment enchantment. Has the crown not ordered any such magic to be placed over the area?"

Amell frowned. "Concealment magic? Not that I'm aware of. Why would we do that? We want to reveal what's hidden, not hide anything. The location of the prison isn't a secret."

The dragons were silent for a long moment, their gazes locked on one another, and their expressions unreadable.

"He's telling the truth," Dannsair commented.

Rekavidur gave a rippling shrug that caused his scales to tinkle. "As far as he knows it, anyway."

Feeling slightly disgruntled, Amell shifted in the saddle, causing both dragons' eyes to flick back to him.

"Where are you going, out here all alone?" the yellow dragon asked suspiciously.

Amell shrugged. "To a site I wished to explore further. There's a large clump of trees that's so thick I couldn't see inside it, and the area didn't seem to match the map."

"Did you leave this trail, leading to that site?" Dannsair asked.

Amell inclined his head in assent, and had the dubious satisfaction of seeing surprise cross both dragons' faces.

"Perhaps he is more intelligent than he appears," Dannsair mused.

"Thank you," Amell said dryly, unable to help himself.

Dannsair nodded distractedly in acknowledgment of his gratitude.

"If you are minded to explore this...clump," Rekavidur said, "we will not hinder you."

Amell blinked. "Thank...you?"

The dragon had sounded like he was choosing every word with care, but Amell wasn't at all sure what he was getting at. If he didn't know better, he would almost think the dragon wanted to offer help, but that was impossible. Dragons didn't help humans with human-cast enchantments. Assuming there was an enchantment on the area Amell was heading for.

He fell silent, thinking over the dragons' words and his own observations. Was it possible the concealment magic they sensed came from that clump? Could some of the escaped prisoners have cast an enchantment to hide themselves, one strong enough to conceal not only them but the area in which they were sheltered? That would explain why the terrain didn't match the map.

"But if there's a concealment enchantment, I won't be able to find a thing," he muttered, mostly to himself. "I don't have magic."

"True," Rekavidur said briskly. "You need an artifact."

"A powerful one," Dannsair agreed. "Given the strength of concealment magic we felt."

Amell nodded dejectedly. Even if such an item could be found in Fernford, and even if his father was willing to give him access to it, he was going to have to abandon his hopes of searching the area on this trip. By the time he traveled to the capital and returned to the prison, any fugitives might well have left their hiding place.

"I don't have one with me," he said sadly. "So I suppose there's not much point continuing."

"No matter," said Rekavidur, his voice placid. "Your cloak will do. I know from experience that such garments are capable of being excellent receptors for shielding magic."

"Shielding magic?" Amell repeated blankly, running the thickly embroidered fabric of his traveling cloak between his finger and thumb.

"You need to be shielded from the concealment magic," Rekavidur said, with a touch of impatience. "Now take it off."

"Take it...but..." Amell started, more confused than ever.

"Where is the infamous hastiness of humans when it's wanted?" sighed Rekavidur to Dannsair. The purple dragon gave a guttural chuckle that sounded like rocks being scraped violently together.

Equally bemused and intrigued, Amell slipped the cloak from around his shoulders and held it out to Rekavidur. In an alarmingly abrupt motion, the dragon seized it between his teeth and threw it up into the air. Amell was sure it would get snagged on a branch, but somehow it drifted free, floating down to the ground as if it was no heavier than a feather. During its journey down, Rekavidur opened his mouth like he had with the horse. But this time, when he breathed powerfully upon the cloak, the air shimmered with the heat of his breath.

After repeating the exercise a few times, the dragon snagged the falling cloak from the air like a dog pulling a stick from a stream. His expression serene, he snaked his neck forward and offered Amell back his own cloak.

Mouth and eyes both wide from the excitement of witnessing more dragon magic, Amell took the garment from the dragon's outstretched jaws.

"This is an artifact now?" he asked, awed.

"That's right." Rekavidur confirmed. He didn't say it, but the shimmering heat still lingering in the air reminded Amell that it wasn't just any artifact. It was a dragon-made one, which meant it was incredibly strong.

"It will shield me from concealment magic?" he pressed. "So that it just…won't apply to me? I'll see whatever is supposed to be hidden?"

"That's right," Dannsair chimed in.

"Thank you," said Amell, running his hand fervently over the doubly precious fabric. "But…" He looked up with a frown. "But I don't understand. I didn't ask you to do that. Don't get me wrong," he added hastily, "I'm extremely grateful. But I thought dragons weren't supposed to help humans with magical problems."

"Well met, Prince of Fernedell," said Rekavidur tonelessly, as if Amell hadn't spoken. "We wish you success in your investigations."

And without another word, the two dragons took to the air. The gust of wind caused by their departure was so strong, Amell had to lie flat against his horse's neck to avoid being blown off. He felt branches whipping violently around him, but by the time he looked up, blinking, the forest was once again still. He gazed up in amazement. How the dragons had taken off through that thick canopy—and apparently without breaking a single branch—he couldn't imagine. But they must have, because they were gone, leaving no sign whatsoever of their presence.

Amell gazed down at his cloak, trying to make sense of the bizarre encounter. One thing was certain, he thought fervently. He was glad he hadn't included anyone else in this expedition. Having reminded Furn of the agreement between humans and dragons, it would be hard to explain the fact that he'd just broken it.

Not that he'd asked the dragons for help, he defended himself internally, as an image flashed before his eyes of the horrified outrage that would cross his father's face if he found out the truth about Amell's cloak.

The prince's first instinct was to hurry straight on to the site in question, but a moment's consideration made him regretfully abandon that idea. Even under the dappled shade of the trees, he could tell that the light was beginning to fade. Tora would be long gone by now, and Furn would undoubtedly be looking for him. He felt a squirm of conscience at the thought of his friend's worry. They were camping at the prison overnight. He would have the opportunity to return the next day, with more light to explore. He just had to hope that any fugitives hiding under the concealment enchantment would stay put until then. It wasn't like they had anywhere else to go, not with the protective perimeter still in place.

Turning his horse's head, Amell started back toward the clearing where the prison was situated. By the time he reached the camp, the sun was slipping below the horizon, and fires were springing up in preparation for the evening's simple meal.

Amell had barely slid down from his horse when a familiar voice hailed him.

"Your Highness! Where have you been?"

"Hi Furn," said Amell, trying to sound casual. "Just exploring a little more."

"I thought you were going to find us a place to sleep," Furn demanded.

"I got sidetracked," said Amell, with a shrug.

Furn's eyes searched the prince's face carefully, the distraction that had dogged him most of the day clearly gone. "And what did you find?"

"Lots of trees, mainly," Amell said cheerfully. But he couldn't quite meet his friend's eyes, and he knew Furn had noticed it.

He couldn't remember the last time he'd lied to his guard, even if it was a lie of omission.

"I've been too distracted," Furn said unexpectedly. "His Majesty was wrong to trust me with your safety."

"What?" Amell said, startled. "Nonsense! I'm perfectly safe, Furn, look at me. You're the best guard any royal has ever had, and Father agrees with me."

Furn didn't respond, something in his eyes that almost looked like bitterness. Amell's guilt rushed up again, and he gripped the other man's arm. "I really am fine, Furn. And I won't wander off again. I'll stick with you."

Furn nodded, still looking more troubled than the occasion called for.

"What's going on, Furn?" Amell rallied him. "You've never been ruffled by my escapades before, and we both know how outrageous they've gotten."

The guard gave a perfunctory smile, but it didn't reach his eyes.

"Come on," said Amell, starting to feel troubled himself. "Let's find a place to camp. For real this time."

Nodding dejectedly, Furn followed Amell across the camp. The prince noticed a pair of enchanters from the guild glancing curiously at him as he passed, and he pulled the cloak around his shoulders self-consciously. They could probably sense the magic on it, he realized, and it occurred to him that the dragon had chosen his object well for the artifact. Any enchanters would probably assume that the shielding enchantment on the prince's cloak was intended for his general protection. Not a bad idea, really, with twenty-five magic-using criminals on the loose. Especially if he was going to lose his faithful guard. He would need all the protection he could get.

Amell faltered slightly, alarmed by the stray thought. Of course he wasn't going to lose his guard. Furn's strange moment of self-doubt didn't signify his intention to resign from Amell's detail. Furn would never desert him.

And yet, the uneasy feeling that something was changing between him and his most trusted friend lingered so powerfully in the prince's mind, he struggled to fulfill his father's prediction of a good night's sleep on the simple pallet laid down among the soldiers.

His megrims of the night before were forgotten instantly upon awaking, however. The camp was bustling with activity, and a sense of looming adventure hung in the air. Amell had slept with his cloak pulled tightly around him, and he settled it on his shoulders with excitement. He was going to explore that clump of trees today, if he had to defy every guard in Fernedell to do it.

His eyes fell on Furn, who looked like he hadn't slept nearly as well as his charge, and he remembered his promise the day before. Well, not every guard. He'd told Furn he wouldn't wander off, so that was one guard he'd need to take with him.

It was no surprise to Amell that, in spite of his father's talk of including him, the opportunity soon presented itself for him to slip away. The moment the king's investigations required any delicacy of approach, he was only too happy to send Amell on a meaningless errand out of the way.

Pushing down a vague sense that he should be sticking around and demonstrating to his father that he wasn't as unreliable as the king believed, Amell took the offered out. Within minutes he was saddling his horse, a resigned Furn beside him.

"We're going back to the strange clump of trees, aren't we?" the guard asked placidly.

Amell grinned at him. "You know me too well, Furn." He twitched his cloak around him. "We might just find something this time, you never know."

Furn said nothing, a faintly indulgent smile on his face. He may not look well rested, but his manner had thankfully returned to normal with the advent of the sun. There'd been no more disquieting talk of being unworthy of his role, and he no longer seemed unduly alarmed by the idea of danger. Perhaps he figured there was little trouble they could get into within the protected grove.

He did show a flash of concern when he realized Amell was following a previously marked trail through the forest, however.

"Did you leave these markers yesterday?" he asked. "I didn't even notice."

"Yes, I was being impressively sneaky," Amell confirmed cheerfully.

Furn grimaced, but the expression lacked any force, and Amell's grin grew.

The prince's excitement mounted as they passed the place where he'd met with the dragons the evening before. No more than a quarter of an hour later, they reached the end of his trail, and the infamous clump came into view.

"I'm not sure what you're hoping to find, Your Highness," Furn commented.

Amell barely heard him. He'd already slipped from his horse, one hand on his cloak as he scanned the trees intently. Furn dismounted as well, and Amell absently handed his friend his own horse's reins. Approaching the trees, Amell ran a hand over their trunks, looking for any sign of the magic that he couldn't sense. It was possible, of course, that this area wasn't the source of the concealment enchantment the dragons had felt. Had they said it was, or had he just speculated?

Frowning, Amell noticed a gap between two of the trees that he hadn't seen the day before. He slipped sideways through it, and found another similar gap. Perplexed, he realized that the trees were no longer as thickly grouped as he'd thought. In fact, it had become quite easy to walk between their trunks. He paused, glancing back the way he'd come. Again, the trees were a reasonable distance apart, and there was no sign of Furn.

Amell hesitated for only a moment. The guard would be fine, and he wasn't about to miss this opportunity. Pushing forward, he saw with growing excitement that the trees were thinning up ahead, the morning light slanting between their trunks and suggesting a sizable clearing nearby. Were there fugitives hiding there? He placed one hand reassuringly on the hilt of his sword, and crept forward more stealthily.

The trees ended quite suddenly, and Amell found himself gazing out at a clearing that certainly hadn't shown up on the warden's map. It wasn't as big as the one in which the prison stood, but it was significant enough that it should have been marked. All at once his ears picked up the faint sound of a woman singing. The voice was light, pleasant. He didn't recognize the tune, but the cheerful lay certainly wasn't what he'd expect from a hardened criminal hiding from the biggest manhunt Fernedell had ever seen.

Hardly aware of his movements, Amell stepped out into the open, his eyes passing in amazement up the stone side of a lone tower, standing in the precise center of the clearing. The singing was surely coming from there, and it was hard to believe any of the fugitives could be cohabiting with the innocent sound.

Moving across the clearing as if in a daze, Amell's eyes settled on the sole window set into the tower's uppermost level. Suddenly, a figure appeared in the opening, a broom held loosely in one hand, and a sweetly wistful expression on her face as she gazed out at the clearing. Amell stood frozen, staring in utter astonishment at the most beautiful woman he'd ever seen.

Here, undoubtedly, was the damsel of his foolish childhood imaginings. Beautiful, sweet, simply waiting for him to appear and sweep in to her rescue. He blinked, half expecting her to disappear when he opened his eyes. Was this girl—impossibly beautiful, painfully vulnerable in her proximity to a dangerous prison break—simply a figment of his imagination? Was there perhaps a second layer of enchantment on this hidden place, one that addled the observer's mind, turning their daydreams into reality and thereby distracting them from impending danger?

Whether real or wraith, the girl was still there. Amell found himself moving forward without conscious thought, his eyes fixed on her face, and his ears still full of her lighthearted song. His movement must have drawn her attention, because all at once her head swiveled around, and her gaze latched on to him, round blue eyes widening in an astonishment that matched his own as her mouth fell open in a silent exclamation.

CHAPTER EIGHT

Aurelia

Aurelia woke slowly, confused by the unfamiliar shuffling sound near her ear.

"Oh, Aurelia, you're awake. Good. You said Cyfrin willingly gave you the key?"

"What?" Aurelia pushed herself to a sitting position, rubbing her eyes in confusion. "Mama Gail?" She blinked from her mother's bleary eyed face to the thin light coming through the un-curtained window. "What time is it?"

"I don't know, it's very late," said Mama Gail, with a touch of impatience. "Tell me about the key."

"Very late?" Aurelia stretched painfully, realizing as she looked around her that she'd fallen asleep on a settle in the living area instead of in her bed. She vaguely remembered sitting there, waiting in growing concern as her mother hunted for answers in Cyfrin's study with a franticness that Aurelia couldn't understand. "I think you mean very early. Mama, have you been rifling through Cyfrin's study all night?"

"Have I?" Her mother glanced distractedly at the window, surprise showing faintly on her face at sight of the weak sunlight. "I guess I have."

Aurelia grimaced as she stretched her back. She couldn't remember ever sleeping not in a bed before, and she didn't intend to repeat the experience.

"Did you find anything?"

"All sorts of things." Mama Gail rubbed her eyes impatiently, tension still visible in every line of her body. "But nothing that will help us get out of here."

"Help us get out of here?" Aurelia demanded. "I thought we gave up years ago on finding anything in his study that would help us break the restraining enchantment. Is that what you were searching for?"

"Not initially," sighed her mother, biting her bottom lip. "Initially I just wanted to understand Cyfrin's new project, but…"

Aurelia began to feel impatient herself as the other woman trailed off. "But you figured out his project, and whatever it is has you desperate to get out of here. You can say what you're thinking, Mama Gail. I'm not an idiot, and I'm not as fragile as you think."

Mama Gail sat down heavily on the settle next to Aurelia. "I know you're not an idiot, darling. And I don't think you're fragile. But that doesn't change the fact that I want to protect you."

"I don't understand," Aurelia said, extending her hands appealingly. "You were so desperate to protect me from Cyfrin last night, but he honestly didn't do anything to me. I know he's a monster for locking us in here, but he's already done that, so it's not exactly a reason to be scared of him. He's never tried to hurt me physically. What is it you're so afraid of?"

Mama Gail's expression was almost anguished as she met Aurelia's eyes. "If I explained what I'm afraid of," she said softly, "I *wouldn't* be protecting you."

"Honestly, Mama Gail," Aurelia said in frustration, "the thing that's frightening me the most right now is your behavior."

Her mother groaned softly, running a hand down her own

face. "I'm sorry," she said. "I'm scared as well, to tell the truth. I don't like not knowing what's coming, and I don't like feeling powerless to stop whatever it is." Her voice took on an edge of desperation. "I wish I could get you out of here. I wish I could do it *today*."

Aurelia frowned, placing her hand over her mother's on the settle. She wasn't used to the older woman showing such vulnerability, but she welcomed it. Her experience the evening before had bolstered her, making her dare to believe she was stronger than she'd always feared. "Don't be afraid, Mama Gail. You've always been strong for me, and I'm old enough now to be strong for you as well. Whatever's coming, we'll weather it together, like we always do."

To her amazement, moisture welled up in the other woman's eyes. Mama Gail leaned forward to wrap Aurelia in a quick hug, effectively hiding the emotion, although the thickness in her voice betrayed her.

"You're so good, Aurelia. I wish sometimes I had your gentle spirit."

Aurelia laughed. "Don't wish that. Who would stand up to Cyfrin if we were both gentle?"

"You would," said Mama Gail firmly. "And I trust you always will."

"Of course," said Aurelia easily. "Now tell me what you learned about his project."

Mama Gail let out a frustrated breath. "Nothing clear. Tell me again, what happened with the key?"

Aurelia cast her mind back over her strange encounter with the enchanter the night before. "He said that giving it to me was a sign of goodwill." She frowned. "And something else. What was it? Something about a key being a fitting gift."

"Fitting," Mama Gail repeated grimly. "Hm." She sifted

through the papers in her hands, her eyes scanning the pages rapidly as she turned them.

Aurelia leaned forward curiously, but she was only able to catch a glimpse before her mother turned them upside down.

"Why are you hiding them?" Aurelia demanded. "I saw something about giving me the key. What does it say?"

"I don't understand it yet," said her mother pleadingly. "Let me make sense of it before I try to explain it to you."

Aurelia frowned. "Can't we try to make sense of it together?"

Her mother blinked several times in quick succession. "Maybe that's wisest," she muttered to herself. "Maybe best to be forewarned…or maybe it'll just make it worse."

"You're muttering, Mama Gail," said Aurelia, a little alarmed. With great resolution, she drew a deep breath, swallowing her impatience at her mother's reluctance to confide in her. Time was something they had in abundance. "You're not thinking straight. Why don't you get some sleep, and we can talk in a few hours."

"You're right," said Mama Gail, glancing longingly at the door to the bedroom. "I can't think clearly in this state." She smiled at Aurelia, but the expression was strained. "We'll talk it all through when I wake up."

Aurelia nodded, hoping the older woman would sleep long enough for the anxiety to ease from her visibly tense body. Aurelia, meanwhile, would use the hours to come up with a series of unassailable arguments for why her mother should tell her everything she'd discovered, and everything she suspected about Cyfrin's plans.

Any hope of sneaking a look at Cyfrin's notes while her mother was asleep was dashed when Mama Gail returned the papers to the study before seeking her bed. No matter. Aurelia preferred to convince her mother to confide in her rather than finding the answers behind the other woman's back.

It was earlier than Aurelia usually woke, but she didn't try to go back to sleep herself. Her thoughts were too full. She moved around quietly, making herself a simple breakfast from the eggs Cyfrin had brought the night before. By the time she'd eaten, the sun was shining brightly, and she could hear birds singing in the grove outside her window.

A peek into the bedroom showed that Mama Gail was sound asleep, so Aurelia closed the door gently, and set about her usual morning tasks. There was some mending to do, but she spurned it for the moment. She didn't feel like sitting still, not on such a glorious morning. She retrieved her pruning shears, and moved around the circular living area, tending to each of the plants she and her mother had managed to cultivate in their tower over the years. As she worked, she passed Mama Gail's words and behavior over in her mind. Something had certainly changed, and although Aurelia couldn't for the life of her figure out what, it was something significant enough to have Mama Gail more worked up than she'd been in years.

What had Aurelia glimpsed in the quickly covered notes?

Give Honeysuckle the key? Risk vs reward.

She frowned over the strange words, not entirely sure she'd remembered it correctly. Cyfrin's face swam before her mind's eye, as it was when he'd handed her the key. It had seemed like the whim of the moment to her. But if it was mentioned in his notes, it must have been something he'd planned.

A slight shudder went over her. She'd never wanted to be part of any of Cyfrin's plans, and that hadn't changed. But she tried to push the fearful reaction down. Mama Gail had said she didn't like feeling powerless, and yet having a role to play surely meant that Aurelia wasn't entirely powerless. And if the enchanter had decided to give her the key, he must have concluded that the rewards—whatever they were—outweighed the risks.

A flash of resentment passed over Aurelia, some rebellious inner voice noting that even Cyfrin seemed to be trusting her with a role, while Mama Gail wouldn't even tell her what she'd found. The thought was fleeting, but it unnerved Aurelia all the same. She would do well not to forget who her real enemy was.

Still, she was determined to show Mama Gail that she could handle whatever sinister plot Cyfrin was hatching now. She glanced at the silver key, sitting on the counter next to the copper kettle. Perhaps it had been more than a gesture. Could it be an artifact? Aurelia sighed, running a hand over her unrestrained hair. She had no need of extra magic. With all the power Cyfrin had poured into her hair, she was basically a walking artifact.

The feel of the loose dark waves gave Aurelia her next task. Mama Gail had been too distracted the night before to re-braid her hair after Cyfrin's departure, and it was tugging painfully at Aurelia's head. Not to mention it was trailing behind her gathering dirt, which would make her job of sweeping the floors impractical.

She settled herself on a chair by the window, gazing out at the lovely scene before her eyes. A familiar wistfulness washed over her at the beauty that was, as always, just out of reach, but she was determined not to give in to melancholy today. There was a gentle breeze blowing, she had a rare moment to herself, and Cyfrin wouldn't be coming near them for hours and hours.

More significantly, Aurelia was still heartened by her recent discovery of her own ability to stand up to her persecutor.

Mama Gail might feel helpless at their continued captivity, but Aurelia was feeling—for the first time in her life—like she might have some power in the situation. Her eyes fell again on the key as she began the rather tortuous task of braiding her own unmanageably voluminous hair. Cyfrin had given her something, even though doing so apparently carried some risk to himself. He undoubtedly had a sinister purpose behind it, but that didn't change the fact that he'd given it to *her*. If she was smart about it, she might just be able to figure out how to use it to fight back.

Taming her hair took a full hour. Although the result was nowhere near as neat as Mama Gail's usual creations, it did succeed in making it possible for Aurelia to move freely about the room. As quietly as she could, she eased the door to the bedroom open. Pleased to see that Mama Gail remained deep in a much-needed sleep, she closed it again, and took up the broom.

Still gripped by her new feeling of purpose, she sang as she swept. It was a simple, foolish ditty, one Mama Gail often sang while doing household tasks. Aurelia put her heart into the cheerful tune, her thoughts on the beauty of the day, on her dreams for a future free of the tower, and on her determination to use the power and confidence that was only just beginning to emerge within her.

She swept the room clean in no time at all, making a pile of dust near the window. Before going to fetch the tray into which she would sweep that dust, she paused, leaning on the windowsill and gazing out at the quiet clearing.

The birds had fallen silent for the moment, and even the breeze had died down. All was still, nothing indicating that the quaint stone tower was actually a prison. A movement at the edge of the trees drew Aurelia's attention, and she turned her head, expecting to see a fox, or perhaps a rabbit so late in the morning.

Instead, her eyes fell on a tall, lean figure, emerging from the tree line with an energetic step Cyfrin had never used. Aurelia's heart seemed to stop, her eyes widening at the sight of the second man she'd ever seen in her life. Even the obvious, world-shattering considerations of who he was and how he'd entered the hidden clearing were momentarily subsumed by her fascination with the person himself.

He was young, much younger than Cyfrin. She was no judge of the age of strangers, but his face looked as bright as her own did in the mirror, no sign of the lines that crinkled Mama Gail's face when she smiled. His hair was tawny, close to the color Cyfrin often complained that Aurelia's should be. Not unlike the honeysuckles that grew up the side of the tower. It was short compared to Aurelia's, of course, but longer than Cyfrin's closely cropped style. It was disordered as well, and she couldn't quite tell whether it was curly, or simply heavily tousled.

The eyes that were locked on to hers in a reflection of her own shock were gray, like the color of clouds before a summer storm. And every line of his frame suggested energy and vitality.

He was, quite possibly, the most beautiful thing Aurelia had ever seen.

She felt her face suffuse with color as her heart picked up speed. If simply the sight of a well formed stranger caused this reaction in her, perhaps she was as foolish as Cyfrin always said, and as in need of protection as Mama Gail seemed to think. The man was probably an escaped inmate from the prison, not a figure of daydreams.

The thought reminded her that he may very well have dangerous magic, and she drew in a breath. All the questions her shock had temporarily held at bay flooded back. Who was he, and how had he gotten past Cyfrin's enchantments? She was on the point of calling to Mama Gail when the stranger suddenly spoke, arresting her tongue.

"Hello."

She blinked. She wasn't sure what she'd been expecting, precisely, but that casual greeting wasn't it.

"Hello." The reply was out of her mouth before she'd thought about it.

"Who are you?" the man asked, his voice carrying clearly through the still air up to her window. He looked around him. "What is this place?"

Aurelia frowned, shaking her head. "You first. Who are you? Are you one of the escaped prisoners?"

The man looked surprised. "You know about the escaped prisoners?"

"Yes," said Aurelia, lifting her chin slightly. "I know all about it."

"Well, that's a relief, I suppose," he said doubtfully. His eyes traveled up the tower. "I suppose you're fairly safe up there."

"I know that you have magic if you're from the prison," Aurelia said suspiciously. "But you won't be able to get in here, if that's what you're thinking."

"I'm not from the prison," he said quickly. "I'm from Fernford."

"The capital?" Aurelia repeated, instantly distracted. "What's it like?"

Again the man seemed surprised by her question. He paused for a moment, thinking it over. "It's...busy," he said. He glanced around. "Nothing like here. There are lots of buildings, lots of people. And it's very colorful."

Aurelia couldn't quite hold in a sigh. It sounded wonderful. "Why is it colorful?" she pressed. "Are there lots of green trees?"

"There are trees," he said, smiling a little. "But it's the people who are colorful. Everyone wears bright fabrics in Fernford." He gestured to his own garments, which consisted of tightly fitted leggings in a deep blue, and a tunic the color of a summer sky. Even the cloak over the top wasn't black like Cyfrin's traveling cloak. It was a deep red, with gold embroidery glinting in the sunshine. "Like this, but in every color of the rainbow."

"I've seen rainbows," Aurelia said, feeling a little defensive. "I know what colors there are."

"Oh," he said blankly. "That's...good."

Realizing she'd made a bit of a fool of herself, Aurelia hastened on. "If you're not from the prison, why are you here?"

"I am here because of the prison break," he clarified. "I'm part of the group searching for the fugitives."

Aurelia relaxed slightly, then frowned. That made sense, and she didn't want to believe this newcomer was a criminal. But she couldn't just take his word for it. He might be unerringly honest, like Mama Gail. But he also might be a total liar, like Cyfrin.

"How do I know you're not an escaped prisoner?" she asked doubtfully.

He glanced down at himself, a smile tugging up one corner of his lips. The expression made his face, already pleasant, even more appealing. He gestured to his garments again. "You clearly haven't seen the prison uniform if you're asking me that."

Looking him over, Aurelia decided he was right. She didn't know much about fashion, beyond the pictures she'd seen in the few illustrated books contained in Cyfrin's study. But his clothes certainly didn't make him look like a prisoner.

"You could have stolen your clothes," she said, narrowing her eyes. "I know all about stealing, so don't think you can trick me."

"I don't want to trick you," said the man. For some reason he was smiling again, in spite of being accused of deception. But it was such a different smile from Cyfrin's mocking sneer, Aurelia couldn't help but relax further.

"How did you get in here?" she asked abruptly. "This place is supposed to be hidden by powerful enchantments."

He nodded, drawing his thick cloak around his shoulders. "I gathered that. There was no sign of it when I was in this area yesterday. But I came back today with this cloak. It's a powerful magical artifact, and it's designed to shield me against concealment magic."

Aurelia's eyes widened. She hardly dared to believe such a thing was possible, but the very presence of this stranger seemed to demonstrate that it was. This might be their chance to escape! Her heart beat more quickly, and again the thought flashed through her mind that she should wake Mama Gail. And yet, she made no move toward the bedroom.

"But...why did you get it?" she asked. "Did you know about this place?"

He shook his head. "I didn't, but I could tell something was strange about the area. To be honest, I thought there might be fugitives from the prison hiding in here." His eyes passed to her braid, most of which was hidden below the windowsill. "But something tells me you're not from the prison." He sent her a good-natured grin. "I don't suppose you're hiding any escapees in there, who I could round up?"

She shook her head.

"But who are you?" he pressed. "Why are you here, hidden away by concealing magic?"

"You first," Aurelia said again. "What's your name?"

"I'm...Amell."

The hesitation was so brief, she probably would have missed it if she hadn't been suspicious already. Congratulating herself on her astuteness, Aurelia looked him over. Had he given her a false name, like Mama Gail had done to Cyfrin?

"What's yours?" he asked.

"Honeysuckle," said Aurelia casually, not to be outdone. The foolish name sounded bitter on her tongue, but she was sure it was the right decision not to give this stranger her true name, and whatever power might come with it. Even if he wasn't from the prison, he might still have magic. That artifact he was wearing had come from somewhere.

"That's an unusual name," Amell said, his eyes passing over the honeysuckle growing up the outside of the tower. He looked up at her again, his eyes dwelling on her hair. "You weren't very aptly named, were you?"

"You have no idea," muttered Aurelia.

"What was that?" Amell was craning his neck to look at her, and he lifted a hand to rub the back of it. "It's a little hard to talk like this. Do you...do you want to come down?"

Sky above, did she. Aurelia was silent for a moment, taken off guard by the wave of emotion that washed over her at the simple question. As it so often did, her imagination ran away with her, picturing how it would be to descend from the tower, to feel the grass, walk under the trees, travel somewhere far from this quiet, monotonous clearing.

Except now there was a new figure in her imagination. A handsome young stranger waiting for her at the bottom of the tower, ready to spirit her away to his bustling city, where bright colors swirled from every side, and adventures surely happened on a regular basis. And perhaps he would look at her like the hero had looked at the heroine in that storybook Cyfrin had brought her a few months ago, before Mama Gail had declared it foolish and thrown it away. He would gallantly lift her hand to his lips, and—

Flushing in private embarrassment, Aurelia shook off the foolish fantasies.

"I can't," she said curtly.

"Why not?" Amell asked.

She sighed. "There's another enchantment here, beyond the

concealment one that hides the clearing from the world. There's a restraining enchantment, too. No one but my captor can enter or leave the tower."

Amell's eyes were wide with horror by the end of this simple explanation. "You mean you're a prisoner? You're trapped up there?"

Aurelia nodded mutely.

"But we have to get you out!" Amell said, clearly aghast.

Even as her head told her she should still be suspicious of this stranger, Aurelia couldn't help the bubble of hope that began to inflate inside her at his words. She also noted that his reaction didn't support Cyfrin's claims that the world was an evil place. Rather, it matched Mama Gail's insistence that only a monster like the enchanter would steal two women away and lock them up for seventeen years, and anyone else who heard of it would be horrified. And although she didn't know this Amell enough to trust him, she did trust Mama Gail. Perhaps he really would help them.

"If you know how, please do," she said, spreading her hands in a silent appeal. "I'm extremely ready to be free."

"How long have you been up there?" he demanded.

She shrugged. "As long as I can remember. More than seventeen years."

"Your whole life?" he repeated, horror once again in his eyes. His voice dropped so that Aurelia barely caught the words. "And I thought *my* life was restricted."

His look of dismay was so exaggerated, it was almost comical. But as his eyes once again traveled up the tower, they became determined.

"I'm coming up," he said. "Where's the door?"

"There isn't one," Aurelia replied. "And I already told you, no one can get inside except the man who trapped me here."

Amell's face lost none of its determination. "So you say, but

I've never been good at following restrictions. You said your captor gets in and out. How does he do that if there's no door?"

"He comes in through the window," Aurelia said.

Amell seemed to be waiting for more, but she didn't elaborate. "How does he get to it?"

"Well, he climbs up my...my hair." Aurelia could feel her face heating. She didn't need to have experience of the world outside to know that Cyfrin's method of entering the tower wasn't normal behavior.

"Your what?" Amell's face was completely blank.

With a sigh, Aurelia reached back and pulled on her dark braid. Grunting, she tugged it over her shoulder and dropped it out the window, being sure to hold on close to her scalp, to avoid the hair tugging too painfully at her head. Confined as it was in its complicated triple braid, the hair didn't fall to the ground like normal, but she knew it was still shockingly long.

"I don't...understand."

A little amused by the look of utter astonishment on Amell's face, Aurelia reeled her hair back in and untied the bottom of the braid. Once she'd tugged the dark locks loose, she threaded them through the metal hook with a practiced flick, feeding it all the way down. Freed from the braid, her hair reached the grass, the odd strand waving idly in the breeze, but the bulk of it too heavy to do more than just hang limply.

"He climbs it," she repeated.

"Doesn't that hurt you?" Amell asked.

She shrugged. "Not anymore. I've gotten good at bracing myself."

Amell stepped up to the dangling hair, looking fascinated. Craning his neck again, he looked up at her as he lifted a hand. "May I?"

Aurelia blinked, surprised and pleased by the question. Cyfrin had certainly never asked her permission to touch her hair. The thought of the familiar feel of his hands tangling through his beloved vessel made her shudder slightly, but she nodded to Amell.

With a touch so light she couldn't feel it at all, the stranger picked up a loop of hair. He ran his hand over it, shaking his head.

"It feels just like normal hair."

She laughed. "It's not exactly normal, but it is still hair."

He grinned up at her again. "It looks like a dark waterfall."

"Does it?" Aurelia asked, her smile a little twisted. "I wouldn't know."

"Do you..." Amell hesitated. "Do you want me to try to climb it? See if I can get inside?"

Aurelia stared. He was asking what *she* wanted? Another pleasant surprise. She bit her lip, thinking. She didn't think he'd be able to get past Cyfrin's enchantment, but then, she hadn't thought anyone would be able to get past the concealment magic that disguised the clearing. What did she have to lose, after all? Nothing that compared with the chance, however slim, that he might be able to help her and Mama Gail escape.

"If you want to try, I don't mind," she said. "I know what I'm doing. As long as you don't let go, I won't let you fall."

Something unreadable passed over Amell's face, although his voice was perfectly polite. "Thank you."

Hesitantly, he grasped hold of two thick fistfuls of hair. But he made no move to pull himself up.

"What's wrong?" Aurelia asked. "Aren't you able to pull your weight up?"

"No, I...I'm sure I can," Amell said. "I just don't want to hurt you."

Aurelia's heart picked up speed again, and she told it firmly to calm down. If Mama Gail was right, that level of basic consideration was the minimum one person should be able to expect from another, not a sign that this Amell was the type of hero childhood daydreams were made of.

"You won't," she assured him. "I'm taking the weight with my arms, not my head. And you don't look too heavy."

A rueful look passed over Amell's face, but without further protest, he placed one foot on the wall of the tower and pulled himself up. Aurelia felt his weight transfer from the ground to her hair, and her arms quivered from the strain. Bracing herself against the wall under the windowsill, she focused on the familiar task of perfecting the tension required to enable her visitor's ascent.

Her position didn't allow her to watch through the window anymore, but she could feel Amell drawing closer, and hear his occasional grunts of effort. All at once, he appeared in the windowsill, and the tension on her hair slackened as he shifted his weight onto the stone, crouching in the opening with apparent disregard for the sheer drop behind him.

"Well," he said, breaking into an endearing smile that seemed to laugh at himself rather than at her, "I think that was the strangest thing I've ever done."

"For me, on the other hand, it was utterly mundane." She nodded. "Careful now. You don't want to fall backward when the enchantment stops you from getting through."

"Oh, I forgot about that," said Amell. Casting his eyes around, he spotted the metal ring through which Aurelia's hair was still threaded, and gripped onto it with one hand. Narrowing his eyes in anticipation, he leaned forward, clearly expecting resistance.

Except, to Aurelia's amazement, he met none. Apparently he was also taken off guard, because he lost his balance, toppling forward into the room with a clunk that Aurelia feared would wake Mama Gail.

She glanced at the doorway to the bedroom, but there was

no sign of movement. When she turned back around, Amell had straightened, and for the first time she had to look up to see his face. She froze, her heart pounding erratically and her color once again rising, able to do nothing but stare at the young, attractive, and very *real* man standing impossibly in her tower.

Amell

Amell's breath caught in his throat at the way the girl—Honeysuckle—was looking at him. He'd never felt so conspicuous, but her gaze didn't seem critical. On the contrary, she was looking at him like he was the most impressive thing she'd ever seen, and it made him uncomfortably aware of how far from the truth that was.

She, on the other hand, was perfect, at least in appearance. Her dark hair flowed around her slim form and up to the hook, like a voluminous train, mesmerizing in its strange beauty. She raised a hand to tuck a loose strand behind her ear, and Amell found himself staring back at her delicate features, and striking blue eyes. The unusual combination of coloring struck a chord in his memory, but he couldn't put a finger on it. He was too distracted by the woman in front of him, more dreamlike and fantastical than anything his overactive mind had ever made up, and yet as real and solid as himself.

Not that solid was the word he would choose to describe her. She wasn't much shorter than him, but she was willowy, her slight frame belying the strength it must have taken to half pull him up that tower wall.

"Well," he said, clearing his throat, "I guess the enchantment didn't work on me."

She opened her mouth, then closed it without speaking. When she tried again, her voice came out a little hoarse. "How did you do that?"

Amell shrugged. "I don't know. I just...could. There was no barrier that I could sense." He twitched the fabric of his cloak. "Maybe this artifact shields me against the restraining enchantment as well."

He wasn't convinced, however, and he could tell it came through in his voice. The dragon Rekavidur had been quite specific about the function of the cloak. And he hadn't known about the restraining enchantment, so it was unlikely he would have molded his magic to counteract it.

"Or maybe there is no enchantment keeping people out," Honeysuckle mused quietly. "It's just the kind of lie he'd tell, wanting me to think he was protecting me. Maybe he didn't think it was necessary, given the whole place is hidden."

"Plus there's no easy way up without using your hair," Amell chimed in, feeling absurd as he said the words.

Honeysuckle—could that ridiculous name be real?—nodded slowly. "You did well to pull yourself up without practice," she commented. "You're stronger than you look."

Amell smiled ruefully. "I'm not sure if that was a compliment or an insult."

Honeysuckle gave a sudden laugh, surprising herself as much as him if he was any judge. "Neither am I, to be honest."

"I'm amazed that it didn't hurt you," said Amell, his eyes on that unbelievable hair, still dangling out the window. Looking self-conscious, Honeysuckle drew it quickly through the loop and gathered it into her arms as he continued. "Or that it didn't break."

"Yes, well, I think the magic makes it stronger than normal

hair," she said matter-of-factly. "In addition to making it, you know...grow really long."

"The magic?" Amell asked, comprehension dawning. Of course her hair was affected by magic. He should have realized it.

Honeysuckle nodded. "Plus you're lighter than Cyfrin."

"Cyfrin?!" Tensing instantly, Amell took an unconscious step toward her. "Did you say Cyfrin? Is that the name of the enchanter who's been holding you captive up here?"

Honeysuckle nodded again, her expression suddenly wary. "Do you know him?"

"I heard about him just a couple of days ago!" Amell said, his mind reeling at the unexpected connection. "He was thrown out of the Enchanters' Guild almost twenty years ago because of his unsanctioned experiments."

The girl spread her arms wide, her expression suddenly grim. "Behold me."

Amell felt his eyes widen. "You're saying his experiments continued? He pursued his idea of using a human as a vessel, with *you* as the vessel?"

Honeysuckle shrugged. "Basically, yes. But from what we can gather, he hasn't put the magic in me so much as in my hair. I mean, it's not in my core. You see, the thing is that using living creatures as vessels instead of artifacts has the potential for much greater power, but it also has risks. One of those risks being that when the magic is extracted, the living vessel usually, well..."

"Dies," Amell supplied heavily, remembering Bartholomew's account.

Honeysuckle nodded sagely. "Precisely. Cyfrin seems to think a human wouldn't die like animals do, but he's just guessing. Putting the magic in my hair instead of into my core seems to be one of the ways he's trying to prolong my potential for greatest use."

"He told you all this?" Amell asked, feeling appalled. Not that it would be better for the enchanter to conceal the truth of his experiments, exactly, but the idea of him being so cold as to not even feel ashamed of gambling with this girl's life made Amell sick to his stomach. And the most heart-breaking part of it all was the matter-of-fact way she was describing how she'd been exploited.

"Hardly," Honeysuckle said dryly. "He told me he's putting magic in my hair, but that's about it. The rest we found out from reading his notes when he's not here."

"We?" Amell pressed, glancing around the open space.

It was a neat and pleasant living area, ringed with flourishing indoor plants, and showing every sign of being a home. To all appearances, they were alone. But he noticed that the space wasn't a perfect circle, one side flattened by an interior wall with two doors. Both were currently closed, and he assumed whoever Honeysuckle was talking about must be behind one of them.

"Cyfrin isn't here right now, is he?" Amell demanded, his hands straying to the hilt of his sword.

Honeysuckle's eyes widened slightly as they followed the gesture, and he hurriedly lowered his hand again, not wanting to frighten her.

"No, he doesn't live here," Honeysuckle explained. "He comes at sunset every evening, threads more magic into my hair, and then leaves. The rest of the time it's just my mother and me."

"Your mother?" Some of the tension leaked from Amell's shoulders. "You're not alone up here?"

"Thankfully not," said Honeysuckle, with a smile. "Or I think I'd go mad, don't you?" She lowered her brilliant eyes, fidgeting with the sleeve of a rather worn gown. "She's the only mother I've ever known, anyway. Cyfrin stole us both together, and locked us up here, and she's taken care of me ever since."

For a moment Amell was silent, unable to find a response. "You were serious when you said you know all about stealing," he said at last, his voice gentle. Her very life had been stolen from her.

She smiled painfully as she raised her head again. "I might not know much, but I know I shouldn't really trust you when I've only just met you. The thing is, I'd *rather* tell the truth than lies. I'd rather be like Mama Gail than like Cyfrin. And I'd risk just about anything if there was some chance you might actually be able to get us out of here."

"Of course I'm going to get you out of here," Amell declared. "If it's the last thing I do. You and your mother." He glanced again at the closed doors. "Is she trapped as well, or can she leave?"

"She can't leave," said Honeysuckle. "She's here, she's just sleeping right now."

Deciding not to pry, Amell just nodded. "Should we wake her up?"

Honeysuckle hesitated for a moment, looking a little guilty. "No," she said at last. "Not yet."

Amell's mind whirled with questions, but again he didn't pry. "If the enchantment supposedly stopping people from entering is just a lie, is it possible the one stopping you from leaving is a lie as well?"

Honeysuckle gave him a look. "Do you really think we've never tested it, in seventeen years?"

"Right," he said sheepishly. "Well, you've never tested it with my help, though. Maybe it will make a difference, since I'm not trapped here."

Honeysuckle bit her lip. "I hope you're not," she said. "I

hadn't thought about that. If the restraining enchantment only goes one way, then all you've achieved by getting in is to be stuck in here with us."

"Good," said Amell flippantly. "That will give me plenty of opportunity to give this Cyfrin a piece of my mind."

Honeysuckle visibly shivered. "You absolutely mustn't still be here when he arrives at sunset. I don't even want to think about what he'd do."

This sign of the girl's fear of her captor caused a wave of fury, sudden and intense, to rise up within Amell. He struggled to keep it at bay, again worried about frightening her. When his breathing calmed, and he thought he could speak normally, he tried to reassure her.

"I'm not afraid of Cyfrin, magic or not. And I'm not helpless."

"I'm not helpless either," she retorted, with a flash of spirit. "I have power in the situation."

"I'm sorry," Amell stuttered, taken aback by her suddenly defiant tone. "I didn't mean—"

"And you're foolish not to be worried about his magic," she told him frankly. "He's more powerful than you realize, and if I'm in the room—which I always am—he'll have an unbeatable source of magic. I, for one, don't want to give him cause to extract it in order to kill you, thereby killing me in the process."

"Of course I don't want that either," said Amell quickly. "I just meant that I would fight back if—"

"Fighting isn't just about swords and armor," scoffed Honeysuckle, once again cutting him off. "Mama Gail and I have been fighting for years, with no weapons except a stubborn refusal to give in to despair. And that's *much* harder than some paltry sword fight, believe me."

"I do," said Amell, as enchanted as he was astonished by this sudden burst of fire from the apparently docile girl. "I do believe you."

Honeysuckle nodded with lofty grace, and a slow grin spread across Amell's face.

"You're stronger than you look as well."

She sniffed. "I know I am." She was trying to sound superior again, but Amell could tell that she was pleased with the compliment. His grin grew.

Honeysuckle surveyed him doubtfully, the appealing pink of her cheeks suggesting that she wasn't entirely impervious to his smiles.

"Well, shall we try it?" Amell asked pleasantly, extending his hand.

Honeysuckle stared at it with as much wary fascination as one might regard a rearing snake. Her gaze traveled to his face.

"Try what?"

"Getting you out of here," Amell said, bouncing slightly on the balls of his feet. He'd stumbled into an adventure more strange than even he could imagine, and he was wasting it standing around talking.

Honeysuckle apparently caught his restlessness, because without another word, she slipped her hand into his, a reckless air about the gesture. Her fingers were cool under his warm ones, and trembled slightly in his grip. For a moment Amell forgot what he was doing, every sense focused on the point of contact. Then, with a slight shake of the head, he turned toward the window, tugging her gently behind him.

It was only when he reached the casement that he remembered there was only one way down.

"I suppose we'll have to use your hair again," he said apologetically.

Sighing, Honeysuckle let go of his hand and gathered her

hair in her arms. She slipped it through the hook, lowering it gradually toward the ground.

"It's not going to work," she told him. "I've tried many times."

"Try once more," Amell coaxed. "Just to humor me."

Shaking her head a little, Honeysuckle climbed nimbly up onto the windowsill, her skirt pooling around her as she crouched. Amell could see the expert way she gripped her hair on both sides of the hook, but when she tried to lean out of the window, she just stopped.

She turned to him. "Like I said. I can't leave."

Amell frowned. "Let me try." He pulled himself up onto the windowsill beside her. It was cramped with two, and their legs were pressed against each other's. Trying not to get distracted, Amell gripped the metal hook and leaned outward. He swung forward so quickly, he almost lost his grip on the hook. Looking down, he swallowed at the sight of the ground, twenty feet below.

"So I can leave," he said thoughtfully, his eyes passing to Honeysuckle. He swallowed again at the realization of how close their faces were. She looked dejected, and he felt a rush of guilt for getting her hopes up. "Maybe it's the cloak. Here."

Without giving himself time to think too hard, he extricated one arm, lifting his cloak with it. Passing his hand over Honeysuckle's shoulder, he draped the voluminous cloak around her, so that it encompassed them both. They were even closer now, and he could smell the flowery scent of her hair. It was a little intoxicating, and he turned quickly away. Scaling sheer drops called for a clear head.

But when he leaned out, he could no longer swing far enough to be suspended in the air. One half of him moved cleanly, but the arm that was around Honeysuckle's shoulders held him back. It was as if he was trying to pull her through a solid wall instead of open air.

Glancing at her, he caught her wince as he tugged, and he quickly reeled himself back in with a hasty apology. Once he'd scrambled down from the windowsill, he reached out to help her return to the safety of the stone floor. Blushing furiously, she took his hands, letting go as soon as she'd stepped down, so she could gather her hair to her again.

Amell frowned at the window, his thoughts on the challenge before him. "I see what you mean about the restraining enchantment," he mused. "And clearly it's not the cloak that's allowing me to get past it. Unless it only works on me...but that's not how artifacts usually work, from what I know." He drew his eyes to hers with determination. "I think I *had* better stay here, confront Cyfrin. We'll just have to make him lift the enchantment."

"You can't do that!" Honeysuckle said, aghast. "He'll kill you!"

"I'm not going to give up just because there's danger," said Amell firmly. He didn't think even Cyfrin would dare to murder him once he discovered who he was, but there was no need to tell Honeysuckle that detail just yet.

"But what will you achieve?" Honeysuckle demanded. "If he kills you, I'll be just as stuck as ever. And even if you get away, he'll know this clearing has been discovered, and he'll move me to somewhere else, and I'll *still* be just as stuck as ever."

Amell frowned, not convinced, and she pushed on.

"That is, provided I'm not dead from him extracting magic from my hair in order to kill you."

Amell let out his breath in a sigh. That point was unarguable.

"But what am I supposed to do?" he protested. "Just...leave? And do nothing?"

"For now, yes," she said. "Can't you get help and come back tomorrow? Cyfrin's never here during the day."

He frowned, and not just because it was such a tame suggestion. The idea of Cyfrin coming that very evening and forcing this girl to be a passive vessel for his magic, knowing the process might kill her, was unendurable. Of course Amell knew it had been happening for seventeen years, and that one more night shouldn't matter so much. But there was a crucial difference—he hadn't known about it before, and he did now. And that being the case, he couldn't be comfortable doing nothing.

"Amell," Honeysuckle said seriously, and her first use of his name caused him to still, meeting her eyes and listening not just to her words but to the earnest plea in her voice. "I don't know why or where you got that cloak, but I do know that you are the best—no, the *only*—chance we've had to get out of here, in seventeen years. Please don't mess it up by doing anything rash."

Amell swallowed, suddenly overwhelmed by the seriousness of the situation, and the weight of his own responsibility in it. He'd been chasing excitement all his life, but this wasn't some adventure. This *was* Honeysuckle's life. And she couldn't afford for him to be his usual reckless self.

He nodded meekly. "If you think it's best for me to leave and come back tomorrow, that's what I'll do. But if I'm going after help, it's best for me to know as much as you can tell me about what Cyfrin's up to. What's his role in the prison break?"

"None whatsoever, as far as I know," said Honeysuckle, sounding surprised. "He was furious when they built the prison so close to our tower, and he was raging about the break out when he came last night. He said he had to reinforce the protective enchantments as a result, and he clearly felt it was a waste of his magic."

She brightened. "He talked like he was worried about the escaped prisoners, but I realize now that he must have been afraid the area would attract extra notice because of the break out." Her eyes shone as she looked up at Amell, and he once again had the uncomfortable sensation of being far from the hero she thought him. "And he was right. We attracted your attention."

He gave her a tight smile. "Of course he was right. The whole region is being combed. There were even dragons searching the woods today."

"Dragons?" Honeysuckle's eyes were as round as coins. "I've never seen one, and Mama Gail doesn't know much about them. What are they like?"

Amell's smile became more genuine. "They're irritatingly cryptic, and a little surly, if I'm honest. Now what else can you tell me about Cyfrin's activities?"

It wasn't much, he reflected, once Honeysuckle had told him what she knew. Her experiences aligned with Bartholomew's account of the enchanter's intentions all those years ago. With a start, Amell realized that there had been no delay. Given Honeysuckle's age, Cyfrin must have stolen her away and started experimenting with her hair soon after the guild expelled him. If only they'd kept better track of him, instead of letting him disappear!

"So your hair is carrying seventeen years worth of magic?" Amell said at the end of her account, his awed gaze passing over the dark tresses.

Honeysuckle nodded, her expression troubled as she gathered up a stray loop. Amell had noticed that she was protective of the hair, as if she wanted to keep it out of reach of danger.

"But what's he planning to use all that power for?" Amell asked uneasily. "I can't believe his interest in the concept of storing magic in living vessels is purely theoretical."

"Definitely not," agreed Honeysuckle. "He's planning something, and every now and then he makes veiled comments about how they'll all regret it. But I don't know what he intends to do." She hung her head slightly. "I'm sorry I don't have more details to give you. Mama Gail has read every note in his study, but it's not like he writes out all his dastardly plots. He just makes notes about the practical aspects of his magical experiments, and stores some of his theory books there. We put the pieces together as best we can."

"Don't apologize," Amell reassured her. "Even just knowing that he *is* planning something could be enough to prevent disaster." She lifted her head again, and he was suddenly locked in her brilliant blue eyes. "But dealing with his plans is secondary," he said, his voice coming out a little gruff. "The first priority is getting you and your mother safely out of here."

She nodded gratefully, a shy smile spreading across her face. Glancing at one of the closed doors, she took a step toward the window. "I think you should go now," she said. "There will be time to talk tomorrow."

Amell didn't argue, feeling he'd been given plenty to think about and plenty to do already. Getting the sense that it might make her uncomfortable, he didn't help thread Honeysuckle's hair through the hook, instead waiting politely until she nodded him toward it.

"I'm glad to have met you, Honeysuckle," he said, as he climbed up onto the windowsill.

She bit her lip, looking suddenly troubled. "You will help us, won't you?" she asked. "You're not lying, or making false promises? I mean, you are going to come back tomorrow?"

"I swear it," he said solemnly. "I'll help you get free of Cyfrin, or I'll die trying."

She looked a little alarmed. "That sounds very dramatic."

"Well," Amell said, grinning, "I'm hoping it won't come to that." As gently as he could, he took hold of her hair, testing his weight before planting his feet on the outside wall and swinging carefully free of the window. "Until tomorrow, Honeysuckle."

"Until tomorrow, Amell," she agreed, disappearing from his sight as she braced herself.

He descended as quickly as he could while still being careful, releasing her hair as soon as his feet were on the ground. Craning his neck, he looked back up at the window, and was rewarded by the sight of a beautiful face appearing in the opening. With a wave, he turned toward the trees where he'd entered, his thoughts flying suddenly to poor long-suffering Furn. Who knew what he thought had become of his charge this time?

When Amell reached the tree line, he looked back. Honeysuckle was leaning on the windowsill, one delicate hand cupping her chin, and some loose tendrils of dark hair floating out around her. She made such a striking picture Amell caught his breath involuntarily. But the whimsical moment was soon driven out by his determination. Honeysuckle's setting might look picturesque, but her situation was actually a nightmare. And he wasn't going to rest until he'd freed her from it.

He remembered the sweetness of her smile when he told her he'd help her, and the hesitation in her eyes when she'd asked him if he was making false promises. A pang went through his heart. He was always being told he wasn't responsible enough, and didn't take anything seriously. But not this time. For all his father's lectures on a prince's duties, no one had ever actually been relying on Amell before. They'd always had their king at the helm. But this time, Honeysuckle was counting on him to help her escape a life of imprisonment.

And this time he would do whatever it took.

CHAPTER TEN

Aurelia

Aurelia watched Amell disappear into the trees, her heart in her throat. Did he mean what he said? Would he really make it his mission to see them set free? Had she done right to send him away—to trust him?

She hadn't told him her real name, she reflected. So that was something, if he proved to be false. But she couldn't believe he was false. She couldn't bear to think that the candor in his clear gray eyes had been a pretense, that his appealing smile and light laugh hid an evil heart.

She was being foolishly sentimental, she supposed. But there was a simple way to tell. She would wait and see if he followed through with his big promises. *Judge a person by what they do, not what they say,* Mama Gail had told her, whenever Cyfrin subjected them to a lecture on his beneficence in shielding Aurelia from a harsh world. And her mother was right. His magnanimous words had confused Aurelia as a child, but reflection had shown her the truth. Someone who meant well by her wouldn't keep her trapped against her will.

So, as much as her heart wanted to take Amell for exactly

what he appeared to be, she would wait, and reserve judgment until she saw whether he really was going to help them.

No more than half an hour after Amell had left, Aurelia heard the creaking of a wooden bed, followed by a soft groan. A moment later, Mama Gail appeared in the doorway, rubbing a hand over her face and smiling blearily at her daughter.

"Good morning, Aurelia," she said. "Or is it afternoon now?"

"Just past noon, I think," Aurelia smiled. "I was about to have lunch. Do you feel better?"

"Much better," Mama Gail said firmly. "I'm sorry I left you to do the morning chores alone. It was very irresponsible of me to stay up all night, and I won't do it again."

Aurelia's heart sank slightly, and she scolded herself for it. It was a bit of a shock to realize that, unacknowledged, she'd been harboring the hope that she might again be alone when Amell came the next day.

"No need to apologize," she said lightly. "The chores were no trouble. But I wouldn't mind your help with my hair."

"Of course," said Mama Gail repentantly. "You've been stuck with it like that since last night, haven't you? Poor Aurelia."

Aurelia said nothing, turning to the kitchen to hide her flushed face as she thought of what she—and her hair—had been up to that morning. Guilt burned through her at her deception in not telling Mama Gail about Amell's visit immediately. It made little sense—she would have to tell her, and soon. But she felt strangely reluctant to do it.

Perhaps it was because she suspected Mama Gail wouldn't trust him, and she didn't want to hear her own fears articulated. Or perhaps it was because she'd never before, not in all her life, had anything she *could* hide from Mama Gail. Prior to Amell's appearance, the previous evening's interview with Cyfrin was the only occasion in her life when Mama Gail hadn't been present. And that paled in significance compared to her interaction with Amell.

Remembering the tingling warmth that had spread through her when she'd taken his hand, Aurelia felt her face burn again, for different reasons this time. Mama Gail would definitely question Aurelia's ability to objectively assess Amell if she knew how disordered her thoughts were, and perhaps she'd be right. It was on the tip of Aurelia's tongue to confess the whole thing, and ask Mama Gail what she thought, when her eyes fell on the key, still sitting by the kettle.

Give Honeysuckle the key? Cyfrin's notes had said. *Risk vs reward.* And Mama Gail still hadn't told her what she thought it meant, or what else she'd found in the study. After all, even without any lying involved, Aurelia wasn't the only one who wasn't being entirely forthright.

"Can we talk about last night now?" she asked, turning abruptly back around. "About whatever you found in Cyfrin's notes?"

Mama Gail's expression was sober, and she looked at Aurelia for a long moment before she spoke. "Yes, let's talk about it. Come and sit, so I can fix your hair while we do."

Some of the tension leaked out of Aurelia as she lowered herself into a chair in front of her mother. Her every nerve felt painfully alive, her mind a jumble of the last twenty-four hour's worth of new and overwhelming experiences. It was hard to believe that only the evening before she'd been so astonished and confused by Cyfrin wanting to speak to her alone. That incident was absolutely nothing compared to the appearance of a stranger in her clearing, in her actual tower. It was so life-changing, she could still barely wrap her mind around it.

"You've brushed it already," Mama Gail observed, pulling Aurelia's mind from its chaotic spiral. Her hands were firm but soothing as they worked, bringing order to Aurelia's trailing hair.

Aurelia nodded. "I had some time on my hands," she said dryly. "But I don't want to talk about my hair, Mama Gail. I want to talk about last night."

"All right," said Mama Gail, clearly a little surprised at Aurelia's firmness. "About what?"

"Why were you so terrified at the idea of Cyfrin speaking with me alone?"

There was a moment's silence. "I was afraid of what he would do to you."

Aurelia frowned. "But you were still so worked up, even after I told you he didn't try to hurt me." She half turned in her chair, to look her mother in the eye. "I told you everything we spoke about. Did he do whatever it was you were so afraid of?"

Mama Gail bit her lip. "I don't think so," she said, her expression troubled. "Not yet, at least."

"Not yet?" Aurelia felt a spike of fear, but she pushed it back ruthlessly. She wasn't going to let the feelings of powerlessness back in. Instead she pinned her mother with an insistent look. "Let's talk about what happened next. What did you find in his study, Mama Gail?"

The older woman sighed. "Just the usual cryptic ramblings. The only notes I found that might relate to this new project of his were talking about a key."

"That key, do you think?" Aurelia demanded, her gaze flying to the silver key on the counter.

But Mama Gail grunted dissent, gently turning Aurelia's head to face away from her again, and resuming work on her hair.

"I don't think that key is anything more than a key. I couldn't see any notes about a new artifact. The notes talked about the role of a key in storing magic. I think giving you that physical key was just a whim, but one that tickled his fancy given how it reflects his more theoretical plans."

"What's the role of a key in storing magic?" Aurelia asked, attempting to turn back to face her mother only to have her head gently steered forward again.

"I'd never heard of it before," Mama Gail acknowledged, "so I don't really know. But it seemed to have something to do with unlocking the magic after it's been stored."

"Unlocking it?" Aurelia repeated, startled. "Does that mean he's ready to extract the magic from my hair?" Perhaps she'd been hasty in telling Amell to leave. Perhaps he was right, and they should have confronted Cyfrin that very evening, in spite of the risks. What if tomorrow was too late?

"I don't know," said Mama Gail, sounding as troubled as Aurelia felt. "But it all makes me uneasy. I didn't realize any particular ceremony was required for extracting it."

"Neither did I," Aurelia agreed. "I thought he could just pull it out at will."

"I think...I think he can," Mama Gail said, and her hesitance told Aurelia there was more she wasn't saying. "His notes show that he's exploring ways to increase the potency of the magic he's already stored. It sounds like this idea of fashioning a magical key might be one of those ways."

"Why does he need to increase its potency?" demanded Aurelia. "He's stored so much magic in my hair, he could do just about anything. Will it never be enough for him?"

"Truly, sweetheart, I don't think it ever will," said Mama Gail heavily. "Some people are like that. No matter how much they get their hands on, they're never satisfied. In fact, it's as though the more they acquire, the less content they are."

Aurelia rubbed her temples, thinking. "What kind of thing can be a magical key?"

"It's not things so much as actions, if I've understood his scribbles," Mama Gail said. "Your hair is already acting as a cage of sorts for his magic...it looks like there's a complex type of enchantment he can perform that would build in a triggering action which would act to release the magic from its cage, without him even needing to specifically extract it. And I imagine it could be just about any action. The type of action will depend on lots of factors, and I'm not familiar enough with the theory to know what they might be."

"But why did his notes mention giving *me* the key?" Aurelia asked. "Surely he'd want the action to be something he could control."

Mama Gail was silent for a moment, and Aurelia had the distinct impression that she was debating whether to answer.

"Honestly, Aurelia," she said at last, her voice strained, "I think he believes that you *are* something he can control."

Aurelia gave a little huff of annoyance. "He's certainly always talked like he has every right to order whatever details of my life he wants," she agreed.

There was silence for several minutes, as she thought over her mother's words. She supposed it was worthwhile to know that Cyfrin's new project involved fashioning some kind of magical key, but without knowing what the relevant action was, or understanding its purpose, they hadn't really gained much.

"There was more though, wasn't there?" she asked abruptly, as Mama Gail tied off the completed braid. "You found more than that in his notes."

It wasn't a question, and Mama Gail didn't deny it. With a sigh, she dragged her chair around so that she was facing Aurelia.

"There was more, but I don't want to tell you about it."

Aurelia frowned. "I can handle it, Mama Gail. I'm stronger than you think I am."

The other woman reached out and placed a hand gently on her daughter's cheek. "Impossible," she said softly, "since I already believe you to be the strongest person I know."

Aurelia stood abruptly, somehow unable to find the usual solace in her mother's reassurance. "You're the one who told me to judge people's actions, not their words. If you think I'm so strong, why are you hiding the truth from me in some misguided attempt to shield me?"

A flash of pain crossed Mama Gail's features, but she met Aurelia's eyes unflinchingly.

"It's not misguided, Aurelia. There are different kinds of dangers. I know we don't face many physical threats up here, but there are things you can't un-learn once you know."

"But if I want to take the risk and you won't let me, aren't you just locking me in a tower of ignorance?" Aurelia challenged. "I'm not a child anymore, Mama Gail. I don't need to be shielded—I need to fight back. If Cyfrin is giving me some kind of key to unlocking the power he's stored in me, shouldn't we be using every bit of information we can to try to understand it and use it?"

She expected her mother to agree, but she didn't immediately answer. "Some kinds of power I wouldn't want you to use, Aurelia, even if you could."

Frowning, Aurelia sat back down. "What are you saying? You think he's creating a situation where I can access his power if I invoke some kind of dark magic?"

Mama Gail shook her head quickly. "Nothing like that." She leaned forward. "And let's keep one thing straight. Nothing I read contradicted what we've learned before—you can't be anything but a passive vessel. No matter what this key is, even if you're the one with the ability to unlock his magic, it's still his magic, and it will still be him using it. Holding the key won't give you the ability to wield it."

"That's a pity," sighed Aurelia. "But I suppose if it was any other way, he'd never give me the key." She bit her lip in thought. "Perhaps I want to learn what the key is so that I can make sure *not* to do whatever action will unlock his magic."

"That may be best," Mama Gail agreed. "Unfortunately, I think he'd still be able to extract it. But it wouldn't be as powerful."

"That makes no sense to me," said Aurelia, frustrated.

"I don't understand it either," Mama Gail said helplessly. "Because I don't really understand the theory behind it. But that's what his notes said. He's been researching ways to increase the potency of magic, according to 'the foundational principles of power', whatever they are. Apparently one principle is that power willingly given is stronger than power coerced or forcibly taken."

"So he thinks if he just forcefully extracts the magic from my hair, it will lose some of its potency compared to if I willingly unlock it through the use of this key action," Aurelia said.

Mama Gail nodded. "That's the best I can ascertain from his notes. But he'd made a note underneath, that if giving you the key didn't work, he could still extract the magic as planned, with less potency."

"Risk versus reward," Aurelia muttered.

"What?"

"Nothing." She sighed. "And what was the other thing you found? The one that's making you so nervous?"

Mama Gail chewed on her lip, looking at her daughter with troubled eyes.

"Was it another of these foundational principles of power?" Aurelia guessed. "Another way for him to increase the magic's potency?"

Slowly, her eyes locked on Aurelia's, Mama Gail nodded.

"And are you going to tell me what it was?" Aurelia pressed, when the silence stretched out.

Mama Gail let out a long breath. "Not yet. Not if I don't need to."

"Mama Gail, that's infuriating," Aurelia complained.

Her mother winced. "I know it is," she acknowledged. "But I'm not trying to infuriate you. Can't you trust me on this?"

Aurelia clenched and unclenched her hand over the fabric of her skirt, trying to still her agitation. "Honestly, I don't know," she said flatly. "I trust your intentions, but I still think you should tell me everything you read. I think I'll be better able to fight back against Cyfrin if I know what I'm up against."

"Well," said Mama Gail, her voice gruff, "I can understand that perspective. I'll...I'll give it some thought. But in the meantime, our safest route is to prevent Cyfrin from getting you on your own again."

Aurelia didn't answer. She couldn't remember the last time she'd felt so out of charity with her mother, and any guilt over her failure to confide in her about Amell's visit had fled. If Mama Gail didn't trust her, she thought petulantly, she wasn't going to share her secrets until the last minute either.

The afternoon passed uncomfortably, neither woman speaking much. Their daily chores took much less time than they had, and Aurelia spent the hours before sunset curled up on a settle, pretending to read over her notes from the physician's guide, while in reality wrestling with the day's events.

When the hated voice called up to her from the clearing below, Aurelia almost welcomed it. She was ready for the day to be over, and it couldn't end until Cyfrin's visit was done.

"Honeysuckle, throw me my rope."

Grumbling, Aurelia tugged her hair free and looped it through the metal hook. As she felt Cyfrin's weight leave the ground, it was impossible not to compare the experience with another visitor she'd helped ascend that day. This time there was no asking permission, no hint of caring what she wanted, and no gentleness in the way Cyfrin pulled himself up, hand over hand, as if her hair really was nothing more than an inanimate rope.

When he appeared in the window, she found herself examining his form with disfavor as well. Did he always wear such a sour expression, or only in the tower? It was really very unflattering to his features. And why did he cut his hair so close and tight? It gave him such a plain appearance compared to Amell's general exuberance.

It was unfortunate for him, she thought dispassionately, that he was not only lacking in both personality and character, but in appearance as well. Not that she'd ever particularly considered him ugly before, of course. But that had been before she'd set eyes on someone so undeniably handsome.

"Well," Cyfrin said, depositing the usual meager parcel of supplies on a table. "Good evening."

"Good evening," Aurelia said flatly.

He raised an eyebrow at her tone, but didn't comment. "Shall we begin, child?"

Aurelia stepped forward, flicking her hair behind her in a defiant gesture that she knew meant little. But it made her feel better. A moment later she felt one of his hands tangle in her hair. Suddenly, his other hand was planted on her midriff, and she let out an involuntary gasp.

"What are you doing?" Mama Gail asked sharply, appearing instantly at Aurelia's side. "Get your hand off her."

"Begone, crone," said Cyfrin carelessly. He turned his gaze to Aurelia. "Honeysuckle doesn't mind, do you, child?"

Aurelia's skin crawled uncomfortably under the hand that

was still sprawled across her stomach, but she met his gaze steadily.

"As a matter of fact, I do mind not knowing what you're doing. Why is tonight different?"

To her surprise, Cyfrin neither showed anger, nor dismissed her question out of hand. He lowered his arm, considering her thoughtfully. "Do you want to understand my process, Honeysuckle?"

"I do," she said, surprised but more than ready to take the offered opening.

"She doesn't want to hear anything *you* have to say, Cyfrin," Mama Gail interjected hotly.

Aurelia turned to her mother, frustrated. "Actually," she said, widening her eyes meaningfully, "I do."

An edge of desperation entered Mama Gail's eyes, and Aurelia's frustration grew. Why couldn't the other woman see how good an opportunity this was? If Cyfrin was in the mood to talk, they might be able to find out what this key was going to be.

"It seems you're not needed here, Abigail," said Cyfrin, sounding infuriatingly delighted at their conflict. "Why don't you step into the next room again?"

"Absolutely not," gasped Mama Gail. "And you can't lock me in this time, so don't think you're going to—"

"Honeysuckle," Cyfrin interrupted her, sounding bored, "where's that key I gave you?"

Aurelia hesitated for a moment, her eyes passing to her mother. Mama Gail's fear and anger were written all over her face, and Aurelia could tell the other woman wasn't able to consider the situation clearly. The thought of Amell's visit decided it for Aurelia. He was coming back tomorrow, and at the very least, she needed to be able to tell him more about Cyfrin's plans than the embarrassingly small amount of information she'd been able to impart that day. And clearly Mama Gail wasn't going to help her find out more. Meaning Cyfrin was her only option.

Sending her mother a silent apology, Aurelia stepped over to the kitchen and retrieved the key. Making as little contact as physically possible, she slipped it into Cyfrin's outstretched hand. His self-satisfied smirk made her want to snatch it back, but she forced herself to wait, motionless, as he turned to Mama Gail.

"Well then," he said pleasantly. "Time to step out for a minute." With a sudden gesture, and a few muttered words, he seized Mama Gail's arm. Aurelia could tell that his grip was stronger than was natural as he pushed the older woman into the bedroom and once again locked her in. This time, Mama Gail didn't yell or pound the door, but the betrayal Aurelia had seen in her eyes was worse than any shout.

Cyfrin turned back to Aurelia, who swallowed nervously. Hopefully this wasn't a terrible mistake.

But the enchanter showed no more sign of violence than he had the night before. Strolling back toward her, he gave her a smile that made her want to wince. She remembered fleetingly how Amell's grin had seemed to laugh at himself rather than her. Well, when Cyfrin smiled at her, it couldn't have been plainer that it was himself he was pleased with, not the person standing before him.

"Thank you for your assistance, Honeysuckle," he said smugly. "I'm glad we're beginning to understand one another." His eyes searched her face, that unpleasant smile growing. "With me, you have the opportunity to be part of something magnificent, you know."

"Part of what?" she blurted out. "What's all the magic for?"

She barely hid her wince as Cyfrin raised an eyebrow. She knew she'd been too obvious. But as wonderful a mother as

Mama Gail was, subtlety was one thing she'd never taught Aurelia.

"I'm glad to see you taking an interest, child, but I don't think you're ready for that level of insight yet."

The words were maddeningly reminiscent of Mama Gail's attitude, and Aurelia found herself scowling before she could help it. "If I'm the one storing all the magic," she argued, "don't you think I should at least know its basic function?"

Up went that thin eyebrow again, but this time Cyfrin laughed. "Perhaps you're right," he conceded. "I suppose there's no harm in you knowing my intentions in broad terms. Its purpose, my dear, is to overwhelm and overpower all other enchanters. To show them that I am and always have been greater than their narrow minds could imagine."

His voice had become darker and harder as he spoke, and Aurelia found herself drawing back involuntarily. But Cyfrin didn't seem to notice, his eyes unfocused as he looked at some imagined future where he emerged victorious over all his critics.

Selfish pride, Aurelia reflected. That was all the motivation he'd ever shown, and it was no surprise that his plans for the excessive amount of magic he'd stored were in the same vein.

"And to that end," Cyfrin said, his voice once again mild as he stepped up to her, "let's try again."

It was all Aurelia could do not to squirm as Cyfrin laid one hand back on her midriff, the other reaching for her hair. As he muttered, a strange sensation moved slowly over Aurelia's scalp, as if her hair was growing marginally lighter. She turned her face to the side, not liking Cyfrin's nearness, but thankfully he wasn't in the least focused on her. His whole attention was on whatever magic he was using.

When the enchanter finally stepped back, looking exhausted, Aurelia ran a nervous hand over her tresses, half expecting them to be lopped shorter.

"What is it?" Cyfrin asked eagerly. "What do you feel?"

Aurelia stared at him in surprise. It was unusual for him to show any interest in what she experienced. Was he trying to make it seem like he cared? If so, he little realized how unconvincing his efforts were when compared with the passionate declaration of her recent visitor, that he would free her or die trying.

Forcing her thoughts away from Amell, Aurelia took stock of the sensation that had come over her while Cyfrin worked. "I don't know how to describe it, exactly," she admitted. "It feels like...my hair is lighter, but I'm heavier."

"Fascinating," breathed Cyfrin, his eyes passing over her hair with their usual fervor. "Hopefully that means it's working."

"What's working?" Aurelia asked uneasily, unsurprised to find that his interest had been in the success of his project after all, not the effect on her.

Cyfrin's smile was back. Apparently he was genuinely unaware of how unappealing an expression it was, because he was clearly trying to make his voice pleasant.

"I'm giving you power you can hardly dream of, Honeysuckle. I'm transferring some of the magic from your hair into your core."

"What?" Aurelia gasped, taking a step back. "Why...why would you do that? I thought..." She cast around, struggling to remember what she could and couldn't say.

"To give you the opportunity to take part in my plans," Cyfrin said enthusiastically, unmoved by her change in demeanor. "To give you a role. You can't unleash power that's stored in your hair, my dear. But power that's stored in your core, willingly unlocked by your own choice...Ah, how potent it could be."

Aurelia's mouth opened and closed a few times, panic clouding her mind. She was terrified of saying the wrong thing, and revealing how much she knew. What had Cyfrin told her over the years, and what had she learned from Mama Gail's snooping?

Mama Gail. All at once she was overcome by the certainty that her mother should be here, not locked away against her will. How could Aurelia have helped that happen?

"I want the key," she demanded.

A look of shock passed over Cyfrin's face, but it quickly faded as he took in her outstretched hand. "Oh, that key," he said, with a grating little laugh. "Certainly, my dear. I gave it to you, didn't I? Goodwill and all that." In a lazy motion, he held out the key, and Aurelia snatched it from him.

Stumbling in her haste, she hurried across the room, fitting the key into the lock on the bedroom door. Mama Gail was standing right on the other side, but this time she didn't burst through the opening as soon as she had the opportunity. She stepped out slowly, her face pale as she looked from Aurelia to Cyfrin.

Abandoning dignity, Aurelia threw herself on her mother, remorse washing over her. "I'm sorry," she whispered, as Mama Gail's arms came up instinctively to receive her. "I should never have helped to lock you up. I know better than anyone...I should never have..."

"It's all right," Mama Gail said soothingly, her frame relaxing at the apology. "I'm all right. What happened?"

Aurelia pulled herself together, straightening and turning to face Cyfrin. "He did something a little different tonight...I didn't fully understand..."

She waited, hoping Cyfrin would repeat what he'd said, but he didn't. His expression was disapproving as his gaze passed between the two women.

"You are still such a child, Honeysuckle," he said coldly. "I'm disappointed."

For some reason, Mama Gail seemed to relax even further at these critical words. "What did you do differently?" she demanded, with something of a return to her normal manner.

"Sharing my process with you is no part of my plans," said Cyfrin icily.

"He said he was transferring magic from my hair to my core," Aurelia interjected, her voice not quite steady.

"What?" Mama Gail's head whipped around to face Cyfrin again, her expression furious. "You'll kill her! If it's in her instead of her hair, she'll die for sure when you extract it!"

Cyfrin narrowed his eyes. "How do you know that?"

"You told me," Mama Gail said impatiently. "When Aurelia was, I don't know, six or seven, I accused you of being willing to murder a child, and you said she wasn't going to die when you extracted the magic, because it was in her hair instead of in her core, whatever that means! So why are you moving it to her core? Don't you care if she dies?"

Aurelia let out a silent breath of relief. She'd known Mama Gail wouldn't lose her head, that she'd be able to push for the information they needed without revealing anything dangerous.

"On the contrary," said Cyfrin, who had also visibly relaxed at Mama Gail's explanation. "I care more than ever for Honeysuckle's survival. I never accepted the theory that extracting magic would kill her, as if she was a common rodent or dog." His eyes dwelt mockingly on Aurelia, although he continued to speak to her mother. "As you know, Abigail, she is far from common."

Aurelia frowned, confused both by his meaning, and by the sudden stiffening of her mother beside her. With a nasty little laugh, Cyfrin went on.

"The hair was only an extra precaution. But it was never necessary, and it's even less so now, given my new project." His gaze still rested on Aurelia. "These changes are to benefit you, Honeysuckle, not harm you."

Aurelia remained silent, not trusting herself to speak.

Cyfrin let out a sigh. "I see I have yet to win your trust, child. But we'll get there. We have time." He ran a hand over his own short hair, still looking weary from whatever magic had been involved in the transfer of power from Aurelia's hair to her core. "I'm too tired to work in my study tonight. Lower me down."

Aurelia hastened to comply with the curt command, only too eager to be rid of the enchanter. The moment he was back on the ground, she yanked her hair through the ring and turned to her mother.

"I'm sorry," she said. "I shouldn't have been part of restraining you."

"Thank you, Aurelia," said Mama Gail quietly. "I can't tell you how I appreciate that." She studied Aurelia with her usual clear gaze. "Can you acknowledge now that I might have my reasons for wanting to protect your mind as well as your body? Can you admit how easily Cyfrin manipulated you?"

Aurelia's frustration rose back up, but she forced herself to speak calmly. "I don't think he did manipulate me, Mama Gail. I was the one manipulating the situation, because I wanted answers."

Mama Gail didn't look in the least convinced, and Aurelia couldn't help the scowl that crossed her face.

"I still stand by what I said before," she informed her mother. "You should be telling me everything you know, so we can figure it out together."

Mama Gail sighed, clearly hesitant, but Aurelia didn't wait for a reply. She couldn't let her resentment over their disagreement once again stop her from doing what she should have done hours before. Even if admitting her deception gave Mama Gail yet another reason not to trust her judgment.

"There's something else I need to tell you," she said. "It was petty of me to keep it from you, but I was irked that you weren't being open with me."

"What is it?" Mama Gail asked, alarmed.

"It's big." Aurelia swallowed. "Really big. Maybe you should sit down."

CHAPTER ELEVEN

Amell

With the tower now out of sight behind him, Amell pushed his way through the trees, heading for where they seemed the most clumped. When there was only one small gap visible, he turned sideways, and was unsurprised to emerge back into the normal forest.

"Your Highness!" Furn's familiar voice was equal parts relieved and exasperated. "Where have you been? Do you realize how long you've been gone? I couldn't find you anywhere."

Amell blinked, some detached part of his mind noting that it was nice to have the normal, hard-to-ruffle Furn back, instead of the strangely uptight version of himself the guard had been the day before.

But in all honesty, he hardly knew how to answer his friend. He had only a very hazy idea of how long he'd been gone. When he thought about it, it must have been no more than an hour, but it felt like he was emerging from a dream.

"Furn, you honestly won't believe what I found," he said fervently.

The guard instantly stilled. "You mean you actually found

something?" he asked sharply. "There really are fugitives hiding out here?"

"What?" Amell latched on to the words with difficulty. He'd forgotten about the fugitives. "No, not that. Something much more extraordinary. I found—"

His tongue stopped.

"Found what?" Furn pressed, looking bewildered.

"I found—" Amell tried again. But again, the words just wouldn't come. "I can't believe this," he said, aghast. "I can't tell you."

"What do you mean?" Furn looked utterly lost now, and Amell didn't blame him.

He opened his mouth, trying again to tell Furn about Honeysuckle, the tower, Cyfrin, any of it. But his mouth simply wouldn't form the words. He ran a hand over his face, horrified at this complication in his plans to help Honeysuckle.

"I've heard of this kind of thing," he realized suddenly. "Prince Bentleigh mentioned it, at the council Basil called. And so did the Mistran prince. Protective enchantments that prevent you from saying what you've seen or heard." He thumped the heel of his hand against a nearby tree trunk. "Why didn't any of them mention how infuriating it is?"

"What do you mean an enchantment?" Furn asked, sounding alarmed now. "Are you telling me you were cursed while you were...wherever you were?"

Amell shook his head. "No, I haven't been cursed. I've suffered no harm, Furn, don't worry. You won't be executed at dawn."

"A great relief," said Furn, his lips twitching.

Amell let out a groan. "But I didn't plan for this. If I can't tell anyone what I saw..." How was he going to bring back help, like he'd promised? He bit his lip. "Perhaps Bartholomew can help me."

"From the Enchanters' Guild?" Furn asked, trying valiantly to keep up.

Amell nodded. "But he's back in Fernford, and I—" He was going to say that he'd promised to return the next day, but the magic wouldn't let him. He supposed it would imply that there was a someone to whom he'd made the promise. He let out another groan. "Let's return to the prison," he said.

"Gladly."

Furn handed over the reins of Amell's horse, which he was still holding, and within moments the two of them were riding back toward the prison clearing. Amell's thoughts whirled, trying to adjust his plans based on this new development. He should have known it wouldn't be so easy. Cyfrin clearly had all kinds of nasty tricks up his sleeve. Amell still had no idea how he'd gotten past the restraining enchantment, but it seemed there were some aspects of the concealment magic that his cloak didn't protect against.

Amell was a little surprised when they emerged from the trees to see that it was only about an hour past noon. It felt like a different day that he'd welcomed the chance to sneak off from his father's inspection of the prison, hoping to heroically discover some of the fugitives with the help of Rekavidur's gift.

He was struggling to remember why he cared about the fugitives now, but he received a brutal reminder the moment they entered the prison compound.

"Whoa, something's going on," Furn commented, his gaze passing mildly over the kerfuffle that greeted them.

"We'd better find my father," Amell said grimly, dismounting and handing his horse to a hovering soldier. The two of them strode toward the ruined section of the prison, where King Bern could be seen deep in conversation with the warden.

"What's happening, Father?" Amell asked sharply, alarmed by the look on his father's face.

The king turned to his son. "Two of the fugitives have surfaced," he said grimly.

"They've been caught?" Amell asked. "That's excellent news, isn't it?"

"They haven't been caught, Your Highness," the warden said heavily. "We know for certain that they were five leagues east of here three hours ago. But where they are now, we couldn't say."

"How do you know they were..." Amell trailed off as it suddenly clicked. "What did they do?"

King Bern's face was as grave as Amell had ever seen it. "They attacked a farmhouse. The farmer is gravely injured, and his family were held in a cellar with a restraining enchantment. The two fugitives stripped the house of all the valuables they could carry."

"Which means they now have horses," the warden interjected. "So they'll make better time."

"They could be halfway to Bansford by now," Amell said.

His father nodded. "I've already sent an express to King Rhinehart."

Amell frowned, thinking of Honeysuckle trapped in her tower with all these criminals on the loose. She was supposed to be hidden, but he'd managed to find her, with his artifact.

"You said they used a restraining enchantment?" he said. "That's powerful magic, isn't it? How strong are these fugitives?"

"I'm almost certain I know who we're dealing with, Your Highness," the warden answered. "And unfortunately they have considerable power. They were some of our most magically gifted prisoners. This latest news answers the question as to whether the explosion destroyed their individual restraining enchantments, which prevented them from using magic. If they were still in place, they'd never have been able to perform the magic necessary to restrain people in a cellar."

"But how could an explosion destroy individual restraining enchantments without harming the people to whom they were attached?" Amell objected.

"I think it's clear to say that the explosion was more than it appeared," the warden said. "It must have involved targeted magical attack."

Furn shifted beside Amell, and he glanced at the guard. "What is it, Furn?"

"Nothing, Your Highness," Furn said self-deprecatingly.

"If you have any insights, I'm sure my father would like to hear them," Amell told him.

King Bern looked up. "What's that?"

Looking uncomfortable, Furn bowed. "I didn't mean to intrude, Your Majesty. I only wondered, from what was just explained, if the explosion might have been more of a diversion. Perhaps it wasn't the attack so much as a way of hiding the true attack, which was magical in nature."

King Bern considered the guard thoughtfully. "A concept worthy of further consideration, Sir Furnis." He looked at the warden, who murmured something to one of the prison guards, standing close at hand. The man took off at a smart trot.

"It will be considered, Your Majesty," said the warden, bowing first to the king, then inclining his head respectfully to Furn.

"Good thought, Furn," Amell said brightly. He turned to the king. "Father, I searched the forest again this morning. And I found—" He ground his teeth in frustration as the words were blocked by the magic. "I think the area is worthy of further exploration."

"The woods have been thoroughly searched," the king said, with a touch of impatience. "And, as this morning's unfortunate event has shown, the fugitives haven't hung around this close by. They've taken off across the continent."

A shout drew all three men's attention, and Amell's heart lifted at the sight of a dozen prison guards, escorting two men and one woman, all with unflattering billowing clothes, and roughly shorn hair.

"Three more!" he cried in delight. "That only leaves...what? Twenty-two?"

"Only?" King Bern repeated, but his face was a little lighter as he turned to the guards. "Well done."

Amell realized, as he looked the prisoners over, their capture indicated not all the escapees had fled further afield. Some of them must be hanging about the general area, unable to make a clean escape. Which meant that Honeysuckle was doubly vulnerable. What if one of them had magic strong enough to counteract Cyfrin's concealment enchantment, as Amell's cloak could do?

The rest of the afternoon passed in a strange sort of tension, the camp torn between dismay at the news of the attack on the farmer and his family, and delight at the unrelated recapture of three more fugitives.

Amell, meanwhile, couldn't focus on any of it. When his father once again refused to allow him to attend the interrogation of the newly captured prisoners—citing his clear distraction as the reason—he tried to pull his mind back to matters of the prison. But all he could think about was the beautiful girl trapped in the tower, and how she was trusting him to help her get free. All attempts to tell Furn, or anyone else, about any aspect of what he'd seen in the clearing led to the same result. The magic was stopping his tongue, and he had no idea how to get around it.

"Well, I have good news, Your Highness."

Furn's voice pulled Amell from his reverie.

"What's that?"

"Some action," the guard said, in a heartening tone. "There's been a report of magical activity only an hour's ride north. His Majesty is sending a squadron to investigate, and I've talked the captain into letting us form part of it."

Amell raised an eyebrow. "Why, Furn. It almost sounded like you were happy about a report of criminal activity."

His guard grinned appreciatively. "Of course not, Your Highness. I just thought you'd welcome the opportunity to actually do something."

He glanced pointedly down, and following his gaze Amell realized that he was jiggling his leg. He hadn't even noticed himself doing it, and he stilled it at once. But a moment later, his foot was tapping.

"I'm not sure, Furn," he said, glancing at the sky. "If it's an hour's ride, we'll be arriving as the sun is setting."

The guard raised an eyebrow. "Are you worried about riding in the dark, Your Highness? I wouldn't have guessed it."

Amell laughed reluctantly. "Of course not. It's just…" He trailed off, and Furn's forehead creased in thought.

"It's to do with whatever you found in the woods, isn't it?"

Amell tried to nod, but his head wouldn't move. Clearly his friend understood, however.

"You're sure whatever it is has nothing to do with the prison, or with any of the fugitives?" Furn pressed, not for the first time.

"Positive," Amell said curtly.

"And you're not in any danger?"

Amell made an impatient noise in his throat. "Of course I'm not."

Furn nodded. "Well then, if you'll excuse me saying so, Your Highness, I really think we should focus on what we came here to do. There are still twenty-two inmates out there in the community, and this might be a chance to help capture one of them."

"You're right, of course," Amell sighed. He glanced toward the distant trees, his foot once again tapping. It was hard to accept that Cyfrin would be approaching the tower within the hour, and Amell was just going to stand by and let it happen. He knew Honeysuckle had been determined he leave before the enchanter arrived, but he'd had vague thoughts of hiding in the grove and following Cyfrin, perhaps finding out where he lived.

Or maybe confronting him in a blaze of righteous wrath.

Amell sighed again, acknowledging the folly of his own daydreams. He couldn't forget the earnest entreaty in Honeysuckle's face when she'd told him he was the first real chance she'd had, and begged him not to mess it up. Real people were on the line, and as much as he wanted to engage in heroics, he couldn't give rein to his imagination.

Fleetingly, he wished his father could see inside his mind, and realize how capable Amell was of showing restraint. But of course the one time Amell was making a sensible choice, he was magically prevented from telling his father about it. Instead the king had been impatient with his son all afternoon for his inability to concentrate on the crisis before them.

"All right, let's saddle up," he said, turning abruptly to Furn. "And thank you for making it happen," he added, reminding himself that it wasn't Furn's fault that he was uncharacteristically reluctant to join a mission.

Still looking a little confused by Amell's manner, Furn nodded.

When the group departed the prison, Amell and Furn were positioned at the center of a full squadron of the soldiers who had traveled from Fernford with them the day before. Two enchanters from the prison guard occupied the protected central space with them. They traveled by the main road, so

Amell could only glance in the general direction of the hidden clearing as they passed through the trees. With a sigh, he turned his attention northward, trying not to wonder if Cyfrin was already on his way to the tower.

For the next hour, he and Furn rode in silence, as the tension in the group rose palpably. They heard the hubbub before they saw it. The group rode into the chaos of what had clearly been a twilight market, although now it more closely resembled the site of a stampede.

"There were two of them," a merchant told the captain, his voice unsteady. "They demanded my horses, and when I refused, they said they were cursing me to fail in everything I put my hand to. It's not true, is it? They can't...I mean, they can't actually do that?"

One of the enchanters rode forward, speaking reassuringly to the man. He explained the process by which he could seek assistance from the Enchanters' Guild, which would examine him and his family for any sign of lingering magic, and ascertain a way to counteract any curse they might have suffered.

"Two people caused all this chaos?" Amell said to Furn. "They must have strong magic."

"I don't know, Your Highness." Furn sounded skeptical. "People love to panic. I suspect they made a little mischief, and the crowd did the rest."

Amell nodded. "You're probably right." The merchant was telling the captain that the two prisoners—both men—had taken clothes and supplies in addition to the horses, and had ridden north.

The captain turned to two of his soldiers. "Pursue," he said curtly. "But don't engage. Just recon, then return."

They nodded their understanding, spurring their horses on. The rest of the squadron set about assisting in bringing order to the pandemonium.

"It's a stupid thing to do, isn't it?" Amell commented to Furn, as the two of them righted a vegetable cart. "Make such a scene, I mean. Surely they should be trying to lie low. And I know they've been on foot, but how have they only made it this far since the break out?"

"It doesn't suggest a very good plan, does it?" Furn agreed. "Some of them have been in that prison for ten years, of course. They might not have many contacts or resources outside anymore. But you'd still think that if they'd known the break out was coming, they would have a better plan for what to do once they were out."

Amell frowned, puzzling once again over who could be behind the break out if it wasn't one of those who were liberated by it. Honeysuckle had seemed very certain it wasn't Cyfrin, but perhaps she was wrong.

The scouts returned before the sun had fully disappeared below the horizon. The market was in decent order, and the soldiers gathered behind their captain as the two riders delivered their report.

"The trail disappears a short distance to the north, Captain," one of them said. "They rode into a creek, and we couldn't find where they left it. But we did find these." He held up a clump of formless gray garments.

"So they're no longer in prison uniform," the captain said grimly. "And they're in the wind."

"Their hair will still identify them, though," Amell chimed in. He hesitated. "Unless they've grown it out magically."

"They shouldn't be able to do that, Your Highness," responded one of the prison guard enchanters. "Their hair isn't cut in the natural way. When they arrive at the prison, their hair is shorn by magic. It shouldn't be able to grow again until the length of their sentence is served. As far as I know, that will still apply, even if they've escaped the site."

Amell nodded, and the conversation moved to more immediate concerns.

"We'll ride back to the prison," the captain decided. He pointed to half a dozen soldiers, including the two who had scouted ahead. "Except you, who will stay and see if you can pick up the trail from the creek. Send word to me at the prison immediately if you find anything."

The soldiers lost no time in heading northward again, and the rest of the group turned south, moving at a smart trot along the darkening road. They were only about halfway back to the prison when one of the enchanters nudged his horse toward the front of the group, where the captain was riding.

"Captain, I think I can sense a faint signature." He gestured to their left.

"What does that mean?" the captain asked, a touch irritably.

"It means we think there's someone with magic out there," the other enchanter chipped in. "It's faint—I'll admit I hadn't noticed it. But now I'm searching, I can feel it, too."

The captain followed the direction of their gaze with interest. "Is that so?" He cast his eyes back over the group, then turned to the soldier on his right. "Take several men and follow the enchanters, as quietly as possible. I'll continue toward the prison with the group. It seems unlikely it's the inmates. I can't think why they'd be heading back toward the prison. But just in case, we don't want to draw attention to the fact that we've noticed them. We'll go slowly, though, and if you need us, we'll be ready."

The soldier nodded smartly, weaving his horse expertly through the ranks and picking up others as he went. When the group detached silently from the main contingent, Amell nudged his horse after them.

"Come on, Furn," he said quietly. "Let's go with them."

"Your Highness," Furn said calmly, "I think we should let them do—"

But Amell was already emerging from the formation, and with a sigh his guard followed him. They attached themselves to the back of the small group now riding slowly across a dark field, the enchanters in the lead.

They'd been riding for several minutes when a sudden shout ahead told Amell that action was happening at the front of the group. He spurred his horse into motion, Furn close beside him as they drew alongside the enchanters.

Several soldiers were spreading out, trying to surround two men in simple clothes, whose raggedly cut hair gave away their identity. The enchanters were hanging back out of reach, muttering words Amell couldn't understand, clearly preparing magic of some kind.

One of the soldiers who'd drawn close to the prisoners pursed his lips, a thin whistle emerging. But it cut off a moment later, when one of the fugitives slashed a hand in front of him like an ax, shouting something unintelligible as he did so. The soldier toppled over, bleeding from a jagged gash along his collarbone, and the fugitive leaped forward to snatch up the man's sword. Turning, he ran toward the enchanters who were still gathering their magic.

With an angry cry, Amell surged forward. He was dimly aware that the rest of the soldiers were all closing in on the other enchanter, who seemed to be holding them off with gestures that caused them to bounce back as if hitting an invisible shield. Amell disregarded that scuffle, focusing instead on the prisoner who had slashed the now moaning soldier. He'd never seen magic like that—used in its raw form as a literal weapon—and he was determined not to let such a magic-user roam free across the countryside.

The prisoner had taken advantage of the soldiers' distraction to creep around behind the enchanters in the darkness. He'd just raised his stolen blade when Amell threw himself off his horse, placing his body in between the prisoner and the enchanters and raising his own blade. The two weapons clanged, causing the enchanters to gasp and stumble out of the way.

The prisoner turned his full attention to Amell, growling. Amell knew no hesitation. He was well-trained with a sword, and he rained down blow after blow on the man's head, each only just intercepted in time. Furn was at his side in a flash, his blade in his hand as the two of them pressed the prisoner hard.

The man clearly wasn't going to last long. He fought savagely, but he wasn't trained with a sword like Amell and Furn were. Amell wasn't even out of breath yet when he twisted his sword in an expert flick, sending the other man's stolen weapon flying.

The prisoner let out a cry of fury, but as his eyes locked on Amell's face, the expression changed.

"It's the prince!" he shouted, drawing everyone's attention. The other prisoner took advantage of the soldiers' distraction to shove one to the ground, sprinting to his companion's side.

He gave a cackle. "Thanks for saving us a ride to Fernford, Your Highness. Let loose!"

Before Amell well understood the words, both prisoners had raised their hands, shouting in unison as they slashed them down again.

Instinctively, Amell raised his sword, although he knew it wouldn't defend him against this type of attack. He braced himself for pain, but it didn't come. Instead, two things happened in such quick succession, he could barely make sense of them. The first was that Furn threw himself bodily in front of Amell, and the second was that the two enchanters behind him shouted as loudly and as unintelligibly as their opponents.

Furn fell like a stone to the grassy ground, and with a cry, Amell dropped to his knees alongside him.

"Furn!" he cried, trying to comprehend what had happened. "Are you all right?"

Furn groaned, pushing himself to a sitting position and running a hand over his chest. "I'm fine, Your Highness. Are you hurt?"

"You know I'm not," Amell snapped, an illogical anger taking hold of him. "Because you threw yourself in the way. What were you thinking?"

Furn didn't bother answering. "Thank you," he said instead, his eyes on the enchanter who'd knelt down as well. "I'm guessing that was a powerful shield you both constructed."

The enchanter nodded. "Good thing it was, too," he said grimly. "I reckon they put all the magic they had into that attack. That one was aiming to kill for sure."

Amell followed the man's eyes to where the prisoners, looking spent and exhausted, were being bound by some of the soldiers. A glance around showed two soldiers down, but neither of their injuries looked life-threatening.

"Fortunately shield magic is our bread and butter in this line of work," the other enchanter prison guard interjected matter-of-factly.

"Well, thank you again," Furn said with his usual calm, as he pushed himself to his feet.

"Yes," Amell agreed, more shaken than he wanted to admit. "Thank you."

"You saved my life first, Your Highness," the enchanter reminded him.

Furn turned to the senior soldier. "Did you hear what they said? They were heading for the capital."

"But why?" Amell demanded. He glanced at the prisoners, who stared sullenly back at him.

The soldier followed his gaze. "Revenge, I'm guessing. They weren't running, they were gathering what they needed to strike a blow at the kingdom which put them in prison. Makes sense of why they hadn't gone further."

Furn nodded sagely. Amell felt his anger once again rising at his friend's calm demeanor.

"Furn!" he demanded. "What were you thinking? If those enchanters hadn't shielded you, you would've been killed!"

Furn looked at him in surprise. "And if neither I nor those enchanters had shielded you, *you* would've been killed."

"Well that would be on me!" Amell declared.

Furn gave his familiar light chuckle. "You're wrong there, Your Highness. It would have been on me." Taking in Amell's expression, he frowned. "Why are you so surprised? This is the job, Your Highness. This is my role."

"What, to leap to your own death?" Amell demanded.

"If I can't defend you any other way, then yes," Furn said, still sounding bemused. "Absolutely."

Amell realized his mouth was open, and he closed it. A strange mix of emotions were churning inside him. Furn's very calmness chastised him even more than his friend's words. The guard wasn't even scolding his charge for riding off after the soldiers when he wasn't supposed to be there, when doing so had almost led to disaster.

"Furn," he said. "I don't want you to die for me."

His guard clapped him on the back. "It hasn't come to that yet, Your Highness."

And with that he turned away, speaking again with the senior soldier. Amell could only stare at his friend's back, trying to grasp the reality that Furn had almost just died as a result of the prince's determination to be part of the action.

One of the soldiers rode back to the main contingent, and

before long others arrived and began to assist with restraining the prisoners and assisting the wounded.

"You fought well, Your Highness," the senior soldier from the scouting group told Amell. "It was a good instinct to protect the enchanters."

Amell smiled in acknowledgment, but his thoughts were troubled. He had an uncomfortable feeling the soldier was just pandering to him because of his status. He might have saved the enchanter, but it had almost cost Furn his life. And furthermore, Amell's very presence had invited further attack from the prisoners.

He thought back to his realization earlier that day about how his recklessness might cost Honeysuckle her chance at freedom. He'd flattered himself that he was learning to be sensible, but then he'd immediately chased adventure again, this time endangering his most faithful friend.

"Furn," he said quietly, as they rode back toward the prison, with the rest of the group. "I don't think I said thank you, did I?"

"No need to thank me, Your Highness," Furn said cheerfully. "I'm just doing my job."

"There's every need," Amell contradicted him. "You might see it as simply your job, but to me, you're not just a guard, you're a friend."

"Thank you, Your Highness," said Furn, clearly taken aback. "If I may say so, I feel the same way. And it's my honor to protect you."

Amell nodded, his thoughts still too troubled for further speech. When they reached the prison, and he had to listen to the captain giving his father a glowing report of his performance, he could hardly keep from wincing. Never had his heroics seemed more foolish, or the responsibility of his position weighed more heavily on him.

"Well, Amell," said King Bern, sounding a little surprised by his son's apparent prowess. "You've seen some action after all. There's a contingent heading back to Fernford tomorrow, to swap out with reinforcements. I daresay you'll want to take the tale of your daring back to the castle."

"What?" Amell demanded, speaking up at last. "Return home? No Father, I want to stay and see this crisis out."

"I see," said the king, again sounding surprised. "I'm glad to hear you're committed to the task. You may stay for the moment. I won't be heading back for another day at least."

Amell nodded, a flash of guilt shooting over him at his father's misconception. It wasn't the prison break he was determined to see through. It was Honeysuckle's plight. But it wasn't as though he was hiding the truth from his father out of rebellion. He wanted to tell her predicament to anyone and everyone, but he wasn't free to do so.

He was free to keep his promise to return to the tower, however. As he eased himself into his bedroll in the camp, he resolved to do just that as soon as he could slip away the following morning.

CHAPTER TWELVE

"Checking the window every two minutes won't make him come any faster." Mama Gail's voice was skeptical. "If he's coming at all, that is."

"He's coming," said Aurelia firmly. Then she sighed. "Who am I kidding, I have no idea if he's coming. But I hope he is." She turned pleading eyes to her mother, who was pruning a rather aggressive devil's ivy that was taking over one corner. "He seemed so sincere. He *swore* he was coming back today."

"Well, then, his honor is on the line, isn't it?" Mama Gail replied calmly. "If he doesn't come, we'll know his word can't be trusted."

"Yes, true," Aurelia agreed, tapping her fingers on the windowsill. "But if he does come...imagine the possibilities, Mama Gail! He just came right in, as if Cyfrin's enchantment didn't exist. What if he can help us get out of here?"

"Then I'll be forever grateful to him," said Mama Gail.

But her voice was clipped, and Aurelia knew she was feeling tense from the reminder of just how much she'd missed. Her alarm at discovering that a stranger had actually entered the tower and Aurelia hadn't woken her had almost rivaled her fear over the idea of Aurelia being alone with Cyfrin.

"You said you told him I was here?" Mama Gail asked suddenly.

Aurelia nodded.

"And why exactly was it that he didn't want you to wake me?"

"That's not at all how it was, Mama Gail," Aurelia explained patiently. "He suggested we wake you, and I'm the one who said no."

"But why?" her mother demanded.

Aurelia turned fully to face her. "To be frank, Mama Gail, because I'd never had a single experience without you in my entire life, and it seemed like a rare opportunity."

Her mother was silent for a moment. Aurelia half expected her to be hurt, but she just sighed. "Well, that's actually quite understandable," she acknowledged, a little begrudgingly.

"If it helps, he looked very relieved when he learned I wasn't trapped up here alone," Aurelia added.

Mama Gail nodded slowly. "It certainly doesn't hurt. He said his name is Amell?"

"That's what he said," Aurelia confirmed. "But he hesitated. I think it might be a false name." She looked hopefully at her mother. "Like I gave him."

Mama Gail smiled in amusement. "Yes, you keep mentioning that."

"Well, I know you think I was foolish to speak with him alone," said Aurelia defensively. "And I don't want you to think that I blindly trusted a total stranger just because he was handsome."

"Because he was what?" Mama Gail demanded, alarm crossing her face.

Aurelia winced slightly. "Well, he seemed handsome to me,"

she said frankly. "But then, I don't have much basis for comparison, do I?"

"That's precisely my concern," muttered Mama Gail.

Before Aurelia could respond, she caught a flash of movement in the corner of her eye, and spun back around.

"He's here!" she cried, and Mama Gail appeared beside her so quickly, Aurelia half suspected her of flying across the room.

"Well?" Aurelia demanded, as the two of them watched the tawny-haired figure cross the clearing. "Is he handsome?"

Mama Gail gave her a long-suffering look. "Yes," she admitted. "I'd have to say he is. But that tells us absolutely nothing about his character."

"I know," Aurelia assured her lightly. Cupping her hands around her mouth, she called out, "Amell!"

He looked up quickly, breaking into a smile at the sight of her.

"Oh dear," muttered Mama Gail beside Aurelia, as the expression transformed Amell's face. "He's far too handsome."

Aurelia chuckled at her mother's dismayed tone, already pulling her hair from the floor and threading it through the hook. She'd released it from her braid an hour before, in faith that he would come as promised.

"I thought you said he was going to bring help," Mama Gail commented, her eyes passing over the otherwise empty clearing.

Aurelia paused with her hair halfway down the tower. "Yes, that's right." She frowned at the tree line. "It looks like he's alone though, doesn't it?"

"Hm," Mama Gail was skeptical again. "I wonder what his explanation is."

"Good morning, Honeysuckle," Amell called up, having reached the base of the tower. He bowed in Mama Gail's general direction. "Good morning, ma'am."

Aurelia lowered her hair the rest of the way, then poked her head out the window. "Climb up, Amell, and we can talk more easily."

He hesitated, looking between her face and the hair now hanging in front of him. "You're sure it didn't hurt you yesterday?"

"Not this again." Aurelia rolled her eyes. "Just climb up already."

She'd already pulled her head back into the tower, but she heard a low chuckle wafting up from the direction of the ground. For once Mama Gail didn't offer to help her with the weight, instead watching carefully as their visitor climbed the outside wall. Aurelia braced herself, noting again how much lighter this younger man was than Cyfrin.

Old codger is getting chunky in his middle age, she thought to herself, her heart impossibly light at the vindication of her faith in Amell.

When a tousled golden head appeared over the windowsill, she almost dropped her hair in her excitement. Forcing herself to focus on the task, she waited until he'd fully climbed through the opening, his clear gray eyes passing from her to Mama Gail, who'd stepped back out of the way.

"Ladies," he said, bowing low again. "Thank you for inviting me into your home."

Mama Gail said nothing, her chin slightly raised as her eyes completed a slow pass over his form. Aurelia noticed that in spite of his gracious words, one of his legs was bouncing a little. Nervous, or just full of energy? Perhaps both.

"You came back," she said, smiling brightly at him.

"Of course," Amell replied easily. "I said I would."

Aurelia sent a triumphant look at Mama Gail. "This is my mother, Abigail," she said, with a gesture. "Mama Gail, this is Amell." It occurred to her how ridiculous it was to perform introductions when they might very well all be using false names, but she supposed the niceties had to be observed.

"How did you get in here, Amell?" Mama Gail asked, her tone neither friendly nor hostile.

"I'm very pleased to meet you," said Amell, bowing again. "Having missed you yesterday. As for how I got in here," he glanced around the space, "it's a bit of a mystery, to be honest. I found the clearing in the first place with the help of this shielding artifact." He lifted his cloak slightly then let it drop. "But I don't think that's what got me past the restraining enchantment, because it didn't help Honeysuckle when she tried to get out."

"Yes, she's told me all that," said Mama Gail, her tone slightly defensive. "And it seems highly convenient that the one person who's ever found us is apparently immune to the restraining enchantment."

Amell shrugged. "I know it makes no sense. I wish I had an answer."

"Did you find out anything that might help us get out of here?" Aurelia asked hopefully.

A regretful look came over Amell's face, and Aurelia could almost feel the suspicion rising once again in Mama Gail.

"I have bad news there," Amell said, biting his bottom lip in a troubled expression. Aurelia's eyes were drawn to the gesture, fascinated. Mama Gail did that sometimes when she was thinking, but it looked very different on Amell. Much more distracting.

"What's the bad news?" Mama Gail pressed.

Amell sighed. "I couldn't tell anyone about you."

"Why not?" Aurelia demanded.

"The magic," Amell said. "At least, I assume it's that. When I tried to speak of any aspect of what I saw in here, I just... couldn't. The words wouldn't come out. I couldn't even nod in answer to a question." He looked incredibly frustrated. "I've actually heard of such things before. A friend of mine experienced something similar, also connected with a powerful concealment enchantment."

"It actually makes sense," Mama Gail said, again sounding begrudging. "I've read in Cyfrin's notes about his layered concealment magic, and I didn't understand what it meant."

"So..." Even as Aurelia lowered her head, her eyes darted up to study Amell's face, trying not to let her disappointment show. "So there isn't anything you can do, then? Did you come to say goodbye?"

Amell had been staring at her with a strange expression, but he started visibly at her words. "What?" he protested. "Of course not! I swore I'd get you out of here, and I will. It's just going to be harder than I initially hoped."

Aurelia brightened, lifting her head and smiling warmly at him. "I knew you weren't full of false promises." She gestured toward the seats ranged around their little wooden table. "Why don't we sit down?"

"Wait." Mama Gail threw a hand up. "First, I want to know who you are." She frowned at Amell. "Who you *really* are."

"What do you mean?" he asked, sounding cautious.

"My daughter told me you hesitated before giving your name. I want to know your real name."

Amell's eyes darted to Aurelia, and she felt herself coloring. "I did tell her that," she acknowledged. "It sounded like you hesitated."

He laughed. "I did, and I don't in the least resent you saying so. But Amell is my real name. I only hesitated because I wasn't sure whether to use my title."

"What title is that?" demanded Mama Gail.

"Well," said Amell, his leg bouncing again, "I suppose it's...

Prince Amell." He looked a little sheepish. "Crown Prince Amell, if we're being precise."

Aurelia felt her mouth fall open. "You're a prince? You're Fernedell's prince?" She folded her hands in front of her, then unfolded them, suddenly not sure what to do with any of her limbs. "Why didn't you tell me that yesterday?"

"Yes," Mama Gail pressed. "Why?"

Amell grimaced. "To be honest, it was just because I had no idea what I was dealing with. And," he glanced apologetically at Aurelia. "I thought it might spook you."

"I have no idea why you'd think that," she said with dignity, as she crossed her arms, then changed her mind and folded them behind her back instead.

Amell's lips twitched slightly. "I apologize for my error," he said gravely.

She narrowed her eyes in suspicion, then let out a laugh. "All right, I'm a little intimidated," she admitted. "But that's really not saying much. You're the third person I've met in my life, so chances were always high that I would be intimidated."

Amell laughed as well, but apparently Mama Gail remained unimpressed. "That's all very nice," she said curtly, "but what is Fernedell's prince doing wandering around the woods out here?"

"Searching for the inmates who escaped from the prison nearby," Amell answered her seriously.

"It does make sense," Aurelia argued, her eyes on her mother.

Amell nodded. "It's the biggest crisis we've seen in decades. My father is overseeing the response himself. He's camped at the prison right now."

"The king?" Aurelia gasped. She shook her head. "No wonder Cyfrin was annoyed about it all." She looked at Mama

Gail, a hint of dryness in her voice. "Is His Highness allowed to sit now?"

The older woman grunted her assent, and the three of them sat.

"Please just call me Amell," the prince said, with a disarming smile. "It's so much simpler."

"If you're a prince," Mama Gail cut in unceremoniously, "you should have all the resources we could need to get out of here."

"That was my hope as well," Amell responded gravely. "But my inability to communicate your situation to anyone does complicate things. Given the nature of the protections on this place, military force won't help free you. And I'm not versed in matters of magic myself, so I'd be dependent on our Enchanters' Guild to find a solution. How to achieve that without telling them the details of your plight has me in a puzzle."

"Well, at least you can still get in," Aurelia said brightly. "That's much better than nothing."

"I'm glad you feel that way," Amell smiled. "And I fully intend to find a solution. If I can't break the magic that's silencing me, I'll have to find a way around it." He flashed her a grin that made her stomach flutter strangely. "I've always been good at finding a way around the rules."

"I'm sure," Mama Gail cut in dryly.

"Oh Mama," Aurelia said, reproachfully. "He's been as good as his word so far."

"I reserve the right to be skeptical," the older woman said unapologetically. Her eyes were still on Amell. "I come from Albury, so I don't have a great deal of trust for royals."

Amell grimaced. "That's understandable," he said heavily. "If you've been stuck in here for seventeen years, you're probably thinking of the former king. I never met him myself, thankfully, but by all accounts he was a hard and cold man." He brightened. "But his son is king now, and he's much more reasonable. Since his marriage, he's considered almost kind."

Mama Gail looked surprised. "Albury's king is married?" she demanded. For some reason she glanced at Aurelia. "I must have missed that day's news."

Amell nodded. "He was married immediately after his curse was broken. The girl in question broke the curse, and it seems they fell in love in the process."

"That's nice," said Aurelia brightly.

"And it explains how I missed it," Mama Gail mused. "Cyfrin was very interested in that curse." Again she threw a look at Aurelia. "He took to keeping his news book with him, instead of leaving it here." She frowned. "Such a shame there's no way to access old announcements."

Aurelia saw that Amell looked confused, and she hastened to explain. "Cyfrin has an enchanted book in his study that mirrors the royal announcements of each kingdom in Solstice each day. Mama Gail checks it most evenings."

"That's handy," said Amell, sounding intrigued. "I'm surprised he doesn't lock his study."

Aurelia chuckled. "He doesn't think he needs to. There's an enchantment designed to keep us out, by name, but he doesn't know Mama Gail's real name, so it doesn't work on her."

Mama Gail shot Aurelia a sharp look, and she shrugged. "It's not like I can tell him your real name by accident."

Amell was looking uncertainly between the two suddenly tense women, and Aurelia brushed the old argument aside. She didn't know how long their visitor—the prince!—would stay, and she didn't want to waste a minute on unrelated matters.

"You might not be able to tell anyone about us, but you can bring us news, can't you?" Her eyes widened. "And items, even."

"Yes, I imagine so," said Amell. "What would you like me to bring?"

"What wouldn't we like?" Aurelia countered, delighted. She turned to her mother, their moment of conflict forgotten. "We could ask for anything!"

Amell chuckled. "Well, within reason. I suppose it has to be something I can carry."

"Well, Mama Gail?" Aurelia pressed, hoping to elicit some enthusiasm from the older woman. "You first."

"Well..." Mama Gail hesitated, her voice a little gruff. "I was very fond of cheesecake."

"Done," Amell said promptly. He turned to Aurelia. "And you?"

"I don't know," she laughed, feeling almost giddy with excitement at the vista of opportunities opening before her. "I don't know what I'm missing, because I've never known anything that's not in this tower. I suppose some new books would be nice."

"What type of books?" Amell asked. He was watching her with such rapt attention she felt almost self-conscious, but the soft smile that curved his lips awoke an answering one in her.

"I like storybooks," she admitted. "Or at least, I liked the one I read."

Mama Gail shifted slightly beside her, and Aurelia was sure she was remembering how she'd thrown that book away.

"But any new book would be fascinating, really," Aurelia finished quickly.

Amell's smile grew. "Well, I'll see if I can find something you'll like." His tone turned businesslike. "Now. It's unfortunate that instead of a host of helpful advisors you've only got me to help get you both out of here. But I'm going to do my utmost. So is there anything new I need to know since yesterday?"

Aurelia nodded eagerly. "There is, actually." She looked at her mother. "Tell him about the key."

The other woman looked back at her skeptically, her finger

moving rhythmically back and forth over the rim of a plate Aurelia had left on the table. Clearly the promise of cheesecake hadn't been enough to fully thaw her toward Amell.

"Come on, Mama Gail," Aurelia sighed. "Can you honestly tell me we have anything to lose by trusting him?"

Her mother let out a long breath. "All right," she said, raising her hands in surrender as she turned to Amell. "Cyfrin changed tactic last night. He's now moving some of the magic he's stored in her hair into her core."

"What?" Amell was suddenly on his feet, and Aurelia stared at him in amazement. "But won't that kill her when he extracts it? This is terrible! We have to act now!"

"By all means," said Mama Gail, looking at him with raised eyebrows. "Act."

Amell slumped back into his seat, his eyes troubled as they rested on Aurelia. "I don't know how," he admitted, "as you already know. But I don't like this. I don't like this at all."

"Goodness," Aurelia said mildly, her eyes passing between the prince and her mother. "You two are a matching pair."

Mama Gail sent her a look, but didn't comment. "Cyfrin is still optimistic that extracting the magic—either from her hair or her core—won't actually kill her. But honestly no one can know if he's right, because the experiment has never been tried on a human before."

"With good reason," Amell said forcefully, and Mama Gail nodded.

"There is, of course, a reason he's suddenly decided to change his approach."

"What is it?" Amell demanded.

Mama Gail was fidgeting with the plate again. "He's been researching a magical concept called a key." She shot him a look. "Do you know anything about that?"

Amell shook his head.

"Well, from what we can tell, it's basically a way to set stored magic to respond to a trigger action which, when performed, will unlock the magic like a key."

"All right," said Amell, looking between them, apparently lost.

"His plan is for it to be an action I perform," said Aurelia helpfully. "It seems his research has led him to believe that magic willingly given by me will be more potent than magic forcibly taken from me."

"What's the action going to be?" Amell asked, looking unaccountably alarmed.

"We don't know," Aurelia answered, frowning in thought. Once again, his reaction seemed eerily similar to her mother's.

"And how's he going to force you to undertake it?" the prince pressed.

Aurelia wrinkled her nose. "I think he's under the impression I'll do whatever he says." She lowered her head in shame. "I haven't generally been as good at defying as Mama Gail has. I'm not as brave."

Suddenly Amell's hand was on hers where it rested on the table, and she looked up, astonished.

"To have survived up here your whole life with as cheerful an attitude as you have shows the greatest bravery I've ever seen," he said quietly, and with every appearance of sincerity.

"That credit belongs to Mama Gail," Aurelia said, flushing both from pleasure at the compliment and from the delightful tingling that was spreading out from Amell's warm hand on hers.

"It's a credit to both of you," Amell said, removing his hand a little hastily. Following his gaze, Aurelia saw that her mother was giving him her hardest look yet.

"So that's the key," Aurelia said quickly. "Or as much as we know about it for sure. I found something else out, too."

"You did?" Mama Gail looked surprised.

Aurelia nodded. "While you were...in the other room, I asked him what all the magic was for."

"And he told you?" It was her mother who spoke, but both of her listeners looked equally skeptical.

"Sort of," Aurelia shrugged. "He didn't want to give me specifics, but he seemed to be bizarrely pleased that I was taking an interest. He's been acting very oddly lately, as if he's trying to be nice or something."

She realized that both Mama Gail and Amell looked suddenly tense, and she stared between them. "What? What is it?"

"What did he say about his magic?" her mother asked, dodging the question.

Aurelia frowned at her, but didn't press in front of Amell. "He said its purpose is to overwhelm and overpower all the other enchanters. Something about showing them that he's the greatest."

"That sounds like his target is the Enchanters' Guild," Amell interjected, his forehead creased. "Because they kicked him out."

Aurelia nodded. "That would be my guess as well."

The prince rubbed both hands over his face. "And I can't even warn them properly."

"Well," said Aurelia reassuringly, "I think it's safe to say he's not ready to move yet. He's still putting magic into my hair, and he's only just begun shifting some across to my core. Plus he said something last night about having plenty of time to earn my trust, remember, Mama Gail? I guess he was thinking of persuading me to unlock his magic."

"None of that makes me feel better at all," Amell declared firmly. "It sounds to me like time is of the essence."

"Well, we're agreed on that," Mama Gail cut in, her voice brisk. "So what's our next step?"

Amell frowned thoughtfully. "I'm not suggesting you do this," he said slowly. "I just want all the information. Have you ever considered trying to...eliminate Cyfrin?"

"The thought has crossed my mind," Mama Gail said curtly. "But I'm not sure I could, even if I was willing. Who knows what type of magical protection he carries on himself? He's clearly the suspicious type. And more to the point, I don't know what would happen to his enchantments if he died. It's possible they'd remain in place, at least for a while. And we wouldn't survive up here without the food he brings us."

Amell nodded. "Not a viable option then, at least not without more information." He pushed himself to his feet. "I think I'd better return to Fernford. I may not be able to explain it all, but I can still speak to someone from the Enchanters' Guild. Surely I can find a way to get the relevant information without contravening the silencing magic."

"When will you be back?" Aurelia asked, aware that her voice sounded anxious, but unable to prevent it.

Amell smiled down at her, and she could see nothing but sincerity in his gray eyes. "As soon as I possibly can. Tomorrow, I hope."

Aurelia nodded, her cheeks a little warm under his sustained gaze. Amell turned to Mama Gail, bowing with a stately grace that was almost humorous in the energetic young prince.

"Until tomorrow, Miss Abigail."

Mama Gail nodded, her expression conflicted. "Can I write you a list?" she asked abruptly. "There's a type of cake I've often told...my daughter about." Aurelia had noticed that while her mother wasn't giving away Aurelia's true name, she didn't seem able to bring herself to call her Honeysuckle, either. "There are just a few ingredients I can't get from Cyfrin. Perhaps you could acquire them in Fernford."

"I would be delighted," said Amell.

Mama Gail bustled to find fresh paper, and Aurelia had a sudden thought. If Amell was going to the Enchanters' Guild, she had questions of her own she'd like answered. She stepped close to him, lowering her voice.

"Can you ask something for me, at the Enchanters' Guild?"

"Of course," he said, leaning his head toward her, and speaking softly as well.

"I'd like to see a list of something called the foundational principles of power," Aurelia told him. She searched his eyes a little anxiously. "Can you remember that?"

"The foundational principles of power," Amell repeated obediently. "I won't forget."

She nodded in gratitude and stepped back. A glance at the kitchen showed Mama Gail still writing. Aurelia felt a little guilty at her deception, but she pushed the feeling down. Mama Gail had definitely said that whatever it was she didn't want to tell Aurelia from Cyfrin's notes related to another one of the foundational principles of power. If the other woman wasn't going to tell her what else she suspected Cyfrin of planning, she left Aurelia little option but to make inquiries behind her back.

"Here," Mama Gail said, handing Amell two pieces of paper. She cleared her throat. "I doubt it will work—I'm guessing Cyfrin's magic won't allow such a simple workaround. But the second paper is a letter. If you can send it to Allenton, well...I figured it was worth trying."

Aurelia caught the name *Gustav* on the front of the paper, and her heart twisted. Her life in the tower with Mama Gail was all she'd ever known—it was so easy to forget that the other woman had a family out there, whom she would be desperate to contact. Of course she wanted Amell to pass a message from her if he could.

"I'll try," he promised. Leaving the letter folded, he glanced over the list of ingredients. "Only three items?" he asked. "That shouldn't be too hard." He smiled at the two women. "I'll leave straight away, the sooner to be back."

With a smile of thanks, Aurelia began to thread her hair through the hook. After taking leave of them, Amell lowered himself down, hand over hand. Giving them a final wave, he disappeared into the tree line, leaving Aurelia gazing silently at an empty clearing.

"Well?" she asked, turning to her mother. "What do you think?"

Mama Gail grunted. "He seems genuine," she admitted. She glanced at her daughter, her expression troubled as she ran a gentle hand through Aurelia's long hair, untangling a knot. "But things aren't always as they seem, Aurelia."

"I know," Aurelia said. She shot her mother a look. "You sound a little like Cyfrin, you know. You've always told me that he's lying when he says I should be afraid of everyone and everything out there in the world. But the first time we actually encounter someone, you're so suspicious anyone would think he was a monster."

Mama Gail grimaced ruefully. "You have a point," she acknowledged. She sent the younger woman a sly grin. "And if he brings me back cheesecake, I might even have to forgive him for being so dangerously handsome."

Aurelia's light laughter rang out across the clearing.

CHAPTER THIRTEEN

Amell

Amell picked his way through the grove, his thoughts on the two women in the tower. Honeysuckle's mother was clearly suspicious of him, and he didn't really blame her. If he had someone like Honeysuckle under his care, he'd probably be overly protective as well. It was equal parts endearing and alarming how completely innocent the girl was. An image flashed before his eyes, of the hopeful way she'd looked up at him through her lashes as she asked forlornly whether he'd only come to say goodbye.

It was downright distracting, and she was all the more enchanting because she had no idea of her charm. As a prince, Amell had been targeted by his fair share of flirtatious young ladies hopeful of climbing the social ladder. He couldn't count the number of times one of them had looked at him in carefully crafted imitation of the precise expression Honeysuckle had worn. But in her case, it couldn't have been clearer that there was no guile, no art. She was completely genuine, and completely entrancing. Not to mention she was possibly the most beautiful girl he'd ever laid eyes on.

And the sick, evil enchanter who'd trapped her in a tower all her life was suddenly trying to be kind to her, and modifying his plans to rely on her willing involvement.

Amell didn't have to be an expert either in magic or in human behavior to recognize the signs of a particularly unsavory type of danger approaching the isolated girl. Honeysuckle had grown from a child into a breathtaking young woman before the enchanter's very eyes. It had been clear that Honeysuckle's mother was perfectly aware of what the nature of Cyfrin's plans might be, and equally clear that no such thought had yet entered Honeysuckle's head.

Amell suddenly realized that the muscles in his arm were strained, and his hand had closed into a fist, crushing the letter he was holding. He smoothed it out, determination filling him. He would just have to get both of them out before Cyfrin could do anything to destroy the innocence that drifted out from Honeysuckle's every movement. And before the enchanter could extract any magic from her, thereby endangering her life.

Glancing down at the now crumpled parchment in his hand, Amell frowned. He was sure there'd been a name on the letter Abigail had given him, but now the top of the folded billet was blank. He flipped it open and sighed at the sight of empty parchment. It was disappointing, but not surprising. The other paper was blank too, and Amell squeezed his eyes shut for a moment, trying to commit the three ingredients to memory. It was a good thing it hadn't been more.

And what had Honeysuckle asked for? In addition to books, she'd wanted a list of the foundational principles of power, whatever they were. And Abigail had asked for cheesecake. Amell scratched the back of his neck. It was a lot to remember. He might need to write a list of his own.

When he emerged back into the clearing where the prison sat, he was met by a resigned looking Furn.

"Did you really have to sneak off from me, Your Highness?"

he asked wearily. "I wouldn't have tried to stop you. Your father will replace me if he thinks I'm not serving my function anymore."

Amell gave him an apologetic smile. "Sorry, Furn. But you would've been bored standing around again. And you were busy when I left."

"If by busy you mean relieving myself for two minutes, then yes," Furn agreed dryly.

"Well, I'm back now," said Amell shamelessly. "And I'm hoping you'll come with me this time. I want to return to Fernford."

"To Fernford?" the guard asked, surprised. "I thought you wanted to stay here."

"Change of plans," said Amell. "I'd better tell my father."

It didn't take long to find the king, who listened with an unmoved expression to Amell's announcement that he intended to return immediately to the capital after all.

"What a surprise," said King Bern tonelessly. He cast a look over his son and sighed. "You know, Amell, at some stage you're going to have to stick with a task for longer than five minutes."

Amell frowned, feeling that the criticism was most unfair. He'd been at the prison for days now, and his father had been the one to offer him the option of returning to the capital the day before. But he didn't give voice to these complaints, aware that his mind hadn't exactly been on the crisis at hand, and that he couldn't explain his distraction to his father.

"I intend to come back, Father," he said instead. "I just want to visit the Enchanters' Guild, and ask Bartholomew for more information that might help with my...search."

"Is that so?" The king eyed him. "As it happens, I'm returning myself this afternoon. I received a message from my steward an hour ago, and it requires my personal attention."

"I'll be glad to see you there," said Amell politely. "Do you mind if Furn and I leave now, and ride on ahead?"

"Go on with you," said the king, waving a careless hand. "I imagine I'll see you for dinner." His voice turned stern. "Make sure you stay on the main road, and go straight back to the capital. That's the only route that's been fully cleared and maintained by the combined teams."

Amell nodded, needing no more opening. In a matter of minutes, he and Furn were on the road, heading south east toward Fernford.

"What do you really plan to do in the city?" Furn asked, no hint of accusation in the casual question.

"I really am going to speak to Bartholomew at the Enchanters' Guild," said Amell, a little aggrieved. He considered the list he'd scribbled on the blank parchment before they left the prison. "And I might visit the market as well."

"The market?" Furn sounded bemused, but when Amell didn't elaborate, he let the matter drop.

"Are there things you need to attend to as well, Furn?" Amell asked. "It was a paltry trick, pulling you away on this mad venture a day after we arrived back from Entolia."

Furn smiled. "Not at all. I have nothing tying me down, so I can afford to be dragged across the continent by my charge."

Amell chuckled, but he thought there was a slight edge to Furn's voice. "Do you want something tying you down, Furn?" he asked, considering the matter for the first time. "I suppose you'll get married sometime, won't you? Have a family, settle down. Then I'll be in the basket."

Furn's laugh was a little forced. "I wouldn't worry just yet, Your Highness."

When Furn fell silent, Amell pushed the matter from his mind. He had plenty else to think about. They reached the city in good time, having stopped for a simple lunch on the road. After they'd handed off their horses to grooms at the castle's entrance, Amell paused, looking up at the building. Perhaps it would be as well to go straight to the guild. If he went into the castle first, there was no telling how long his mother might keep him there.

Before commencing the short walk, he sent Furn off, sternly ordering him to go home and rest. For all his protestation, the guard looked happy to do so, and soon Amell found himself once again traversing the cobblestones on the short walk to the guild.

He pushed his way through the door, emerging into the lobby with his habitual abruptness.

"Your Highness." It was a different clerk on duty today, but he looked just as astonished as the previous one had to see the prince.

"Good afternoon," said Amell. "Is Bartholomew here?"

"Of course, Your Highness," said the clerk, standing. "I can fetch him."

"Can you take me to him instead?" Amell asked.

After only a moment's hesitation, the clerk gestured for Amell to precede him into a corridor. "I believe he's in his study, Your Highness. It's the fourth door on the left."

"Thank you," said Amell, striding down the hallway. At a sharp rap on the door in question, he was rewarded by the sound of a familiar, slightly quavering voice.

"Enter."

When Amell poked his head in, Bartholomew struggled up from his chair. "Prince Amell! You've sought me out again. I'm honored."

"Don't stand," Amell said hastily, coming fully into the room. "Do I interrupt?"

"Not at all." Bartholomew waved Amell into a chair, only

sinking back into his own once the prince was seated. "Is all well?"

"With the prison, you mean?" Amell asked. He ran a hand through his travel-tossed hair, glancing around the neat study. It couldn't look more different from the chaotic room at the castle where he was supposed to undertake his more mundane duties. "As well as it can be with twenty inmates still on the loose."

"That's fewer than last I heard," Bartholomew said encouragingly.

Amell's nod was a little absent. "Bartholomew, I have some questions for you about magic."

"Is this about the possibility of a conspiracy?" Bartholomew asked, dropping his voice. "Because I've conducted some discreet inquiries since our last conversation. If any of the guild's governing members have had involvement in these magical attacks, I would own myself utterly astonished."

"No, it's not about that," Amell said, "although that's heartening to hear." He drummed his fingers on the table, trying to find a way around the silencing charm. "Do you remember who we spoke about last time?"

Bartholomew frowned in an effort of memory. "Cyfrin, you mean?"

"That's right," said Amell. He tried to say more, but no matter how he phrased it in his mind, the words wouldn't come. He gave a grunt of frustration.

"Are you all right, Prince Amell?"

Amell closed his eyes, blocking the sight of the older man's concerned face. "I'm fine," he said through gritted teeth.

He cast his mind over the events of the previous few days. "Are you familiar with the magic in use at the prison?" he asked.

"We all are now," Bartholomew assured him. "We've spoken of little else at the guild since the break out. And we've been sending enchanters and enchantresses to help reinforce the protections, as you would know."

Amell nodded. "Of course. I understand that there's some kind of...restraining enchantment around the property, that prevents certain people from leaving."

"That's right," said the enchanter. "Although properly speaking, it's called a fencing enchantment. Restraining magic is more...I don't know how to phrase it without getting technical. Let us say more aggressive."

"Would it require powerful magic to have a restraining enchantment around the whole building?"

"Oh yes," Bartholomew said, with a little chuckle. "Extremely powerful."

Amell frowned. "Unbreakable?"

"Well..." Bartholomew drew out the word. "Nothing is unbreakable. But to break it would require even more magic than to cast it. More resources than we have readily available, at any rate. I daresay a dragon could do it with ease, but we're not speaking of dragons."

"No," Amell agreed ruefully.

If only he dared to seek out Rekavidur and Dannsair, he could probably break Honeysuckle and Abigail out that afternoon. But the beasts were virtually unknown to him, and dragons were unpredictable. They might help him again...or they might declare war on Fernedell for breaking the agreement, and wipe his kingdom off the face of the continent.

"Could you try?" he asked. "Could you, I don't know...make an artifact that would make someone immune to any restraining enchantment?"

"Why would you want to do that?" Bartholomew asked, taken aback. "Surely we don't want any of the prisoners to be able to evade the restraints?"

"Of course not," said Amell casually. "This is nothing to do with the prisoners. I'm asking as a personal favor. Are you willing to try?"

"Yes, I'm willing," said Bartholomew slowly. "For you, Your Highness, I'm willing. But it will take finesse, and a great deal of power, which I can't spare all at once. Even if I'm able to create such an item, it won't be ready anytime soon."

"I understand," Amell said. "I'd be grateful for anything you could come up with."

Bartholomew nodded, still looking puzzled, but respectfully asking no questions.

"What about concealment magic?" Amell asked.

"What about it?"

"Well..." Amell could feel the magic closing on his throat, and he again hunted for an unrelated route into the topic. "When I was in Entolia, Prince Bentleigh of Bansford mentioned something that piqued my interest. He talked about concealment magic which acted to stop his tongue, preventing him from speaking about the thing that was concealed."

"Interesting," said Bartholomew, with all a scholar's fascination. "Complex magic, indeed. That is an unusual layer of concealment magic, because it requires great finesse as well as great force." He made a wry face. "Not as common a combination in the magic community as you might think."

"How would you get around it?" Amell pressed.

"Oh, I don't think you could get around it," Bartholomew said, settling his shoulders more comfortably in his chair. "It would lift with the breaking of the whole concealment enchantment, of course."

Amell let out a frustrated huff. "How would you do that?"

"With a great deal of magic, once again," said Bartholomew. "And not just a great quantity. A high level of skill would be involved. Or the enchanter or enchantress who created it could undo it fairly simply."

Amell frowned. Not much hope for release from either of those quarters, what with Cyfrin being a vile snake, and all the other enchanters in the kingdom focusing their efforts on the prison break.

"But surely," Bartholomew said mildly, "Prince Bentleigh is no longer under this enchantment?"

"Of course not," Amell said.

"And how was he freed?"

Amell sighed. "It was all part of the Listernian princess's curse, which was broken altogether, as you'd know."

Bartholomew nodded thoughtfully. "A very interesting aspect of the curse," he mused. "I hadn't heard about that detail before." He sent an amused glance at Amell. "For a moment I was concerned these questions weren't theoretical. That you had yourself been exposed to some kind of malicious magic."

Amell didn't even try to answer this time. He could feel in his throat that he wouldn't be able to. He just stared unblinkingly back at Bartholomew, willing the man to put the pieces together by himself.

Unfortunately, the enchanter seemed oblivious to his silent communication.

"But then I realized the power I'm sensing on you comes from that cloak." Bartholomew glanced at the article in question. "The amount of magic leaking from it is positively garish. What is it, by the by?"

"It's an artifact designed to shield me from concealment magic," Amell said with a touch of irony. He slipped it from his shoulders and threw it into an empty chair. "What do you feel now?"

Bartholomew clucked his tongue. "That's no way to treat a valuable artifact, dear boy." His gaze passed from the cloak to the prince. "What do you mean, what can I feel? I still sense the magic. It's just...coming from that chair instead of from you."

Amell frowned. It seemed that whatever layer of concealment magic was silencing his tongue was too subtle for even Bartholomew to sense. He couldn't help but be rattled by the thought. He considered Bartholomew one of the most skilled enchanters in Solstice. It wasn't good news if Cyfrin's capability was high enough to fool him. And, now he thought about it, it didn't tally with Bartholomew's own description of Cyfrin's mediocre strength.

But then, none of the enchantments surrounding Honeysuckle and Abigail tallied with that old description. Something definitely didn't add up.

With a sigh, he shook off the thought. So Bartholomew wasn't going to be able to help him dodge the silencing restriction. That wasn't the only matter he wanted to raise.

"What can you tell me about keys in magic?" he asked abruptly. Thankfully, without any context whatsoever, the magic allowed him to ask the question.

Bartholomew leaned back, processing the change in topic. "That's very advanced magic. Tricky to do, but not difficult to explain. In essence, a key is an action that will trigger the release of magic for a preconstructed purpose."

"So the action doesn't control what the magic does?" Amell asked.

Bartholomew shook his head. "The function of the magic is decided at the time the key is fashioned. Then when the action is performed, the magic is released onto its pre-approved path."

"What kind of action could be a key?" Amell asked.

"Any action at all," said Bartholomew simply.

Amell groaned internally. That didn't help narrow down Cyfrin's plans.

"You know," Bartholomew added thoughtfully, "I'm sure you have heard of keys before. Just not by that name."

"What do you mean?"

"Well, you've heard of a counterforce, surely?"

Amell nodded.

"Tell me what you know," Bartholomew urged.

Feeling like he was back in lessons, Amell recited, "The magic we know isn't the strongest force in existence. Therefore all curses can by nature be broken. We call that counteracting force a counterforce, and it acts as a remedy for a curse. A sensible magic-user will build in a counterforce intentionally when casting an enchantment, so that he or she can control what action or situation will counteract their magic. But if they fail to do so, the natural counterforce still exists, and can be used to break the enchantment if one can figure out the natural opposite of whatever motivated the curse in the first place."

"As good an explanation as any," Bartholomew said approvingly.

Amell frowned. "But what does that have to do with a key?"

"Well, it's the same sort of concept, isn't it?" Bartholomew explained. "The counterforce, whatever it might be, is a key of sorts. It's usually an action, and by performing it, you trigger a specific magical outcome, in that case breaking the relevant curse."

"I suppose that makes sense," said Amell.

Not that it really helped him. Honeysuckle wasn't exactly under a curse. She was hemmed in by a restraining enchantment, which was a different kind of magic altogether, and who even knew what to call the magic that had been stored in her hair? He doubted even Bartholomew could explain the ramifications of that, given no one had ever done it before.

"Thank you, Bartholomew," Amell said, suddenly feeling very weary. The activity of the last few days was catching up to him. "I appreciate your assistance." He was on his feet before he remembered his final question. "Oh, are you familiar with something called the foundational principles of power?"

"Of course," said Bartholomew blankly. "I'm a senior enchanter."

Amell couldn't help but laugh at the hint of haughtiness on the kind old man's face. "My apologies," he said. "What I should have asked is whether you would mind writing them down for me."

"Gladly." Bartholomew pulled a blank sheet of parchment toward him, and lifted an extremely long feather quill from an ink pot on his desk. Scratching in an unhurried way, he wrote out a list of six principles. Before handing the parchment to Amell, he rolled it up neatly and tied it with a blue ribbon.

Containing his impatience with difficulty through this careful process, Amell received the scroll with a word of thanks. "And you'll work on that artifact idea? The one to counteract restraining magic?"

"I will indeed," Bartholomew assured him gravely.

The afternoon had worn away by the time Amell left the guild, but he didn't think the market would be cleared out altogether. Enjoying being once again in motion, he walked briskly through the streets, taking it all in with new eyes. Was it only a matter of days since he'd reflected that the bustling city was a place of frustration and restriction? He tried to see it through Honeysuckle's eyes, imagining how it would look to him if he'd spent his entire life in one room.

Suddenly the marketplace was a wonderland of opportunities, a veritable whirlwind of sensations. The tantalizing smells, the shouts of children running between the legs of the market-goers, the sight of so many vivid colors.

It was beautiful.

Amell was lucky to acquire a cheesecake from a baker's cart so late in the day, and he didn't mind paying the higher price he knew was only quoted to the nobility. Some children ran past, laughing, and one accidentally knocked Amell's leg.

"Sorry, My Lord," the urchin squeaked out, clearly not recognizing the prince.

"It's all right," smiled Amell. He spotted the other children, congregating near the sweets stall next door. "Here." He handed the merchant several coins. "One for everyone." He smiled as the children squealed, shoving the treats into their mouths with a speed that suggested no such bounty was secure until eaten.

"And a few for me," Amell added, handing the merchant another coin. "Wrapped, please."

Once he'd deposited the parcel in the paper box given him by the baker, he wandered on, collecting anything that caught his eye for Honeysuckle. By the time he returned to the castle, he barely had time to change his raiment before he would be expected at the dining hall. Which suited him just fine. Less time for mind-numbing conversation.

To his surprise, when he left his rooms to head toward dinner, he found Furn waiting for him.

"Furn," he exclaimed. "I thought I sent you home.'

"You did, Your Highness," Furn acknowledged. "But I wanted to check whether there was anything else you needed tonight."

"No, consider it a long overdue night off," Amell smiled. "I'm hoping to ride for the prison again at first light, though."

Furn nodded. "I'll be ready, Your Highness."

A laugh sounded from around the corner ahead, and they rounded it to see a tall and graceful figure leaning on the arm of a well-dressed young man, and laughing at something he'd just said.

"Tora!" Amell called, genuinely pleased to see his sister. "Did you miss me?" His gaze passed to Tora's companion in some surprise. "Ah, and Lord...My Lord," he said hastily, the man's name escaping him. Amell recognized him as one of the more ridiculous members of his own generation among court. Even for a Fernedellian, the young nobleman dressed with rather astonishing flamboyance. His leggings were bright yellow, and his velvet doublet the color of a ripe plum. It was a somewhat startling combination.

"Your Highness," the nobleman swept an elegant bow, "I rejoice at your safe return."

"Uh...thank you," said Amell blankly.

"You've been a truly impeccable companion, My Lord," Tora said, casting a look up at the nobleman that was uncomfortably reminiscent of the manner of the scheming damsels Amell had been thinking about only that afternoon. "I look forward to further such walks."

"Not as much as I do, Your Highness," said the nobleman, a glint in his eye that Amell didn't quite like. He felt Furn shift beside him as the man lifted Tora's hand and pressed his lips to it for an unnecessarily long moment.

"Yes, well, thank you, My Lord," Amell said flatly. "I'll escort my sister to dinner."

"Of course, Your Highness," said the nobleman, bowing again and prancing away down the corridor.

Tora turned to the pair of them, her expression bright and entirely unabashed. "Amell, Furn. I'm so glad to see you back. It's been dull here without you."

"Not dull enough, apparently," Amell said grimly. "Tora, what on earth were you doing with that fool? He was utterly ridiculous."

"Ah, there's no accounting for taste, Amell," said Tora brightly. "And he pays me the most extravagant compliments."

Her eyes were twinkling in a way Amell knew well, and he frowned at her. "You're up to something, Tora. What is it?"

She just laughed at him. "I don't know what you mean." She turned to Amell's guard. "How was your journey, Furn? I hope my brother isn't making you act as his manservant at dinner again."

"No, Your Highness," said Furn quietly. "I was merely bidding His Highness goodnight." He bent in a slightly stiff bow. "And to you as well, of course." And without another word, he turned on his heel and strode away, toward the castle's distant entrance.

"Well," said Amell, staring after him. "That was a little abrupt." He turned back to his sister, his eyes narrowing. "What was all that nonsense before, Tora? I don't think I've ever seen you flirt before in my life. Why would you choose that idiot?"

She sighed, looking suddenly quite dejected. "You have seen me flirt, Amell. And the fact that you think you haven't is utterly depressing." She slipped her hand into his arm, steering them toward the dining hall. "I chose that idiot, as you so politely phrase it, because he's perfectly safe. His family is all to pieces, and he's quite ineligible, so Mother won't get any grand ideas."

"Were you so desperate to flirt with someone?" Amell demanded.

Tora winced, even as she let out a reluctant laugh. "Must you use the word desperate? Be kind to your old sister, up here on my shelf."

Amell nudged her, laughing himself. "Now you're being ridiculous. But I still don't understand what you're up to."

Tora just smiled. "I have my reasons, little brother. Now, I want to hear about your time at the prison."

They'd reached the dining hall by this time, however, and their conversation was suspended. Amell hadn't especially been looking forward to the meal—he'd never much enjoyed sitting around talking. But even the private family dinner took on a new light in his eyes. He couldn't help but reflect that it was pleasant to have three members of his family, instead of being restricted to one companion all the time. King Bern had also returned, as expected, and most of the meal was occupied with his account of the doings at the prison, for the benefit of the queen and princess.

"Amell was involved in the capture of the most recent two fugitives," he added toward the end of the meal, nodding at his son. "The captain said he acquitted himself well."

"So it was worth camping out over there all this time," Tora grinned.

Amell shook his head, still rattled whenever he thought about the incident. "The captain overstated my achievements," he said. "I was more foolish than heroic. And I almost got Furn killed."

"Goodness," said Queen Pietra mildly. "Don't do that, Amell. I don't know how we'd replace that man. He has the patience of a saint."

"What do you mean, Furn almost got killed?" Tora demanded, ignoring her mother's light words. "Is he all right?"

"Yes, he's fine," Amell assured her. "But only because the enchanters got their shielding magic up in time. He dove right in front of me when the prisoners were attacking."

"I'll see him commended for exemplary service," said King Bern, as placid as his wife. He looked up from his plate to see both of his children frowning at him, and raised an eyebrow. "Why do you look so outraged? That is his job, you realize."

"Yes, that's what Furn said, too," Amell acknowledged, troubled. "I'm not sure how I feel about being someone who has people employed to die in my place."

"Well, you'd best get used to the feeling before ascending the throne," King Bern said briskly. "I for one think I will retire early tonight. The warden's quarters, although perfectly acceptable, are not what I would call comfortable."

"Yes, I'll do the same," Amell commented distractedly. "I'm planning to head back at first light."

The king raised an eyebrow. "So early?"

"I have a task to see through, Father," said Amell with dignity.

King Bern didn't quite manage to hide his smile as he rose, and it did nothing for Amell's confidence. The queen left with her husband, and Amell found himself alone with Tora.

"I can't believe Furn almost died," she said repentantly. "And there I was plaguing him earlier with my stupid jokes."

"What stupid...oh, you mean Lord What's-His-Name?" Amell said. "I wouldn't worry about it, Tora. I mean, you were behaving a bit embarrassingly, but I doubt Furn even noticed, let alone felt plagued by it."

Tora scowled at him, apparently not softened by this reassurance. "If you're in a disagreeable mood, I think I'll retire early as well." And she flounced out of the room, leaving Amell feeling bewildered.

"Sisters," he muttered, heading for the library before seeking his own rest. It had been some time since he'd read a storybook, but he still remembered perfectly where they were kept. And perhaps in the morning, he'd visit a dawn market and pick up some fresh flowers.

Not honeysuckles. Something rare and beautiful, like the poorly named girl in the tower.

CHAPTER FOURTEEN

Aurelia gave the broom one final, vigorous flourish. "There," she said, satisfied. "It's the cleanest it's ever been."

"Somehow I doubt Prince Amell will notice the floors," commented Mama Gail from where she sat with her mending.

Aurelia sent her an innocent look. "Who said anything about Prince Amell?"

Her mother didn't even grace that question with a reply. "How do you feel after a night's sleep?" she asked instead. "Does your hair feel different? I don't understand the process, but it seemed to me like Cyfrin pulled a lot of magic into your core last night."

"Did it seem that way?" Aurelia asked absently. "I didn't really notice."

Her thoughts had been elsewhere. It was the first time she could remember being so genuinely unconcerned by the enchanter's visit. She'd just tuned him out altogether, her thoughts on Amell, wondering if he'd find answers while he was gone, and if he'd really be able to return the next day.

"Yes, it did," Mama Gail said flatly. "And he was acting very strangely, I thought."

"I did notice that," Aurelia said, frowning in memory. "He hardly snapped at all." She chuckled. "Maybe he's found an enchantment for gaining an altogether new personality."

Mama Gail grunted. "Somehow I doubt it."

Aurelia didn't answer, already having lost interest in the topic of the enchanter. She glanced out the window, her thoughts returning to the one person who seemed to dominate them now. He said he'd try to come today. But he hadn't been any more specific than that. It couldn't be much later than ten o'clock, and it was unlikely he'd come in the morning. She should probably—

"Honeysuckle? Abigail?"

Aurelia flew to the window with a gasp, a smile spreading across her face at the sight of the prince.

"You made it!" she cried, as Mama Gail joined her at a more sedate pace. "Let me pull you up." She threaded her hair quickly through the loop, dropping it more hastily than was comfortable.

Amell grasped hold of it without hesitation this time, just waiting for her to confirm that she was ready. He seemed to pull himself up with extra speed. Was he as eager to see her as she was to see him?

"You came earlier than I expected," she told him, once he stood in the tower room.

He flashed her the smile that made it hard to think. "I left the city at first light, and rode straight here."

With interest, she watched as he swung a satchel from his shoulder and placed it on the small table. He'd never brought a bag before.

"I've done my best to find what you requested," he said brightly, his smile encompassing Mama Gail as well. "Miss

Abigail, for you." With a flourish, he extracted a paper box, and Mama Gail took it eagerly. She peeked inside, and her eyes lit with more excitement than Aurelia had seen her show in a long time.

"I'll cut it up at once," she said, hurrying to find a plate. "Au—darling, you're going to love it!"

Aurelia saw Amell look quickly between the two women, and knew he'd caught the slip. She bit her lip, feeling a prickle of guilt at her continued deception. Perhaps she should just tell him her real name. After all, he'd shown himself true to his word so far. But as she watched her mother bustling around, she knew what the other woman would say. A few days wasn't long enough to know someone could be trusted.

"I also got the ingredients you asked for," Amell told Mama Gail. "I hope I remembered them correctly, because the list disappeared. Unfortunately the letter was wiped clean as well."

She sighed, beginning to slice up the cake. "I expected as much."

Amell smiled at Aurelia, reaching back into his bag. "I thought you might like these," he said, pulling out a small packet. "They're from one of the best sweet stalls in Fernford. I brought enough for us all." He gave a cheerful chuckle that made his eyes dance. "They're popular with the children. You should have seen these little ragamuffins crowding around the stand at the market. They were like a swarm of bees."

"I saw a bee once," Aurelia told him brightly. "But I've never seen a whole swarm."

Amell's smile faltered the tiniest bit, but his voice remained just as cheerful. "Well, they're loud, and they're busy. Never still. And bright."

"What else did you see at the market?" Aurelia asked eagerly. She listened with fascination as the prince described one of Fernford's markets—the colors, the smells, the barking dogs, and shouting vendors. He pulled a number of other food items from his bag as he described the stalls where he'd acquired them. They all looked incredible, and the cheesecake was delicious, but she could hardly focus on any of it, her eyes locked on the prince's animated face.

"You describe it so well," she said wistfully. "I wish I could picture it, but too many of those things I've never seen." She smiled. "It's as fantastical as something out of a storybook to me."

"Speaking of which," Amell said brightly, reaching back into his bag. "I brought you books." He slid a stack of five books onto the table, and Aurelia's eyes widened.

"So many!" She gathered them up as gently as if they were breakable eggs. "A storybook," she lifted the top one, "and another, and a book on the history of Fernedellian fashion—"

"You seemed interested the first time we met," Amell interjected, "when I mentioned how brightly everyone dresses in the capital. I thought you might like to learn more about how our customs developed."

"I would," Aurelia breathed, her heart in her eyes as she looked up at him. "Thank you, Amell, thank you from the bottom of my heart."

"It's nothing," he said, a little gruffly. His face had taken on a hint of color, but she thought he looked pleased by her thanks.

She looked through the other books, running her fingers down the spines. One appeared to be a traveler's account of other lands, and the last one was a book on dragon lore. She could hardly wait to read them.

"These are very fine books," she said, with a touch of anxiety. "Were they expensive? We have no coins to pay you for them."

Amell laughed. "I don't want your coins, and if I took them,

I'd be a thief. I didn't actually purchase these books. They come from the castle library."

Aurelia looked up in alarm. "But won't they be missed?"

"I'm allowed to take whatever books I like from the library," Amell assured her. "I'll just take them back once you're finished. And there's no rush," he added quickly.

Aurelia nodded, her heart seeming to inflate. He was planning to come back, the borrowed books were proof.

"I, uh...I brought you something else," Amell said, his voice definitely gruff now. Mama Gail had taken their plates back to the sink, but Aurelia saw her glance over. "I'm afraid they got a bit crushed by the ride, but hopefully they'll still brighten the place up for a while."

He pulled a final item from his satchel, and Aurelia's eyes widened at the sight of a delicate bunch of vibrant pink flowers, wrapped carefully in paper.

"What are they?" she asked reverently, running her fingers along the long petals of one of the flowers. There seemed to be two types of blooms in the bundle.

"They're roses and lilies," Amell said. "They're both very popular types of flowers. They caught my eye in the market, and I thought you would both like them. I didn't know if you had any growing within sight."

"They're beautiful," said Aurelia, drinking them in. "And I've never seen either of them before."

"It's a long while since I saw a rose," Mama Gail commented, lowering herself into the seat next to her daughter. "Very thoughtful of you. Although we'll have to be careful to hide all this when Cyfrin comes."

Aurelia frowned at her mother, thinking she was showing less enthusiasm than the occasion called for.

"Did you discover anything about the magic that's keeping us here?" Mama Gail asked, her eyes on Amell.

He sighed. "Nothing terribly helpful, I'm afraid. I spoke with one of the guild's most senior enchanters. Apparently true restraining enchantments are very strong. He agreed to work on an artifact that might counteract it, but he wasn't very optimistic, and he told me not to expect results anytime soon."

"Were you able to tell him about us, then?" Aurelia asked, sitting up straighter.

Amell shook his head regretfully. "I wasn't. The magic wouldn't let me. If I could have, I imagine the project might take more priority, even with the prison break. Still, I was able to find other ways to ask for the information I wanted."

"That was very clever of you," she encouraged him, but his answering smile was a little strained. She could tell he was disappointed he hadn't been able to achieve more, and it warmed her to him even further.

"He confirmed what we already knew about keys," Amell added, his eyes drifting to Mama Gail. "The action could be anything, so not much help there. He also said they're a bit like counterforces. Do you know about those?"

Mama Gail nodded. "I didn't before we were locked up here. But Cyfrin has a book about them in his study, so we have a pretty good grasp of the concept."

"Can I see this study?" Amell asked, standing. "You said the enchantment is limited to those named, so I should be able to go in, right?"

Aurelia stood as well, feeling a little forlorn as she wandered toward the study behind the other two. She was used to the frustration of being kept out while Mama Gail went in, but it was much harder to take when Amell was in there, too. It was a decent sized room, one side of it filled with bookshelves which jutted out into the space. The pair disappeared behind them while searching, and Aurelia walked back to the table, touching the flowers again. She tried to picture Amell walking the markets, seeing the beautiful blooms, and thinking of her. Color flooded her cheeks, but it wasn't an unpleasant sensation.

Mama Gail and Amell came back out of the study after several minutes, and Aurelia couldn't help being suspicious at the thoughtful look on the prince's face. She had no doubt they'd been having a private word, and she couldn't help feeling a little aggrieved.

"Well," said the prince, not speaking quite naturally. "I shouldn't linger too long today. I've left poor Furn wandering the woods. Turning gray before his time because of my constant disappearing, no doubt."

"Who's Furn?" Aurelia asked, her heart sinking at this prompt departure.

"He's my personal guard," Amell explained. "His name is Sir Furnis, but we call him Furn. My sister and I, that is. He's a good sort, and I don't usually keep things from him. But thanks to the magic, I can't even tell the poor fellow what I'm up to."

"You have a sister?" Aurelia asked, fascinated.

"We know that," Mama Gail reminded her. "King Bern and Queen Pietra rule Fernedell, and their children are Princess Tora and Crown Prince Amell."

"Oh yes, of course," said Aurelia. She smiled at Amell. "Mama Gail has drilled me on the royalty of every kingdom in Solstice, although I'm not sure why I need to know. We have a lot of time up here, you see, so we're always looking for new things to do. I just forgot about your sister, because it's hard to comprehend that our Amell, the handsome stranger who appeared magically in our clearing, is actually *Prince* Amell."

Amell's neck turned red, and Mama Gail cleared her throat. Watching in dismay as they exchanged a meaningful look, Aurelia realized she'd erred.

"Did I say something strange?" she asked, inwardly cursing her inexperience when it came to interacting with anyone but her mother. The truth suddenly dawned on her, and she felt her face heat furiously. "I shouldn't say you're handsome to your face, should I?"

Amell suddenly laughed, lightening the tension. "I don't mind," he assured her, a twinkle in his eye. "But I'm sure my aforementioned sister would tell you not to give me a big head."

Aurelia smiled, his casual air easing her embarrassment. "She sounds fun. I wish I could meet her."

"You will," Amell promised, collecting his bag and moving toward the window.

"Plus," Aurelia added reflectively, as she lowered her hair down the side of the tower, "you shouldn't really get a big head, you know. I probably only think you're handsome because I have no basis for comparison."

"That certainly puts me in my place," Amell said gravely, his eyes dancing merrily.

"Thank you," said Aurelia softly, as he took hold of her hair. "For bringing all those wonderful things."

"It was nothing," he said, his tone equally gentle. "I wish I could do so much more. Oh," his voice dropped even lower, "I almost forgot. I got the other thing you asked for." He drew a tightly scrolled piece of paper from an inner pocket of his cloak, and Aurelia took it hastily, slipping it into her sleeve.

"Thank you," she said again, grateful that he hadn't asked her any questions. She searched his eyes a little shyly. "Will you come back soon?"

"Tomorrow," he promised. "And every day, until we can find a way to get you out of here."

Her face glowing and her heart light, Aurelia stepped back and braced herself against the wall. Once Amell was safely on the ground, she leaned on the windowsill, watching his lithe figure until he disappeared into the trees. Then she turned suspicious eyes on her mother.

"You talked about me while you were in the study, didn't you?"

Mama Gail acknowledged it unashamedly. "Of course we did."

"What did you say?" Aurelia demanded.

"I just wanted to make sure he knows that although you seem alone and vulnerable up here, you're not unprotected." Mama Gail gave her a tight smile. "Parents are always protective of their children, Aurelia, we can't help it."

Aurelia gave her a look. "Mama, I truly don't think he means me any harm."

Mama Gail sighed. "I don't think he does, either," she admitted. "But that doesn't mean he won't do you harm unintentionally." For some inscrutable reason, she threw a disgruntled look at the flowers still lying on the table.

Aurelia frowned. It didn't make much sense to her, but she was glad Mama Gail was at least acknowledging Amell's good intentions. It seemed the cheesecake had worked.

"Well, it's a shame that enchanter from the guild didn't have better news about getting through the restraining enchantment," Aurelia commented. "But at least I won't be bored today!" She turned eager eyes to the stack of books.

"Yes, I'm looking forward to something new to read as well," Mama Gail smiled. She gave her daughter a teasing look. "That is, assuming you intend to share your bounty with me."

Aurelia laughed. "You shared the cheesecake, so it's only fair."

The day passed in a blur, sunset approaching all too soon. Aurelia grumbled to herself as she stashed all her new treasures in hiding places around the tower. It was hard to remember that so recently she'd felt fearful every time Cyfrin approached. Now she just felt irritated at the interruption.

But his presence didn't have to interrupt her thoughts. She

barely heard his forced attempts at pleasant conversation, her mind on Amell, reliving every expression, every look. He'd brought her flowers. And books. Those wonderful books! She'd made it halfway through one of the storybooks before she had to stop and hide it. She thought she might read the one about dragon lore next.

Her distraction wasn't enough to prevent an involuntary shudder passing over her when Cyfrin laid his hand on her midriff again, and the enchanter apparently noticed.

"Why do you shy away from me like I'm a snake, Honeysuckle?" he chastised. "Have I ever hurt you?"

She stared at him in bemusement. "Is that a joke? You locked me up in this tower when I was only a baby, and you've kept me here against my will ever since."

The enchanter looked like he couldn't decide whether to be astonished or angry at her matter-of-fact response. Aurelia felt a slight surprise herself at his reaction. Was it really such a short time ago that she'd been too cowed to defy him openly?

"I have fed you, and clothed you, and protected you from a hostile world," Cyfrin snapped. He controlled his voice with an effort. "The violent criminals now running loose across the countryside are excellent proof of why you need me."

"What is the update on the prison break?" Aurelia asked, realizing that she'd forgotten to ask Amell about it.

"They continue to roam across the land, ravaging at will," Cyfrin sniffed.

Aurelia raised an eyebrow. "Haven't they caught any of them?"

"No," said Cyfrin impatiently. "Now hold still so I can work."

He closed his eyes, putting all his attention into his magic, and Aurelia and Mama Gail exchanged a look across the room. Little did the enchanter know that his lies had been exposed by another source.

It wasn't until late that night, after Mama Gail was asleep, that Aurelia dared to light a candle from the embers of the fire, and pull out the scroll from where she'd stashed it.

Loosening the blue ribbon, she unfurled the paper and smoothed it on her lap.

The Foundational Principles of Power
1. All forces have a counterforce.
2. Love is stronger than any destructive force.
Note: when misapplied for destruction, love is therefore capable of unparalleled devastation.
3. Power willingly given is more potent than power forcibly taken.
4. An aptitude for power is either present or absent—it cannot be developed.
5. Multiple sources of power united are stronger than the sum of their separate parts.
6. Power in itself is neither good nor evil.

"Power willingly given is more potent than power forcibly taken," Aurelia read in a whisper. That was where the key came in. That was why Cyfrin was moving the magic to her core, with the intention of making it more potent when she willingly released it to him.

Which she had no intention of ever doing.

But what was the other principle that her mother had seen mentioned in Cyfrin's notes? She'd said it also related to increasing the potency of the magic. Perhaps number five? Maybe Cyfrin thought that if she controlled some of his stored magic, and he controlled the magic still within him, together they would count as two sources of magic.

With a sigh, she rolled up the parchment and hid it under

her mattress. No obvious answers, but at least she had the information. It was a start.

Aurelia's life had always moved according to a predictable routine, and the weeks that followed were no exception. Except now her day was dominated by an event she anticipated with great excitement, instead of one she dreaded. Amell's visits weren't always at the same time, but he always came in the morning, and he always brought the sunshine with him into the tower room, regardless of the weather.

He enchanted her with tales of the world outside, made her laugh with stories of his own childhood antics, and fascinated her with descriptions of the places he'd been and the things he'd witnessed. He told her all about Furn, and Tora, and his friend Basil, who was already king in Entolia, despite being not much older than Amell himself.

At first he only stayed for a short time each day, casting the odd shifty look at Mama Gail that convinced Aurelia her mother had given him a lecture in the study that day. But as the days turned into weeks, he relaxed, and his visits were longer and longer, until it wasn't unusual for him to spend most of the morning with them.

Even Mama Gail seemed to warm to his cheerfulness, and his endless energy.

"You look like you're dancing on hot coals," she told him one morning, about two weeks into his daily visits. "You don't sit still much, do you?"

"Rarely," Amell acknowledged, with a rueful grin. "I've always suffered from an excess of energy. It drives my mother spare."

"I can imagine," said Mama Gail, the words softened by a smile.

"I don't mind it," Aurelia assured him. "I know the feeling, in fact. I've often told Mama Gail that I have an endless amount of energy."

"You have a good excuse though," Amell pointed out, "since you're denied the opportunity to use that energy. I spend my life bouncing from one thing to another—according to my parents —without ever seeming to satisfy my desire for action."

"That's not fair," Aurelia said, offended on his behalf by this criticism. "You've stuck with us all this time, and with the crisis at the prison. And I've never heard you complain of being bored."

Amell's grin softened into something gentler, and Aurelia found herself locked in his gaze. "Not a fair comparison," he told her lightly. "I'm never bored when I'm with you."

Aurelia's heart began to pick up speed, but the moment was broken by Mama Gail's practical voice.

"Well, we can't exactly be bored when you're here, either. You're much too energetic."

Aurelia laughed. "That's her way of telling you that your visit is the best part of our day." She smiled warmly at him. "Which is true."

A shadow passed over his face. "I'm glad I can cheer you up a little, but it's not making any real difference." He struck one hand against his own knee. "I wish I knew how to get around the restraining magic."

Aurelia just laughed again. "The only reason you think your presence isn't making a real difference is because you have no idea what it's like to be locked in a tower for seventeen years."

"She's right," Mama Gail chimed in from where she was tending to the plants. "You're a spectacle of which we won't soon tire."

That description drew the smile back to Amell's face.

"Even Cyfrin's visits are easier to take now," Aurelia said brightly. "With something to look forward to."

Amell's expression darkened again. "What's he up to? What does he do when he comes?"

Aurelia shrugged. "The same as normal. Puts power into me, moves it about a bit, talks about how great he is." She lifted a hand. "Not much to tell, really."

"So he came last night?" Amell pressed.

"Of course," said Aurelia, surprised. "Right on sunset, as always." She narrowed her eyes suspiciously at the prince. "Why?"

Amell stared at her for a moment, then said in a rush, "Because I hid in the grove in the hope of catching him when he passed."

"Amell!" Aurelia protested, aghast. "That's dangerous! You promised you wouldn't confront him!"

"No I didn't," Amell said quickly. "I never promised that. I just said I agreed that it would be wise to be cautious. Besides, I wasn't going to confront him. I was going to follow him, to see if I could find where he lives. Then surely I could find a way to alert the Enchanters' Guild to his location."

"That's actually not a bad idea," Mama Gail mused.

"I don't like it," said Aurelia anxiously. She wasn't entirely sure when Amell's safety had become a greater priority to her than getting out of the tower, but somehow it seemed to be so.

"Well, it doesn't matter," said Amell heavily. "Because I couldn't see any sign of him. He's obviously good at avoiding detection—he must be, to have been able to keep frequenting the area when the prison break first happened, without being seen by any of the search parties. Where does he spend his time when he's not here?"

"If we knew that, don't you think we would have told you before now?" Mama Gail asked dryly. "From what we can gather, he has a home not too far away. And he certainly must attend a market or something in order to get our food and other supplies. I don't think he works—from comments he's let drop, his family had money, and I suspect he's relying on that. Although, he clearly chose an area where he wasn't known, because he's never shown any hint of concern about being recognized."

Amell nodded slowly, his eyes passing to Aurelia. "To tell the truth," he admitted, "it's not the first time I've tried to catch sight of him, and always with the same result. I don't know if he's using some kind of cloaking magic, or if he's just using a different hidden entrance." He frowned. "This clearing seems to be very close to the edge of the prison's protected ring. His entrance into it must be outside the ring, or he'd get caught within it, and wouldn't be able to leave. Perhaps I should hide somewhere in the clearing. Then I could follow him as he leaves."

"No," said Mama Gail, to Aurelia's relief. "That *is* too dangerous. And not just for you. There's nowhere to properly hide in the clearing, and if he finds out about your visits, there will definitely be repercussions." Her eyes flicked to Aurelia.

"You're right," said Amell heavily. "The last thing I want to do is to endanger either of you." His eyes were troubled as they rested on Aurelia. "But I can hardly stand to do nothing."

"I've told you," she said firmly, "you're doing much more than nothing."

Amell still didn't seem satisfied, but Aurelia's life had never been happier. Another fortnight slipped by, and still the prince came every day. He'd made only a few trips back to the capital since they first met, each time visiting before he left, and returning in time to come the next day. Aurelia had devoured every book he'd brought her, not to mention the treats he always retrieved from the markets. He'd never repeated the flowers, however, and secretly she was a little disappointed.

But she couldn't really be sad, not when Amell's presence continued to brighten her days.

"Did you find what you wanted in those notes?" he asked her quietly one day, when Mama Gail had stepped into the bedroom, and they had a rare moment of privacy.

It took Aurelia a moment to figure out what he was talking about. She'd all but forgotten the foundational principles of power that she'd shoved under her mattress. She'd stopped trying to badger Mama Gail for an answer about what she'd read in Cyfrin's notes. The enchanter's plans didn't seem all that important anymore, somehow. Other matters occupied her mind so fully that she barely even minded his visits. They were so brief compared to Amell's.

Although, she reflected, distracted for a moment from Amell's question, she didn't like how caressing Cyfrin had become with her hair. It was nothing new for his fingers to tangle through it with uncomfortable boldness, but it had always been well down its length. Lately he'd begun placing his hand on the back of her scalp, as if he wanted to put magic into her hair right at the roots. She could still feel the sensation from the night before, and she suppressed a shudder. Pushing the thought aside, she returned her mind to Amell's question.

"I suppose so," she said with a shrug. "I don't really know what I was looking for, to be honest." Her gaze became a little anxious. "I hope it wasn't a lot of trouble for you to get them."

"Of course not," Amell told her, smiling in the way that made her stomach flutter. She'd noticed he never looked at Mama Gail like that, but he was doing so to her more and more often. "I'd be glad to do much more than that if it would help you, Honeysuckle. Even if it would just cheer you up."

She lowered her eyes, torn between delight at his words, and distaste at the sound of her foolish false name on his lips.

"You're so kind, Amell," she said, her voice a little constricted.

His fingers appeared from nowhere, their touch on her chin sudden and gentle. Obedient to their invitation, she raised her head again to find him watching her with eyes half serious, half warm.

"I'm really not as wonderful as you seem to think, Honeysuckle," he said. "It's you who radiates goodness. You're just the type of person who makes it impossible not to be kind."

"Cyfrin seems immune to that logic," Aurelia said, trying to smile naturally while her heart attempted to escape her chest. Amell's fingers were still on her chin, their contact sending shoots of warmth out into her whole body.

"Cyfrin is a monster," said Amell, his voice dark. "And he will be brought to justice for what he's done to you." His eyes dropped to hers again, and one side of his lips quirked up in a wry smile. "I can't take credit for your good opinion of me if he's the only comparison."

Aurelia searched his face, confused by what she saw there. His tone wasn't that of the light banter she was used to from him. He seemed genuinely troubled, and all at once she was overcome by a desperate desire for him to know how well she truly thought of him, how completely she trusted him.

"Honeysuckle isn't my real name," she blurted out. "It's the one Cyfrin gave me, and I hate it. When we're alone, Mama Gail calls me by the name I was born with."

Amell dropped his hand, surprise wiping away whatever he'd been wrestling with. She could see the curiosity in his eyes, but he didn't press, didn't try to force her confidence.

Aurelia took a deep breath, ready to trust him with her real self, but the sound of approaching feet drew both of their attention to the other side of the room, where Mama Gail was emerging.

"Here it is," she said, holding up a book Aurelia had hidden and then forgotten the location of. She stopped, looking between the two of them, and Aurelia realized they were standing too close. She took a step back, flushing guiltily.

"Thank you," said Amell, his voice impressively natural. "You've saved me from execution by librarian, which I've heard is not a nice way to go."

Aurelia gave a slightly hysterical giggle, and Mama Gail shook her head indulgently.

"I can't imagine even such a formidable figure as a librarian would dare to lay a finger on a prince."

"Probably not," Amell agreed cheerfully, stowing the book in his bag. "There have to be some perks to my position, to balance out all the dull responsibility."

"Hm." Mama Gail considered him, her voice coming out strangely careful. "I'm no expert on royal life, but I am a little surprised you're able to be here so often."

"I wouldn't normally have so much leisure," Amell assured her. "It's because of the prison break. When my father moved permanently back to Fernford a few weeks ago, I requested to be placed at the prison as his liaison while the crisis is still being managed. I'm able to act as his representative, but the truth is that the warden is very capable, and doesn't need much from me." He flashed a grin. "And he's much less likely than my mother to notice if I slip off when he's otherwise occupied."

Mama Gail shook her head again, but she was smiling, and Aurelia couldn't help laughing.

"Well, we're glad to have you close by," she said. "What's the latest on the escaped fugitives?"

Amell's expression sobered. "Nothing good, I'm afraid. A group of four were caught by the Listernians a few days ago, trying to cross the mountains. But that still leaves sixteen at large, and this morning we received some terrible news."

"What was it?" Aurelia demanded, alarmed.

"A murder was committed," he said gravely. "One of the escaped prisoners tracked down the man who reported his initial crime, and killed him for revenge."

Aurelia's hands shot up over her mouth. "That's terrible! What a horrible thing."

Amell nodded heavily. "And to make it worse, the murderer escaped. I'm actually going to be traveling back to the capital this afternoon, to discuss the development with my father. I may have to stay longer than normal, unfortunately. I don't know for certain what will be required of me."

"Of course," said Mama Gail quickly. "We understand. You do what you need to, and we'll be all right here."

"Of course," Aurelia echoed, without much enthusiasm. She scolded herself for her selfishness in not wanting to release Amell for such an important task. The safety of the citizens exposed to the escaped criminals was more important than her entertainment. So why did the prospect of a few days without Amell's company seem unendurable?

"I don't want to leave, either," Amell said quietly, his gaze much too knowing as it rested on Aurelia's face. "And I'll come back as soon as I can."

A delightful shiver went over Aurelia at the promise. "I'll be here," she joked. "Waiting."

CHAPTER FIFTEEN

Amell's thoughts weren't on the road as he urged his horse toward Fernford, the long-suffering Furn beside him. Truth be told, his thoughts weren't even on the terrible crime that had been committed, or the summons he had accordingly received.

As always, they were on the tower, and on Honeysuckle.

But no, not Honeysuckle. It wasn't a surprise to learn that Honeysuckle wasn't her real name. How could it be? But the fact that she had told him so made his heart swell. He knew the significance of Abigail keeping her real name secret, and he understood what a sign of trust it was for Hon—for *her* to decide to tell him the truth. Such a shame they'd been interrupted.

But what should he call her now? She'd said she hated the name Honeysuckle, and he was determined never to use it again. But he couldn't call her the girl in the tower anymore. Not now that he knew her. Perhaps when next he saw her she'd tell him her true name, he thought hopefully. And until then...he smiled as a sudden idea occurred to him. He'd think of her as Princess. Yes, that was fitting. Her origins might be humble, but she was absolutely the princess of his tale, no question. And perhaps one day...But he wouldn't get lost down that track, not yet.

"You seem happy, Your Highness," Furn commented, when they dropped to a walk to rest their horses.

Amell glanced up to see his guard watching him closely. "I shouldn't be, should I?" he asked lightly. "Terrible news about the murder."

"Indeed," Furn agreed gravely. He raised a questioning eyebrow. "Will we stay in the capital, do you think, Your Highness?"

Amell shook his head. "I'll return as soon as I'm released."

For a moment his guard was silent. "Your Highness," he said abruptly, "I know it's not my job to pry into your activities, only to keep you safe. But you've done me the honor to call me a friend."

"I do consider you a friend, Furn," Amell said, looking at his guard in surprise. "You're free to say anything to me."

"I'm concerned about you," Furn said simply. "I don't know where you go, or what you do there, but it has you distracted. And it's been going on for a month now."

Amell sighed. "You're absolutely within your rights to be concerned," he acknowledged. "And frustrated." He noted ruefully that Furn was unflatteringly taken aback by this concession. "If I could tell you, I promise I would. And I truly am not in danger." He could see his guard was still troubled. "If it makes you feel better, I've got Bartholomew assisting me with the...problem." The magic would allow him to be no more specific. "I intend to seek an update from him while we're in Fernford."

"Master Bartholomew?" Furn repeated, his expression lightening. "From the Enchanters' Guild? That does make me feel better, I admit."

A shadow passed overhead, and Amell glanced up. "Is it just me, or are there a lot more dragons about since the break out?"

"It's not just you," Furn said, his eyes fixed on the creature flying far above. He frowned. "That one looks old. Is that one of the dragons who visited the prison when your father was there?"

Amell studied the beast, receding into the distance. "I think it was," he said, surprised. "What were their names? Idric? And Tanin?" He frowned. "But they were elders, weren't they? Surprising that they're out in the human realm again so soon."

Furn nodded thoughtfully, following the dragon with his gaze.

They reached the capital with a couple hours to go before sunset, and Amell decided to pay a quick visit to Bartholomew on his way to the castle. After flicking a coin to a pair of nearby children only too eager to hold the well-trained royal horses, Amell strode into the guild's lobby, Furn close behind him.

The guard looked around with interest. "I've never been here before," he commented. "Impressive building, isn't it?"

Amell nodded vaguely. "Is Bartholomew in his study?" he asked the clerk. "No, that's all right, I know the way."

Leaving Furn to his observation, he hurried down the corridor and knocked at Bartholomew's door. He was halfway in before the enchanter had finished his reply.

"Prince Amell," Bartholomew smiled. "Please sit."

"Thank you," said Amell, doing so. "I don't have long, I'm afraid. I'm expected at the castle, but I was hoping you could give me an update on our project while I'm passing."

Bartholomew nodded. "Of course. I've been storing magic gradually since last we spoke, as much as I could spare given current events." He opened a drawer, and pulled out a simple ring. "I've settled on this as an appropriate vessel."

"Is it an artifact?" Amell demanded.

"It will be," the enchanter said calmly. "I've only just begun to weave magic into it, though. And it's still just a test. I'm perfecting the parameters, and I imagine it will go through several iterations before we can properly tell whether it will work."

Amell nodded. He would have liked things to move faster, but some progress was better than none.

"Keep me updated," he said, making as if to stand.

"You know," Bartholomew said, causing him to pause, "you said it was for you, but it occurred to me after we spoke that you shouldn't have any need of protection against restraining enchantments. Not unless you're leaving our borders."

"What do you mean?" Amell asked.

"Well, you're the heir to Fernedell's throne."

Amell blinked at the old man. "What does that have to do with anything?"

Bartholomew smiled. "Either your education was lacking, or your memory fails you. Remember that I told you that the magic we know isn't the strongest force in this world?"

Amell nodded.

"Well, then, that will give some context for our basic understanding that there is a more foundational type of magic on this land, which runs through your royal blood."

"I have magic?" Amell asked, startled.

The enchanter chuckled. "Not the type of magic you're thinking of. I'm afraid you'll never be a magic-user like me. But there is a certain magic that ties a ruler to his or her land, a power older and subtler and much harder to study than that of the dragons and the humans. As Fernedell's heir, you should have absolute capability to move freely around your own land. I don't believe our magic could stop that, even in its most potent form."

Amell stared blankly at him, and the enchanter clarified.

"Even a dragon couldn't cast an enchantment to keep you restrained within your own kingdom."

"Dragon's flame," muttered Amell, amazed. "I had no idea I had such a protection." It certainly made sense of his ability to enter and exit the tower, regardless of the enchantment that prevented anyone else from doing so. "Does that mean that the protective enchantments wealthy people have on their homes wouldn't keep me out if I chose to enter?"

"It does," assented Bartholomew. "Provided those homes are in Fernedell." He smiled. "So please don't abuse the knowledge. Just because you *can* do something, doesn't mean you *should*."

Amell's nod was vague. "I wasn't planning a career as a housebreaker," he said mildly. He ran a hand through his hair. It was one question answered, but it didn't help Abigail or Hon— Princess, since neither of them were rulers or future rulers of Fernedell.

Well, not by blood, anyway.

"Do you still want me to continue with the project?" Bartholomew asked, watching him carefully. "Even though you are unlikely to have need of it?"

"What?" Amell looked up, glad of the interruption to thoughts that had been heading into dangerous territory. "Yes, absolutely. If you don't mind."

"I don't mind, Your Highness," said Bartholomew. "It's a challenge, and I enjoy a challenge."

Amell nodded. "Thank you."

He made his way to the castle, hoping his father would be too distracted by the latest disaster to scold him for how late in the day he'd arrived. It was frustrating to not be able to tell his father where he'd spent the morning, but then again, he wasn't sure the king would be inclined to be more lenient if he'd known his son had come later than requested because he was visiting a beautiful girl of anonymous origin.

She certainly was beautiful, Amell reflected as he strode through the familiar halls. He'd thought so on first sight, and the impression had only increased since then. The sweetness in her eyes enhanced a naturally pleasant face, and she moved with incredible grace considering both her restricted environment and her absurdly impractical hair.

Furn had disappeared to his own home by the time Amell reached the wing of the castle where the royal suites were to be found. He changed quickly out of his traveling clothes, then hurried toward his father's study. He was halfway there when he caught up to his sister, clearly bound for the same destination.

"Tora," he said, smiling. He cast a wary glance around the corridor. "No overdressed lords in tow this time?"

"What?" Tora asked, looking confused. Her expression cleared. "Oh, that." She shook her head. "No, you were right. I was behaving embarrassingly, and I knew it at the time. Vapid flirting isn't for me. I won't be doing that again." She sighed. "I'll just have to find another way."

"Another way to what?" Amell demanded, completely at sea.

She sighed again. "I love you, Amell, but you're incredibly dense sometimes."

"Hey!" Amell protested, but she just linked her arm through his again.

"On your way to Father's study?"

"That's right," said Amell.

"Terrible about this murder, isn't it?" Tora asked quietly. "It's exactly the sort of thing we were all afraid of when the break out happened."

Amell gave her arm a squeeze, his eyes fixed reassuringly on hers. She was almost as tall as he was, so he didn't have to look down to do so. "We'll round them all up, Tora, don't worry."

"Well, it's starting to look like we might," she said. "Or haven't you heard?"

"Heard what?"

"Father received an anonymous letter just before lunch, regarding the location of escaped prisoners. He's sent three squadrons to three different locations. We're hoping to hear good news any minute."

"That's fantastic if the tips are legitimate," Amell said. "But why would someone report it anonymously? Isn't there a hefty reward offered?"

Tora nodded. "It's all very mysterious."

They'd reached their father's office by now, and Amell knocked quickly on the door.

"Enter."

One of the guards opened the door for the royal siblings, who hurried inside to find not only their father, but their mother seated before the enormous desk.

"Amell," the queen said, rising with a smile. "I'm glad to see you back. It feels like we hardly ever see you anymore."

"It has been a bit like that, hasn't it?" Amell responded cheerfully, bowing over her hand. His smile dimmed. "Wish I was here under better circumstances, though."

She sighed as she resumed her seat. "Don't we all."

"Are we absolutely certain an escaped prisoner was the murderer?" Amell asked his father, as soon as they'd exchanged greetings.

"As certain as we can be," the king said. "Witnesses described the man's unevenly cut hair, and the body showed signs of magical attack."

A shudder went over the queen, and Tora looked as troubled as Amell felt.

"The worst of it is that this particular prisoner has been spotted several times, but managed to elude the soldiers on each occasion," said the king. "He's obviously very skilled in evasion."

Amell groaned.

"I've been discussing the matter with my captain," the king went on. "And I'm inclined to follow his recommendation."

"Which is?" Amell pressed.

"To issue the order to kill any fugitives on sight," said the king, his voice heavy. "If that order had been in place when this prisoner was pursued the first time, the murder wouldn't have occurred."

Amell chewed on his lip, thinking. It was a grim situation to find themselves in, but he could certainly see his father's point.

"What do you think, Amell?"

"Me?" The question startled Amell so much, he froze, stilling his tapping foot. "You want my opinion?"

"Of course," said King Bern smoothly, as if he asked his son's advice on matters of state every day. "You're my liaison to the prison. You're the one closest to the whole situation."

Amell squirmed. He didn't feel close to the situation. Physically, he might be near the prison most of the time, but his mind was almost always far away. He brought it into line now, trying to consider the question dispassionately.

"I don't like the idea of hunting them down like animals," he said. "But letting innocent citizens be killed by them is even worse. It would be different if the whole prison was on the run. But the ones who escaped were all high security, and, from what the warden says, almost all violent offenders."

His father nodded slowly. "I see your thoughts align with mine," he said, sounding pleased.

Amell gave him a tentative smile. He was glad to bond with his father, but he wished it could be over something other than ordering citizens to be killed on sight, whatever crimes they'd committed.

"I'd like you to stick around Fernford for a few days," his father told him. "I'm going to send the warden some reinforcements along with the new order, and I'd like you to travel with them."

"Yes, Father," said Amell, his heart sinking a little.

His lateness meant that he'd missed the official briefing from the captain, but the king summarized it for all three members of his family. It was with sober steps that Tora and Amell left the study a short time later.

"Furn." Tora's greeting drew Amell's attention to a familiar figure standing respectfully halfway down the corridor.

"Furn, I didn't expect you," Amell said. "I thought you'd want the afternoon."

The guard bowed slightly. "I've been home and changed, Your Highness, and I'm ready to assist as needed."

"You're far too dedicated to your role, Furn," said Amell, who still hadn't quite forgiven the guard for being willing to die in his place a month before. "You should be resting while you have the chance."

Furn smiled. "Thank you, Your Highness, but I'm perfectly rested."

"I can see that," said Tora, her head tilted strangely. Amell stared at her, wondering whether she had something in her eye. "You look in excellent health, Furn. And that's a very nice color on you."

Furn swallowed visibly, shifting his feet in a way Amell knew denoted discomfort.

"Stop teasing him, Tora," he told his sister sternly. "You know he doesn't like being the center of attention the way you do."

"I wasn't teasing," she protested. "He really does look good."

"If you don't need me, Your Highness," Furn interjected in a slightly strangled voice, "I think I will return home after all."

"Yes, of course," Amell said. As soon as Furn was gone, he frowned at his sister. "What did I tell you?"

Tora scowled at him, but he could have sworn he saw a hint of moisture in her eyes as she turned away. Puzzled, he took a step after her, but was stopped by a voice from behind him.

"Amell, walk with me?"

He turned to see his mother leaving the king's study, her eyes fixed on her daughter's retreating back.

"Of course, Mother," said Amell, offering her his arm.

She took it with a smile. "What do you think about Tora, Amell?"

"Uh...I like her," said Amell blankly.

His mother sighed. "That's not what I meant."

"What did you mean?"

"I mean, what do you think about her marriage?"

"What marriage?" Amell demanded.

"Precisely," said the queen, in dark accents. "She's being particularly difficult about the matter. The two of you have always been as thick as thieves. I thought perhaps you could help talk sense into her."

"I don't think you should give me that role, Mother," Amell said. "To be frank, I'm with Tora. I don't see why she has to get married if she's not ready. I think making sure she marries someone who'll make the rest of her life better not worse is more important than the age at which she settles down."

"Of course you think that," scolded his mother lightly. "You're a man. And two years younger than she is. But Tora is a princess, Amell. People are starting to talk."

"I don't see why that should matter in the least," said Amell staunchly. He hesitated, casting a glance at his mother's profile. "I know Father thinks I'm too young to think about marriage, Mother. But you said you thought it might steady me, didn't you?"

"If you married the right girl, absolutely," she said, looking up at him keenly. "Are you gaining interest in the idea?"

"Maybe," Amell said, fidgeting slightly. "I mean...what would you think if I wanted to settle down?"

"To be frank," the queen answered, borrowing his own words, "that would depend entirely on the girl."

"Her personality?" Amell asked hopefully.

She gave him a look. "Certainly. And her connections."

Amell sighed. He'd been afraid of that. "You have your heart set on a princess for me, don't you?"

"Not necessarily," his mother smiled. "But someone from the right circles, Amell. These things matter."

Amell was silent. He remembered his mother's words about it being unfortunate for Albury that their queen was a commoner, raised with no knowledge of court matters whatsoever. He didn't like to think what her opinion would be of a future queen for Fernedell who was not only common, but had been raised in an isolated tower. He could call her whatever nickname he liked in his head, but it didn't change who she was. Amell's lips twitched as he remembered Princess declaring defensively that she'd seen a rainbow, so she knew what colors there were in the world. Or telling him that she'd once seen a bee. Or commenting casually, and completely without guile, that she found him handsome.

He sighed. "Well, it's a moot point anyway."

"What is?" the queen demanded.

"Nothing," said Amell hastily. "I'll see you at dinner, Mother."

He took his leave, his thoughts still on the ineligible girl in the tower. It didn't matter what his mother thought, he reminded himself. Because *her* mother had made his position very clear. He could recall perfectly the uncompromising words Abigail had said to him in Cyfrin's study, the second time he'd met her. She'd reminded him, somewhat forcefully, that her daughter had seen nothing of the world, and knew no one but herself and the evil enchanter. She was bound to be taken with any personable young man, and she was in no position to judge her own heart.

Amell had seen the truth of Abigail's words, and he'd sheepishly acknowledged that bringing flowers for Honeysuckle—as he'd then known her—was a little too lover-like to be appropriate. He hadn't done so since, and he'd tried to be circumspect in all his interactions with her, not leading her on, or encouraging her to think of him romantically.

He hoped his restraint was benefiting her in some way, because it had done nothing to stop his own headlong descent. He hadn't lived his life in total isolation. On the contrary, he'd been chased and courted by every girl in Fernedell's court, and he had no reason to doubt his own heart. He knew he'd fallen hard for his Princess, and who could blame him? She was the kind of girl any man might dream of, but she was real, and fascinating, and unashamedly full of admiration for him.

He groaned aloud as he hurried toward his suite. He knew he didn't deserve her admiration—she thought him wise and reliable, of all things! He'd joked that his sister would warn Princess against giving him a big head, but the truth was that her high opinion of him did the opposite. He'd never been more aware of his shortcomings, of how unworthy he was of such a pure-hearted woman.

And yet, he argued with himself, surely he was better than Cyfrin. When he'd dared to make such a hint to Abigail in the study, she'd gone pale, and taken a moment to reply.

"I won't let that happen," she'd said through gritted teeth. "Not while I'm alive."

"Neither will I," Amell had promised.

She'd nodded firmly, but her gaze had become no less piercing. "I'm determined she'll be free one day. And when that day comes, I want her to be free in every way, to have the opportunity to discover her options."

Amell had nodded, chastened. The older woman was right. But surely it wasn't wrong of him to hope that when that day came, he might have as good a chance as anyone.

As sorry as he was to be away from the tower, he enjoyed spending a night in his own bed. The soldiers were no longer camped at the prison, so he'd been accommodated in the guards' quarters. It was comfortable enough, but nothing compared to his own luxurious rooms.

He rose early the next morning, hoping he might be given leave to return to the prison sooner than expected. Furn had obviously risen even earlier, because he was already in the training yard when Amell arrived, looking to spar. His time at the prison had interfered with his usual training, and he was getting out of practice.

"Good morning, Your Highness," said Furn cheerfully, showing no hint of the discomfort that had sent him running home the evening before. "Care for a bout?"

"You took the words out of my mouth," Amell smiled, already stripping off his tunic.

They sparred for a solid hour, at the end of which time both men were spent enough to be ready to call it a morning and seek out breakfast. They were still toweling their faces, however, when a cheerful voice hailed them.

"Amell, Furn, what good luck to find you here."

"Hello Tora," said Amell, looking at his sister in some surprise. "Don't let Mother catch you near the training yard."

"I never let Mother catch me," said Tora comfortably. Her eyes flicked to Furn, whom Amell noticed had hastily slid his tunic back on. "Furn," the princess said pleasantly, "I was wondering if you could help me."

"Help you, Your Highness?" Furn asked, his eyes slightly

narrowed. Clearly he also found her innocent air suspicious. Amell's gaze traveled to the bow clutched in his sister's hand, his confusion growing.

"Yes, I'm determined to improve my archery. It's the only kind of fighting princesses are allowed to learn, apparently, and I'm quite out of my depth." She smiled serenely at the guard. "I've heard you're an excellent archer, and I thought perhaps you could show me how."

"Oh," said Furn, looking momentarily flummoxed. "That's... that's very kind of you to say, Your Highness. But I'm not much above average with a bow, to be perfectly honest."

"Nonsense," she said brightly. "I've heard excellent things. And you must be a very patient teacher if you can put up with Amell."

The guard's lips twitched as if in spite of himself, and he seemed to hesitate.

"The archery yard isn't in use by the guards at present," Tora pressed, raising her bow and pulling back a hand in imitation of releasing an arrow. "We could practice for a quarter of an hour before breakfast."

"I can give you a refresher, Tora," Amell offered helpfully. "Last I saw, you weren't at all bad. But if you want to go over some pointers, I'd be happy to help." He stepped up to his sister, pointing at her hand. "First off, your grip isn't quite right." He yanked her hand up to the level of her eyes, then leaned down to elbow her hip into place. "And your hips should be angled this way, not—"

"Amell," she hissed in his ear, so quietly he doubted Furn could even hear, "if you don't butt out, I will stab you with an arrow."

"But," protested Amell, straightening, "I thought you said you wanted—"

"Prince Amell is right, Your Highness," Furn cut in, his

expression a little strange. "He'd be a better choice to teach you. His marksmanship is at least as good as mine."

With a bow, the guard took off, striding away down the corridor with more haste than dignity.

"Amell!" Tora burst out, the moment the guard was out of earshot.

"What?" Amell asked, totally perplexed. "What did I do?"

"Ruined everything, that's what," she told him. A glance around the training yard seemed to remind her that several guards were watching them with interest. Dropping the bow onto a bench with so much force it clattered to the ground, she powered toward the door.

"I was helping," Amell protested, pulling on his tunic as he followed her. "I don't understand what the fuss is about. And why do you need practice in archery? You're almost as good as I am."

"I'm better," Tora snapped. "Always have been."

"Then why—?"

Tora raised her hands before her face, balled them tightly, and took a deep breath. Releasing both the air and the fists, she turned a long-suffering look on her brother.

"Sometimes I find it hard to believe you can really be so completely oblivious, Amell."

"Oblivious to what?" Amell demanded.

"You keep him away constantly," his sister ranted on, "barely showing your faces in the city, and whenever you are back, you mess up my every attempt to—"

"Him?" Amell repeated, wondering which of them had gone mad. "This is about Furn?"

"Yes, it's about Furn," Tora groaned. "Obviously it's about Furn."

"But..."

Tora's strange posture from the evening before flashed

through Amell's mind, when she'd tilted her head. Suddenly he realized why he'd noticed it. It had almost looked like she was trying to look up at Furn through her lashes, the way many girls had done so pointedly to Amell, and the way Princess did with total artlessness. Only it didn't really work in Tora's case, given she was about as tall as the man in question.

"Tora," he said, a feeling of horror creeping over him. He glanced around at the bustling corridor and lowered his voice. "Tora, are you in love with Furn?"

"Of course I'm in love with Furn, you dolt," Tora said calmly, without the slightest hint of embarrassment. "I have been for years. And I think—I really think—he likes me too. Maybe he's not as deep as I am, but sometimes he looks at me like...well, never mind that."

"I do mind," said Amell, reeling from this revelation. "He looks at you like what?"

"Like I'm the one he wants to protect, not you," Tora shot at him.

Amell blinked, processing this. "He was certainly very jumpy about your safety the time you came to the prison with us." He frowned. "But Tora, you can't steal my guard and best friend away from me. He's off limits!"

"Don't I know it," Tora grumbled. "You think you'd be enough to scare me off, when I have Mother to contend with?"

A slow grin spread across Amell's face. "Not quite a prince, is he? But how dare Mother think some stranger would be better than our Furn? He's the best man alive! Dragon's flame, it would almost be worth losing him to have him join the family. Not to mention you'd be able to stay in Fernford instead of being married off to one of the Mistran princes."

"Thank you for your unwavering and unselfish support," Tora said dryly.

Amell ignored her, thinking over her bizarre behavior the

last month or so. "If you've been in love with him for years, why have you started acting like a lunatic all of a sudden?"

Tora made no attempt to argue his choice of words. "Because things are getting desperate. Mother's become obsessed with marrying me off, and if I can't get Furn to admit his feelings to himself soon, it will be too late."

"Hm." Amell frowned, thinking of his mother's words the evening before. "You might be right there." He felt a rush of sympathy for his sister. The state of his own heart made it easier for him to understand why Tora might go to such ridiculous lengths in an attempt to win the man she was in love with.

"But nothing I've tried has worked," Tora said despairingly. She lifted her hands, counting on her fingers. "I tried getting myself into danger so he'd have to heroically rescue me. But even at the site of a violent prison break, I couldn't find a sniff of real danger!"

Amell nodded sagely. "It's maddening how difficult danger is to come by when you really need it," he agreed.

"I tried flirting with someone else to make him jealous," Tora went on. "I tried paying him overt compliments on his appearance." Her voice turned dry. "If Lord Fancypants is anything to go by, that's what men like. And just now I tried pretending feigning helplessness so he could show me how to do something. And I think it was actually working until you elbowed your way in!"

She glared at him, rubbing her hip as if in memory of when he had literally elbowed her.

"Sorry about that," said Amell, unable to help grinning again. "Want me to put in a good word, make up for it?"

"Don't you dare!" Tora gasped. "You will absolutely and unequivocally make things worse if you try to talk to him about it."

Amell raised his hands in surrender. "All right, all right, I'll keep your secret. But all of those ideas you just listed were stupid. Why don't you try being yourself? Seems to me you're the kind of girl Furn would like without any playacting."

"You mean too tall, lacking in curves, and with unflatteringly large teeth?"

Amell blinked. He could see the truth of all those descriptions, if he was being brutally honest. But he'd never thought of his sister as unattractive, and he'd had no idea she was dissatisfied with her own appearance.

"No, that's not what I meant," he said carefully.

Tora sighed. "I've tried being myself, Amell. I've been doing that for twenty years. The point isn't whether he likes me. If he doesn't, he doesn't, and I'm not foolish enough to think any silly stunts will change that. The point is how to get him to admit it if he does."

"Well, I don't know what to suggest," Amell said apologetically.

"I know you don't," Tora assured him. "I wasn't expecting you to solve my problems." She sent him a sisterly glare. "Just stop getting in the way."

And with that, she tripped lightly away, leaving Amell blinking after her, unsure whether to feel sorry for her or for Furn.

CHAPTER SIXTEEN

Aurelia screwed up her face in distaste, wishing Cyfrin would hurry up. He had his hand on her scalp again, and it made her skin crawl.

"Why are you flinching away from me?" the enchanter demanded. "I'm being gentle."

"It's taking a long time tonight," Aurelia said by way of answer. "Haven't you moved all the magic from my hair to my core yet?"

He gave a patronizing laugh. "Honeysuckle, you foolish child. I've moved less than half. And I'm not going to move it all. I prefer not to have all my eggs in the one basket, just in case." She couldn't see his face, but she could hear the smugness in his voice. "Not that I anticipate any hitches. You just need a little more time."

"Aurelia," said Mama Gail sharply. The older woman was hovering nearby, glaring not at her daughter but at the enchanter. "Do you think you could fetch a brush from the room? I think I left it near the bed. Your hair needs neatening after all this carry on."

Aurelia frowned. "But—" She encountered a look that made

her decide it wasn't worth arguing. It wasn't as though she was sorry for the excuse to pull away from Cyfrin.

"I'm not finished yet," the enchanter complained, as Aurelia moved away from him, her hair trailing behind her as she crossed the tower toward the bedroom.

"That can wait," Mama Gail snapped, her voice so quiet Aurelia could barely hear it from the bedroom. She could see no sign of the brush on her mother's bed, so she got down on her hands and knees, searching underneath. Still nothing.

She could hear her mother's low, angry voice from the other room, and sighed. Mama Gail had gone a surprisingly long time without ranting at the enchanter. But it had always been only a matter of time. Perhaps her mood had been bolstered by Amell's visits, the same as Aurelia's had. For a moment Aurelia forgot what she was looking for, her thoughts drifting to the prince. It had been three days since they'd seen him, and it felt like an eternity.

She finally hunted the brush down in a drawer next to her own bed. Clutching it, she moved back toward the main room, pausing in the shadows next to the doorway at the sound of her mother's words.

"—and I tell you, it's gone far enough, Cyfrin. Too far."

"On the contrary," said the enchanter coldly. "I've barely begun the process."

Aurelia frowned. What process? Was he talking about transferring the magic into her core?

"Are you really stupid enough to think you can convince her to willingly—"

"Why should she not wish to?" he retorted. "It would be an excellent thing for her."

"Over my dead body," Mama Gail burst out, her voice quiet but passionate. "Do you understand? Over my dead body will you—"

"What an apt choice of words." The enchanter's voice was as smooth as glass. "You wondered how I would convince her if it came to that—you have your answer. I think a threat to the life of her dear *Mama Gail* would be enough, don't you?"

Aurelia froze in horror at the cold words, but Mama Gail just let out a harsh laugh. "I thought it had to be her choice."

"Did I say that?" drawled the enchanter. "I don't think so. Certainly an easier process is preferable, but her choice is still her choice, however we arrive there."

Aurelia frowned, thinking of the principle stuffed under her mattress. *Power willingly given is more potent than power forcibly taken.* She had no doubt that coercing her with a threat to a loved one's life would count as forcibly taking. But it was also easy to believe that Cyfrin wouldn't be convinced of that. He'd always had the attitude that whatever he wanted was his by right.

For a moment panic clouded Aurelia's mind. She'd been so sure she'd never perform whatever action Cyfrin chose as the key, and thereby give him extra potent magic. But if the alternative was letting him kill Mama Gail, how could she refuse?

She took a deep breath. She wouldn't give in to despair. She had a choice. Whether Cyfrin truly believed that or not, she did, and that would have to be enough. She wasn't alone. She had Mama Gail to help her, and Amell. They would find a way.

"So I'm sure you don't need me to tell you," Cyfrin was saying in a tone of finality, "that it would be in your own interest to encourage her in that direction."

"Here it is," Aurelia interrupted brightly, emerging from the bedroom with the brush held aloft. Her gaze passed to Cyfrin. "Can't we stop for tonight?"

"Very well," snapped the enchanter. His eyes dwelled nastily on Mama Gail. "I think we all have enough to think about."

Neither woman answered him, and within record time,

Aurelia had lowered him to the ground below. "Good riddance," she muttered, as he made his way across the clearing. She turned back to her mother. "Are you going to tell me what you chivvied me out of the room to talk about?"

"I'd rather not," said her mother, smiling faintly in acknowledgment that Aurelia had seen through her.

"Suit yourself," said her daughter lightly. "I'll start on dinner, shall I?"

Mama Gail nodded, and Aurelia busied herself with the supplies Cyfrin had brought. The enchanter was right about one thing. They all had plenty to think about. Aurelia realized how foolish she'd been to let her enjoyment of Amell's company dull her sense of urgency regarding Cyfrin's plans. Her thoughts flew out the window and away to the south east, toward Fernford.

"Hurry back, Amell," she whispered. "We might need your help sooner than I thought."

Aurelia woke before dawn the next morning, an unusual occurrence for her. She'd slept uneasily, hearing her mother toss and turn in the bed beside hers all through the night. It was a relief to see that the other woman was sleeping deeply now. She needed it.

Moving silently, Aurelia dressed and slipped out to the main room. She stoked the fire, fishing the exotic tea leaves Amell had brought from their hiding place. Something hot would help dispel the chill of the pre-dawn air.

There was still no sound from her mother when the sun began to peek over the top of the trees, but a soft voice from the clearing below sent Aurelia running to the window, her heart swelling.

"Amell," she gasped, quietly enough to make him look questioningly at her. She smiled. "My mother is still sleeping," she called softly. "I don't want to wake her before she's ready." She paused. "It was a bit of a rough night."

Looking concerned, Amell nodded. He moved more slowly than usual as he climbed, clearly trying to be quiet. He'd barely set his feet on the stone floor of the tower when he gripped her shoulders, his eyes boring into hers.

"What happened last night?" he asked, his voice quiet but intense. "Are you all right? Did Cyfrin do something?"

"We're both fine," Aurelia assured him, matching his volume. "She just had an argument with him, and she was lying awake worrying, if I know her." She smiled. "I didn't know if you'd come today. I certainly didn't expect you so early."

He smiled back, but the expression was strained. "I arrived at the prison last night, and I couldn't wait this morning. I left while it was still dark. What was the argument about?"

Aurelia sighed, turning back to the kettle, which had begun to boil. "She sent me out of the room, but I overheard the second half of it. I think they were arguing about the key, whatever it is. She said I'd play my part over her dead body, and he basically told her that was his plan."

"What?" Alarm radiated from Amell, his eyes searching hers more frantically than ever.

"He meant he was willing to threaten her life in order to coerce me if it comes to that." She chewed thoughtfully on her lip. "I can't deny it has me feeling anxious, Amell. How will I fight back against that? I don't want to help him, but I can't let him kill her."

"Of course we won't let him kill her," Amell said forcefully. "And we won't let him have your help, either." His voice darkened. "Or anything else he thinks he can take from you."

Aurelia smiled blissfully up at him, his use of the word *we* lightening her heart more than she could say. She'd known she wasn't alone. She'd known he'd never abandon her.

"My name is Aurelia," she said simply, and felt a weight lift from her shoulders. It was indescribably wonderful to be known.

"Aurelia," Amell breathed, his eyes lighting up like the fireflies she'd seen dancing across the clearing. "It suits you."

"You think so?" she asked, pleased.

He nodded, still looking at her with something close to reverence. "It's the most beautiful name I've ever heard." Hesitantly, he lifted a hand and tucked a strand of hair behind her ear. "Like you."

Aurelia felt her face flush with pleasure. "You think I'm beautiful?"

Her question surprised a laugh out of Amell. "I suppose you'd have no way of knowing, would you?" he mused. "Well, let me tell you, Aurelia," the name dropped deliciously from his lips, "I've been chased by half the girls in the kingdom, and I can assure you that you are breathtakingly beautiful."

A thrill of pure delight went over Aurelia at the words, and she found herself reaching tentatively for him. Shivering at her own daring, she placed a hand on his chest, feeling the thickness of the embroidered fabric, and the way his muscles tensed under her touch. This man came with so many sensations, she reflected. So many sights, and sounds, and smells, and textures. So many things that had been missing from her restricted life.

"Aurelia," he whispered, and she raised her eyes to his.

"Yes?"

He hesitated, their eyes locked in intense but wordless communication. "I'm not as wonderful as you seem to think I am."

"Of course you're wonderful," Aurelia said calmly. "I don't understand why you can't see it as clearly as I do." She tilted her head to the side. "But I'm getting the sense that it's often hard for people to judge that about themselves." Her smile was warm as her eyes lingered on his face. "You'll just have to take my word for it."

"Aurelia, I'm not...I'm not supposed to..." He swallowed.

"Not supposed to what?" Aurelia prompted. "Not supposed to kiss me?"

His breath caught audibly, and his eyes dropped to her lips. She waited hopefully, but the moment stretched out, long enough that she began to feel embarrassed.

"I'm sorry," she said, lowering her gaze, but not quite able to bring herself to remove her hand from his chest. "I see I made a mistake. I thought you felt the same way I do."

Suddenly Amell's hand was on her chin, and she found her face being gently raised to his.

"I do," he assured her, the earnestness that she loved back in his eyes. "I do feel the same way. I just...I know I shouldn't assume...I shouldn't take advantage of the fact that—"

His rambles remained unfinished. Aurelia had heard enough, and once again gathering her courage, she pushed herself onto her toes and pressed her lips against his.

Two things happened at once. The first was that Amell's arms wove instantly around her, and he pulled her gently against him as his lips responded to hers. It was magical, and toe-tingling, and more incredible than Aurelia could possibly have imagined. She could almost hear her heart singing as Amell held her, and she knew herself to be loved back by the man who'd claimed her heart.

The second thing was less pleasant. As their lips connected, Aurelia became aware of a strange draining sensation that seemed to originate in her midriff. At first she ignored it, too lost in the sensations exploding from the point where Amell's lips met hers. But all too quickly, the feeling spread, until a heavy weakness had settled over her whole body.

She pulled back with a small groan, sagging in Amell's arms.

"Aurelia?" he asked, alarm clear in his voice. "Are you all right? What's happening?"

"I'm not sure," she admitted, lifting a hand to her forehead. "That storybook Cyfrin brought me once had a girl who went weak at the knees when she was kissed. Maybe this is what that feels like."

Amell's eyes searched hers in growing concern, clearly finding no humor in her joking words. "You look pale," he said. "We'd better wake your mother."

With an effort, Aurelia shook off the fogginess clouding her mind. She straightened, shaking her head. "No, I'm fine," she said. "I think I just got overwhelmed by the new experience." She smiled shyly up at him. "The very nice new experience."

He still looked a little worried, but he smiled at her as well. "Aurelia," he said. "That was...you're...I've never in all my life met anyone so..."

"I don't think your lips are at their best when they're talking," she informed him solemnly, grasping hold of his shoulder and pulling him back toward her.

He needed no further encouragement, and a moment later she was back in his arms, one of his hands gently cupping her cheek, and the other flat against her back. Aurelia still felt strangely weak and foggy, but she was encouraged that the draining sensation didn't happen again. She was ready to abandon herself to Amell's kiss when his hand traveled, apparently unconsciously, up from her back to tangle into her hair.

The moment his fingers spread across her scalp, a feeling of repulsion raced over her, and she pulled back with an involuntary gasp.

"Don't touch my hair," she cried, pulling it out of his reach.

Amell looked as horrified as if she'd slapped him, and she felt instantly repentant.

"I'm so sorry," he said, clearly aghast. "I didn't mean to... please forgive me. I should never have—"

"It's all right," Aurelia told him shakily, the weakness rushing back now that her mind was no longer distracted. "I shouldn't have snapped at you like that. It isn't your fault. You didn't do anything wrong. I suddenly just—"

Just what? What exactly had happened in her mind when he'd touched her scalp? Some horrible realization had exploded across her consciousness, but she couldn't grasp it, couldn't articulate it.

"It's not you," she assured him, her voice coming out distressingly faint. "I don't know exactly what's happening, but I promise it's not you."

Without warning, she slumped against him, and he caught her, his fear palpable.

"Aurelia? Aurelia, what's wrong?"

She couldn't find the energy to answer him, but inwardly she marveled at the strength of his arms. They quivered with tension, seeming even more full of energy than usual.

"Abigail!" Amell shouted, so loudly Aurelia started in his arms. "Abigail, we need your help!"

With a grunt and a crash, the familiar figure of Aurelia's mother appeared in the bedroom doorway.

"What is it?" she asked, clearly struggling to pull her mind from sleep to wakefulness. "Prince Amell? What are you doing here? What happened?"

"I...I..." The prince seemed to be struggling to find words.

Aurelia tried to pull herself together and come to his rescue. "I'm fine, Mama Gail. I'm not entirely sure what happened, but all of a sudden I just became so incredibly tired." She sagged slightly as she said it, and Amell's grip on her tightened.

"Lower her into a chair," Mama Gail commanded, sounding more like her usual self. "Let me look at her."

Aurelia felt herself placed gently into a chair, and she blinked at the fuzzy sight of her mother's face peering carefully into her eyes.

"Do you feel sick?" Mama Gail demanded.

She shook her head.

"Is your vision going black?"

Aurelia blinked, considering the point. "No," she said. "It's a little fuzzy, but not going black." She blinked again. In fact, now that she was sitting, her vision was clearing. She still felt unaccountably weary, but not as though she was deteriorating further.

Mama Gail let out a relieved breath, although her face was still lined with tension. She rounded on Amell. "What did you do?"

"Mama Gail," Aurelia protested.

The prince swallowed. "I…"

"You kissed her, didn't you?" Mama Gail accused.

"Actually," Aurelia interjected with dignity. "I kissed him."

Mama Gail groaned, actually covering her face in her hands. "We talked about this," she said, her voice coming out muffled.

Aurelia stared at her in confusion. She didn't remember talking about anything of the kind. But apparently her mother wasn't speaking to her.

"I know," Amell said, sounding guilty. "I'm sorry. I never meant to…I just…"

"Hang on," Aurelia protested. With a flash of spirit, she struggled up straighter in her chair. "What do you mean, you talked about it?"

"Aurelia," Mama Gail said, ignoring both her question and her false name, "did you start feeling weak when you kissed Amell?"

Flushing furiously, Aurelia nodded. "But only...only the first time," she said.

Mama Gail raised an ominous eyebrow but didn't comment on the information that there had been more than one kiss.

"He must have used the kiss as the key," she said, so quietly Aurelia questioned her own hearing.

"What?" It was Amell who gave voice to her confusion. Although his voice had a definite edge of anger as well. "What did you say? What do you mean he used the kiss as the key?"

Mama Gail looked between them. "It was one of the options he considered, judging by his notes. He was looking for ways to increase the power, remember? One of the principles is that power willingly given is stronger than power forcibly taken, which seems to have given him the idea of the key. Another principle is that—"

"Love is stronger than any destructive force," Aurelia whispered, horror washing over her as she began to grasp what her mother was saying. Love? As in, romantic love? With *Cyfrin*?

"How did you—?" Mama Gail shook her head. "Never mind. Yes, precisely that. I believe he'd already formed the intention of marrying you, for other reasons. But from his notes, I got the impression that he'd fixated on your first kiss as a good option for the key, because it would ignite both the principle about power willingly given, and the principle about love being strongest. Alongside it he'd scribbled out some old wives' tale regarding first kisses carrying magic. I think he was trying to cover as many bases as possible."

"He's planning to marry me?" Aurelia repeated, horrified. "He thought he could get me to willingly kiss him?" She pictured it, unable to help herself, and a shudder of pure revulsion ran over her. "How could he ever think I could be brought to love him, after what he's done?"

A vivid memory gripped her, of the horror she'd felt when

Amell's fingers brushed her scalp. Forgetting her weakness, she leaped to her feet, then swayed so violently her mother had to help her sit again. Suddenly she understood her unconscious reaction. Some part of her had recognized in Amell's caress—one motivated by genuine tenderness—the type of touch Cyfrin had been trying so unsuccessfully to mimic.

"That's what he was doing all this time?" she gasped. "With the attempts to be nice, and giving me that physical key, and..." She shuddered again. "And caressing my hair? He was trying to...to woo me?"

She looked between her mother and Amell, noting that the prince looked no more surprised than Mama Gail at this information.

"You knew?" she whispered.

"I guessed." His eyes were hard. "It was bound to occur to him sooner or later. But believe me, I would kill him myself before I let him take advantage of you like that."

"But I would never have willingly agreed," Aurelia said, aghast. "Never." The truth suddenly dawned on her, and she stared in horror at her mother. "But he's willing to coerce me, by threatening you."

"How do you know that?" Mama Gail demanded.

"I eavesdropped on your argument last night," said Aurelia impatiently. "Did you really think you could have a private conversation in this place?"

Her mother grunted. "Well, I don't think he really expects it to come to that," she said. "He's clearly confident he can convince you." She glanced at Amell. "Of course he never dreamed of a rival."

"Wait."

Aurelia turned to see Amell looking at her with an expression of dawning horror.

"If Cyfrin really did make Aurelia's first kiss the key, then..."

"Then she's just unlocked all the magic he's stored in her core," Mama Gail finished. "And, unless I'm mistaken, given it to you."

Aurelia's mouth fell open. That was what she'd felt draining from her when she kissed Amell. That must also be why he seemed to have double even his usual energy.

"But that could kill her!" Amell cried, his panic visibly rising. "Is that what's happening?" He clutched at his chest, as if he could physically rip the power out of himself. "How do I give it back to her? What's the key now?"

"There is no key," said Mama Gail, sounding exasperated. "Aurelia couldn't exactly build one in when she unconsciously gave you the power, could she?"

"So what do I do?"

His terror tugged at Aurelia's heart, but she was too exhausted to reassure him.

"Get her out of here," Mama Gail said grimly. "Before Cyfrin comes tonight. Because there's no way he'll fail to notice that half his magic is missing."

"Bartholomew's artifact to counteract the restraining magic," gasped Amell. "He was working on a test version. Maybe it will be enough."

"Go," Mama Gail said. "It can't be much past seven. If you ride straight to Fernford and straight back, you should be here well before sunset."

Amell was halfway to the window before Aurelia's thoughts caught up. "Wait!" she cried. "Don't leave."

He was back at her side in an instant. "I'll be back as soon as humanly possible, my darling," he whispered, and the endearment sent a thrill coursing through her.

"Promise?" she whispered, grabbing his arm.

"I promise." He lifted her hand, just like the hero in her

storybook, and pressed his lips to it with the intensity of all his suppressed energy.

Then he was gone.

Aurelia sank back against the chair, closing her eyes in exhaustion. It took her a full minute to realize what was missing. "How did he get down?" she demanded, opening her eyes.

"He climbed down the wall," Mama Gail said, from where she stood at the window, peering down. "He sort of fell the last several feet, but he doesn't seem to have been injured."

"Goodness," said Aurelia mildly. "He was in a hurry."

Mama Gail crossed to her side, lifting Aurelia's hand and pressing it between both of her own. "I think perhaps he cares about you," she said softly.

A smile flitted across Aurelia's face. "What gave you that impression?"

"The fact that he didn't show even a moment of interest at the news that he might have just acquired an excessive amount of power," said Mama Gail simply. "He just wanted to get it back into you so you would be safe."

"Does that mean you've forgiven him for being handsome?" Aurelia quipped.

There was no answering laugh. Mama Gail's expression was tense, strained. "I was afraid of this," she muttered. "I was afraid the prince would complicate everything."

"Things would have been much less complicated," Aurelia told her frankly, "if you'd just been honest with me. If I'd known there was a possibility the key was my first kiss, this wouldn't have happened."

Mama Gail rocked back on her heels, anguish crossing her face. "I know," she whispered. "You're right, of course you are. But...you've always been so beautifully innocent, Aurelia. As hard as your life has been, you've been wonderfully unaware of the depths of depravity some people can sink to. Can you understand why I didn't want to tell you that...that..."

"That Cyfrin was going to try to seduce me," Aurelia said flatly. Her mind flew to the enchanter. She felt something within her curl in on itself at the thought that the man who had figured all her childhood as some kind of evil version of a parent wanted to entangle her romantically. "Of course I can understand why you didn't want to tell me," she told Mama Gail. "But you should have overcome your reluctance. How long have you known what he was up to?"

"I've been afraid of it for years," Mama Gail admitted. "You don't realize this, darling, but you're uncommonly beautiful." Aurelia flushed a little, but said nothing. "That became clear three or four years ago," her mother went on, "and I started watching Cyfrin for the moment it would occur to him that he might gain in more than one way if he forced you to marry him. That moment didn't come until several months back. When he brought you that storybook with the soppy love stories, I was worried."

"That's why you threw it out," Aurelia realized.

Mama Gail nodded. "I knew he was up to no good. When has he ever brought you something just because he thought you might like it? He was beginning to plant seeds. And then a couple of months ago he started wanting to speak with you alone, and talking as though he thought you welcomed his company, and I felt like my worst fears were coming true. And trapped in here as we are, I had no way to protect you."

"I used to be so afraid of him," Aurelia mused. "Perhaps you were right that knowing the truth would have paralyzed me a few months ago." She met her mother's eyes. "But I think you should have seen more recently that I was ready to know everything."

Her mother's eyes were filling with tears, but she made no

attempt to deny it. "I should have," she agreed. "Being a parent is harder than you know, Aurelia. I have no rulebook for how to do this." She reached out and touched her daughter's cheek gently. "You're growing up before my eyes, and it's hard to remember that you're not the child who sheltered behind me every evening. Sometimes I wish you could stay innocent and unaware forever." She pulled her hand back, wiping an arm across her eyes. "But it's only now dawning on me that such a desire is tantamount to wishing you could stay locked in this tower forever. And you know I don't wish that."

"Of course I do," Aurelia assured her. "And I know it's been hard on you. Part of the reason I wish you'd confided in me is because maybe it would have been easier together."

"Your generous spirit doesn't come from me," her mother said, halfway between laughing and crying.

But Aurelia was still caught on something she'd said earlier. "What did you mean Cyfrin would benefit in more ways than one if he married me?"

Mama Gail's face sobered, and she let out a long breath. "I mean that allying himself with you could gain him a great deal of influence and credibility."

"What?" Aurelia demanded. "Why?"

"Because of the identity of the parents who brought you into the world."

"And who—"

"King Justus and Queen Racquel of Albury," Mama Gail cut her off. "The kingdom might believe you dead, but you are still Albury's princess, Aurelia."

The world seemed to spin around Aurelia as she tried to grasp this fresh revelation. She was a princess? Her parents had been the king and queen? So many tiny pieces fell into place. No wonder Mama Gail had been able to find news of her parents' deaths in Cyfrin's news book!

She remembered the conversation between Mama Gail and Amell about Albury's royals, their reputation for coldness, and a shiver went over her. That was the family from which she came? Amell had said the new king was supposed to be kinder than his father. That was Justin, her brother.

Amell. What would he think of all this? Dimly, she grasped that her identity might change everything between them, hopefully for the better. But she couldn't focus on that now. She still felt so weak it was all she could do to remain upright in her chair, and with all the information she was absorbing, her hold on reality felt more fragile by the second.

"Aurelia?" Mama Gail sounded anxious. "Are you all right?"

"I'm not entirely sure," Aurelia admitted. "Why didn't you tell me?"

Her mother drew a shaky breath. "Perhaps it was another mistake," she said. "I don't know. I was afraid of the knowledge, of how Cyfrin would use it, how he might manipulate you, play on your desires and expectations. I also thought it might make it much harder for you to be trapped up here, knowing everything you should have had. Your desires have always been so simple— just freedom, nothing more. I didn't want to destroy that, and perhaps destroy what little peace you had along with it." She hesitated, watching Aurelia's face. "Was I wrong?"

Aurelia shook her head helplessly. "How can I possibly know, Mama Gail?"

"Imelda."

"What?" Aurelia blinked at the other woman. "What did you say?"

"My name is Imelda."

Aurelia stared at her mother, seeing the moment of release as the older woman's last secret fell away.

For a moment, Aurelia just sat in silence. Nothing was what she'd thought it—she was a princess, and Mama Gail's name was Imelda. Cyfrin had been trying to seduce her, and Amell now carried the enchanter's hated magic, thanks to Aurelia giving him her first kiss. She'd survived the extraction of the magic, but her strength was gone, and she didn't know when or even if it would return.

And yet, she realized, as she looked into the eyes of the only mother she'd ever known, the things that really mattered were exactly as she'd thought—they hadn't changed at all.

"Mama Imelda," she said softly, taking her mother's hand and squeezing it. "It's good to be known."

CHAPTER SEVENTEEN

Amell

Amell's poor horse was lathered in sweat as he pushed it harder than was reasonable down the familiar road. Furn was beside him, saying nothing, but clearly able to read his charge's panic. Even if the magic hadn't been preventing him from speaking, Amell didn't think he would have had the words to tell Furn what he was feeling.

Aurelia. Aurelia Aurelia Aurelia.

He felt like he'd just found her, just discovered her true self. And now she was in danger of being ripped away from him. She'd seemed so weak when he left. Was she still breathing? Would he be too late? No one knew what the effect would be of her releasing the magic Cyfrin had stored within her. But it had done something to her, that much was clear.

No, he had done something to her. He had done this. If he'd just stuck to his resolution to keep some distance between them, she would be safe now. Or as safe as she could be with Cyfrin's plans. But instead he'd lost his head, and kissed her.

And what a kiss it had been. Heat rushed over him at the memory, and he could feel again the intoxicating sensation of holding her in his arms. She'd looked at him with such trust, such admiration. She'd told him so calmly and confidently of his own worth, only for him to prove himself a selfish fool a moment later.

Pain lanced across his mind as he remembered the look in her eyes when she'd pulled away from him, telling him not to touch her hair. He didn't understand exactly what had happened, but he knew he'd been at fault. He'd tried so hard to moderate the intensity of emotion and desire that had rushed in on him when she'd so unexpectedly kissed him—he'd tried so hard to make every movement gentle, knowing how sheltered she'd been, how new every sensation would feel. But still, he'd managed to cross a line, to make her feel unsafe in some way. The thought was utterly unbearable, and it was made even worse by how quickly she'd forgiven him, how earnestly she'd assured him that he'd done nothing wrong.

A memory flashed into his mind, of his old fantasy, where he swooped in to rescue a damsel in distress, and she looked up at him with eternal love and gratitude. Well, Aurelia certainly had long, flowing hair and sparkling eyes. And the trustful way she looked at him was everything his childish self had imagined.

But even before he'd so stupidly kissed her, even as she'd gazed up at him back in the tower, he'd felt to his very core how shallow his own desire for heroics was. Aurelia truly was in danger, and truly was looking to him for a rescue she was magically prevented from pursuing herself. And he took no pleasure from either her plight, which was nothing short of a nightmare, or her trust, which only highlighted how incapable he was.

He couldn't fail her, he told himself over and over. Not this time. He had to get her out. He completed the ride to Fernford in record time, but it felt the longest it ever had. No thought of the castle or his family entered his head as he sent his exhausted horse clattering over the cobblestones toward the Enchanters' Guild.

Still offering Furn no explanation, he threw himself from the saddle and through the doors of the lobby.

"Bartholomew?" he gasped, almost startling the clerk right out of his chair.

"He's at the castle, Your Highness," the clerk said nervously. "Consulting with the king."

Without a word, Amell raced back through the door, mounting his horse and turning its head toward the castle. It was unlucky that Bartholomew was with his father. He wouldn't be able to avoid seeing his family.

Fortune was with him, however. He was just running up the castle steps when the enchanter emerged from the entrance.

"Bartholomew!" he called, seizing the old man by the shoulders. "The project. Did you do it? Can I have it?"

"Whoa, slow down, Your Highness," Bartholomew protested in alarm. "What's happened?" His eyes widened as they passed over Amell's form. "What have you done to that cloak? The magic around you has increased by about a hundredfold."

Amell groaned at this reminder of the power he'd unknowingly taken from Aurelia. "I can't..." he puffed, "never mind what..." He drew a deep breath, pulling himself together. "Bartholomew, I need that artifact. Urgently."

The enchanter looked dismayed. "But it's not ready, Prince Amell. I told you—it's only an early test. I've put very little magic into it, and I'm still perfecting the theory. I'm not even sure if it will work at all, and even if it does, it only has enough magic to sustain a single use, for testing purposes."

Amell groaned. A single use? Did that mean that at best, only one of the women could use it to get out of the tower? "That's better than nothing," he said desperately. "It will have to do. Where is it?"

"Back at the guild," said Bartholomew, his forehead creased with concern. "Prince Amell, what's going on?"

Amell shook his head, feeling slightly sick. He knew he'd never be able to tell Bartholomew what was happening. There was no point trying.

"I'll come to your study now," he said. He turned to his guard. "Furn, can you get us fresh horses? We're going straight back."

Furn looked utterly perplexed, but he asked no questions, bless him. He was just stepping lightly back down the castle steps, his face turned toward the royal stables, when a clear voice issued from the castle's entrance.

"Amell. I've just been informed of your arrival. Excellent timing."

Barely holding back a groan, Amell turned to the king. "I can't stay, Father," he protested. "I need to return to the prison immediately."

"Nonsense," said King Bern, frowning. "I've just received an urgent missive, important enough to require the attention of every member of my family."

"Can't it wait, Father?" Amell asked desperately.

"Did you not hear me say it was urgent?"

The king's voice was unyielding, and Amell couldn't bear to waste such precious time arguing.

"I'm sorry, but I just can't, Father," he said curtly. He turned back to his guard, who was hovering, watching the two royals uncertainly. "Furn, fresh horses, please."

"I tolerate a great deal from you, Amell," said the king, anger under the calm words. "But I won't tolerate open defiance in the castle courtyard."

Amell glanced around, seeing that they had indeed gathered several onlookers. Frustration rose to boiling point within him. Why did his father have to take a stand on this issue now of all times?

When he still failed to give in, the king turned to his son's guard. "Sir Furnis, Prince Amell will not be needing a fresh horse this afternoon. I trust *you* are not minded to defy your king?"

Amell saw the horror behind Furn's suddenly frozen expression, and the sight undid him. It would be unforgivable to put Furn in the position of either defying him or defying his father. He couldn't do that to his friend.

"Very well, Father," he said stiffly. "I'll join you."

The king searched his son's eyes for a long moment, then gave a curt nod before mounting the steps back into the castle.

Amell turned to his two companions the moment his father disappeared. He told himself not to panic. Aurelia had said she was only weary, and she hadn't seemed to get worse in the time he'd been there. And there were many hours still to go before sunset. He would just have to complete whatever his father wanted from him quickly. Still, he didn't intend to take any chances.

"Bartholomew, give the artifact to Sir Furnis and explain what it is, and its...limitations. Furn." He slipped his cloak off and threw it at his friend, who barely caught it in time to avoid his face being enveloped. "Go back to the grove, the trees I like to explore. You know the place. I'll follow as soon as I can, but I don't know how long that will be, and we can't afford to wait. Take the artifact Bartholomew will give you, and make sure you're wearing this cloak. I'll just have to trust you to figure out the rest." He met his friend's eyes seriously. "I'm always asking too much of you, my friend, but please...don't fail me this time."

"I won't, Your Highness," Furn assured him, looking lost but determined.

With a grateful nod, Amell turned and took the steps up to the castle two at a time. He found the king in his study, Amell's mother and sister already gathered.

"What is it?" Amell asked without ceremony, the moment he'd burst through the door. "What was so urgent?"

"Amell!" scolded the queen, aghast. "That's no way to speak to your father."

"I was in the middle of something, Father," Amell pleaded, his eyes flicking to the letter in the king's hand. "What's the urgent missive? If it's another anonymous tip about the location of escaped prisoners, I don't see what you need me for. The last ones turned out to be genuine, and the soldiers rounded the prisoners up without any help from me."

"Sit down, Amell," said his father calmly. "And stop making a spectacle of yourself."

Breathing hard, Amell looked from his father to the two women already seated. His mother still looked a little shocked, and even Tora was watching him with astonishment. Drawing a deep breath, Amell lowered himself into a chair. His thoughts flew to Furn. Had he acquired the artifact yet? Was he leaving for the prison? Surely he'd know where to go. He'd followed Amell to the clump of trees enough times.

"As a matter of fact," the king continued, when satisfied Amell wasn't going to interrupt, "I did receive further anonymous tips, yesterday evening. The prisoners in question have already been rounded up. Only nine now remain at large."

"That's great, Father," said Amell, half rising from his seat.

"*However*." The king's unyielding voice sent Amell back onto his chair. "That is not the missive I referred to. I have received a message of some delicacy from King Justin of Albury. And as it is in essence a family matter as well as a state matter of potentially great importance, I wished for you all to hear it immediately."

Amell raised an eyebrow, his interest caught at last. It was rare for Albury's monarch to reach out to his fellow sovereigns. Amell's first thought was that it related to the theory they'd all discussed at Basil's wedding, of an organized group behind the various attacks against royals. But that didn't quite tally with what his father had said.

"A family matter?" Amell repeated. "Has Queen Felicity had the baby?"

The king shook his head. "Not yet, as far as I'm aware. This matter relates to King Justin's sister." He scanned the thick parchment in his hand, and now that he was paying attention, Amell could see the Alburian royal crest on the outside of it. "Although, by a peculiar chance, it relates to Queen Felicity's family as well."

"What does it say, Father?" Tora asked, a touch of Amell's own impatience in her voice.

King Bern cleared his throat. "Do you all remember that King Justin had a younger sister, who died in an accident as an infant?"

The queen nodded, but both of her children frowned in thought.

"I don't think I knew that," Amell said.

"I remember hearing something to that effect," said Tora. "I don't actually remember when it happened, though."

Queen Pietra nodded. "Neither of you would remember. Amell, you were only one at the time, so Tora, you must have been three."

Amell stared at his mother. "That's a very specific thing to remember."

"A queen makes it her business to know the ages of the children in other royal families. And the princess was less than a year younger than you."

"She means she was already plotting a marriage of alliance when you were a one-year-old," Tora supplied helpfully.

"I wasn't plotting anything," said the queen, a touch crossly. "But of course I wished to be aware of the royals of similar ages to my own children. And Princess Aurelia, as I said, was—"

"Princess who?" Amell demanded, flying out of his chair. His heart was pounding, but he couldn't make sense of the information flying around his mind.

"Princess Aurelia," said the queen, staring at him in bemusement. "That's the name of the princess who died as an infant."

"Actually," King Bern cleared his throat, his expression long-suffering as he attempted to reclaim his family's attention, "she may not have died. Amell, for the last time, sit down. You're not going anywhere until we formulate a response to this letter."

Amell lowered himself back into his seat, his eyes wide and his mind completely incapable of forming words.

"What do you mean, she may not have died?" Queen Pietra demanded.

The king flourished the letter. "King Justin says that although he has always believed his sister to be dead, he has recently received information that suggests that she may be alive, but that if she is, she is definitely somewhere outside of Albury. He has sent letters to the monarchs of each of the other kingdoms in Solstice, begging us—"

"Begging?" Tora interrupted skeptically. "King Justin?"

"That was his precise choice of word," said the king calmly. "He begs us to use whatever resources we can to ascertain whether Princess Aurelia and her companion might be concealed somewhere within our kingdom."

"Good gracious," said the queen faintly. "Do they suspect the accident to have been staged, and the princess kidnapped?"

"Something along those lines," assented her husband.

Queen Pietra shook her head. "It would be a terrible thing if such a crime had been concealed within our borders all these years." She frowned, clearly calculating. "Seventeen years...the princess would be nearing her eighteenth birthday if she's alive.

She would have spent her whole childhood at the mercy of her abductor."

Amell opened his mouth, then closed it. Nothing would come. He was utterly unable to think of a single thing to say that the magic would allow.

"Is that the companion they mean?" Tora asked. "Whoever abducted her?"

The king shook his head. "She was with a minder when she fell into a ravine—or at least, when they thought she did. The woman was to be her lady-in-waiting, or some such. She also is believed to be alive, but outside the kingdom." He cast his eyes over the letter again. "By some bizarre twist of fate, she was the mother of the commoner King Justin married."

"Dragon's flame," Amell muttered, the color draining from his face. Could this be real? But it must be. It was impossible that his Aurelia could be a different one, also kidnapped as a baby and hidden away her whole life with one faithful companion whom she called mother but knew wasn't the mother who'd given her birth. Abigail—or whatever her name really was—had even told him she was from Albury. And now he thought about it, her copper hair was just like Queen Felicity's.

He suddenly remembered, with a physical start, how Aurelia's striking coloring had reminded him of something. He could picture King Justin, sitting at the council table in Basil's castle, little more than a month before. That dark hair and those piercing blue eyes were such an unusual combination...

Aurelia was King Justin's sister. Aurelia was a princess.

"I'm glad you grasp the gravity of the situation," Amell's father said. "The matter is clearly delicate, and our relationship with Albury may be substantially affected by our response. But I'm reluctant to commit to anything costly. King Justin's request, although heartfelt, is vague. Are we to scour the entire country, interview every girl between fifteen and twenty? Of course I will start inquiries, but we're already in the midst of a different type of manhunt, one which is more urgent, given the very real risk to our people's safety."

I know where she is! Amell wanted to cry. *And the danger she's in is imminent, too!* But he couldn't say anything at all. Perhaps if he just hinted that the area around the prison would be worth examining. Perhaps he could confess that he'd spoken with dragons, and they'd told him of the concealment magic they'd sensed in the area.

But no matter what he decided to say, the words simply wouldn't come. He was sure he could have told his father all about his interaction with the dragons at the time. If only he'd done so! But he hadn't, and once he'd crossed into Cyfrin's hidden clearing, and been engulfed in its magical protections, he'd lost his opportunity to be open with information that had turned out to be of grave importance.

"Father," he said, his voice coming out unsteady. "I want to help with this search. Let me take a group. Some soldiers, a few enchanters. Perhaps Bartholomew will consent to come. I could...could look for..."

"I appreciate your enthusiasm, Amell," said the king. "But we're not ready for that yet. I'll start with more discreet inquiries, see what that brings up. My hopes aren't high. We must remember that even if King Justin is right, Fernedell is only one of five kingdoms where the princess could be concealed."

"I understand," said Amell, trying to hide the frustration coursing through him. "Thank you for telling me this news, Father. I'll just—"

"Sit down, Amell," said his father impatiently. "You're not going anywhere until I've written a response to King Justin. With such a delicate matter, I don't intend to send my reply with a courier. I thought perhaps you could lead a small delegation, convey our goodwill to King Justin along with a written commitment of assistance."

"What?" Amell cried. "You want to send me to Albury now? No, Father, you can't!"

"I think you'll find I can," said the king, scowling. "I thought you'd be glad of a task to do. You can't pick and choose the duties that seem interesting to you, Amell."

"That's not what I'm doing," Amell insisted. He drew a breath, trying to project calm. He just had to get Aurelia out of that tower, and then everything would make sense to everyone. "Very well, Father. If you want me to take the message, I can. But first I think I'd best return to the prison, inform the warden of my intended departure."

"For the last time, Amell, *sit down*," his father growled. "Any messenger can fulfill that function. You are not going anywhere."

So Amell was forced to sit, his leg bouncing frantically, his mind even more so, while his father composed a tortuously slow response to King Justin's letter. Queen Pietra and Tora seemed very interested in the process, interjecting with suggestions, and arguing over wording. But Amell couldn't focus on any of it.

All he could think about was Aurelia. Aurelia weak and fading, in danger because of him, because he'd kissed her. Aurelia the victim of Cyfrin's repulsive schemes. Aurelia a princess, sister to Albury's intimidating king.

No wonder the enchanter thought he would gain from marrying her! He would rise drastically in status from the union. But Amell would never let that happen. Even if she hadn't kissed him, even if she had no interest in him whatsoever, he would never allow Cyfrin to carry out his plans. He realized his hands had balled into fists in his lap, and he smoothed them out.

Pushing all those other considerations to the side, Amell wasn't sure how to feel about this revelation of Aurelia's identity. It would make her eligible in his mother's eyes. That much was certain, even without the court training. She'd actually been toying with the idea of their marriage when Amell was still a baby! But how would it affect Aurelia's feelings?

Amell was ashamed to discover that some part of him had been overconfident, sure of his success with Aurelia once she was out of the tower. Because as far as he'd known, she had no one else, and he was, well...the words made him wince even in the privacy of his head. But however conceited it made him sound, it was still the truth that he was the most sought-after young man in Fernedell.

What a vain fool he'd been.

Aurelia was a princess, from one of the proudest houses in Solstice. Amell knew her brother thought him a frivolous fool, although King Justin had never been so vulgar as to say so to his face. And Aurelia would find that she had all the options in the continent when it came to choosing a husband. Surely it couldn't hurt that Amell was a prince, but it was no guarantee.

By the time Amell was finally released, having been forced to endure a luncheon, it was past one o'clock in the afternoon. Furn had been gone for almost three hours. For all Amell knew, the guard was already on his way back to Fernford with Aurelia. Although even if Bartholomew's artifact had worked, it was hard to imagine Aurelia would be willing to just leave the area, with Abigail still trapped in the tower.

Either way, Amell had no intention of sitting around, waiting to find out. He hadn't told his father that he'd sent Furn on an errand, allowing the king to believe that the guard was standing by, ready to accompany Amell on a journey to Albury. But when the prince rode out of the city a short while later, his father's letter tucked into a pocket, his destination was most definitely within Fernedell. By the time his father realized Amell had taken off on his own, he hoped to be out of reach.

The road was busier than he was used to, due to a large seasonal market being held in the capital. In frustration, Amell directed his horse off the main road, choosing a narrower and less used route. He knew that in doing so he ran the risk of missing Furn in passing. But he thought it unlikely that his guard had made a clean departure from the tower. Chances were high that they were all still in the clearing, arguing about who would use the artifact.

Either way, Amell should be there well before sunset. And if the worst came to it, and neither of them could get out, well... Amell touched the hilt of his sword reassuringly as he rode. Cyfrin would find himself confronted with an unexpected visitor when sunset came.

CHAPTER EIGHTEEN

Aurelia

"How are you feeling, Aurelia?"

"I'm all right," Aurelia answered her mother. It was true. She still felt weak, but it hadn't gotten any worse. A little better, even, from sitting in stillness all morning. "I really don't think I'm dying. I guess Cyfrin was right."

"Words no one should ever say," the other woman responded dryly. "But I know what you mean. I've read in his notes about the animals he used as vessels. They all died instantly upon his magic being extracted. The fact that you didn't is a good sign."

"A very good sign," Aurelia agreed, unable to help laughing a little. She looked at the small patch of sky she could see out the window. "It must be about noon. Amell could be back any minute, if he made good time."

Her mother stood, moving to the window and surveying the clearing. Aurelia couldn't see the ground, but her mother's sharp intake of breath told her that something was happening.

"What is it? Is he here?"

The other woman shook her head. "It's someone else. But that's the prince's cloak he's wearing, I'm almost certain."

"What?" Aurelia pulled herself out of her chair. Had something happened to Amell?

"Uh...hello?" The unfamiliar voice carried faintly up to their tower room. Aurelia reached the window to see a tall man, several years older than Amell, staring up at them in astonishment. He was indeed wearing Amell's cloak, but underneath it he appeared to be in some kind of uniform.

"Who are you?" Mama Gail—or rather Imelda—demanded. "How did you get here?"

The man bowed. "My name is Sir Furnis, ma'am. And I was sent by Prince Amell to...well, I don't know exactly what I'm supposed to do, to be honest."

"Furn!" Aurelia cried. "We've heard all about you. Where's Amell?"

The guard blinked, apparently taken aback by the information that his reputation had gone before him. "He was detained in the capital, miss," he said. "It was unavoidable, but he seemed quite frantic that no time be lost. He wasn't able to explain the situation—I admit I had no idea what I would find here—but he sent me with this." Sir Furnis held something up, and squinting at it, Aurelia realized it was a small ring.

"What is it?" she asked doubtfully.

"According to the enchanter who gave it to me," the guard explained, speaking carefully as though reciting something from memory, "it's an artifact to counteract restraining magic."

Aurelia drew in a sharp breath, exchanging an excited look with her mother.

"But," Sir Furnis added hastily, "I was exhorted most strictly to warn you that it's not finished. The enchanter wasn't sure if it would work—he hasn't yet tested it. And it has very little magic imbued in it, so it will probably sustain one attempt only."

"Only one?" Aurelia repeated, looking at her mother in

alarm. She didn't like the sound of that. "Do you think we could both use it at once?"

"I don't know," said Sir Furnis doubtfully, trying valiantly to keep up, even though he clearly had no idea what was going on. "The enchanter told me that in order to activate the magic, you just put the ring on your finger."

Mama Imelda let out a breath. "It's designed for one, Aurelia," she said briskly. "We can't both wear it. But after you get down, you can send it straight back up to me. You never know, perhaps the enchanter misjudged how much magic was in there, and it will last to get us both out."

"Mama," Aurelia said warningly. "I'm not going to do that. There's no way I'll—"

"Don't argue, Aurelia," her mother said, in a voice Aurelia hadn't heard since she was a child. "This is not open for debate."

Aurelia bit her lip, searching the other woman's face. She knew when it was hopeless to fight, and this was undoubtedly one of those times.

"All right," she said quietly, and Mama Imelda let out a breath of relief.

She seized a fistful of Aurelia's hair and threw it out the window, not worrying about the metal hook.

"You'd have to use the ring to get in," she called to Sir Furnis, "and that would be a waste of its limited power. Just tie it onto the hair, and we'll pull it up for Aurelia to use."

The guard was staring at the dark locks in front of him with open astonishment, but at her words, he hastened to obey. Within moments, Mama Imelda had pulled the artifact up, and untied it from the makeshift rope.

"Well," she said, holding it out to Aurelia. "Here goes nothing."

Aurelia took it, turning it over in her hand. It wasn't fancy jewelry. Nothing more than a simple brass circlet. It was sized for a bigger hand than either hers or her mother's, but it would have to do.

She threw her arms around her companion, squeezing tightly. "I love you, Mama," he said quietly. Mama Imelda's arms came up, and Aurelia felt no guilt at her deception as she threaded her own hair gently through the other woman's belt.

Her task done, Aurelia pulled back, taking her mother's hand and pressing it as if in emotion.

"Don't be angry," she said softly.

A look of confusion passed over Mama Imelda's face. "What do you—?"

The question died on her lips as Aurelia thrust the ring over the thumb of the hand she still held, then pushed her mother bodily out the window. Mama Imelda's gasp was lost as she toppled, and leaping back across the room, Aurelia brought both hands up to seize as much of her hair as she could, close to the scalp.

Even so, it was agonizing when her mother's weight transferred to her hair. Letting out an involuntary cry of pain, Aurelia was tugged mercilessly back against the window. Ironically, the only thing that kept her from falling straight out was Cyfrin's restraining enchantment. But not a strand of the magically reinforced hair broke. Once her vision stopped swimming, Aurelia looked hastily down, to see her mother lying stunned on the grass, next to a bewildered Sir Furnis.

Mama Imelda struggled to her feet, horrified but clearly unhurt, and Aurelia let out a sigh of relief. It seemed she hadn't erred in her calculations. The knot around her mother's belt didn't seem to have held, but it had jerked her to a temporary stop, so that the final fall had been short and gentle.

"Aurelia, what have you done?" Mama Imelda cried in anguish.

"I'm sorry, Mama," Aurelia called. "But you would never

have agreed, and I couldn't let you die for me. Cyfrin would kill you if I wasn't here, you know he would. But he has more than one reason to keep me alive."

"This is madness!" Her mother cried. "I'm coming back up."

"Oh no, you're not." Aurelia began to tug her hair, but Mama Imelda seized it.

"Mama," said Aurelia sternly. "In the unlikely event that there's more magic left in that ring, are you going to waste it climbing back *into* our prison?"

Mama Imelda seemed to see the logic of this argument. Her fingers fumbling, she tied the ring back into Aurelia's hair. Without much hope, Aurelia reeled it up, and put the ring on her own finger.

She stuck her head tentatively out of the window, but when her shoulders reached the invisible barrier, she was unable to move.

"I'm afraid not," she called down, her voice light. "The magic's all gone." She pulled the ring off, considering it dispassionately. It was no longer an artifact. Nothing but a worthless piece of metal.

"Aurelia, you can't stay there alone!" Mama Imelda cried desperately.

Aurelia didn't point out that there was by now no other option possible. "I'll be all right," she said instead, cheerfully. "You go with Sir Furnis back to the capital. Find Amell, and tell him what's happened. Maybe he can get another of these artifacts."

"I won't leave you to face Cyfrin alone," Mama Imelda declared. "I'm staying right here until—"

"Don't do that," said Aurelia, exasperated. "What will that achieve? You need to be long gone by the time he comes. I'll lock the door to our room and tell him you're sleeping. Maybe he'll come and go none the wiser."

Mama Imelda hesitated, and Aurelia pressed her point.

"It's not much past noon, Mama. If you go now, you might even be back again before sunset with a solution." She glanced at the stupefied guard. "I'm sorry to add to what must have been a hard day of riding already," she commented. "But do you think you could get my mother back to the capital?"

"Of course," he said, bowing hastily. "It would be my pleasure."

"Good," said Aurelia briskly. "It's decided." She pulled her head—and her hair—fully back inside the tower, indicating she was done with further argument. After several minutes she peeked through, and ascertained that they were gone. Clearly Mama Imelda had decided to take her advice and spend the time finding a solution before sunset instead of wasting it arguing.

Free of witnesses, Aurelia let her calm mask drop, and slid to the floor. Her scalp felt like it was on fire from Mama Imelda's weight, and her whole body was shaking, both from the weakness that still plagued her, and the enormity of her situation.

She was alone. For the first time in her life, she was truly, genuinely alone. And Cyfrin was coming.

Overwhelmed by her emotions, she let herself cry for several tension-releasing minutes. Then she picked herself up, dusted off her hands, and set determinedly to work tidying the space and preparing herself some lunch. She wasn't a helpless child, and she would not fall apart. Life would go on.

Amell had told her that it took two hours to ride to the city, so she knew she would have to wait at least four before her mother might be able to return. So she almost jumped from her chair in amazement when she heard a shout below after only two. Was it possible Amell had left the capital only two hours after his guard, and was here now? She should be able to pull him up easily enough. Her head still hurt, but her weakness had improved substantially as the time wore on.

But when she reached the window, horror washed over her at the sight of a far less welcome figure than the prince.

"Cyfrin!" she gasped. "It's hours before sunset. What are you doing here?"

The enchanter raised one disapproving eyebrow. "That is entirely my own affair."

"But…" Aurelia swallowed. "But you've never come during the day before."

"Well," said Cyfrin crisply, "the situation has changed. I will explain it all when I don't have to crane my neck to do so. Now pull me up."

Aurelia's mind whirled. He sounded like his usual irritable self, but there was no sign of the fury he'd feel if he knew how the situation had really changed. Was there a chance he'd poured so much magic into her hair that he wouldn't notice the power missing from her core? She needed to behave as naturally as possible.

"I'd…I'd rather not," she said. "It's just…my mother is resting, and it's difficult to pull you up on my own." She made her voice hesitant. "I think she's fallen asleep, but I suppose I could wake her."

Predictably, Cyfrin's eyes gleamed at the news that his hated critic was out of the way. "Asleep, is she?" he said eagerly. "No, don't wake her child, let her rest. We can manage without her."

Now that Aurelia understood the motivation behind his eagerness to be alone with her, it was all she could do not to gag. But she hid the reaction, still trying to sound casual.

"I don't think I'm strong enough, Master Enchanter."

Cyfrin made a gesture of impatience. "Of course you are. Now throw down your hair. You know from the years when your hair was too short that I have other ways of getting up if I need to. And if you put me to the effort of using them, I will not be pleased, believe me."

Aurelia did know it, and she did believe it. Resigning herself to the inevitable, she fed her hair through the loop and threw it down. In her weakened state, the ascent that was usually mildly uncomfortable was agony, and she couldn't keep in a whimper as she braced herself against the wall.

At least it was brief. In no time at all, Cyfrin stood before her, his eyes instantly passing over the space in confusion.

"Something's different," he declared. "What's missing?"

"Well, my...my mother is sleeping," Aurelia reminded him.

Cyfrin waved her off impatiently. "Not her. I don't care about her."

"You said the situation has changed, Master Enchanter," Aurelia said quickly, trying to turn his thoughts. "What's changed?"

"Ah, yes." Cyfrin turned to face her, a gleam coming into his eyes. "An unexpected development, my dear. I confess, at first I was angry, but then I decided I would turn it to good account." He gave her a solemn look. "My child, it's time."

"Time for what?" Aurelia demanded uneasily. "And what development?"

"Time to extract the magic I've stored within you," Cyfrin said simply. "Time to make my move at last."

Aurelia stared at him, too stunned to speak, and he went on blithely.

"I don't know how, but it seems your brother has become aware of your survival. He has sent messages all over the land, encouraging his neighbors to poke and pry and examine things that don't concern them. We can't have that, I thought to myself. You wouldn't like it, my dear—your father was a nasty man, everyone knew it. And your brother is just the same. I knew I had to protect you from him. But then I realized...what does it matter if they find our tower, if we've already emerged from it?" His eyes were gleaming once again. "What do you think, child? Would you like to emerge from your seclusion, re-enter the world in triumph at my side?"

Aurelia drew back involuntarily. "I don't want to go anywhere at your side," she said simply. "Not even if it meant finally leaving this tower."

Cyfrin's eyes narrowed in anger. He took a step toward her, but Aurelia didn't pull back this time. She stood tall, looking him in the eye. Her defiance had given her the boost she needed, and she didn't even feel fear.

All her life she'd been trapped by this man, with no control. But the knowledge that she could have escaped that very day, that she had chosen to remain in order to set her mother free, made her feel empowered, strong. Cyfrin might not realize it, but he no longer controlled her. She had been given a choice, and she stood by her decision unreservedly. Somewhere in her heart she knew, whatever happened, she would never truly be in his power again.

"Honeysuckle, do not defy me, or I—"

"That is not my name," she said coldly. "My name is Aurelia, and I won't respond to anything else."

He gave a nasty laugh. "You think you're so—" The enchanter broke off, his eyes widening as they roamed over Aurelia's form. "Where is it?" he demanded. "Where's the magic?"

"What do you mean?" Aurelia asked, in an attempt at confusion that she knew had fallen flat. She drew her hair into her hands. "The magic in my hair, you mean?"

"No," snarled Cyfrin, his rage growing. "The magic in your hair is still there. Where is the magic I transferred into you?" He stepped forward, seizing her by the shoulders and shaking her roughly. "Where is it?" he roared. "Tell me!"

"It's gone," said Aurelia, her face white but her voice quite calm. "You gave me the key, and I unlocked it. I set it free, where you can never claim it. Its power would never have been yours. You ensured that the moment you put it in my core."

"WHAT?!"

Despite her sudden confidence, Aurelia had to admit to herself that Cyfrin's fury was terrible to behold. For a moment she was sure he would hit her, but instead he seized a chair and threw it forcefully against the wall. Aurelia flinched as the wood splintered into pieces, but still she stood firm.

"But this is impossible," Cyfrin declared, calming down as his mind caught up. He ran a hand over his closely cropped hair. "You can't have used the key. There's no one to—"

"No one but you?" Aurelia asked coldly. "You had the audacity to think, after everything you've done, that I would willingly give my first kiss to you? That I would *marry* you? You are as foolish as you are evil. I would rather die than marry you. And you're too late. I've already given someone else my heart, and my kiss. Your power is his now, and I would trust him with it as I would trust him with my life."

Cyfrin's face drained of all color. He stepped up to her again, but there was no more shouting. Now his voice was low, almost too quiet to hear. And infinitely more terrifying.

"Who?"

The single word made Aurelia's blood run cold, but she forced herself to look her captor in the eye.

"Someone who is a hundred times the man you are."

"You will pay for this," Cyfrin said, his lips white with rage. "You've taken what I care about, and I'll take what you care about. I'll kill that servant woman you call mother, and then I'll find the man who dared to claim what was mine and kill him too!"

"I don't think you'll find that so easy, in either case," said Aurelia coldly.

Without a word, Cyfrin strode across the room and tore open the door to the bedroom. His eyes scanned the empty space, and he let out a cry of fury.

"Where is she? Where?"

"Far away," said Aurelia, hoping fervently that the words were true.

"Impossible!" Cyfrin cried.

Aurelia shrugged, spreading her hands wide. "And yet..."

Cyfrin began to pace, his rage momentarily held at bay as his mind began to work, clearly trying to figure out how to salvage the situation.

"My plans have been compromised," he muttered angrily, to no one in particular. "It's time to move." He glared at Aurelia. "With half—HALF—of the power I should have had!"

Leaning into her face, he growled. "You are a simple, weak child. What a mistake it was to ever think you could be trusted with the smallest role. But don't think you've bested me, little rat. The power in your hair isn't dependent on you doing anything. It's mine, and I'll take it. *And* I'll see you pay for what you've done!"

Without warning, his arm snaked around Aurelia's neck, and he pulled her against his side.

Gasping and choking, she grabbed blindly at his arm, trying to dislodge him. He ignored her movements completely, dragging her toward the kitchen area. Before Aurelia's horrified sight, he seized a knife from the counter and brought it up toward her. She squeezed her eyes shut, bracing herself for death, but she felt no sting. Instead she heard a strange sound by her ear. Forcing her eyes open, she realized what Cyfrin was really doing. She struggled harder, not wanting him to access even half his stored power, but he had her in a stranglehold, and stars were beginning to burst before her eyes.

All at once, he released her, and she fell heavily to the wooden floor. She saw a thick coil of hair in front of her, and followed it with her eyes. Reaching the end of the line, she looked up in a daze at the unnerving sight of her own long tresses, detached from her head, and held in the enchanter's hands.

Aurelia reached up and felt her head, her trembling fingers finding nothing but short, uneven spikes protruding from her scalp.

"What a fetching style you're sporting, my dear," Cyfrin said nastily. "You never believed me that the world is a cold hard place. Let's see who's right—let's see how our lovely community receives you."

Aurelia blinked at him, confused. Before she could ask what he meant, Cyfrin had placed one hand on the hair in his fist. Muttering angrily, and with increasing speed and volume, he brought his hands—hair and all—up in front of his face. Suddenly, with a furious shout, he flung his arms wide, and the walls exploded.

At least, that's what it felt like to Aurelia. She felt herself thrown violently outward, and the sensation of something bursting open was so potent that she was sure the tower had been blown to pieces.

But the next thing she knew, she was lying on her back in the clearing, staring up at a very unfamiliar view of a very familiar building. The tower was intact, and somehow so was she. But something had definitely been destroyed, and with terrible force.

Cyfrin's head appeared at the window. "If you're still in my sight in one minute," he snarled, "I'll kill you and be done with it."

Aurelia didn't need telling twice. She'd dreamed her whole life of being free from the tower, and she had no intention of staying anywhere near it now she finally was. She clambered to her feet, instantly falling in her weakness. But a moment later she was back up, stumbling toward the tree line.

She blundered through the trees, marveling at the feel of the bark on her hands, not even caring as it shredded her sensitive skin. The plants were soft under her slippers, the birdsong was so close she could almost touch it, and the wind whipped about her from all sides. She was so overwhelmed by all the sensations that she could barely grasp what had happened. Cyfrin had cut off her hair, removing the last of his magic from her person. She could feel it, too. It wasn't as intense as the draining feeling she'd experienced when she kissed Amell, but its cumulative effect was alarming.

Physically, she felt more weakened than ever. But emotionally...she felt lighter than she ever had in her life. And she moved so easily, without any encumbrance, her balance a little off, but her movements delightfully unhindered. She was free of the tower, free of Cyfrin, free of his magic. Even free of that ridiculous *hair*.

But with that realization came another. If she didn't carry the hair, and the magic stored within it, that meant Cyfrin did. And he'd said it was time to make his move. Whatever attack he'd been planning, it was now imminent. And no one knew that except Aurelia.

"I have to warn them," she muttered, looking frantically around her.

She had no idea where she was, and no idea how to find her way. She stumbled through the trees for what felt like an age, knowing only that she needed to move away from the clearing with the tower. When she finally burst out into open ground, the sight of so much space took her breath away.

She looked up at the sun. By now it must be three hours or more past its zenith. Thanks to Amell's information, she knew that Fernford was south east of her tower. But she didn't know enough about such things to find direction from the sun in the sky.

She set her face toward the grassy expanse before her. She would just have to keep going until she found another human being. Surely anyone she found would be happy to point her toward the capital.

CHAPTER NINETEEN

The horse Amell had grabbed at random from the royal stables picked its way through the woods surrounding the prison. The animal was clearly grateful for the slower pace, and the prince felt a flash of guilt. He hadn't given the creature nearly enough breaks on the ride. But it had been worth it. In spite of the stretch where he avoided the main road, he'd made good time. The clearing wasn't far away, and it couldn't be later than three in the afternoon. Still plenty of time before sunset.

It wasn't until he spotted the familiar clump of trees that Amell suddenly realized his own foolishness. He didn't have his cloak. He'd given it to Furn, and now he had no way to find the clearing.

He struck a hand against his knee in frustration. He shouldn't have left the main road and risked missing Furn. What if the guard was halfway back to the capital by now? Or what if he was still in the clearing? Amell had no way to find out.

But to his amazement, as he pulled his horse to a stop next to the well-known trees, he saw that they didn't seem to be growing as closely together. They weren't an impenetrable wall at all—he could see straight through. Frowning, he glanced around him. Had he come to the wrong place? But no, this stretch of forest had become incredibly familiar over the last month. He knew where he was.

Dismounting, he led his horse toward the close-growing trees. The stand was noticeably denser than the trees around it, but not impassable by any means. The pair moved through it slowly but easily, and the trees soon thinned out again.

Unease prickled through Amell as he saw the point up ahead where the trunks ended and the clearing began. He'd gotten in without his cloak. What did that mean? Was it a good sign, or a bad one? Perhaps because he'd found the clearing before, it was always open to him...or perhaps it was his royal blood.

But neither of those things explained the change in the trees. It was more like the concealment magic had lifted. Surely that must be a good sign. He should be free to speak of Aurelia's plight now, if nothing else. But how had they achieved such a victory? And did that mean the restraining magic was lifted as well?

He entered the clearing cautiously, but there was no sign of anything or anyone but the lone tower, its conical roof pointing toward the afternoon sky.

"Aurelia?" he called anxiously. "Abigail?" Doubtfully, "Furn?"

No face appeared at the window, but suddenly a familiar cascade of dark hair came shooting out of the opening, bypassing the metal ring completely and hanging free all the way to the ground.

"Aurelia!" he cried, relieved by this sign of life. "Brace yourself, I'm coming up." Hoping that Abigail would help take most of his weight, he ran to the foot of the tower and seized the tresses. Hand over hand, he climbed the wall, reaching the opening out of breath and eager.

For a moment he balanced on the windowsill, expecting to be greeted by two familiar faces, but then his eyes traveled the length of the dark hair and he gasped, dropping it as if he'd been holding a snake.

It was no longer attached to Aurelia's graceful form. In fact, there was no sign of either woman. Instead, Aurelia's hair was held loosely in the hands of a tall, broad-shouldered man with hair as dark as the tresses he was clutching.

"Cyfrin!" Amell breathed, dropping fluidly into the room and pulling his sword free in one swift motion. "Where are they? What have you done with them?"

"I hoped you would come," the enchanter hissed, his eyes full of malice. "Oh, how I hoped you would come. I wanted to set eyes on the viper who dared to climb my tower and claim my prize."

"Aurelia was never yours," Amell ground out, through clenched teeth. "You are a thief and a liar."

"Never mine?" Cyfrin cried, looking quite mad in anger. "Do you know how much effort I've poured into that girl these last seventeen years? How much *magic*?"

Amell's lip curled, revolted by the inhumanity of the man before him, who saw a lively, intelligent, warm-hearted girl as nothing more than an object, a passive vessel to be used for his own ends.

"You're a monster," he said simply, spitting on the floor. "Now where is she?"

The enchanter laughed coldly. "That's none of your concern. Your only part in this endeavor is to die for your insolence."

Amell raised his sword, not at all reluctant for it to come to a fight. The enchanter's eyes settled on the beautifully wrought blade, his gaze passing slowly across Amell's costly clothes, and resting finally on his face.

Comprehension dawned. "I recognize you," he breathed. "You're the prince."

"What of it?" Amell snarled.

"How in the world did you find…" Cyfrin shook his head. "Never mind. It matters little now. I suppose you were in the area looking for those cursed prisoners." He frowned. "It is a complicating factor, however."

Amell raised an eyebrow. "What's wrong?" he spat. "You have no hesitation in targeting defenseless infants, but you're too afraid to fight a grown man with the resources to hold you to account?"

"Someone with my power has no need to be *afraid* of anything," snapped Cyfrin. He ran a stroking hand over the hair now draped across one arm. The sight made Amell feel sick. The hair was too associated with Aurelia, and seeing it wrapped around the enchanter was horrifying. But where was she?

"Having the death of the prince on my hands might be a little awkward once I take over the guild," Cyfrin mused. With a shrug, he seemed to flick the thought off. "No matter. There's no reason anyone will associate your death with me. It shouldn't be too difficult to pin it on one of those escaped prisoners."

He nodded in satisfaction, his decision clearly made. Then, in a movement so swift Amell barely saw it, he flicked out the hand that had been resting on the hair, as if casting something across the room.

Amell felt something invisible collide with his chest, and he was pushed backward. But the blow did no damage, the sensation neither sharp nor especially forceful. It reminded him somehow of the attack by the two escaped prisoners, when they'd used their magic like weapons, and he and Furn had been protected by a shield from the prison guards.

"What...?" Cyfrin was clearly as confused as Amell, but wasted no time. Once again drawing power from the hair, he tried again.

The result was the same. This time, braced for it as he was, Amell wasn't even pushed backward.

"Hm," he said provokingly. "It's not doing much. Looks like you need more fuel."

"That's impossible," snarled Cyfrin. "I have an incredible amount of power here, and I—"

"True, true," Amell interrupted casually. "The thing is, I have a fair bit of power over here as well."

Cyfrin's eyes widened, then narrowed. "Of course," he breathed. "You tricked her into using the key, and unlocking the power for your benefit." He sneered. "I must say, you're more intelligent than you look."

"I would never trick her," growled Amell. "And I don't want your filthy power."

Cyfrin's laugh was scornful. "Everyone wants power, you childish fool. Or were you ignorant of what was at stake? Perhaps your head was simply turned by a beautiful face." His expression was mocking. "She did grow to be quite beautiful, didn't she? But you had to come and ruin all that."

"You would never have won her," Amell told him furiously. "Even if she'd never set eyes on me, she'd never choose a snake like you."

"Relax, Your Highness," Cyfrin said indulgently. "Obviously I don't want her now." He stroked the hair in his arms again. "I have the only part of her that has any worth right here."

Fury clouded Amell's senses, and he lunged forward. Too late, he realized that the enchanter had been baiting him in order to distract. Draping the hair quickly around his neck, Cyfrin threw wide his arms and shouted. Amell felt what seemed to be an invisible noose close around him, and he gave a cry. But the next moment it had loosened, drifting away into nothing.

Cyfrin's scream of rage cut through Amell's confusion. "I can feel it!" the enchanter cried. "My own power, fighting back against me. But you're no enchanter—you can't control it. Why won't it obey me?"

Amell ignored his rant, rushing at him with weapon raised. But Cyfrin repelled him almost lazily, drawing magic from the hair that created a formless shield through which Amell couldn't penetrate, no matter how hard he tried.

"Enough," Cyfrin snapped. He shot his hands out again, and Amell felt himself thrown backward with such force that he hit the far wall. For a moment he wobbled, unable to get his balance, then he toppled back, out of the window.

His arms flailed wildly as he fell, grasping at air in an effort to slow his descent. But it seemed the power still hanging around him was primed to do just that. He felt himself slow slightly as the ground approached, and he bounced off a cushion of pure power, landing gently on the grass, his sword falling several feet away.

"You are a nuisance, Prince."

Cyfrin's voice drew Amell's gaze to the tower. The enchanter was in the window, and before Amell could do more than struggle up, he'd looped Aurelia's hair through the metal hook, gripping it on either side and sliding down.

"It seems it won't let me kill you," Cyfrin grumbled, looking Amell up and down. "But it will wear off with time. For now, perhaps it will allow something less drastic. A good old-fashioned curse, perhaps."

He lunged forward with surprising swiftness. Amell, bereft of his sword, raised his arms in defense. But Cyfrin made no move to strike him, merely tapping the side of his head.

Something seemed to descend over Amell's face, and he clutched at it, confused.

"I'd best say the words, make it official, hadn't I?" Cyfrin's voice was a hiss in Amell's ears, and the prince struck out blindly, trying to connect with the enchanter. "You are doomed to blindness, Your Highness. I think you'll find it difficult to run to your little guards if you can't find them. And just know that I take great delight from the best part of this curse—you'll never see *Aurelia* again."

With a cry of rage, Amell swung his arms around, searching for his enemy. There was nothing but a ghostly laugh on the wind.

"Cyfrin!" he roared into the blackness. "Cyfrin, where is she?"

"Oh, she's out there somewhere," the enchanter said lazily, his voice seeming to drift from far away. "I hope she's received kindly by whoever she meets. I'm afraid she looks a bit of a fright. I cut her hair in something of a hurry, you see, and I'm afraid it wasn't quite neat."

Amell drew in a horrified breath as he grasped the enchanter's meaning. The monster had shorn Aurelia's hair like a prisoner's, and then thrown her into a community still jumpy from the threat of escaped and potentially violent enchanters.

And the king had given the order to kill fugitives on sight!

"WHERE IS SHE?" he demanded, fear clutching at his throat.

This time there was no answer. The enchanter was gone, and Amell was alone in darkness. He clawed at his face, but there was nothing covering his eyes. He was genuinely blind. Panic clouded his mind, and he stumbled over the grassy ground, desperate for he hardly knew what.

His foot hit something hard, and he knelt, feeling his way across the grass. His sword. Carefully, he picked it up, returning it clumsily to its scabbard. What was he going to do? He was blind, without even Furn to help him. And worst of all, Aurelia was once again in danger, and he had no idea how to find her.

After a moment's thought, he decided his best hope was to make for the prison. The route was so familiar, he might be able to feel his way there.

He made it to the tree line without serious mishap, but as soon as he was between the trunks, he knew it was hopeless. Without his sight, he had no idea where he was going. And yet, even as he moved, he felt that energy swirl around him, the same buoyancy that had gripped him when he'd kissed Aurelia. At the time he'd thought it was just elation at her touch, but now he knew it had been Cyfrin's magic, draining from her and pouring into him.

Blinking frantically, he realized that the fog was beginning to clear. Blurry shapes were appearing in front of him, slowly solidifying into trees.

"Yes," he muttered, willing the magic to keep going. "Fight back! Fight it off."

Whether in obedience to him or in accordance with a predetermined path, the power lingering around him broke down the last of Cyfrin's attack. With a gasp, Amell lurched forward, his vision restored.

A soft nicker brought his attention to his horse, grazing nearby between the trees. He hurried toward it, leaning for a moment on a nearby tree trunk as he drew in breath after breath, his mind trying to recover from the terrifying experience of sudden and absolute blindness. When he pulled his hand away, he was astonished to see a smear of red. He examined the skin, but could find no sign of an injury. Peering at the tree, he realized with an uncomfortable flop of the heart that it wasn't his blood.

Looking around, he saw another smear on a nearby tree,

and another beyond. The ground was trampled as well, as though someone had blundered through here before him. Who had it been? Not Cyfrin—Amell knew from experience how stealthily the enchanter moved through the trees.

Seizing his horse's bridle, he followed the signs of passage. He had only a rudimentary level of training when it came to tracking, but some indication of direction had to be better than none. He had to find Aurelia before any well-meaning soldiers caught sight of her, and this was the best lead he had. If there was any chance Aurelia was at the end of it, he would follow this trail to the edge of the world.

CHAPTER TWENTY

A urelia hugged her shoulders miserably, wishing she had better protection against the chill of the evening air. As desperately as she'd wanted to be outside of her tower, the idea of being truly outside through the hours of darkness was a little alarming. She walked as briskly as she could over the strange terrain, the brown dirt striped with row upon row of green plants, reaching halfway up her legs.

She'd thought it would be such a simple thing to ask for directions, but so far she'd only encountered one person, and it hadn't gone well. Unease raced over her at the memory of how the man had started when she spoke, dropping the long handled tool in his hand and running at full speed toward what seemed to be his dwelling, a short distance away.

Aurelia had debated following him, but some instinct warned her that she'd do better to keep moving. At least the sinking sun had given her a better idea of what direction she should be traveling in. It was mostly behind her now, giving her the sense of walking into gathering gloom. Fear prickled at her, and with it came a stab of grief. She'd waited her whole life for this moment. She should be celebrating, not wandering miserably, fighting off fear. At the very least, her mother should be with her.

But the thought of Mama Imelda bolstered her. The other woman might not be with Aurelia, but she was safe, and free of the tower, and that was what really mattered. They would find each other sooner or later, and then they would be able to celebrate their liberation.

In spite of the early hour, weariness tugged at Aurelia, her limbs still gripped by the weakness that had come over her when Cyfrin's magic was extracted. But she was alive, she reminded herself fiercely. She'd survived the experience, when no one had known whether she would, and now no part of her belonged to the enchanter. That was worth any weakness.

A clomping sound drew Aurelia's attention to a row of trees up ahead, and she picked up her pace hopefully. As she drew close, she realized with a rush of excitement that there was a road on the other side of the trees. She might never have seen one before, but she still knew what a road was, and that it meant people. And people meant help.

Hurrying forward, she wove her way through the small stand of trees, emerging onto a wide, flat space that continued out of sight in both directions. A cart was going past, pulled by a large horse. Aurelia gasped at the sight of it. Mama Imelda had drawn pictures for her, but they couldn't compare to the reality. It was magnificent. Her gaze passed from the horse to the two people sitting up on the cart behind it. They were the oldest people she'd ever seen, one a man, the other a woman.

"Hello!" she called excitedly. "Can you help me, please?"

The woman screamed, her eyes widening as they latched on to Aurelia's form. "Look, Jim!" she cried, pointing. "We'll be killed! Go faster!"

The man was gaping at Aurelia, but at the woman's words, he slapped the reins he held, calling to the horse to move. The cart lurched into faster motion, the woman still clutching at the man's arm as she cast fearful eyes back over her shoulder.

Aurelia was left standing in the middle of the road, tears of confusion and loneliness welling up in her eyes. Why were they afraid of her?

More feet were approaching, and she whirled quickly to see a trio of men on foot, chatting cheerfully. As soon as they caught sight of her, they all stopped dead.

"Good...good evening," she said, clearing her throat nervously. "I wondered if you could help me. I'm trying to find my way to the capital."

"Don't let her speak to you!" one of the men cried to his companions, covering his ears. "Don't listen! Run!" Giving Aurelia a wide berth, the men edged around her, breaking into a run as soon as they were clear.

"Don't think you'll get away with it!" one of them called back, from what he seemed to consider a safe distance. "We'll be reporting you."

"But—" Aurelia cried, fear and frustration warring within her.

"Yeah, *and* we'll tell them you're heading for the capital!" another of the men yelled.

"Get away with what?" Aurelia demanded miserably, well aware that they couldn't hear her. "I haven't done anything!"

Fear gripped her as the men disappeared from sight. Had Cyfrin been telling the truth about the world after all? Had Mama Imelda's assurances that people were generally kind been another of her misguided attempts to shield her daughter from painful knowledge?

Drawing a shaky breath, Aurelia looked up and down the road. At least she'd found a thoroughfare. The sun had almost disappeared, but its location was enough to tell her which direction would lead her to the city. She started walking, shivering in the cold and no longer knowing whether she wanted to encounter more people or not.

After a similar experience had been repeated with a lone traveler, a group in a carriage, and a family passing in a wagon, she knew the answer. She never wanted to see another unfamiliar face again. Every single one of them was unfriendly, full of fear and anger. She kept her thoughts on Amell. He was kind. He would never shun her like all these people.

But did she want a life here with him, if the people she'd met were any indication of Fernedellians? Not that Albury was likely to be any better, she reflected glumly, remembering her mother's words about the royal family from which she came.

She just had to reach the capital, she told herself firmly. She would warn the king about the threat to the guild, and with any luck she would find Mama Imelda. Then they could leave, go somewhere where they could be safe and alone and away from all these people.

With a flash of horror, Aurelia realized she was describing the tower. She'd finally gotten free, and one afternoon of exposure to the world outside had her wanting to run back to the safety of her prison.

Overcome, she stumbled to a stop. It was hard to keep going when she was so very weary, without even hope to sustain her. It turned out Cyfrin had been right. She wasn't strong enough for the world outside. Tears dripping down her face, she turned off the road, pushing into the trees that lined one side of it. She didn't go far before she collapsed to the ground, too exhausted to go on. She pulled her knees against her chest, wrapping her arms around them and resting her head on top.

Thinking of her simple, if restricted, life in the tower, she closed her eyes. The sun had gone down at least an hour before. If she was back there, Cyfrin would have left, and she and Mama Imelda would be preparing dinner. Perhaps she'd spend the evening reading, her mother singing while she washed the dishes.

Her voice thin and miserable even in her own ears, Aurelia began to sing. The cheerful ditty didn't match her mood, but it made her think of her mother, and that was a comfort of its own. She raised her voice, the foolish words irrelevant as she focused on the tune.

She sang loudly enough to miss the noise she now recognized as approaching hooves until it was almost upon her. Frightened, she fell silent. But it was clearly too late to evade notice. As her singing had stopped, so had the movement of whoever was on the road.

CHAPTER TWENTY-ONE

Amell dropped to a walk, giving his horse a well-earned rest. Disheartened, he directed his eyes ahead, trying to make out the road through the darkness. The sun had set an hour before, and he'd been forced to abandon what had become a futile search. His tracking skills had failed him, and he was no wiser as to Aurelia's location than he would be if he was still blind.

Returning to Fernford had seemed like his only option. He had no idea what had become of Furn, but hopefully the guard would be waiting for him, perhaps with answers. He thought Abigail and Aurelia would be likely to attempt to make their way there as well, so he still had some hope. And if they weren't there...well, if he was right about the concealment magic being broken altogether, he'd be able to explain Aurelia's identity to his father. He had a feeling that finding her would suddenly become the king's top priority.

Amell was just thinking that his horse might be ready to canter again when his ears caught an unbelievable sound. A sweet voice, raised in a light song he'd heard before. He pulled his horse to a stop, his heart beating wildly. Surely that was the song Aurelia had been singing the very first time he'd met her.

But his straining ears found only silence. Had he imagined it, because she was so constantly on his mind? He dismounted, leading his horse to the side of the road. It had come from the trees, he was almost certain. A group of riders was approaching from the direction of the capital, but Amell ignored them, tying his horse's reins loosely to a nearby branch and stepping into the trees.

"Aurelia?" he called cautiously. "Are you in there?"

The question was met with an audible gasp, and Amell's heart flooded with relief as a beautifully familiar voice called back.

"Amell? Is that really you?"

"Yes, I'm here!" he cried, his voice shaking with shock and relief. "Where are you?"

"I'm...I'm right here." Aurelia sounded tearful, and Amell felt his heart twist. What had she been through since he'd ridden away from her that morning? Could it really be the same day they'd shared those kisses? It felt like a lifetime ago.

"Aurelia, my darling, it's going to be all right," he promised her. "There's no need to hide. You can come out, I'm going to keep you safe now."

"I knew you wouldn't shun me."

Her relieved words confused him, as did her continued failure to emerge. He peered through the darkness, seeing nothing but trees in the thin moonlight.

"Who's been shunning you?" he demanded. "Surely not your mother. Where is she?"

"I don't know," said Aurelia shakily, her voice sounding louder, although he could still see no sign of her. "She and Sir Furnis left for the capital hours ago. And of course she'd never shun me. But oh, Amell, everyone else has been awful.'

"Aurelia, where are you?" Amell demanded, perplexed.

"What do you mean?" She sounded as confused as he felt. "I'm standing right in front of you."

Amell blinked, but no familiar form appeared. "I...I can't see you," he said, "I can hear you, but I can't see—"

He cut himself off with a gasp as something touched his arm. His hand jumped to the spot, and he felt another hand, placed tentatively on his elbow.

"Aurelia?" he demanded, astonished. "Is that you? Why can't I see you?"

"I don't know," she said, again sounding tearful. "I can see you."

"But..." Something suddenly clicked into place in Amell's mind. "Cyfrin," he said grimly. "He said I'd never see you again. It must have been a separate curse, one the power didn't fight off."

"What?"

He had no opportunity to answer Aurelia's confused question. A shout from behind him made him turn, and he gaped in astonishment at half a dozen soldiers racing toward him through the trees, lanterns in their hands.

"We found her!" one soldier shouted over his shoulder. His eyes flicked to Amell, recognition dawning. "Your Highness!" he gasped. "Step back! She's dangerous!"

"What are you—?" Amell could have slapped himself as he suddenly understood what was going on. "She's not dangerous," he said, exasperated. "I can explain it all."

"She's likely bewitched you, Your Highness," said another soldier gruffly. "Step away now. We had reports one was spotted on the main road, and we've come especially."

"Amell!" Aurelia's voice was full of fear, and he swung back around. Even in the blaze of the lanterns, the grove looked empty, his eyes unable to see the figure the soldiers were staring at. It was beyond bizarre.

"Amell," Aurelia pleaded again. "Please don't let them arrest me." She clutched at his arms, but before he could close them protectively around her, one of the soldiers let out an angry shout.

"Step away from the prince! Step away now!"

He'd raised a bow, an arrow notched to it, and Amell felt his patience desert him.

"Stop," he said sternly. "This is ridiculous."

"You know the orders, Your Highness," said one of the soldiers, his eyes fixed warily on a spot of apparently empty air.

"Of course I know the orders," said Amell, exasperated. "I helped issue them. But they don't apply here. She's not a—"

Before he'd even finished his sentence, he felt Aurelia pull away from him. Whether she didn't have faith in his ability to extricate her, or she just lost her head, he didn't know. But seeing the soldier pull his bowstring hastily back, he didn't pause to think. He was unable to see Aurelia to know if the soldier's aim was true, but it wasn't a chance he was willing to take. With a cry of horror, he threw himself sideways, straight into the path of the oncoming arrow.

The simple projectile did what none of Cyfrin's magic had been able to achieve, and pierced Amell, burying itself into his shoulder. Pain radiated from the spot, and his vision spun as he fell heavily to the ground.

"Amell!"

Aurelia's scream told him that she hadn't run far, and he reached blindly for her invisible form. A hand gripped his, and he suddenly found his head cushioned in a soft lap.

"Amell, speak to me, don't leave," she sobbed.

"I'm...all right," he managed, wincing with the words. "It's just...a bit of blood."

Aurelia made no answer, but he could hear her breathing growing more and more rapid.

"Move away from him!" came the voice of the soldier, clearly aghast at what he'd done.

"NO!" Amell shouted, with the greatest effort of his life. "No one touch her!"

"Your Highness, she's addled your mind!"

"She hasn't," he insisted, attempting to sit up, and instantly falling back.

"Don't move!" Aurelia protested.

"Your Highness—"

"Stop!" Amell interrupted the soldier, in his sternest voice. "Stay where you are, and that's a royal order."

"I'm so sorry, Amell," Aurelia said, disregarding the soldiers, "but this will hurt."

Amell gave an involuntary cry of pain as the arrow came out of his wound, seemingly by itself. There was a loud ripping sound, and a wad of fabric was suddenly pressed to his shoulder. He felt Aurelia's warm breath on his cheek as she bent over him, and something wet fell onto his forehead.

"Don't cry," he said weakly, reaching blindly for her. "It's going to be all right."

"Amell, you shouldn't have done it," she sobbed. "I can't bear to see you hurt for me."

"And I can't bear to make you cry," he said, in an attempt at lightness. "Crying doesn't help anyone."

Aurelia gave a hiccup that might have hidden a hysterical laugh. "I saved someone's life by crying once. If only I could do it again."

Amell was about to protest that his life wasn't in danger, when something hit his eyes. Blinking rapidly, he gasped at the stinging sensation. Steady drops were still hitting his face, and it took him a moment to realize that Aurelia's tears had fallen into his eyes. Unable to see them coming, he hadn't instinctively closed his eyelids for protection.

With a few more rapid blinks, something solid came into view, and he jerked convulsively at the sight of the most beautiful face in the world, hovering over him in tear-stained anguish.

"Aurelia!" he cried. "I can see you! Your tears counteracted the magic somehow."

"Amell," she gasped, relief washing over her face.

"And you claim she's not an enchantress." The skeptical voice came from a nearby soldier, who was watching Aurelia with mistrust.

Amell's senses were swimming, and he could see that the fabric Aurelia was pressing to his shoulder was soaked with his blood. He drew a labored breath, putting as much authority as he could into his weakened voice.

"She's not a prisoner." His eyes passed over the gathered soldiers.

"Your Highness, her hair," protested one of them.

Amell glanced at it, grimacing as he saw how very similar it looked to the standard prison style. Aurelia's anxious face danced before his vision, spots erupting here and there. With an effort, he turned back to the soldiers.

"I can explain...everything..." he panted. "But not...here. Anyone who hurts her...will answer to...me." He closed his eyes for a moment. The pain in his shoulder had become overwhelming, but he willed himself to stay conscious until he could finish what he needed to say. "Take her to...the castle...she won't...resist." His eyes searched Aurelia's pleadingly. "Do you...trust me?"

"Of course I do," she whispered.

He stretched out a hand toward her face, wishing he could wipe the terror from her eyes. But before he could reach her, the blackness closed in, and he knew no more.

CHAPTER TWENTY-TWO

Aurelia

"Amell!" Aurelia clutched Amell's limp form close, terror racing through her. He couldn't die. Not now, not for her. Why had he leaped in front of that arrow? But she understood why. It was the same reason she'd thrown Mama Imelda out the window of the tower. Tears fell freely from Aurelia's eyes, but she knew that this time they wouldn't be enough to save anyone. Why they'd made Amell able to see her again, she didn't understand. But none of that mattered. She'd infinitely prefer him to never see her again than for him to die.

She pressed her hand to his chest, afraid of what she'd find. His heart was beating, but it felt weak to her. And his face was unnaturally pale, even in the yellow glare of the soldiers' lanterns.

"Up you get." One of the soldiers had approached her, his weapon raised and his voice grim. "The prince said you wouldn't resist. If you want to show we've made a mistake about you, you'll do as he said you would."

Drying her tears, Aurelia pushed herself to her feet. She'd

almost forgotten her own weakness in the terror of Amell's injury, but it came rushing back, making her sway.

"No tricks now," said one of the soldiers warily. He approached her the way Mama Imelda inched toward particularly large spiders. "Hold out your hands."

No fight left in her, Aurelia did as she was bid.

"And gag her," one of the other soldiers prompted. "Bind the hands and stop the tongue. They usually use one or both of those in their magic."

"I don't have—" Aurelia started, but she stopped abruptly when the soldiers all raised their weapons.

Satisfied that she wasn't going to speak, one of them—a man older than Mama Imelda, who so far hadn't spoken—put a simple gag around her mouth.

"If we're mistaken, miss, you'll have our apologies," he said calmly. "But we won't take any chances."

Shivering from some combination of shock, fear, and genuine cold, Aurelia allowed herself to be led back to the road. She was lifted onto one of the soldier's horses, and the man urged his beast toward the capital, two others flanking him.

Aurelia caught sight of another soldier wrapping a length of fabric around Amell's injured shoulder, but the prince was soon cut off from her sight. Terror for Amell engulfed her, driving out every consideration. How much blood could he afford to lose? The physician's guide she'd read had claimed that bleeding could kill a person, if it went on for long enough.

The trio of horses moved slowly, but another of the soldiers shot past them before long, riding hard for the capital. They were obviously closer to Fernford than Aurelia had guessed, because it wasn't long before an empty carriage trundled past, led by the same soldier. Hopefully Amell would make it back to the city without doing his shoulder further injury. Aurelia was glad he wouldn't have to travel on horseback. She never would have guessed that riding a horse would be so uncomfortable.

Aurelia knew the carriage would travel even more slowly than her own group, however, and she wasn't surprised that the equipage was nowhere to be seen when they passed a large sign announcing the proximity of Fernford. They'd just emerged from the grove, and Aurelia strained her eyes for her first look at a city. It was disappointing. She could make out very little in the darkness, and she soon gave up trying, too racked by grief and fear.

The weariness was so heavy on her now, it was all she could do to keep her eyes open as the horses clopped their way over cobblestoned streets. A day ago, it would all have been a source of such fascination to her. But now, she wanted nothing more than to sleep.

She did rouse herself enough to look up at the castle when they drew close. The enormous building looked imposing and threatening in the darkness, its turrets uncomfortably reminiscent of her tower. She thought the soldiers would take her in through the grand entrance, but instead they turned their horses toward a nearby building, which seemed to be attached to the castle, but had its own door.

A shout went up from a man at the entrance, dressed in the same uniform as the soldiers in Aurelia's group.

"You've caught another one!" His eyes lingered on Aurelia's head.

"Yep," said the soldier on the same horse as her. "But the prince ordered us not to touch her. He said to bring her to the castle."

"Who's blood is that on her hands?" the soldier asked skeptically.

"The prince's," said Aurelia's rider in a grim voice.

The other man's eyes widened in horror. "Why didn't you follow the order?"

The mounted soldier grunted. "The prince was clear. He said anyone who hurts her will answer to him. Now, is the special holding cell empty? We've got to go back to help escort the prince to the castle. He'll need a physician, and fast."

"Bring her through," said the soldier on the door, stepping aside.

The three riders dismounted, pulling Aurelia after them. She was marched into the building, straight across a small entry space, and toward a winding stair. They'd followed two twists before she grasped what was happening.

"No!" she gasped, but her gag muffled the word. She began to flail wildly, an illogical terror rising up in her. They were taking her up one of those turrets—they were going to lock her in a tower!

"Easy now!" shouted the soldier who'd offered a conditional apology. "Don't give us reason to harm you, lass."

Aurelia's muffled screams only rose in volume. She kicked out with her legs and twisted her arms, trying to elbow the closest soldier in the stomach. She'd been a baby last time she'd been locked up, unable to resist. But this time she wasn't going to go without a fight.

"Dragon's flame, she's a live one!" exclaimed one of the men. "Good thing we bound her properly."

Aurelia began to weep, hot, angry tears of despair. Amell had asked her to trust him, but he was far away, his lifeblood draining out of him, and the men he'd told her not to resist were proving to be exactly like Cyfrin.

In spite of her rush of panic, Aurelia was weak from her various ordeals. The soldiers had no difficulty overpowering her, and they half dragged her up the rest of the stairs. Even through her terror, she noticed they were taking care to be gentle. Clearly the prince's word carried a great deal of weight. She would have to hold on to that.

At the top of the turret, there was a line of three strange rooms, each with metal bars instead of walls. Scanning them, Aurelia was greeted by a sight both terrible and wonderful. She again tried to call out, the gag turning her greeting into garbled nonsense. But it didn't matter. The sole occupant of the tower raced to the edge of her little room, crying in shock.

"Aurelia! Aurelia, are you all right?"

"Know her, do you?" one of the soldiers said to Mama Imelda. "That's a count against you, isn't it?"

"Why are you locking her up?" Mama Imelda demanded angrily. "What could she possibly have done to—" She broke off as her eyes dropped to Aurelia's bound hands. "Aurelia! Whose blood is that?"

"Prince Amell's, as a matter of fact," the soldier told the older woman darkly. "So don't expect any leniency."

Mama Imelda's eyes flew to Aurelia's in horror, but Aurelia could say nothing to reassure her mother that the prince was still alive.

"But what's her crime?" Mama Imelda demanded, a hint of anger in her voice. "You don't understand—you can't trap her up here! She's finally free!"

The soldier grunted. "If she wanted to be free, she should have served her time. It'll be doubled now, if nothing worse."

Mama Imelda's confusion suddenly melted away, and she raised her hands in appeal. "Do you think she's an escaped prisoner? You've got it all wrong! She's not a prisoner. She's a princess! She's a princess of Albury, and she's been trapped in a—"

"Sure, lady," said one of the soldiers indulgently. "Tell it to the bars." One of the others had been unlocking the door of the middle cell while he spoke, and he pushed Aurelia in. "This cell's reinforced against magic-users," he told her, as he locked her in. "So don't get any ideas."

"Aren't you going to take off the gag?" Mama Imelda demanded.

"Nice try," grunted one of the soldiers, and a moment later the three of them had disappeared, leaving the two women alone.

"Oh, Aurelia," Mama Imelda said at once, her voice shaking. "I know this is terrible, but you're alive! And you're free of the tower."

Free? At least in Cyfrin's tower she hadn't been in a cage, gagged and bound. Aurelia cast a meaningful glance around her, and Mama Imelda groaned.

"I know, I know. I'm just so happy to know where you are. Is Amell...is he...alive?"

Aurelia nodded fervently, and some of the tension leaked from Mama Imelda's shoulders.

"He'll work it out," she said confidently. "He'll make it right."

Aurelia swallowed, a lump in her throat. She wanted to believe that, but it was hard to have much faith in anything at that moment.

Her mother seemed to sense it, because her voice turned sorrowful again. "Oh, my darling, I know things are bad right now. But this isn't normal. Most people won't treat you this way. I don't know why they think you're from the prison, but when they realize you're not, they'll release you, I'm sure."

Feeling skeptical, Aurelia tilted her head pointedly toward Mama Imelda's own cell.

"Yes, they locked me in here as well," Mama Imelda conceded. "But there's a reason for that, too."

Aurelia raised her eyebrow in a question.

"Sit down," sighed Mama Imelda. "I think we might be in here for a while. My story is quite simple. Sir Furnis found me a horse at the prison, and we rode here to the city as quickly as we could. But the prince was already gone by then, and when Sir Furnis started asking urgently for him, it created quite a reaction. Apparently the two of them were supposed to be on their way to Albury for a diplomatic visit, and the discovery that Amell wasn't with his guard, and that his guard didn't even know his whereabouts, caused the king and queen to become quite…concerned."

Aurelia grimaced at what was clearly an understatement.

"Sir Furnis guessed that Amell had gone back to the clearing, of course, and he announced that he did know where the prince was after all." Mama Imelda sighed. "That was a mistake. Because try as we might, neither of us could tell anyone where that might be. The concealment magic Cyfrin placed on the clearing stopped our tongues, just like Amell described. We couldn't say anything about Cyfrin, or you, or the clearing, or anything. I have to acknowledge it was all highly suspicious. And then someone realized that Sir Furnis was wearing the prince's own cloak, and everything went downhill from there. It seems Amell's frequent absences hadn't gone as unnoticed as he thought, and everyone now suspects Sir Furnis of some kind of plot. I'm not entirely sure what happened to Sir Furnis, but I was locked in here, and told my case would be considered when the prince reemerged. I can only assume he still hasn't done so."

The older woman frowned, lost in thought for a moment. "I was able to tell that guard just then who you were, wasn't I?" Her eyes searched Aurelia's. "Has the concealment magic been lifted since this afternoon?"

Aurelia considered the point, remembering when she'd thought Cyfrin was destroying the walls of the tower, only to find it intact. Was that what he'd really destroyed? The powerful magic of concealment, and possibly of restraint, that had coated the clearing and the tower for seventeen years?

She nodded tentatively, her mind racing with the implications. If she'd needed more proof that he was preparing to make his move, that was it.

Her thoughts flew to Amell, bleeding on the forest floor, pierced by an arrow meant for her. Aurelia groaned, leaning her head against one of the metal bars. It was a terrible mess, no denying it. And it seemed there was little they could do but wait.

CHAPTER TWENTY-THREE

Amell

Amell's eyes fluttered open, the fuzziness around him settling into his own familiar room. He suddenly became aware of an agonizing pain in his shoulder, and he lifted a hand to it.

"Best not to touch the dressings, Your Highness."

Amell lifted his head, blinking in confusion at the face floating above him, framed by white hair.

"Bartholomew?"

"Who else?" the enchanter said cheerfully. "Do you think I'd let anyone else patch you up?"

Amell laid his head back down, groaning. "What happened?"

"In simple terms, you were shot in the shoulder by an arrow. Accidentally, the soldier in question assures me, but that's not my area. I just do the fixing up."

Amell frowned, trying to remember. His eyes traveled to the window, through which the thin light of early morning was streaming. In spite of his light tone, Bartholomew looked strained and tired, as if he'd been up tending Amell all night.

It wouldn't be the first time.

"Shot with an arrow," Amell repeated, reflecting that this *was* a first. A flash of memory came to him. Fabric soaked in blood, a dark forest around, and a beautiful, terrified face suspended above his.

"Aurelia!" he gasped, sitting upright and instantly grimacing in pain.

"Whoa, Prince Amell!" Bartholomew protested. "You need rest! Lie down again, there's a good lad."

But Amell was back in possession of his senses, and recovering was the last thing on his mind. "Where's Aurelia?" he demanded. "Where did they take her? They didn't hurt her, did they? I have to explain everything."

He groaned. He couldn't explain, could he? The magic wouldn't let him. Then he remembered how he'd found the clearing even without the cloak, and hope grew inside him.

"Does this have anything to do with the truly excessive amount of magic that's lingering around your person?" Bartholomew asked cautiously. "I thought it was your cloak, but that's nowhere nearby, and you're still positively reeking of it."

"It's Cyfrin's magic," said Amell, figuring it was as good an opportunity as any to test whether his tongue was still bound. Apparently it wasn't.

"Cyfrin?" Bartholomew gasped, horror crossing his features.

Heartened, Amell nodded. "He kept going with his experiments in secret. He stole an infant to use as a vessel. An infant who happened to be Princess Aurelia of Albury. He took her with her carer, and the two of them have been locked in a tower not far from the prison ever since. He stored his magic in her hair, figuring that it was less likely to wrap around her core, and kill her when extracted. Not that he really cared about her. He just wanted to prove he was right, I think. And then later he wanted to marry her, for the status." Amell shuddered.

Bartholomew was staring at him, his mouth opening and closing wordlessly.

"But lately he became obsessed with the idea of using a key," Amell hurried on. "He transferred half of his magic into her core instead of her hair, thinking it would sort of be in her control that way. He thought that if she performed the key, thereby willingly releasing the magic to him, it would make it stronger, according to the—"

"Foundational principles of power," Bartholomew finished weakly.

Amell nodded again. "He also wanted to manipulate the one about love, so he linked the key idea into his plan to marry her. He made the key her first kiss, but he hadn't actually told her that." A grim smile crossed his face. "So when she kissed me, completely unaware of its significance, she released all of the magic he'd stored within her core, and it sort of..." He shrugged.

"Wrapped around you," Bartholomew said, looking half fascinated, half horrified. It was an expression he'd often worn when examining Amell's more dramatic childhood injuries. "But you can't wield it, can you?"

Amell shook his head. "I can't control it, but it still seems to be active. It prevented Cyfrin from killing me, more than once. It sort of rebuffed the magic he was using, which was the magic in Aurelia's hair."

"My word," Bartholomew said mildly, passing a hand down one side of his face. "It's a lot to take in."

"I have to find Aurelia," said Amell. "The fact that I was able to tell you all that means that the concealment enchantment must have lifted. I'll be able to explain everything to my parents, and to those soldiers who thought Aurelia was an escaped prisoner because of her hair."

"An escaped prisoner?" Bartholomew repeated sharply. "I've been in here with you all night, so I don't know the details, but I heard something about an escaped prisoner being involved in your injury. There was to be a hearing before your father this morning."

Amell's eyes widened. He couldn't let Aurelia face such an ordeal alone, even if she would now be free to explain it all. Groaning, he swung his feet off the bed.

"Whoa, whoa, whoa," said Bartholomew, alarmed. "You need to stay here, Your Highness. Let me go."

Amell shook his head. "Nonsense," he said through gritted teeth. "I'm fine. You can patch up anything."

"Incorrect," Bartholomew said dryly. "You're no longer in danger, and my magic has certainly accelerated the healing, but I can't fix something this big all at once. You need *rest*."

"I'll rest once I know Aurelia is safe," said Amell firmly. Wincing, he pulled on his boots, then pushed himself to his feet.

Finding he was unable to dissuade the prince, the old enchanter followed him, fussing around him like an agitated hen. Or so Amell told him.

The pair was only halfway to the king's audience hall when a flash of bright purple hurtled across their path, latching on to Amell's good arm.

"Amell!" Tora cried, her voice frantic.

"Ouch," Amell complained. "I have a hole in my shoulder, Tora, careful."

"Sorry," she gasped. She looked him over, then gave him a tentative hug on the other side. "I'm glad you're all right. But what's going on? Why is Furn locked up?"

"What?" Amell demanded. "What lunatic would lock Furn up?"

"Our king and father," said Tora dryly. Her face was unusually pale as she searched Amell's eyes. "Is this because of me,

Amell? Did someone find out how I feel, and...and cause mischief for—"

"Of course not," Amell scoffed. "I'm sure it's nothing to do with that." He frowned. "Is he really in the dungeons?"

Tora shook her head. "Not as drastic as that. He's detained in the guard's barracks. I mean, he's free to move around them, just not free to leave."

"That's not quite locked up," Amell said dryly. "Come on. I'm going to find Father, so I can get to the bottom of this."

Tora fell into step beside him, but she cast a doubtful glance over him as he began to walk again, at about half his usual speed. "Are you sure you should be up?"

"Yes," said Amell.

"No," Bartholomew contradicted at the same time.

Tora sighed. "Sounds about right."

They reached the audience hall to find that, although it was far from full, there were a decent number of spectators already in attendance. Their father appeared to have just taken his seat on the small dais at one end. At the sight of his children, he rose quickly to his feet, however.

"Amell! You're supposed to be resting."

"I'm fine," Amell said, wincing as he said it. "Father, there's been some mistake."

"Amell!" The queen had entered through an antechamber, and she hurried to her son in a rustle of silk. "You were shot! You shouldn't be up."

"I'm all right," said Amell impatiently. "Father, you've got the wrong end of the—"

At that moment, the door to the audience hall swung open. Furn entered, looking tense, and accompanied by a pair of guards who weren't actually laying a hand on him. Behind him came another contingent of guards. They were leading one copper haired woman with a tight, angry expression, and one much younger woman, with unevenly chopped dark hair, a gag around her mouth, and hands that were still covered in Amell's dried blood bound in front of her.

Horror rose up in him at her state. With her mangled hair and blood-encrusted hands, she looked worse than he would have believed possible for such a beautiful woman. Not that it was her appearance that distressed him. The restraints on her wrists and the guards at her side told him that unlike Furn, she had been properly locked up. The thought that his own people had thrown her back into captivity the moment she escaped her prison of seventeen years was unendurable. What must she think of them all? He could only imagine what she'd been through during the long hours of his unconsciousness.

"Aurelia!" Amell cried, genuinely forgetting his injury for a moment as he sprinted across the room. "Release her at once, you fools! What are you doing?"

"Aurelia?" the king repeated, startled. "Amell, who is this? I was informed she was an escaped prisoner who was somehow involved in your injury."

"You were *mis*informed," Amell growled, pulling the gag off Aurelia with his own hands. Snatching a small blade from the belt of the nearest guard, he sliced first Aurelia's bonds, then those on her mother.

"Are you all right?" he asked Aurelia softly, tilting her chin up with his hand.

Her eyes were filled with moisture as she met his gaze. "I don't know if I'd say all right," she said, and his heart broke at the pain in her voice. This whole situation was about as far as it could possibly be from what he would wish for her first experience of the world outside her tower.

Before he could find the words to apologize for everything she'd suffered, her face was softened by a tremulous smile.

"But I'm much better than I was, now I know you're not dying," she whispered.

Amell took her hand, squeezing it reassuringly as unshed tears pricked at his own eyes. "You poor thing, what have they put you through?"

Turning, he slipped Aurelia's hand through his uninjured arm and led her up the room toward the dais.

"Father, Mother," he said with dignity. "This is Princess Aurelia of Albury." He glanced at Abigail. "And her adoptive mother, Ab—"

"Imelda, Your Majesties," she interrupted, sinking into a graceful curtsy.

Amell raised an eyebrow, a smile on his face. It seemed there were no more secrets.

He looked toward the dais to find both of his parents staring in horror between their son and the foreign princess they'd just locked up overnight in their special cell for magical criminals.

"Are...are you sure?" Queen Pietra asked faintly.

"Very sure," said Amell firmly.

He heard Imelda mutter, "Sure, they believe it when *he* says it," and his lips twitched.

"It's a long story," he went on, "but just to be clear, the man who kidnapped her as a baby cut her hair like that because he wanted her to be thought an escaped prisoner. Which she's not."

"My dear," Queen Pietra said, moving toward Aurelia with genuine tears in her eyes. "I cannot tell you how sorry I am for the mistake that was made. We have the prisoners' hair cut in just such a way so as to identify them, for everyone's safety. Our soldiers have been searching for the last fugitives, and would certainly have assumed you to be one of them."

Aurelia smiled shyly, leaning more heavily on Amell than Bartholomew would probably approve of. Not that Amell cared.

"Thank you, Your Majesty. I confess I was confused by everyone's suspicion of me. I didn't know that about the prisoners' hair. Now that I understand, I bear you no ill will."

"That's very generous of you." King Bern's voice wasn't entirely steady as his eyes passed to his son. "She was concealed in Fernedell all this time? How long have you known of her presence, Amell?"

"Only since the prison break," he said. "I found the tower where they were trapped while searching the woods for fugitives. I only realized who Aurelia was when you received that letter from King Justin, though."

The king's eyes bulged. "But you kept this tower a secret? Amell, this was hardly the time to lose yourself in some heroic daydream."

"It wasn't like that, Your Majesty," Aurelia interjected. Her grip trembled slightly on Amell's arm, but her voice was quite steady. "He tried to tell everyone, to get us help. But there was a strong enchantment on the clearing, and it prevented him from revealing anything he'd seen there."

Amell smiled down at her, enchanted by her defense of him. She'd always thought better of him than he deserved.

Apparently she wasn't finished, because her eyes stayed on the king. "Your Majesty, there's a great deal to speak of. But one thing you need to know immediately. The man who locked us up is an enchanter. His name is Cyfrin. And he's just extracted a great deal of stored magic from me, which we believe he intends to use in an attack. We're fairly certain his target is the Enchanters' Guild, and that he plans to act soon. Honestly, I'm surprised he hasn't already struck."

"The guild?" Bartholomew stepped forward, alarm in his eyes. "He's seeking revenge for his expulsion all those years ago, isn't he? What's he going to do?"

Aurelia shook her head apologetically. "I'm afraid I don't know more. He didn't precisely confide in me."

Bartholomew turned to the king. "Your Majesty," he said, in some agitation, "I request permission to return to the guild immediately."

The king nodded. "I will accompany you." He gestured to one of his guards, who hastened out of the room, off to organize an escort. King Bern's gaze passed to Aurelia. "Princess Aurelia, I can imagine you wish for the chance to refresh yourself. We will have our best guest suite prepared for you and your—"

"With respect, Your Majesty," said Aurelia frankly, "I don't wish to be shut away in any room, no matter how luxurious. If Cyfrin is attacking the guild, I intend to see him stopped."

Amell's parents exchanged looks of distress, and he had no doubt they were eager to ensure no further harm came to the princess while she was in their care.

"You've already locked her back up in another tower," Amell said tightly. "Which, incidentally, is the very worst thing you could have done. I suggest you let her freely go wherever she chooses."

Aurelia beamed at him, and his parents let out identical sighs of resignation.

"Well, you need to go back to your rest," his mother said, her eyes dwelling anxiously on his wound.

"Don't be absurd, Mother," said Amell cheerfully, already moving toward the door with Aurelia, and collecting Furn on the way. "I need to stay with my healer, in case I need further patching up. And with my loyal guard by my side, I'll be as safe as I ever am."

"And obviously I'm coming as well," Tora chimed in, hurrying to catch up. Amell shook his head humorously.

Their parents didn't even try protesting Tora's inclusion, from which Amell inferred that they didn't actually expect imminent danger at the guild. He did notice Furn looking sideways at the princess, his expression troubled. Amell had never noticed it before, but he could see what Tora meant. The way his guard moved around his sister, his watchful manner as he scanned her area, certainly conveyed an impression of protectiveness.

They'd gathered quite a crowd by the time they completed the short walk to the Enchanters' Guild, even the queen trailing behind at a dignified distance. Amell entered the lobby just behind Bartholomew, Tora and Aurelia on either side of him, and Furn and Imelda a step behind.

"Is everything all right here?" Bartholomew asked the clerk anxiously.

"I believe so, Master Bartholomew," the man replied, staring at the bizarre group.

"No strange visitors?" Bartholomew pressed.

The clerk frowned. "There is a visitor. He arrived about half an hour ago. He asked for an appointment with the most senior enchanter, and I sent him down to the library to see—"

"What did he look like?" Bartholomew interrupted frantically.

"Fairly tall," the clerk said, clearly alarmed at his superior's tone. "Short, dark hair. He was wearing a strange garment, too. I've never seen anything like it."

"Strange how?" Amell asked, an ominous feeling creeping over him.

"Well, it was a vest, I suppose you'd say," the clerk mused. "It was made of some kind of dark fur...except, it was too long to be fur. It was all braided. I guess it looked like...well, hair."

Amell and Aurelia exchanged looks of alarm. Bartholomew had gone pale, but his voice was quite steady as he rapped out instructions to the clerk.

"A hostile enchanter has breached our guild. Summon every available member immediately, and send them to the library."

On the order, Bartholomew took off sprinting down the

corridor. Ignoring the protests of their various guards, Amell and Tora hastened to follow. Aurelia and Imelda were already hard on the enchanter's heels, clearly intending to see Cyfrin brought to justice. Amell could understand their determination to be involved, but his heart was in his throat as he watched Aurelia running toward the man who had stolen her entire childhood.

Fear was still swirling within him when Bartholomew burst into an enormous library, letting out a cry the moment he passed through the door.

Amell raced in after him, his eyes widening at the sight of Cyfrin, wearing Aurelia's hair like a vest, standing over a prone old man, who seemed to be struggling for air. The most chilling feature of the scene was the enchanter's calm. He wasn't doing or saying anything, just standing with his arms folded so that his hands rested on the hair at his chest, smiling unpleasantly as he watched the power at work.

"Cyfrin!" Bartholomew roared, and the enchanter looked around at last.

"Ah, Bartholomew, isn't it? I remember you. You'll have your turn, don't worry."

Bartholomew raised a hand in a movement Amell would have thought too swift for his frail frame, but Cyfrin's parry was even faster.

"Oh, you won't be able to best me," he said smugly. "I have more power than all the rest of you put together. It's time now. Time to admit I was right in my theories. Time to admit I've outdone you all. The guild is rightfully mine."

Amell growled in anger, and the enchanter's eyes passed to the pair standing just inside the doorway. "Your Highness," he said, raising an eyebrow. His eyes traveled to Aurelia. "Or should I say, Your Highnesses? Such a daring look you're modeling, child."

Aurelia glared back at him. "Leave that man alone," she demanded.

Cyfrin threw back his head and laughed. "Are you giving the orders now, Honeysuckle? How entertaining." His smile instantly dropped, replaced by a look of utter coldness. "None of you have the power to stop me, least of all you, child. You gave up all your chance at power. So I'd recommend you don't get in my way."

"As always, Cyfrin," Aurelia said angrily, "you're a liar and a thief." She yanked a book off a nearby shelf and flung it with all her might.

Taken off guard by the mild attack, Cyfrin did nothing to deflect it, and it whacked him full in the face.

"Well done, Aurelia," said Imelda approvingly, reaching for a book herself.

The enchanter was less impressed. His hand flew to his temple, and he moved away from the downed guild member, growling audibly. The man rolled instantly onto his hands and knees, gasping in air, and Bartholomew ran to kneel beside him.

"You'll pay for that, you useless child," Cyfrin spat, ignoring the elderly men behind him. "I'm going to overpower these feeble narrow-minded enchanters one by one, and then I'll come for you and your little prince."

"Don't speak to her like that," Amell said through clenched teeth.

Cyfrin's eyes narrowed in anger. "I'll speak to her however I want. She's mine to control, not yours."

With a sudden movement, he jerked his hands upward, palms facing the ceiling. There was an almighty crack, and an entire section of stone fell away, raining down on the group by the door.

Amell gave a cry, throwing himself instinctively over Aurelia and Imelda, who stood together beside him. It seemed that the power he'd received from Aurelia's core still lingered in him, because the rocks bounced harmlessly off an invisible shield over his head. It was a good thing, too, because even without being struck, Amell's shoulder was in agony. He was fairly sure he'd reopened the wound.

An ominous rumble announced that the structure of the building had been compromised, and a moment later a further chunk fell at Cyfrin's feet, forcing the enchanter to jump back or risk being struck by the deadly missiles. Bartholomew and the other guild member were also forced to flee deeper into the library, as the falling stone cut them off from the rest of the group.

Scrambling to his feet again, Amell heard the last sound he expected amidst the chaos. A familiar, delighted laugh.

"I did it!" Tora declared. "I actually did it."

Amell looked over, perplexed, to see his sister shielded by Furn's body, just the way Amell had been shielding Aurelia. They seemed to have missed the worst of the falling rocks, for which they could be thankful, given Furn didn't have magic working for him like Amell did.

"I wasn't even trying to put myself in danger this time, and I still managed to get in a situation where you were driven to protect me, Furn!" Tora went on brightly. "Did it work?"

Amell groaned, putting a hand over his face.

"Did it...work, Your Highness?" Furn's voice was a strange mixture of caution and confusion.

"Did saving me from imminent death make you realize your feelings for me?" Tora asked matter-of-factly. "Because I'm practical enough to realize that if that didn't do it, nothing will, and I'll just have to give up."

Furn's face burned, and for a moment he mouthed wordlessly, looking like nothing so much as a beached fish. "Princess, I..." he stuttered. He tried again, his voice quieter. "There's nothing to realize. My feelings are...no secret to me. As I think you've known for some time."

Tora's eyes lit up, but Amell could only stare at his usually unflappable and dedicated guard, who seemed to have entirely forgotten that they were in the middle of a life and death situation. Amell glanced at Aurelia and Imelda, both of whom were staring at the princess and the guard in utter astonishment. Movement on the other side of the room caught his eye, and he realized that Cyfrin was emerging from the wreckage, apparently satisfied that there wouldn't be further collapses.

"Tora, Furn," Amell said sharply. "It's not the time."

"Sorry," Tora said, not sounding in the least repentant. "Life-threatening situations don't come up all that often, though. I had to make the most of it." She followed Amell's gaze and noticed Cyfrin, her frame suddenly stiffening where she still crouched behind Furn's body. "That doesn't mean I think we should repeat the experience, of course," she said darkly.

"Stop," Amell told Cyfrin, in his most commanding voice. "You will answer for your crimes."

Cyfrin's derisive laugh was cut off by a shout from behind Amell. His father had arrived, and the guards who'd accompanied him poured into the ruined room.

"Dragon's flame," the king said, his eyes passing from Cyfrin to the chunks of stone everywhere, then to his children and their companions, half of whom were still crouched in protective poses. "The guild really is under attack."

"King Bern," said Cyfrin, bowing with a flourish. "Don't be dismayed. What you see before you is simply an example of the power your kingdom has available to it. I look forward to working more closely with you in my role as Head of the Enchanters' Guild."

The king stared at the enchanter in evident shock. "Are you mad?" he demanded.

"Certainly not, Your Majesty," said Cyfrin smoothly, sounding not quite pleased. "I am nothing more nor less than the greatest enchanter Fernedell has ever seen. As everyone in this room will soon be brought to acknowledge."

"No." The quiet voice seemed to fill the whole room as Aurelia stepped out from the line of guards and royals, her eyes fixed unwaveringly on the man who had imprisoned her for her whole life. "I for one will never acknowledge that."

CHAPTER TWENTY-FOUR

Aurelia

Cyfrin pinned Aurelia with a glare that would once have frightened her into hiding behind her mother. No longer. She held his gaze steadily, a fire burning within her that no amount of his anger or criticism could quench.

"Nor will I," agreed Mama Imelda calmly, stepping up beside her.

"How dare you defy me?" Cyfrin breathed. "You've both forgotten your place."

"Our place was never in that tower," Aurelia contradicted. "And you will never control us again."

Cyfrin gave a nasty laugh. "You think you have control just because you're out in the big wide world? You were born a princess, Honeysuckle. That means your life will always be controlled by others. Ask your precious prince how much freedom he has."

Aurelia felt Amell step up on her other side, and her heart swelled at his support.

"I have the same freedom every man has," said the prince calmly. "The freedom to choose what kind of man I will be. You chose poorly, and I'm done letting others suffer for that choice."

A shuffling noise made Aurelia flick her eyes to the side of the room, where the two guild members were climbing their way back to the group by the door.

"You are a child, not a man," scoffed Cyfrin dismissively.

"You will show your prince some respect," said King Bern curtly. "Guards, seize him."

The guards hurried forward, but none of them made it more than a few steps. Running his hands caressingly along the braids over his chest, Cyfrin muttered a few words. Instantly, each of the guards froze in his tracks, held in place by an invisible hand.

"How dare you?" the king demanded in outrage.

"How dare I?" repeated Cyfrin, and Aurelia recognized the signs of him losing his temper. "How dare you?"

He extended his hand, but before he could act, the door leading to the corridor burst open, and a dozen guild members poured into the room. Their shouts of anger and alarm rang across the ruined library, several of them gasping Cyfrin's name. Clearly seventeen years wasn't long enough for him to be fully forgotten.

"I'm so glad you could join us, Master Enchanters and Enchantresses," Cyfrin said smoothly. "You're just in time to witness a demonstration of my power. I'm thrilled at the opportunity to show you the results of my...what did you call them? Abominable experiments, was it? See how abominable you find them now."

"Enough playacting," snapped a middle aged enchantress. She lifted her hands before her, palms outward in Cyfrin's direction. As if it was a signal, the rest of the guild members copied the gesture. They began to murmur as they spread out, forming a semi-circle with Cyfrin as the focus.

The rogue enchanter showed no sign of alarm at this coordinated attack. He just smiled lazily, once again folding his arms so that his hands rested on the thick braids crisscrossing his chest. Nausea curled in Aurelia's stomach at the sight of his fingers stretching caressingly over her own hair, detached from her body though it might be. A shiver passed over her frame, and Amell's arm was instantly around her shoulders.

"We should move back," he whispered. "Let the guild members take care of Cyfrin."

Aurelia allowed him to draw her back a little, but her thoughts were troubled.

"I'm not sure they'll be able to," she said.

"They will." Amell's voice was confident. "So many against just him—and these are some of the most powerful enchanters in the kingdom. They train for this as well—they know how to fight together."

Aurelia bit her lip, unconvinced. Cyfrin had been preparing for this moment for seventeen years. And if she was correct, his plan had always been to take on the guild. He must believe he had enough power to defend against a combined attack.

She had no chance to express her doubts. The guild members' muttering had grown to a discordant buzzing, and a senior enchanter suddenly gave a shout. At the sound, the semicircle of magic-users all shouted as well, releasing the power they had been preparing.

Aurelia couldn't sense magic, but she could see from the strain on the enchanters' faces that they were giving the attack everything they had.

And yet, Cyfrin still stood.

He took an unsteady step back, as if he'd been hit hard with something, but he kept his feet. A look of great concentration flitted across his face, but it passed quickly, melting back into the hateful smirk she knew all too well. A quick glance around the room showed the guild members all frozen in shock, their faces telling Aurelia plainly that they had seriously underestimated the power at Cyfrin's disposal.

"Now you see it, don't you?" the renegade enchanter breathed. "The limitless potential. Now you understand that my path was the one of wisdom, not your cautious, narrow-minded—"

"Wisdom?" gasped the enchanter whom Amell had called Bartholomew. "You toy with others' lives like they're playthings to be used and discarded, and you call it wisdom?"

Aurelia applauded his words, but it made her nervous to see how rattled he was. Cyfrin's experiments had clearly had the desired effect—he had exceeded what the guild had believed him capable of. Which meant they weren't prepared.

Cyfrin just laughed at the old man's words. "No lectures today, Bartholomew. Or ever again. I don't believe Fernedell needs an Enchanters' Guild anymore. As you'll soon see, I have enough power to provide the king with all the assistance and advice he could ever require. If I do decide to take on some like-minded apprentices in years to come, you can be assured they won't be subjected to the white-washed drivel you teach your students."

Aurelia could feel the derisive astonishment issuing from Amell, but she didn't find it at all hard to believe that Cyfrin still thought he could muscle his way into a position at the king's side. She knew better than anyone that he believed that having power meant having the right to do whatever you chose with that power. He'd worked for years to demonstrate what he was capable of, and now the time had come, he would see the position as his due.

"Enough!" cried one of the other enchanters. "Again!"

All of the guild members once again closed in on Cyfrin, and he began to laugh. Stroking the braids across his chest, he muttered words of his own. Blow after blow the guild members sent at him, and every time, his stored magic protected him. The king's guards were still frozen in place, unable to move, but Cyfrin showed no strain from keeping up that enchantment while holding off the ongoing attack against him.

Aurelia could feel Amell's alarm growing beside her.

"I think we should get you out of here," the prince muttered, wrapping a hand gently around her arm.

Aurelia shook her head. "I'm not leaving," she said flatly. "I'm not running away."

She could tell that Amell wanted to argue, but at that moment, Cyfrin changed track. The humor fell from his face, and for a moment Aurelia hoped it was because the attack was finally beginning to work. But a second later, a look of determination seized the enchanter's features, and he balled his hands into fists where they crossed his chest.

"I've had enough of this childish play," he said coldly.

Then, with a shout, he brought his fists shooting out in front of him. An invisible wave seemed to sweep the room, and Aurelia braced herself for its impact. But she felt nothing. It was only the fourteen guild members who were struck, each freezing for a painful moment, then toppling one by one to the ground.

With a cry, Amell leaped forward to kneel by Bartholomew's side, rolling the old man onto his back.

"Bartholomew?" he gasped, and to Aurelia's relief, the enchanter's eyes fluttered open.

"So much...power," he muttered.

"Are you all right?" Amell demanded in alarm.

The enchanter grunted. "I'm sorry, Your Highness. My magic is...utterly depleted. It's just...gone. And until it replenishes..." He lifted his head and groaned, immediately letting it drop to the floor again. "I'm so sorry, Prince Amell. We gave it everything we have, but we cannot stop him."

"That's not the point," Aurelia said, her clear, steady voice surprising even her. "It doesn't matter if we can stop him. What matters is that we still continue to defy him. That we don't stop fighting."

She looked up, certainty blazing inside her as her eyes locked on Cyfrin's. She knew the words to be true with all her heart. She had never accepted Cyfrin's plans when she was in the tower, and she didn't intend to start now she was free.

The enchanter wore the smug look she hated so much, the one that said everything would always work out according to his plans, do or say what she might.

"You see what you could have been part of, Honeysuckle?" he told her, running a hand along her detached hair with indecent enjoyment. "But you were too lost in your daydreams to take hold of the power that could have been yours."

Aurelia narrowed her eyes, stepping over the rubble toward him.

"Aurelia!"

She ignored Amell's warning, her eyes still fixed on Cyfrin.

"Enough," she said, and her quiet voice seemed to echo throughout the still library. "You need to stop, Cyfrin."

"Look at you," he scoffed, with a shrill laugh. "Playing at being all grown up. You have no power in this situation, Honeysuckle. You've never had any power, and you never will."

"A strange thing to say, coming from the man who chose to give me access to half of the seventeen years' worth of power he'd been collecting," said Aurelia calmly. "I imagine it still irks you to know that I gave it away to someone else instead of to you."

Cyfrin let out a growl of fury, advancing toward her.

"But you're wrong, anyway," Aurelia continued. "I had power

long before you gave me that key. I had the same power I have right now. The power to choose to defy you. And I will, until my last breath."

"An excellent choice of words, my dear," said Cyfrin smoothly. "I have come to begrudge the effort and expense I went to, providing for you all these years. My plan was initially to simply overpower the guild. But having done so, I find that I have unfinished business. I would have had more than twice the power if it weren't for your duplicity, and I was too generous when I allowed you to walk away unscathed."

Amell let out a cry of anger, launching himself at the enchanter. Aurelia heard the king's warning shout to his son, fear swirling in her own heart. But Cyfrin didn't even look at the prince. With an almost lazy wave of his hand, he lifted multiple heavy chunks of masonry from the debris on the floor. At a gesture from the enchanter, the rubble began to circle around him, flying through the air with increasing speed. Clearly smart enough to realize that attempting to get through would only lead to him being bludgeoned, Amell fell back.

Within a moment, it was difficult for Aurelia's eyes to even make out the individual chunks of rock. She gritted her teeth at the smirk on Cyfrin's face. The rotating shield protected him from physical attack as surely as his incapacitation of all the guild members protected him from magical attack. If only Amell had the aptitude to wield the power Aurelia had unknowingly given him!

"Now where was I?" Cyfrin asked pleasantly, his eyes lingering on Aurelia with malice in their depths. "Ah yes. You were a satisfactory vessel, Honeysuckle, but you've served your purpose. It's time you were disposed of."

With less fanfare, and more deadly purpose, he placed one hand on the hair at his chest, and raised the other in a graceful arc.

Aurelia heard Amell's frantic cry, and Mama Imelda's gasp from beside her, but she didn't look at either of them. She closed her eyes, bracing herself. But instead of pain, she felt the comforting reassurance of arms going around her, first her mother's, then Amell's, as the prince threw himself between the two women and the enchanter, wrapping them both in his embrace.

Aurelia heard an almighty rushing sound, and had the imperceptible sense of something powerful racing toward her. But whatever it was never touched her. She opened her eyes to see Cyfrin, standing in the middle of the damaged room, struggling with some invisible force. His eyes were screwed shut, and his grunt of frustration grew steadily to a scream of rage. Amell stood strong and silent between him and Aurelia, his body convulsing slightly, and his face tight with strain. His shoulder was once again bleeding freely, but his arms remained firm around her.

Aurelia had no words to articulate what was happening. But she could sense an unseen, silent wrestle rising suddenly to fever pitch. Then an explosion went out from the enchanter, reminiscent of the one that had blown her from the tower. Just as on that occasion, there was no smashing stone, no splintering wood. Nothing physical was destroyed, but suddenly, inexplicably, Cyfrin collapsed to his knees.

Aurelia could feel no more struggle. She was looking at nothing more than a loveless man, an enchanter with middling power that was currently utterly spent, sagging weakly on his knees in the middle of a ruined library.

The guards, apparently freed from Cyfrin's magic, raced forward, binding him expertly, and gagging him for good measure.

"Given how much you admire power," King Bern said coldly to the incapacitated enchanter, "I think you'll be quite impressed with the new high security wing we're building at our prison. It's being structured with some truly impressive magical innovations."

Aurelia stared at the man she'd seen every day of her life as he was dragged from the room. She supposed she should feel jubilation at his defeat, perhaps satisfaction at the knowledge that he was about to discover what it meant to be locked away against his will. But all she could muster was a weary kind of relief.

It was over.

CHAPTER TWENTY-FIVE

"Aurelia." Mama Imelda's whisper was so full of emotion, it brought tears to Aurelia's eyes. "I'm so proud of you. We're free, my darling. Truly free."

Aurelia nodded wearily, returning her mother's embrace before swiveling to face the other person who still had an arm loosely around her.

"Do you know what happened?" she asked Amell.

"Not at all," he admitted. "But I think I just got a glimpse of what it feels like to be an enchanter. Except I had no control whatsoever. It was just like...*something* was activated inside me. I could feel it fighting back against Cyfrin somehow."

Aurelia nodded slowly, piecing it together. It seemed that the magic she'd unwittingly given Amell had woken and come to their aid. She drew a shaky breath. So that was how the power Cyfrin had idolized for seventeen long years had been broken. It had fought with itself, one half pitted against the other, and the magic that Amell couldn't wield, but nevertheless carried in his body, had prevailed.

"You saved us, Amell," she said, smiling softly at him. "When you threw yourself in front of us, you saved us with the power in you."

"I can't take credit," Amell contradicted. "The power might be in me, but it didn't come from me." He ran his thumb gently along her cheek, but there was a bemused frown on his face, as his mind clearly struggled to catch up. "I still don't understand it, really."

"Neither do I," interjected another voice. Bartholomew had struggled to his feet, color already returning to his face. "But I would like to. What I can say for sure is that was the most incredible, the most fascinating display of magic I've ever witnessed."

"Yes, well," said Mama Imelda, not sounding entirely impressed. "If you conduct years' worth of illegal experiments, without a care for the potentially fatal impact on those subjected to them, I suppose you're bound to get some fascinating results."

"Naturally I do not condone Cyfrin's actions," Bartholomew said quickly. "But I would still like to understand them." He frowned at Amell. "The power you told me about earlier, the magic released into you when Princess Aurelia unlocked it from her core. I wish you had the magic in your blood to have been able to *fully* sense it as it battled with the magic Cyfrin was pulling from that hair. It was truly a spectacle to behold."

"So that is what happened?" Amell asked. "I don't know why the magic on me did that. I didn't direct it to."

"You couldn't direct it at all," Bartholomew agreed. "It would have operated only on the course set by the enchanter who first molded it from his own core. In this case, Cyfrin."

"He set it on a course to defeat himself?" Mama Imelda asked skeptically.

Bartholomew gave a low chuckle. "I doubt it."

Aurelia frowned. "He told me once that the purpose of the

power he'd stored in me was to overwhelm and overpower all other enchanters. He wanted to show them that he was the greatest one."

"How interesting," Bartholomew breathed. He looked Amell over, noticing the way his shoulder was bleeding. "Your Highness! You've reopened your wound."

"I'm afraid so," Amell said cheerfully. "It hurts like dragon's flame, but it's the least of my concerns right now. I want to understand what just happened."

Clucking his tongue, Bartholomew pulled a wad of bandage from an inside pocket of his robe, redressing Amell's wound as he continued speaking. "What I was about to say was that we can be thankful that once the magic passed into you, it recognized you as its source, not Cyfrin. To be honest, I wouldn't have expected that. I can only speculate that it was the result of Princess Aurelia willingly giving it to you. Perhaps it changed ownership, in a manner of speaking. I doubt even Cyfrin could have predicted that outcome. In any event, it seems the magic considered him to be one of the enchanters it was designed to overcome."

Amell made a noise of comprehension. "So it wasn't protecting me from anything and everything. It was specifically overcoming any magic that was thrown at me. That explains why the arrow was able to hurt me, whereas Cyfrin couldn't kill me." He grinned boyishly. "If he'd picked me up and thrown me out the window the old-fashioned way instead of trying to blast me out with power, it probably would have worked."

Aurelia shuddered, finding no humor in the joke. "So when Cyfrin attacked us just now, the magic in Amell fought back of its own accord?"

"Indeed," Bartholomew nodded. "And overcame, from which we can deduce that it was stronger."

"Of course it was," smiled Aurelia, her gaze passing to Amell. "It was given freely rather than forcibly taken."

"Not to mention," Amell added, returning her smile, "love is stronger than any destructive force." His forehead creased again, and he looked back at the enchanter. "It wasn't able to overcome the blindness completely, though. I mean, it got me my sight back, but I still couldn't see Aurelia."

"Sorry...what?" Bartholomew looked totally lost, and Aurelia listened in belated dismay to Amell's account of his fight with Cyfrin in the tower.

"Then he just sort of tapped my head, and everything went dark," Amell finished. "He told me I was doomed to blindness, although the magic later fought that off. Then he said that I should know he took great delight from the fact that I'd never see Aurelia again."

"That little worm," said Mama Imelda, disgusted.

Bartholomew was looking thoughtfully between Amell and Aurelia. "And how did you lift that final aspect of the blindness, Princess Aurelia?"

She flushed slightly, not used to the title. "Well, I didn't do it on purpose," she said. "I was just weeping over his wound, wishing I could save his life by crying, like I did when...well, it's an old story. The point is, I thought he was going to die because of trying to protect me, and I couldn't bear to see him in pain."

"And her tears fell on my eyes," Amell chimed in. "That's when I could see her again."

"Ah," said Bartholomew, smiling. "That actually sounds quite simple."

"It does?" Aurelia asked blankly.

He nodded. "Well, it's still a bit of a mystery as to why the magic Amell was carrying didn't fight that curse off. I'm guessing here—Cyfrin's work went beyond the boundaries of what we know of magical theory—but I would speculate that he didn't cast it with the magic from your hair, but with the magic in him at the time, like any enchanter casting a normal spell. I doubt he even thought about it, but the fact that it was something so personal makes it likely he drew it straight from his core."

"And that's relevant because..." Amell prompted.

"Because of my theory that the magic from Princess Aurelia's core responded particularly strongly to the magic from her hair. The power was interconnected, equal and opposite, perhaps. I think the power you were carrying, Prince Amell, was particularly effective in fighting back against the power in the hair. Perhaps not so much against a curse cast by Cyfrin in the usual way."

"So why did my tears help?" Aurelia asked, bewildered.

"Oh, that's the simple part. It was a basic matter of a curse with a counterforce. It doesn't seem that Cyfrin built one in on purpose. So the curse was broken by the natural counterforce to the power with which he cast it. Judging by what he said to Prince Amell, he was motivated by sheer malice—quite literally taking delight from another person's sufferings. Your tears were the opposite—you wept in selfless grief over someone else's pain."

"Oh," blinked Aurelia. "That was clever of me."

Bartholomew chuckled. "Indeed."

"Is Aurelia in further danger from the magic being extracted, do you think?" Amell asked anxiously. "She was alarmingly weak when it first happened."

"Well, it clearly didn't kill her," said Bartholomew. "If it was wrapped around her core, it wasn't fatally so. I imagine her body will take some time to rediscover its own energy levels without the presence of the magic constantly buoying it up. She may feel quite weak and tired for some time to come. But I imagine that in time it will equalize, and she'll be as strong as the next healthy young woman."

"What about Amell?" Aurelia asked. "Is the power all gone from him now? Or is he still protected?"

Bartholomew looked the prince over carefully. "It seems to have spent itself in that final struggle," he informed them. "So I'm afraid you'd best refrain from any death-defying exploits from now on, Prince Amell."

"I have no interest in death-defying exploits," said Amell fervently. "I want to stay put, and stay safe. How else can I help keep Aurelia safe, and make sure she's happy?"

"Well, that's certainly music to my ears." Queen Pietra waded into the scene, her eyes passing in distaste over the wreckage of the ceiling. Her gaze softened as it came to rest on her son. "You've certainly been doing some growing, haven't you, Amell? I take it your thoughts about marrying young after all weren't purely theoretical."

"They certainly weren't," Amell said. His eyes sought Aurelia's, and she felt a flush rising up her neck. Amell had spoken to his mother about marriage? Because of her?

"Well, I can't imagine there would be any objection from our end," said the queen, her voice satisfied.

Mama Imelda cleared her throat, and a guilty look came over Amell's face. Glancing around, he drew Aurelia past a clump of fallen stone, so that they were partially concealed by a bookshelf.

"Aurelia," he said hesitantly. But he was clearly struggling to put whatever it was into words, because he bit his lip, anxiety on his face as he searched her eyes.

"What is it, Amell?" Aurelia asked, starting to feel a little concerned herself.

"Well, you know how I feel about you," Amell said, his voice constricted. "I didn't intend to tell you so soon—

certainly not while you were still in the tower—but, well, it happened."

"If by *it*, you mean a kiss that was—both literally and figuratively—magical, then yes," said Aurelia, glowing.

Amell's eyes softened, but the tension didn't leave his forehead. "It was," he agreed, in a low voice that sent a thrill down Aurelia's spine. "*You* are magical, Aurelia, and Cyfrin's power never had anything to do with it. But..." He hesitated again. "But you deserve the chance to experience life a little more before you commit to anything. I mean, if we discount Cyfrin—which we absolutely should—I'm the first man you ever met. I wouldn't be right to expect you to—"

"Will you stop?" Aurelia interrupted, exasperated. "I've had just about enough of people telling me I'm not capable, or thinking that I need to be shielded from life. Who are you to tell me I don't know my own heart?"

Amell's smile was a little sad. "Someone who would rather lose you altogether than take advantage of the generosity of that heart," he said simply, reaching out to gently touch her cheek.

Aurelia captured his hand, trapping it under hers against her cheek. "I understand your concern, Amell," she said quietly. "And I'm grateful for the consideration it shows. But I didn't fall in love with you because you were the first man I met. I fell in love with you because day after day, without fail, you were kind, and thoughtful, and you took me seriously. Plus, you're very handsome," she added as an afterthought. "And a prince."

Amell chuckled, and her eyes sparkled up at him.

"You kept your promises," she said seriously, "which is more important to me than I can say. And you never expected anything in return. You make me feel strong when others call me weak, you make me feel beautiful even when I look like a criminal, and you make me feel worth protecting."

"You are all of those things," he murmured, resting his forehead against hers. "And so much more. I couldn't help falling in love with you as soon as I got to know you."

"Well then," said Aurelia briskly. "I don't understand the problem. Although it might be worth waiting until my hair grows back a little before presenting me to the populace at large."

Amell pressed his lips to her forehead, and she felt his smile against her skin. "Perhaps a long engagement will be enough to satisfy any concerns."

"If we have to," sighed Aurelia.

Amell lowered his head so that his lips brushed her ear. "Not *too* long an engagement," he murmured.

And then his lips were on hers, and she forgot everything, Cyfrin's malice, Amell's wound, her own weariness. All she knew was that she was finally out in the world, and she got to share the endless vista of new experiences with the wonderful man who had become her world.

"So, just to be clear," Princess Tora said, the moment they emerged from the bookcase, clutching hands and looking a little sheepish, "you *are* going to marry a princess, Amell?"

"That's the plan," he said happily, tightening his arm around Aurelia's shoulders.

"And form an alliance with Albury?"

Amell looked a little taken aback. "I suppose so. I mean, I guess King Justin will have to agree to that."

"I'm sure he will," said Princess Tora brightly. She turned to her mother. "If Amell secures an alliance, Mother, does that mean I don't have to?"

"Honestly, Tora," huffed the queen, looking flustered at the public nature of the exchange. "It was never a matter of *having* to. I only suggested that—"

"Because I don't want to marry a prince," Princess Tora

announced over the top of her. "I want to marry a guard." She glanced at Furn. "If, you know…one will have me."

Aurelia watched on in astonishment, sure that there was a great deal of background she knew nothing about. Amell was tense beside her, his gaze fixed on his guard.

"Princess Tora," Furn murmured, looking tortured. "You know I can't…I mean, *I* know I can't. However much I might wish…"

"Might wish to what, Furn?" Princess Tora asked calmly.

The guard met the princess's eyes, and before Aurelia's gaze, the agitation in his frame melted away. His posture straightened, his general air became unruffled, and his eyes were calm.

"And there's our Furn," muttered Amell.

"I have loved you for a long time, Princess Tora," the guard said evenly. "I admire you in every particular. I don't know how any man could fail to do so. I have no expectations. I'm perfectly aware of the futility of my suit. But if it distresses you to think I'm indifferent, it's worth the pain of failure to assure you that I am not."

"Oh Furn," sighed Princess Tora. "That was incredibly romantic."

For a moment the guard looked taken aback, then a slow smile spread over his face. "I'm glad you think so," he said, his eyes warm as they rested on the princess.

"Tora," gasped the queen. "You are making a spectacle of yourself, throwing yourself at a guard in a public place."

Furn's expression set slightly, and Aurelia's heart went out to him.

"I know, Mother, but Furn doesn't even mind me making a spectacle," Princess Tora pointed out. "Surely that's a sign that he's the one for me."

"Tora," the queen said repressively.

"He saved my life earlier, if it helps," the princess offered.

"And," Amell jumped in, "he's my closest and most trusted friend, and the very best man I know. The idea has my full support, Mother, and surely that must help a little."

Furn threw a surprised look at the prince, gratitude clear on his face.

The queen's expression had softened ever so slightly, but she just raised her chin, glancing at her husband, who was distracted with responding to the chaos around him. "We will speak more of it later," said Queen Pietra with dignity.

"That's a foot in the door," Princess Tora informed Furn brightly. "Which, to be frank, is all I need."

The guard made no move toward her, but the look in his eyes as they rested on the princess made Aurelia look away, feeling like an intruder.

"Well." King Bern emerged from the knot of guild members with whom he'd been speaking. "Before anything else, I'd better send an urgent message to King Justin and Queen Felicity, alerting them that we've located Princess Aurelia." He inclined his head toward Mama Imelda. "And Queen Felicity's mother, of course."

Aurelia's eyes widened, a gasp escaping her at these simple words. She whipped her head around to stare at her mother, who was gaping at the king in wide eyed shock.

"Queen...what?" Mama Imelda stuttered. "Did you say I'm the queen's...are you telling me Felicity married..."

"Didn't you know?" Queen Pietra asked, her own eyes widening in ready sympathy. She moved toward the other woman, smiling reassuringly at her. "We're honored to be the ones to give you the very best of news. Your daughter," she glanced at Aurelia, "your other daughter, is the wife of King Justin, and is now Albury's queen."

Mama Imelda's mouth opened and closed several times, but no words came out. The queen was beaming at her, as if she thought she'd just made her day, but Aurelia frowned. She had the distinct impression that her mother took no delight from the news.

"Mama?" she asked softly, stepping up beside the older woman and touching a hand gently to her arm. "Are you all right?"

Mama Imelda turned to face her, and Aurelia could see tears building in the other woman's eyes. "I wasn't there," she said simply. "I wasn't there to protect her, and now she's going to suffer like Racquel, for the rest of her life."

"Racquel?" Aurelia repeated, confused. "You mean...my mother?" She reflected. "Who was the previous queen, wasn't she? I keep forgetting."

Mama Imelda nodded. "It brings me no joy to say it, Aurelia, but the truth is your father was a hard, cold man. Racquel was my oldest friend, and it broke my heart when she married the king for the sake of her family's position. I have no doubt it was his coldness that killed her. Why do you think she wasn't even allowed to be with you that day at the river? All she wanted was to be with her children, and he kept her from you constantly. I could see from the beginning that the union would lead to nothing but misery. You see, Racquel was the sweetest woman alive, but she..." Mama Imelda's face was apologetic. "Well, she wasn't strong enough to fight him. I'm sorry to say she more or less gave up where Justin was concerned. But she hoped that the king would care less about a daughter, and she would therefore be allowed to care more."

In a wave of sudden emotion, she covered her face with her hands. "When I learned of her death, I was almost relieved. It was a release for her. But Felicity is strong. I know it in my bones. She won't succumb—there will be no release for her, but a long life of coldness and loneliness. How could it have happened? How could Gustav have allowed it? How did she even come to the king's attention?"

"Well," said Queen Pietra, sounding a little disapproving. "Allowances must be made for your situation, but to speak so of your former king—"

"No Mother, she's right," Amell interjected. "Being royal doesn't excuse you from treating others with integrity. A king who does whatever he wants simply because he can get away with it is no different from Cyfrin." He glanced at the nearby senior enchanter. "As someone very wise recently told me, just because you can do something, doesn't mean you should."

He turned to Mama Imelda. "But you have no reason to be afraid for your daughter. I've met King Justin and Queen Felicity. They're happy together. He isn't like his father—maybe he was on that path once. But when he got cursed, and Felicity helped him break that curse, everything changed for him. He's kind to her. They married purely because they fell in love."

Mama Imelda still looked troubled, but some of the fear leaked from her eyes. Aurelia gave her hand a squeeze, then leaned against Amell.

"I know you've seen the worst of them, Mama," she said. "But royals aren't always awful." She smiled up at Amell, who squeezed her shoulder. "Sometimes they're positively dreamy."

"Oh dear." Princess Tora's dismayed voice cut across the group. "Amell is going to get a terribly big head if you keep that up, Princess Aurelia."

"Hey." Amell scowled at his sister. "I backed you up in your bid for romance."

"That's true," Princess Tora conceded, sending a mischievous grin toward Furn, who'd said nothing throughout this exchange, but whose eyes had rarely wavered from the princess. "I suppose I can allow it."

"Very generous," grumbled Amell, but Aurelia was laughing.

"I like you," she informed Princess Tora happily. "I've never had a friend near my own age before."

A look of surprise flitted across Princess Tora's face, softening quickly into something Aurelia couldn't quite identify as either happiness or sadness.

"Well," said the other princess, with a friendly smile, "I'm honored to be the first."

Aurelia smiled back, feeling that she had a great deal to learn, and that she couldn't wait to get started. She glanced at her mother, seeing that the other woman still looked troubled.

"Don't worry, Mama," she said encouragingly. "If there's a mess anywhere, you'll straighten it out. I have faith in you." Her mother smiled back distractedly, and another thought occurred to Aurelia. "I just realized," she laughed. "If your daughter Felicity married my brother Justin, she and I are doubly sisters! Through you, and through him."

"That's true," smiled the other woman. She put an arm around Aurelia's shoulder and squeezed gently. "And family is something we'll never take for granted, isn't it?"

Aurelia hugged her back, her heart overflowing with gratitude for the woman who'd had everything stripped away from her, and instead of embracing bitterness, had chosen to love her unexpected daughter with all her heart.

"Never."

EPILOGUE
TWO MONTHS LATER

"He's simply beautiful, Fliss, Justin."

Imelda's warm voice brought a smile to Amell's face. His soon-to-be mother-in-law had come a long way since her initial horror at discovering the identity of Felicity's husband. She looked perfectly at ease now, with her grandson in her arms and a sparkle in her eye.

Amell wasn't surprised—he'd felt no doubt that the woman who'd raised someone as warm-hearted as Aurelia would thaw under the kind and gentle treatment Justin had shown her since the group's arrival in Albury. In spite of his own words of reassurance to Imelda, Amell had been quite amazed to see the depth of transformation in the once cold young king. He'd never known Justin well before—perhaps he'd always placed too much reliance on the Alburian's reputation.

"He's just about perfect, isn't he?" Justin said now, gazing at his newborn son with a warmth that seemed designed to confirm Amell's thoughts.

"Of course he's perfect," laughed Felicity. "He's ours." She cast her eyes around. "Where's his Aunt Aurelia? I promised her a cuddle before the christening."

"I'm here!" Aurelia appeared from behind Amell, where she'd been speaking with Gustav and Ambrose, Imelda's husband and son.

Amell gave the pair a slightly awkward smile. He still hadn't had much opportunity to get to know these new members of Aurelia's family. And he winced a little whenever he thought of how he'd unwillingly witnessed Gustav's reunion with his wife. Eavesdropping had been the last thing Amell intended, but he'd been present when the merchant and his son arrived in frantic haste at the castle in Fernford, and Gustav had seemed unable to restrain himself as he took his wife in his arms and wept openly.

It had been heartwarming as well as awkward, Amell acknowledged to himself. He didn't know their full story, but he'd been moved by Gustav's response when Imelda had burst into tears of her own, then apologized for falling apart. Nothing could have been gentler than the way her husband chastised her for apologizing, or more earnest than his confession that he had been shamefully weak without her, that Felicity had been the one to be strong for them all, and that it was his turn to be strong.

Imelda had wept freely after that, and it had done Amell's heart good to see her leaning against someone for a change, instead of feeling the need to carry so much weight on her own shoulders. He couldn't even begin to imagine the process they would have to go through after seventeen years of separation, but having seen Imelda's strength of mind and heart, he had faith that they would find their way.

He hadn't witnessed Imelda's reunion with Felicity, but Aurelia had, and it had been clear to him that the young Alburian queen had instantly embraced Aurelia as a sister, a fact which brought Amell great joy. He knew Aurelia had been afraid that Imelda's family would resent her for being given a childhood with the mother they'd lost, and he was relieved that they'd shown no hint of reproach.

He shook his head slightly, smiling as his eyes rested on Aurelia. Only she would focus on the gift of Imelda as a mother instead of the theft of everything else Cyfrin had taken. Although, he reflected soberly, thinking of the rumors he'd heard about Justin's childhood with his father, perhaps in some ways, Aurelia had been better off away from Albury's castle.

And now, he thought with satisfaction, he was carrying her away to live in the castle in Fernedell with him. She was to stay on in Albury for some months after the christening, to spend time with Imelda and the rest of their delightfully complicated and multi-layered family. He knew he'd miss her, but he would never begrudge her the opportunity. And when she returned to Fernedell, it would be to make it her home.

Aurelia's delighted laugh brought Amell's attention to the infant in her arms.

"He's so squishy!" she declared. "And soft." She leaned down, nuzzling her face into the wisp of copper hair that curled up from the baby prince's head.

"I told you babies are extremely cuddly, didn't I?" Imelda said in satisfaction. "And I told you that you would get to cuddle one someday."

"You were right on both counts," Aurelia informed her, love shining from her eyes as she gazed at the baby. The image woke something powerful in Amell, and his heart ached with a bizarre and potent combination of satisfaction and longing. There was so much to look forward to, and they had all the time in the world.

"Look at you," came a voice from behind him. "You almost look like you're standing still."

Amell turned to see Princess Zinnia of Entolia grinning at him.

He chuckled. "An illusion, I promise. I still drive my mother crazy with my 'unseemly energy'. Nice that you could come to the christening."

"Entolia must be represented," Zinnia said lightly. She cast her gaze around the pleasant castle garden where the various royal guests had been invited to partake of a luncheon prior to the ceremony. Roses bloomed on all sides, their scent settling over the whole scene. "Besides, I wanted to congratulate you. And to thank you, from the bottom of my heart."

"For what?" Amell asked, surprised.

"For unearthing an extra princess from somewhere, and convincing her to marry you," Zinnia said dryly.

Amell laughed. "Lets us both off the hook, doesn't it?"

She nodded sagely. "Not that Basil would ever push me to marry anyone—it pays having an easygoing brother as your king instead of an uptight father—but that doesn't stop Mother from hinting frequently about eligible princes. Fortunately the only ones left now are Mistrans. We already have a pretty iron-clad alliance with Mistra, so hopefully I'll get a break from all the nudges."

"You and Tora should talk," Amell smiled. "She got more than her share of that as well."

"But not anymore?" Zinnia asked curiously, her eyes passing to where Tora and Furn stood nearby.

Amell followed her gaze. The former guard was no longer in uniform, but he held himself with his habitual alertness, and the way he hovered around the princess left no doubt in Amell's mind that he would spot any danger a mile before it reached her.

"No, not anymore," Amell said, watching the pair in satisfaction. "It took some convincing, but Mother has come around to her choice."

"I recognize him," said Zinnia suddenly. "Wasn't he your personal guard?"

Amell nodded. "Yes, it's cheeky of Tora to poach him. But he was my friend more than my guard. And I decided it was worth losing a guard to gain a brother."

"Very magnanimous of you," said Zinnia, her lips twitching. Her eyes returned to the couple. "Sounds like there's a story there."

"Ask Tora," said Amell dryly. "I'm sure she'd love to tell you all the embarrassing details of her campaign."

Zinnia grinned. "I think I'll do just that," she said, taking a step away.

"Hang on," Amell stopped her. "Before you go...I was hoping Basil might be here, but since he's not, I'll ask you."

She tilted her head questioningly.

Amell glanced around and lowered his voice. "Has he made any progress on his inquiries regarding the idea of a conspiracy of magic-users targeting the crowns?"

To Amell's surprise, a wary look instantly came over Zinnia's face.

"He's been focused on other things. It hasn't even been four months since his wedding."

"Oh, of course," Amell said quickly. "I meant no criticism. I just wanted to check in. I've made inquiries, and I'm pretty confident in our Enchanters' Guild. I spoke with Justin about it, too, and he says the same. If there's a group of enchanters collaborating for mischief, I think they're probably operating outside of any official guild."

Zinnia said nothing.

"I've even wondered if the prison break could be connected to it all," Amell went on. "The power definitely came from outside the prison, and we never identified who was behind it. It makes us all very uneasy, to be honest."

"Were they all caught in the end?" Zinnia asked, her tone stilted.

Amell shook his head regretfully. "Most of them were tracked down, either in the initial hunt, or through the anonymous tips my father received. But there are three still out there. They seem to have completely slipped through the net, unfortunately. I think wherever they are, they're smart enough to keep their heads down."

Zinnia bit her lip, looking troubled, but making no comment.

"What do you think?" Amell asked, his curiosity roused by her manner. "Do you think there's a broader conspiracy going on across the kingdoms? Or is there some other explanation for the excessive amount of power some of the attackers seem to have used?"

Zinnia opened her mouth, then closed it again, a look of great frustration crossing her features. She drew a deep breath, and gave her head a little shake.

"It's not for me to say," she said lightly. "It was good speaking with you, Amell. I'm very happy for you and your princess."

And with that, she moved toward Tora, her steps a little too swift.

Amell frowned after her, his mind full of questions. Something was definitely off with the confident, outspoken Zinnia. Her expression when he'd asked for her opinion struck a chord of memory in his mind, and it took him a moment to place it. Suddenly it hit him—it was like a reflection of his own frustration when he'd been hampered from telling anyone about Aurelia and Imelda.

He drew in a sharp breath. Was it possible that Zinnia had stumbled on some secret of her own, and been exposed to this strange new form of concealment magic that stopped the tongue? It seemed possible—Amell knew he hadn't been the first one to be affected by it, so he shouldn't assume he'd be the last.

But as he watched her chatting cheerfully with Tora and Furn, he couldn't help questioning his guess. It was a bit of a stretch, based on a few strange looks.

A sudden shadow overhead made Amell look up, and a moment later the rosebushes were temporarily flattened in a rush of wind. Two enormous shapes descended, purple and yellow scales flashing in the sunshine as the dragons touched down next to a fountain in an open area of grass.

"Rekavidur!"

"Reka? Dannsair?"

Amell didn't need either Felicity's cry of delight or Zinnia's quieter exclamation to recognize the two dragons he'd met in the forest near the prison. He'd wondered if any of the magical creatures would attend the baby prince's dedication.

"Greetings, Mighty Beasts," King Justin said gravely, bowing to the two dragons.

"Greetings, king of men," said Rekavidur and Dannsair in unison.

The yellow dragon's eyes passed to the young queen. "Greetings, Felicity," he said in his gravelly voice. "I was pleased to receive your invitation." He snaked his head down until it was inches from the child now nestled in Felicity's arms. "Is this your offspring?"

"Yes, this is little Julian," she said happily. Amell noticed that Justin looked a little more tense at the proximity between the baby and the dragon's razor-sharp teeth.

Rekavidur gave a long sniff, his orb-like eyes settled on the child. With a sudden gurgle, little Prince Julian flung his pudgy arm out, grabbing at the dragon's snout.

Several people audibly gasped, and Justin's arms twitched,

but Rekavidur just wrinkled his nose firmly, dislodging the child's grip.

"He seems entirely satisfactory," he commented to Felicity.

"Thank you," said the young queen, struggling heroically to keep in laughter.

Rekavidur straightened. "I have brought a companion, Dannsair. I trust you do not object."

"Of course not," Justin commented, looking marginally more relaxed now the dragon had drawn back. He bowed again to the purple dragon. "We are honored by your presence, Dannsair."

A steward behind Justin cleared his throat nervously, and the king turned to look at him. "Forgive the interruption, Your Majesty, Mighty Beasts," he said, bowing low. "But it's almost time for the ceremony to commence."

Justin turned to speak to the man, and Amell saw Zinnia approach the two dragons. He raised an eyebrow as he watched them all speaking, amazed at how casual she seemed to be. He was even more amazed a moment later, when the yellow dragon turned its head to scan the crowd, its eyes settling on him.

With a few stately steps, the dragon stood before Amell, who bowed low.

"Well met once again, Rekavidur," he said formally.

"Well met, Prince Amell," the dragon responded. He swiveled his head slowly, his eyes passing over Aurelia, who was standing with Imelda. "It seems your cloak yielded significant results."

Amell nodded fervently. "You could say that."

"I did say it," said Rekavidur, sounding confused and a little irritated.

"I meant," Amell amended hastily, "I agree."

The dragon let out a sigh that smelled faintly of smoke, but said nothing.

"I don't feel I sufficiently thanked you for your assistance,"

Amell said, keeping his voice low. "I haven't told anyone about your role, except Aurelia, who understands she needs to keep it to herself."

He waited, but the dragon made no comment, either in thanks for Amell's discretion, or in acknowledgment that secrecy was necessary.

"But I am grateful," Amell finished, a little lamely.

"I accept your gratitude," Rekavidur said placidly. "But it was not for that purpose that I involved myself. It is better to be effective than to be thanked, and sometimes anonymity is the best way to achieve that."

"Anonymity," Amell muttered. A sudden, absurd theory seized him. He remembered thinking how easily the dragons could identify and round up the escaped prisoners if they chose, and what a shame it was that his father wasn't free to ask for their help. "You weren't behind the anonymous letters my father received, were you? Disclosing the location of fugitives from the prison?"

Rekavidur stared back at him in total silence and stillness. Amell felt his mouth fall open.

"Surely not," he protested. "I mean, you're a dragon. You wouldn't do that. It would be against the agreement. You'd be helping us with a problem created by human magic."

"Would I?" Rekavidur asked, his face and voice still utterly expressionless.

Amell's eyes widened. "Are you...are you saying the prison break was caused by," he lowered his voice until it was barely above a whisper, "by *dragon* magic?"

"In point of fact," the dragon responded calmly, "I am not saying anything. What you are inferring is not within my control."

Amell swallowed, shaking his head as if to flick off water. "That can't be what you're saying," he said, trying to convince himself more than the dragon. He glanced around to make sure no one was listening. "You just helped me because you hold the agreement loosely. I know that, because you helped me find the clearing. That was Cyfrin's magic, nothing to do with dragons whatsoever."

Rekavidur's silent stare was so intense, it had a weight of its own.

"Was...wasn't it?" Amell asked helplessly.

"Well met, prince of men," Rekavidur said calmly. "As I said."

With that dismissal, he turned, his attention restored to the new parents and their infant prince.

Amell stood as if transformed to stone, his mind exploding with questions. Had he misunderstood that interaction completely? Or had Rekavidur just implied that there had been dragon involvement, not only in the prison break, but in Cyfrin's schemes?

His shocked eyes passed over the crowd, and fixed on Zinnia, who was looking between him and the yellow dragon with an expression of great strain on her face. As soon as she realized he'd noticed, she looked quickly away.

Amell's limbs unfroze, his foot beginning to tap as he tried to put all the pieces together. Was there some broader picture here? One that Zinnia was somehow aware of? A shudder ran over him. If the shadowy figures behind the supposed conspiracy against the various crowns were dragons, they were all doomed. There was no point even fighting.

"Dragon's flame," he muttered aloud. "What have I stumbled on?"

"Amell?" A familiar voice sounded at his elbow, and he turned to see Aurelia looking up at him questioningly. "Are you all right?"

He nodded. "I just had a very strange conversation," he said. "I'll tell you all about it later."

"All right," she said amicably. "Are you ready to go in? It's almost time."

Amell didn't answer at once, his eyes roaming over her exquisite features. The sense of impending disaster faded away. Dragons were strange and cryptic beasts. He would be foolish to read too much into Rekavidur's heavy silences. The creature hadn't actually said any of the things Amell was concluding.

"Do you know how beautiful you are?" he asked Aurelia suddenly.

She flushed, predictably and delightfully. "I'm certainly getting better to look at now that my hair is growing out. I think it's not too awful now." She touched a hand to her dark locks, which were almost down to her shoulders. They'd been properly styled since Cyfrin hacked at them, and they bounced adorably against her neck.

"It's gorgeous, but you were beautiful to me even when your hair was shorn like a goat's," Amell said simply, and sincerely. Aurelia's laugh brought a grin to his face. He loved making her happy. "But I didn't just mean how you look," he added. "You're beautiful in every imaginable way."

"You're too good to me," she said, leaning against him. She ran a hand through her hair. "And I'm glad you like it. I want to grow it a little more, but I don't think I'll ever let it get really long. It's so much easier like this." She pushed away from him, patting the locks into place.

Amell's eyes roved over the dark tresses, admiring the way they framed her face. She really was breathtakingly beautiful, and he could still hardly believe she was his. He folded his hands behind his back, his leg jiggling a little with the effort of being restrained.

Aurelia smiled knowingly. "You can touch it, Amell," she told him.

"Are you sure?" he asked, surprised.

Since her horrified reaction when they'd kissed in the tower, he'd been very careful never to touch her hair, understanding that it was a complicated and sensitive matter for her. The moment when she'd sprung away from him in revulsion had been among the worst in his life, and he never wanted to do anything that made her so uncomfortable again.

"I'm sure," she said softly. "I want you to."

Amell stared into her eyes for a long heartbeat, grasping the significance of the moment. Tentatively, he reached out a hand, running his fingertips gently over the soft waves. He paused, but Aurelia showed no sign of discomfort. She closed her eyes, a little smile playing on her lips. Encouraged, Amell buried his fingers further into her dark hair, relishing in the softness and closeness. Gently, he stretched his fingers over her scalp, bringing his hand to rest so that he cupped the back of her head.

Aurelia opened her eyes, her gaze settling on him with a look that made his heart beat at double time.

"I don't mind it when you do it," she said softly. "In fact, I very much like it."

Make that triple time.

"Aurelia," Amell said quietly, "I love you."

Her smile grew. "And I trust you, Amell."

His heart swelled, hardly able to bear the intensity of emotion contained within it. He'd somehow stumbled on the most incredible woman in the entire world, and even more amazingly, she wanted him. He didn't think one person in a thousand could go through what Aurelia had, and still come out the other side with such love and kindness in her heart. He knew he had Imelda to thank for the fact that Aurelia was capable of trusting at all, and he would never cease to be grateful for the gift the older woman had given this precious girl in front of him.

There were no words, and he didn't even try to find any. Taking advantage of the emptying garden, he lowered his face, his eyes locked on Aurelia's.

As he pressed his lips to hers, his hand still tangled in her hair, he couldn't help wondering what he'd done to deserve such a partner by his side. Somehow, impossibly, he'd been so lucky as to have his childish dreams transform into the greatest, warmest, most exciting, and most real adventure imaginable.

And he could hardly wait for it to begin.

NOTE FROM THE AUTHOR

Thank you for reading *Kingdom of Locks*. I hope you enjoyed returning to the continent of Solstice! I would be so grateful if you would consider leaving a review on Amazon—it would really make a difference!

If you're wondering what's going on with Zinnia, and want to know the truth behind Rekavidur's hints, check out *Kingdom of Dance*, the sixth and final installment of the series. Adventure, fantasy, mystery, and romance await.

Join up to my mailing list at deborahgracewhite.com to be kept up to date on new releases, specials, and giveaways, such as bonus chapters. You will also receive *Dragon's Sight*, an 8,000 word prequel to my first series *The Kyona Chronicles*, told from the perspective of the dragon Elddreki (who just happens to be Rekavidur's father).

Again, thanks for entering the world of *The Kingdom Tales*! I hope to see you back again.

Legacy of the Curse
Downfall of the Curse
Downfall's Echo

The Kingdom Tales

Kingdom of Beauty: A Retelling of Beauty and the Beast
Kingdom of Slumber: A Retelling of Sleeping Beauty

Kingdom of Cinders: A Retelling of Cinderella
Kingdom of Feathers: A Retelling of The Wild Swans
Kingdom of Locks: A Retelling of Rapunzel
Kingdom of Dance: A Retelling of The Twelve Dancing
Princesses

The Vazula Chronicles (coming 2022)

A Kingdom Submerged
A Kingdom Discovered
A Kingdom Threatened
A Kingdom Restored

ACKNOWLEDGMENTS

So many thanks to my awesome team in bringing *Kingdom of Locks* together. Ray, my husband, continues to be my best support and cheer squad.

To my wonderful betas: Adrian, Mel W, Steph, Mum, and Tamara. Thanks for all your helpful feedback.

And the usual huge thanks to Dad for developmental and copy editing.

Thanks to Karri for the gorgeous cover, and to Becca for the beautifully drawn map.

To you, the reader, thank you for giving me the privilege of being an author.

And most importantly, to God, who adopted us into His family, and who is the source of true freedom.

ABOUT THE AUTHOR

I've been a reader since I can remember, growing up on a wide range of books, from classic literature to light-hearted romps. The love of reading has traveled with me unchanged across multiple continents, and carried me from my own childhood all the way to having children of my own.

But if reading is like looking through a window into a magical and beautiful world, beginning to write my own stories was like discovering that I could open that window and climb right out into fantasyland.

I cannot believe how privileged I am to actually be living that childhood dream and publishing my own novels. I do so from my hometown of Adelaide, Australia, where I live with my husband and our three little ones.

I've never outgrown my love of young adult stories, so the genre of young adult fantasy was always going to be my niche. If you enjoy *The Kingdom Tales*, don't miss my finished YA fantasy companion trilogies, *The Kyona Chronicles* and *The Kyona Legacy*.

Feel free to email me at deborah@deborahgracewhite.com and introduce yourself! Or subscribe to my mailing list at deborahgracewhite.com for free giveaways, sales, and updates.

www.ingramcontent.com/pod-product-compliance
Lightning Source LLC
Chambersburg PA
CBHW060732190726
48285CB00001B/173